T

MW01135285

WR Vaughn

Published by Beta V
Redmond, Washington, USA

http://Betav.com
http://Facebook.com/TimkersNovel
http://WilliamVaughn.Blogspot.com
@VaughnWilliam

ISBN: 978-1530936243

Also available in Kindle™

10 9 8 7 6 5 4 3 2 1 0

The Marshall House, Alexandria, Virginia circa 1861.

§ The Timkers §

The Timkers series begins with *A Stitch in Time*, which follows Sam Harkins as he's transported from modern times back to 1930. *Déjà Vu* continues the story as Sam discovers the real reason why time travel is so critically important and takes him and Avey back to the Civil War era. *Borrowed Time* picks up the story and forces Sam to return to the year 2084.

§ The Author §

WR Vaughn is an award-winning author, dad, granddad and avid nature photographer. He has written over seventeen books and many dozens of magazine articles over the last forty years.

§ The Editing Team §

The final drafts of *Borrowed Time* have been scoured by professional editors and copyeditors including Margo Ayer, Auburn, Washington, Amelia Ramstead, Auburn, Washington and Joanne Erickson, Renton, Washington.

§ Cover Art §

The cover was custom-crafted by the author using photographs he took at Snoqualmie Falls, Washington, and an image from the Hubble space telescope and made available by the Space Telescope Science Institute (STScI).

§ Parents and Teachers §

This book is intended for adult readers. Depictions of violence and explicit adult situations might not be suitable for younger readers.

§ Acknowledgements §

The author would like to thank the steadfast fans of his work for their support, critical reviews, and copious suggestions. The author extends special appreciation to beta readers including Dawn Chellel, Jane and Joel Lippie, JoAnne Paules, Peggy Vaughn and several others. He would also like to thank his steadfast critique group including Margot Ayer, and Melissa Alexander who provided much-appreciated guidance in the early stages. He would also like to recognize the suggestions made by his Facebook friends and members of the Indie Authors group. Finally, he would like to thank Joanne Erickson whose professional attitude, skill and discipline gave the book a far better chance at success.

Thanks.

§ Dedication §

This book is dedicated to those who steadfastly believe that the environmental battle we're fighting today is not lost a cause, and won't require divine intervention or artificial intelligence to resolve.

This is our only chance. Don't blow it.

One—The Specter Returns

*A*vey tried to keep her eyes closed—afraid of what she might see. She wasn't given a choice. Once again, she found herself sitting on a kitchen table in a dimly lit room, her heart hammering as if it was trying to escape her chest. Flickering shadows danced to the tune of the flames peeking out from cracks in the cast-iron cook stove. The bitter taste of fear filled her mouth; the smell of blood and the smoldering fire brushed her nose. Shivering, she pulled together the ragged edges of her torn dress to cover her breasts, bare legs, and hand-print bruises—and then she saw him.

On the floor beside the table, a man's body lay in a dark pool, his eyelids fluttering. His hand slowly beckoned—his mouth moved, but she heard no sound. She gripped the sides of the table as if she would somehow be pulled toward him—like before. *Not again!*

"No!" she screamed. "Leave me alone!"

"Finish me. For God's sake woman, finish me," he gasped, his lips trembling in pain.

Her knife stood like a cross in his chest, with dark blood oozing out around it. *She* had done this. *She* had shoved the blade into him, just as he had tried to impale her with his own erect sword. She found herself standing over him.

The man looked up at her, agony bringing tears to his eyes. "Please. I'm sorry. Just…end it."

Avey wanted to run. She wanted to drag his body into the yard and burn it, to throw it into the privy, but instead she knelt on the wooden floor. Blood seeped through her dress, its warmth touching her legs. She watched in horror as her trembling hand reached out. But before she could touch the knife, his hands wrapped around her throat and pulled her toward him, her lips all but touching his.

"You'll be following me to hell soon enough. I'll be waiting," he said with his last breath.

Avey pushed away and screamed, loud enough to be heard in her next life.

"Avey," she heard someone say. "Avey!"

"No. No, no, no." She fought off the embrace, kicking and trying to get free, but these hands were tender, yielding, and gentle.

"Avey, it's me. It's Sam. You're safe. You were having the dream again."

She refused to open her eyes, worried that she might find herself face to face with *him*. When she realized it was Sam's body pressed against hers, and *his* warm breath on her neck, her heartbeat gradually slowed. It was Sam kissing away her tears. It was Sam, the man she loved, whispering in her ear.

"Oh, Sam. When are we going home?"

"Soon, I hope. Soon."

Two—The Awakening

*B*en Branson found himself sprawled across a bed as if he had ended up there after a binge. It took considerable effort to get his eyes open—an older woman in a high-necked dress was leaning over him, her breath working better than smelling salts to bring him back to consciousness. *Not again.* While used to waking up in strange beds or barns, he tried to make sense of his current predicament, but his thoughts and memories seemed scattered like the pieces of a jigsaw puzzle strewn across the floor by a petulant child.

The small room smelled of pine, perfumed soap, and ladies' face powder. He raised his hand to shield his eyes from the midday sun streaming from a window framed by pressed lace curtains. *Nope, not a bordello.* It certainly wasn't one of the bug-infested hotels or dusty haylofts he frequented on cold, lonely nights. Usually, he remembered the previous night—not this time. This was not the twenty-first century where he was born—at least he didn't think so. Having eliminated where he *wasn't*, all he had to do now was figure out where he *was*.

The last thing he remembered was riding into the foothills above Woodstock, Virginia, in the spring of 1861. He had been sent there to try to find another agent—one Dr. Julijana Streams. How he got *here* was anyone's guess. Across the room, his reflection looked back at him from a mirror on the nineteenth-century oak dresser. His shoulder-length brown hair, trail-worn face, and scruffy three-day beard made him look a lot older than thirty. In modern times, he could have been mistaken for one of the homeless wandering the streets.

He pushed back his mop with both hands and wished he could get into a hot shower. *Not in this century.*

"Excuse me, Mr. Branson, I thought only the lady and her brother were going to be staying," the woman said. Her voice sounded like his mom's when she found him in bed with his latest girlfriend.

She knows my name. "Lady?" he slurred. He didn't recall any lady. *Someone's mother? A madam?*

"Sir, have you been drinking?"

Was I drinking last night? Maybe. He sat up, and his head tried to roll off his shoulders. His wobbles didn't help him appear sober.

"Well? You should know I don't allow no drinking in my rooms."

"I'm sorry ma'am, regretfully, I don't recall your name."

"Well. Perhaps I made a mistake by takin' your lady-friend as a guest. I have very high standards…."

"I apologize. I suspect I've been subject to…tainted food. It's made me a bit dizzy. I assure you, madam, I do not imbibe," he lied.

"It weren't anything *I* gave you," she said defensively, leaning over to smell his breath.

He steadied himself on the bedpost and got to his feet. "Miss?" He hoped her name would jog his memory.

"*Mrs.* Pettigrew. I *own* this hotel."

So, not a madam. "Thank you, Mrs. Pettigrew." Her name didn't unscramble his memory. *Memory…that's it.* Running his fingers over the back of his neck, he felt a hard lump, about the size of a kernel of corn. *Memory eraser.* "Could I have a moment, ma'am? I won't be long."

"Of course, you paid in advance through the night. Do you still want the tea?" she asked, straightening a doily on a tray with three cups, a steaming teapot, and a few cookies smelling of ginger.

"That would be appreciated. And call me Ben. Everyone does."

"All right, *Mr. Branson*, let me know if you require anything."

Once Mrs. Pettigrew's crinoline skirt had swished into the hall, Ben closed and locked the door. Retrieving a thumb-sized device from an inside coat pocket, he touched it to his neck over the raised lump. The floor heaved like a rowboat pushing over ocean swell, but the feeling only lasted a few seconds. A flood of memories—good, bad, and frightening—poured into his consciousness like binge watching a season of *Game of Thrones* in ten seconds. Once his mind had cleared, and he had reassembled the series of events leading him to this room, he found a hurriedly scrawled note.

> *I wish we could have had more time.*
> *Julie*

"Julijana." He shook his head and smiled. *Maybe I should have told her more. Maybe I can still catch that train.*

As Ben reached for the doorknob, someone knocked. *Mrs. Pettigrew?* He opened the door expecting to see another episode of her frown, so he was surprised by the scarred and unshaven face of a large man built like the village blacksmith and smelling of armpits, coal smoke, and horses. His eyes told him the visitor wasn't there to change the chamber pots. *Trouble.* Ben reached for his pistol, but before he could touch the grip, he fell sprawling into the room with the giant's first roundhouse. Rolling to dodge a kick meant for his stomach, Ben pulled the braided rag rug from under his assailant's feet. The man tottered and recovered his balance, but not before Ben had scrambled back to his feet. Reaching for his pistol, the attacker grabbed Ben's hand and a grapple later, the cold steel barrel was pointing at Ben's head. *Shit.*

Ben raised his hands and stepped back. "What's your beef, friend?"

"I ain't no friend o' your'n," the man said, his thumb straining to cock the pistol's hammer. "You hunt down and kilt my brother Darrel like a rabid dog."

"Darrel Crossman? Was he your brother?" Ben remembered tracking Darrel and his ne'er-do-well brothers Larry and the other Darrel. It seemed their Pa liked the name. "You Larry?"

"Yeah. And you kilt him." Unable to cock the pistol, Larry decided to use it as a club instead. As he raised his arm, Ben swept out Larry's leg at the knee. With a loud pop that sounded like a breaking tree limb, the man fell and lay on the floor screaming frustrated epithets. The anger in his eyes could have melted the salt statue of Lot's wife. Snatching up his pistol and unlocking the safety, Ben cocked it and covered Larry from a safe distance. He wasn't about to get any closer to any wounded animal so bent on his destruction. The question crystalizing in Ben's mind was answered before he asked it. He *did* have a partner.

"What did you do?" someone said from the doorway.

Ben looked up to a neatly dressed man who rushed over, kneeling down to cradle Larry's head in his lap. "Oh, my dear child. You didn't try to hurt this man, did you?"

Larry nodded sheepishly. "He kilt Darrel."

Ben held his pistol on the pair. "You Larry's brother?"

"Oh, my heavens no. I'm Maurice, a…friend. Did he try to *assault* you? I told him you were a lawman, but he and his kind…well, none one of them are very nice."

"And you're a friend of his?"

"I try to be. Are all of your friends angels?"

Ben smiled. "No. Some of them are real stinkers."

"Well then. Help me get him on the bed. I don't think he can stand on his own. Just look what you've done to this gentle lamb's knee."

Gentle lamb? We lookin' at the same galoot? Ben lowered the hammer on his pistol, parking it in his holster. He and Maurice strained to get the wounded giant on the bed; all three men and the bed moaned in protest. Before Ben knew what had happened, Maurice had shoved a long, thin knife deep into his side. The last thing he heard over his own scream was, "That's for Darrel."

Three—The Agents

*J*ames Carstairs, a twenty-something with greasy brown hair falling across his face and a trimmed full-faced beard, straightened his hat and tie. He tightened his grip on a small leather bag, and pushed the butt of a Colt Dragoon under his dark coat. He was ready. He politely knocked on Mrs. Pettigrew's boardinghouse door. A disheveled woman appeared almost at once and pulled him inside by his lapels.

"Doc, you took your time," she snapped, using her apron to wipe off dark red stains from her hands.

Blood? "I'm not…there must be some—"

"Come upstairs. Poor Mr. Branson's nearly gone. I did what I could." Leading him up the stairs, she kept talking. "You should see what he's done to my mother's quilt."

At the top of the stairs, two black women stood weeping in a doorway. Mrs. Pettigrew had not stopped complaining about bloodstains, broken furniture, and spoiled linens as if they were Ben's fault.

James pushed by the terrified women to find Ben spread-eagled on an ornate mariner's compass quilt now dyed crimson with what only could be his blood. He was barely breathing. "Ben!" *Fuck.* "Out. Now. All of you. I…need to work," James commanded.

Mrs. Pettigrew and her help reluctantly retreated and James locked the door behind them. As the women whispered and prayed in the corridor, he worked quickly, placing a fist-sized electronic device on the floor. He dug into his leather bag and pulled out a worn weathered portfolio the size of a man's wallet. Inside, he activated his tDAP, a device used by the timkers for everything from managing time threads to messaging to passing the time in long, boring meetings. He took several steps back, tapped on the glowing glass, and the room shuddered as if the building had run over an armadillo in the road.

James watched the last few minutes roll back like pages flipped in a graphic novel. Mrs. Pettigrew came and went, then the Negro servants, and then a man backed out helping another large man walk on a bad knee. Ben lay motionless on the bed. James winced as one of the men un-stabbed Ben with a knife hidden in his boot. The killer backed out; there was a violent scuffle and both men disappeared leaving Ben alone—all in reverse. After that, a short time passed before a woman and a boy backed in.

Julijana. James recognized Dr. Streams at once. Moreover, there was another young person with her dressed as a boy—another redhead—a girl? *Her daughter? What were they doing here?* Julijana had held a special place in his heart—right up to the point where she kissed Ben and injected him. *Shit.* While he wanted to restart time with Julijana in the room, the tDAP threw up a warning message—the rollback had reached its limit. He paused the replay and forward-spaced the sequence until the flashing message blinked off. By this time, Julijana and the girl had left. Pressing an icon on the device, time resumed.

Ben now lay on the bed, still unconscious.

"Ben?" James nudged Ben's shoulder but got no response until he injected his friend's neck with the memory antidote and stimulant. "Hey, bud. Rise and shine." James said with a smile. He glanced at his panel. *No time to dawdle.*

"Jimmy? What are you doing here?" Ben tried to sit

up, but fell back. "Wow, woozy."

"Come on pal, pull it together. No time to catch up now. We have a train to catch."

"If you say so. Did you see those two…."

"Yeah, two redheads. And they seemed a bit more than you could handle. Can you get to your feet? I figure we have about two hundred seconds before Larry and his pal show up."

"*The* Larry? As in Darrel's brother?"

"Yeah."

"Great." Ben smiled.

James half carried and half walked Ben out the door and down the stairs. Mrs. Pettigrew met them, coming up with tea and cookies. Ben, almost walking on his own, took a couple. "Thanks Mrs. P, we won't need the room after all. Just keep the rent. And thanks—yum!" He took a bite and reached back for another pair.

"You are most generous, Mr. Branson. Have a pleasant trip," she said with a smile.

Once they got out on the street, James nodded toward the shadows and Ben followed into a narrow alley, both wary as cats in a dog pound as they made their way to the station.

"What's going on?" Ben peeked around the corner.

"We can talk about it on the train—assuming we can catch it. I don't expect the conductor to wait for us."

"Badger? He's a stickler for his schedule. He would leave his own mother on the platform."

They rounded the corner just as the caboose disappeared into the mist. "See?" James said.

"Any chance to roll it back? All we need is another minute or so."

"The tDAP says TTM's out of buffer space as it is.

You can't write checks on an empty account." The news from Time Travel Management was disappointing—not like the old days where they could snatch him up or transport him to safety at the first sign of trouble. TTM, in charge of the time travel system (and his life, for that matter), always seemed to be upset about something. They hated change, and more recently, chanted their "no interference" mantra on every occasion. They would paint it across the sky if they thought it would help.

"That's a shame," Ben lamented.

You don't know the half of it. James *really* wanted to know why Julijana had been more than friendly with Ben. When next they met, she had some explaining to do.

"How long has it been?" Ben asked.

"Pacific Grove, right?"

"1980? Yeah. That was a close call with Gary Kildall."

"It seems like years," James smiled.

"Well, sort of, three years ago?"

"In base time, yeah."

"So, what's the plan?" Ben looked around nervously.

"We need to lay low until TTM can arrange transport."

"Swell. Got your tDAP?"

"Sure. Don't bother. They're a bit busy dealing with some crisis or another," James said, tapping his tDAP. He stepped back into the alley. "Keep watch."

Ben pulled his pistol, clicked the safety off, and cycled the hammer.

"I noticed Larry couldn't cock your pistol. Did it jam?"

Ben smiled. "Nah. Custom hammer lock, see?" He showed James the hidden lever.

"Sweet." *Impressive.*

Keeping his weapon out of sight, Ben kept his eyes moving as James discretely held the tDAP to his ear.

"Yeah, it's me. I got him. He's okay, but I had to— Yeah, but there was no other alternative," James whispered. Despite the disruption in time, he would have never hesitated to save Ben. Time and again, his friend had proven to be a great agent. Intelligent, imaginative, and with fathomless courage. While he felt comfortable with Ben covering his back, he *wasn't* comfortable with him kissing Julijana. As far as he was concerned, she was *his* girl. No, he wasn't sure she was of the same mind, but he knew she would come around to his way of thinking *eventually*. As to her kissing Ben, that was certainly a setback. He would have kissed her himself, not that the opportunity had presented itself—it wasn't a liberty one simply took, at least not the way he rolled.

"We need to chill. They're having problems." *Thanks to my little adjustment.*

"So what's new?"

"These are more serious than…ever." James's face looked troubled.

"Even as bad as—"

"Worse. The way they tell it, the whole system is collapsing. Everyone is being recalled."

"From all time zones or just here?"

"Everyone—even the researchers in the Jurassic period."

"I'll bet *they're* ready to come home."

"Are you?"

Ben shook his head. "No. The folks here are great, at least for the most part. I don't miss 2084, do you?" He tapped James's arm.

James turned to see a scruffy giant of a man followed

by a smaller, well-dressed dude heading toward the boardinghouse. "Larry and Darrel," James said.

"Really? I don't see the resemblance."

"Well, at least one of them is Larry. The big one nearly clubbed you to death and the dandy shoved a knife into your liver."

"Great. Wait. Really?"

"Yeah, I had to roll it back."

"How far?"

"About twenty minutes, but only locally."

"That should make an ugly hole in the time fabric. No wonder TTM is pissed."

"They're always pissed."

"When do we get out of here?" Ben asked. "And thanks."

"We might be here for a while."

"A while?" Ben said.

"Forever." James kept Larry in sight.

"Fuck."

"Unless we get out of here, we had better get used to being in a southern state in the Civil War. If I have my dates right, it's already started."

"Yeah, today's April twelfth, 1861, isn't it? That's just great. I'm gonna really miss hot showers and HBO."

"Your friends went inside Mrs. Pettigrew's. Let's make a break for the Marshal's office."

James scanned the street. All he saw was a few scattered men on horseback and a handful of people going about their business. Midmorning in Woodstock wasn't Times Square.

"Right behind you." Ben followed James, but kept an eye on the boardinghouse. Before they had crossed the street, Larry the man-mountain appeared at the door with

Mrs. Pettigrew stuffed under his arm like a bleating nanny goat. When he spotted James and Ben, he dropped her in a heap and called back into the boardinghouse. Darrel appeared and watched as Ben and James stepped into the Marshal's office. *If looks could kill.*

The room was small with a one-man cell in the back. Curled up on a bunk, a pile of rags with feet seemed dead to the world. A man with his hat pulled over his face and his shabby boots planted on the desk was taking a nap— or pretending to.

"Marshal?" James doubted if this unkempt young snip was the Town Marshal, but he didn't want to insult him.

"He's in Front Royal on business," he said, without looking up.

"You're the law here in Woodstock?" Ben asked.

"I'm afraid so. I'm Danny...*Daniel* Littlebottom, Assistant Deputy Marshal." Danny pushed back his hat. "What's the problem?" The kid looked *almost* old enough to shave. His badge looked like he had won it at a carnival.

"I'm James Carstairs, U.S. Marshal, and this is Ben Branson of the—"

Ben held up his hand and shook his head.

"I see. A *U.S.* Marshal?" the deputy said, raising an eyebrow.

James flipped out his badge. The deputy scowled back at him as if he had syphilis. The hair on the back of James' neck rose along with his heartbeat.

"Marshal Carstairs, you don't have no jurisdiction here in Woodstock, and 'specially not in Shenandoah County. Perhaps you should go back up north."

"What the fuck are you talking about, boy?" James said.

"Didn't you hear? Virginia stands with Jeff Davis." The boy was now on his feet with fire in his eyes and a hand resting on his holstered pistol.

James just stared into space. He could not believe his own ears. While he had only arrived in this age an hour ago, he was unprepared for the reality of living in a slave state—especially when he felt he was on the losing side of the revolt.

Ben stepped up. "Be that as it may, *Danny boy*, Virginia is still part of the Union, and whether or not Virginia secedes, there are two wanted fugitives raping women over at the boardinghouse."

"We'll deal with the law on our own. I suggest you and your Yankee friend clear out of the county before someone reminds the townsfolk where your allegiance lies."

James had underestimated young Daniel Littlebottom. He had large, solid-brass balls. James had a mind to kick them all the way back to Washington.

"We need to clear out of here," Ben whispered.

James just stood staring at the boy, who glared back at him as if he was daring him to blink first. The boy's hand drifted down, closer to his revolver.

"Come on," Ben said, taking James by the arm. They walked by Danny and out the side door. There was no one waiting to bushwhack them—at least no one in sight. James didn't say a word as they made their way toward the livery stable. They needed transportation and a less antagonistic population.

"You been here long?" James said.

"About five years on and off—about a dozen deployments." Ben kept moving, trying to look nonchalant. He paused to look in the window at the ladies' dress shop to admire the latest fashion and used the reflection to watch the street behind them. He didn't see anyone following them.

"You miss your own time?" James asked.

"Not really. It's pretty bad in 2084. Wait, what's your home year?"

"The same. I lived in a metal cargo container stacked twenty high in the mountains beyond Estes Park—near Grand Lake."

"Colorado?"

James nodded.

"Virginia isn't half bad." Ben waved at the blue sky and puffy white clouds drifting by in the spring sunshine.

"Except for the excitement from time to time, rather nice I would say."

"With clean water to drink and air that doesn't corrode everything it touches, yes, the 1860s aren't bad, but I've had my smallpox, polio, tetanus, typhoid, Zika, and a half-dozen other vaccines."

"Point well taken. So, how long have you known Dr. Streams?" James asked.

"Dr. Streams?"

"Julijana. The redhead you kissed and groped before she slipped you a memory mickey."

"She's a doctor?"

"Two PhDs. Medicine and Anthropology. Didn't you know? I've known her for years."

"She didn't give me her life story. We just met."

"Just met her tongue down your throat?" James wasn't smiling.

Ben didn't respond. James was right. He had acted like a horny seventeen-year-old with Julijana, a woman he had barely met. But after having spent a blissful night with her hip pressing against his on a buckboard, he was ready to go anywhere she cared to lead him—even into her bed if she asked. After all, she kissed *him*—not that he hadn't been thinking about it from the first moment their eyes met.

"You know she's a senior TTM agent—Dr. Vili Streams' sister."

"The one whose grandfather invented time travel? Sam Harkins?"

"One and the same."

"Who was the other one? The one dressed as a man."

"She called herself Avey. I got the impression they're somehow related. She's not from base time, that much I know."

"Let's get some horses. Got any money?" James asked, but he knew the answer—he didn't.

"Wait." James put his communicator to his ear. "Yes? Where? Okay, we'll be there. Give us fifteen minutes—okay, ten. Wait, who are we supposed to—hello?" *Shit.* He looked at the panel and tapped it against the wall as if it had a stuck gear.

"TTM?"

"Yes, our beloved Time Travel Management wants us to go bail out a couple of other agents."

"Where are they?"

"In Alexandria, about a month away. They're going to transport us there the easy way."

"Who are they? Anyone we know?"

"The signal crapped out before they could tell me."

"Great." Ben wasn't smiling.

"And there's more good news. We need to go back to the room where I found you."

"Perfect. What could possibly go wrong?"

Four—The Alexandria Depot

"Today's the day," Vili said as he entered the opulent parlor car and sat across from his sister.

"Why would you remind me? You don't think I know that?" Julijana snapped.

"Sorry."

"I'm sorry, Vili, but you know we've done all we can do. We're not in Seattle, and not in 2020, so everyone should be okay. Let's just get through the day."

"I hope you're right."

"Me, too. Me, too," she whispered.

* * *

Sam Harkins, now about twenty-five, but with the experienced eyes of a much older man, could tell the "train" had stopped again. He knew full well that they had not been riding a conventional 1860s-era train, but a transport camouflaged to look, sound, and smell like a steam train—especially to those watching it slowly chug into the station. His fiancée, Ruth Riley Avenir (he called her "Avey") quietly snoozed in the only rumpled bunk in the compartment. It had been a long night, and it had taken hours to bring Avey back from her nightmare.

While it was hard to know exactly how long, but perhaps ten days ago, he recalled being thrown into the distant future while Avey had been sent into the 1860s. In "real" hours and days, they had been reunited here at the edge of the Civil War for less than a week.

Since their reunion, he and Avey had spent several long, tedious days and nights on the train for reasons no one could satisfactorily explain. As much as they wanted to, they couldn't exactly get off and catch the next American Airlines flight back to Seattle—the Wright brothers' airplane wouldn't be invented for another four decades.

Sam was consistently frustrated when he tried to get a straight answer to a simple question: why didn't they simply return to his time? Vili, in charge of the complex time travel systems, always had some excuse—something about picking up stray agents, or correcting some flaw in the time threads. Sam and Avey were both grasping at the frayed edges of their patience, but as far as Sam was concerned, Vili and his sister Julijana didn't seem to care. Sam felt he should be able to trust them—after all, they were his own grandkids. But he didn't.

Mr. Badger, the truculent train conductor with a permanent scowl to match his name, had repeatedly reminded them the train couldn't stay in any town for long without raising suspicion, so they had pulled into little towns and whistle-stops up and down Virginia's Shenandoah Valley to restock the larder—and feed Vili's bacon addiction. They never stayed more than a few minutes.

Sam wondered where they were stopping this time. He pulled on a pair of pants, pushed the blinds aside, and surveyed the platform—the sign read *Alexandria, VA*. Men and their families were packed into the station as if a foreign army was about to invade the city. Assuming his history references were right, Sam knew that's exactly what was about to happen. The Yankee army would occupy the city any day now. He had been researching the Civil War at every opportunity, despite the simply awful broadband speed he likened to an old telephone-style modem connection.

He spotted a kid hawking newspapers and opened the window. "Hey kid, can I get one of those?" The scruffy newsy pushed a paper up to him and Sam handed him a dime.

The kid smiled and didn't notice the coin was dated 2015. "Thanks, mister," he said with a mossy-yellow smile.

"Hey, what's going on?" Sam asked.

"Didn't you hear? Those damn Yankees are coming. They say the blue-coats will be crossing the river in the morning."

"Really?"

"My Pa says we'll be heading west 'fore noon."

"Thanks," Sam said, tossing him a quarter. "Good luck."

Unlike his hometown *Seattle Times*, the May twenty-third, 1861, edition of the *Alexandria Gazette* was largely ads. On page three, he found an interesting account of today's election. Citizens of Virginia would vote for the state to formally secede from the nation. Once ratified, there would be no going back.

Then it struck him: someone had dropped him and his fiancée off at the dawn of the American Civil War—at ground zero. He had a pretty good idea who (or what) was behind this latest jaunt into history. *Aarden. The ethereal artificial intelligence entity Avey had created and refined, apparently too well.*

"Avey, wake up sweetie. We're here." He kissed her on the cheek.

"Where is *here?*" she said sleepily, pushing her long red hair out of her face.

"Alexandria, Virginia—at least that's what the paper says. Maybe they'll let us walk around this time. It looks like a bigger city."

"And when?"

"Still 1861, I'm afraid, and we've lost another week or so—the paper says it's already late May."

She uttered an intelligible expletive. "So not back home in our time."

"Nope, sorry." Sam felt her pain. They had both had their fill of time travel—he was still rattled from his brief stopover in 2084. He shuddered just thinking about it, and she had nightmares from her harrowing experience in a rustic cabin in the hills overlooking Woodstock. He was not sure of the details, but Julijana said Avey was nearly raped, but somehow managed to kill her assailant. Neither would talk about the details, and he didn't press.

"I hope someone is taking care of Mink." She rolled over, tugging the sheet over her nakedness.

Sam knew Avey had more than their cat on her mind. "Me too. I'll ask Vili why they can't send us home to take care of her."

"And he'll give you the same lame excuse. 'It's not time yet.'" Avey sat up in bed, inadvertently flashing the people on the platform. "Sam, the blinds?"

"Sorry." He closed the curtains, but not before witnessing a woman whack her husband with an umbrella for his visual indiscretion.

"I can't really deal with Aarden from here, unless they have really good broadband and a decent dev system."

"I'll check—don't they have a Fry's here? Perhaps FIOS has reached out this far," Sam quipped. He also laid the blame for their current departure from their own time on Aarden. With any luck at all, Avey could get her back in control. As it was, Aarden seemed to be controlling just about everything imaginable, including their budding relationship. At times, she seemed like the mother-in-law from hell.

"Fry's? Sure, in about a hundred and fifty years. Maybe Amazon delivers to this time zone," Avey said with a smile.

Sam really loved her. She got his wit and fed his spirits like gas feeds a flame. Watching her unwind from the sheets, he was again reminded of another reason he loved this adorable redhead—her green eyes made him crazy. He had memorized their every nuance—the tiny flakes of gold, their kaleidoscope of azure, and the counterclockwise swirls that reminded him of the Milky Way. He resisted the temptation to run his fingers down her slender waist and linger on the warmth of her inner thigh—for about a millisecond. She purred in response, ran her fingers through his brown curls, and rolled over like a kitten wanting someone to rub her tummy. He obliged with his tongue. She soon had his blossoming erection in her hand and then down her throat.

Afterwards, he snuggled up beside her with a broad smile on his face. Sam was happy. So was she—Avey's bright spirits and the sparkle in her mysterious eyes had returned. *Perhaps it's a good time.* "We okay?" he asked. She didn't answer. "Avey?"

"Humm?"

"We haven't talked much about the...the farmhouse." She snuggled a bit closer. "I think if we talk about—" he began.

"Sam, I'm not sure I want to relive that. I'm still processing. I don't really know *how* I feel."

"I'm just trying to understand, and help. You're still having nightmares. Maybe if you talked to Julijana? She's a doctor—" he said softly.

"Sam, he didn't rape me, but I killed him. Even if he had, there is no way you can understand how I feel, there is no way you *could* know. How could you, unless it happened to you? This is not something you can debug like an unhandled program exception."

No, Sam accepted he couldn't know what she had been feeling, what torture she had been going through—alone. How could he? Sure, back in 1930, he had been the victim of a brutal attack that left him battered and bleeding at the foot of a concrete stairway. He knew how it felt to be pummeled within an inch of his life and look into the eyes of a deranged killer—but was it the same? *No, I guess not.*

Sam laid his head on Avey's shoulder and felt her warm skin against his.

"I'm going to hop in the shower, and don't try to join me again. It's hardly big enough for one of us."

"Not even if we stand *really* close?"

"No. Wait until we get home." She closed the bathroom door.

He so wanted to fix her—to fix them. But how do you undo another man's violent assault on someone you love? How do you help someone you love wash away the memory of knifing an attacker—staring into his eyes as the devil's soul was sucked into hell? Given half a chance, Avey had already done what he would have—but it was not enough. Sam was ready to devote his life to making Avey happy—assuming she still wanted him. He had spent the last few days struggling with that very issue. He thought it had been decided, but flickers of doubt kept poking through the veneer of their new relationship. His first step was to get them both back to their own time and their old life.

"You feel that?" Avey asked, stepping out of the bathroom, barely covered with a towel.

"What?"

"There was a strange vibration and a low buzzing noise—like an MRI."

"Not out here. You off your meds again?" he teased. He also knew time travelers often experienced turbulence transitioning from zone to zone. What she felt was probably "normal"—at least for a time-transport.

"Never mind, it was probably a loose steam fitting. You hungry?" Avey asked, drying herself.

"You?" Sam smiled and raised an eyebrow. He was up for another round if she was.

"Later, tiger. Let's recharge our batteries with some breakfast." She flashed him and gave him a dismissive kiss.

Sam nodded and looked for his shirt—it was somewhere in the pile of clothes scattered like shingles after a tornado. Distracted by watching his fiancée dress, he recalled why they were together. Yes, there's a physical attraction—there was plenty of that. It was more. Avey was a unique, complex woman. The instant he thought he understood her, she would do or reveal something unexpected, like a plot twist in a good fantasy novel. She was driven, meticulous, and punctual, but took forever to get ready to go anywhere. Back home in Seattle, she insisted his clothes be segregated to his side of the closet, but only picked up their bedroom when her mom visited or the cleaning lady was coming. She loved cats, but was afraid of kittens. She loved flowers, but hated to get her hands dirty—and especially hated anything sticky. Sure, she said she wanted children and a life together with him, but she also wanted to contribute to the world, not just ride along like a pampered passenger on a cruise ship. And she had a lot to contribute. At twenty-five, Avey had evolved to be a brilliant systems architect and developer, especially when it came to artificial intelligence. AI was her secret power.

Sam couldn't be more proud of her and marveled at how lucky he was that she stayed with him this long. Sought out by scientists and academicians all over the world, Avey's breakthroughs were credited with advancing AI technology far faster than anyone thought possible—it was almost as if some hyper-intelligent entity had whispered in her ear as she coded. She bristled at the suggestion—the last man who implied she had extraterrestrial guidance walked away with a broken nose. She also had a great jab.

"Smell that? I'll bet Vili found someone to cook him bacon," he said.

"What's up with him and bacon?" Avey pulled on some sort of indelicate. She had tried to explain the name of these layered undergarments, but she might just as well have been discussing molecular biology—well beyond his area of expertise. He had a PhD in astrophysics, but was not an expert in dressing 1860s women—only undressing them, based on very recent experience.

"Vili says the bacon in his time is simply awful. Think moldy cardboard dipped in artificial turkey fat. He indulges himself in the real thing whenever he travels into the past."

"Maybe that's why he goes back in time—just for the bacon."

"Or the burgers." Sam pulled on his pants and slipped the leather braces over his shoulders.

"Is that why you invented time travel?" Avey asked.

"Of course. What better cause is there than real bacon?"

"And Kidd Valley burgers."

"And Kidd Valley bacon cheeseburgers."

"Sam?"

"Yes, m'love?"

"You haven't told me much about the future. No, let me rephrase that—you've told me *nothing*."

"You don't want to know." Sam *really* wished he hadn't seen their grandkids' future—where Vili and Julijana lived and worked when they weren't in the past patching time.

"See, I put on my big-girl panties. *Tell* me." She lifted up her petticoat and flashed him again.

Sam glanced down. He wasn't smiling. "Avey, if there was one experience in my life I would roll back and erase, it would be my brief visit to 2084."

"Is that where you were sent?"

"It's where your friend Aarden sent me, yes."

"You're *sure* it was Aarden."

"One-hundred percent. She admitted to it."

"What was it like? Please, tell me." She put on her sad kitten face.

"No. You *really* don't want to know. Just trust me on this."

"It's that bad? *Blade Runner* bad, or more like the movie we watched last night?"

"*Mad Max*?" he asked. During their long days and evenings on the train, Sam had encouraged her (forced, as she put it) to watch a half-dozen time-travel movies. This way they could talk more intelligently about their experiences—without really revealing the actual details. By the time she had seen *Brazil* (which she said was strangely erotic); *The Time Machine* (sappy); *Twelve Monkeys* (true steampunk); and *The Fifth Element* (too much violence, not enough nudity), she put her foot down and made him watch *Gone with the Wind; Her; Colossus: The Forbin Project;* and *The Time Traveler's Wife*. The last one, *Ex Machina* was his favorite—and hers.

Somewhere in between. "No. I'm not going to tell you. Let's make a deal. I won't ask you about Woodstock cabins and you won't ask me about 2084. Deal?"

Avey's face fell. "Okay, deal."

Sam pulled her into her arms and kissed her.

"I don't think Julijana or Vili like me," she said, still in his embrace.

"They love you, hon—like a…sister."

"She's been acting funny…I can't put my finger on it, but there's something—Vili too."

"I'll talk to her. Ready?"

"Do me up, I can't reach the ties for this corset. I have a whole new appreciation for Mammy."

"Mammy?"

"The black woman on *Gone with the Wind* who helped Scarlett O'Hara dress."

"Oh, *that* Mammy. Yeah, I'll check the want ads to see if she's looking for a job as a lady's maid."

"Sure. Just pull."

"Suck in." Sam gave her drawstrings a tug and peeked over her shoulder as the tops of her breasts pushed out over the top of the corset. "'Nuf?"

"Too much—I can hardly breathe." She let a long patterned dress cascade down her arms. When her face reappeared, he kissed her neck and gave her breast a gentle caress.

As Sam prepared to glide his fingers down over her

nipple, someone knocked on the door.

"You kids up?" Vili said through the door.

"Almost," Sam said, repackaging his equipment and buttoning his fly.

Avey rearranged her décolletage, brushed the wrinkles out of her dress, and nodded.

"Come on in, Vili."

"Morning, kids," Vili said with a too-perky voice.

"That doesn't look like 2020 out there," Avey said, nodding toward the window.

"Ah, I…we. I…."

"Great. So when do we get back to our lives?" she asked.

"Good morning, Vili," Sam said smiling. "What's on the schedule?"

Vili raised his hands in surrender. "Sorry, don't kill the messenger. We're just as anxious as you are."

"Sorry," Avey said, "but if you want me to regain control over Aarden, you had better get me back to 2020."

"I wish we could, but there are a few other issues to address first. You could work from the train, but the high-speed links are down, and we need to stay here in Virginia at least a couple more days—but first, breakfast."

"What's the lame <cough> excuse this time?" Sam asked, holding the door open for Avey, who headed for the parlor car. He followed her out, wanting to get between the pair in case a skirmish broke out.

"Well," Vili said, "we also have a couple of agents to collect. We've lost touch with them—no one wants to leave them behind."

"Agents?" Avey asked over her shoulder.

"Yeah. Julijana says Avey met one of them the day

before you got on the train—Ben Branson."

"He's one of your people?" Avey asked.

"Yeah, a good man, and an old friend."

"And apparently, a friend of Julijana's." Avey grinned.

Based on Avey's expression, Sam figured Avey knew more than she had said about their encounter with Mr. Branson. Their time apart had raised as many questions as it had answered—perhaps more.

Julijana was waiting for them in the parlor car. "Good morning, Sam, Avey. Sorry to get you up so early, but the conductor says we need to get off here."

"We were already up," Sam said.

"Get some breakfast, we don't have a lot of time."

Avey fixed her own plate of fruit and a muffin with fresh butter. Sam poured her a glass of orange juice.

"Any sign of Aarden?" Avey asked.

"Not since that first night." Julijana handed Sam silverware and a plate of eggs and Virginia ham.

"Thanks," he said. "Printed?"

"Not this time—the fruit, ham, eggs, bread, and butter are real. Mr. Badger had someone go foraging early this morning."

"There's no bacon," Vili said mournfully.

"Poor baby," Avey said, not showing a bacon bit of compassion.

"When are these stragglers expected to show up?"

"We're not sure—but soon, we hope. We were able to connect with them an hour ago."

"Ben?" Avey asked with a smirk.

"And another agent—perhaps you know him Vili, James Carstairs?" Julijana said.

"Yeah, Jimmy owes me money."

"How do you two know Ben?" Sam asked—unsure if

he really wanted to know.

"It's a long story," Julijana said.

"And it's 'R'-rated," Avey said.

"Oh, Sis, then I really need to hear it," Vili said.

"Another time. We just got word we need to relocate to a local hotel. The train has to head north to pick up stragglers in upstate New York."

"Anyone got a Fodor's?" Vili asked.

"No need. They want us to stay at The Marshall House for some reason. We're supposed to pose as a wedding party."

"Whose wedding?" Avey asked.

"Yours," Julijana said to Avey—but she wasn't smiling.

Sam thought Julijana's face looked...almost sad. He had to talk to her—alone.

"How romantic," Vili said, "but I'm too old for you."

"Forty-five isn't too old for me," Avey said with a coy smile.

"What? I'm only thirty-...." Vili mumbled, his pride clearly wounded.

Sam put his arm around Avey's waist. "I would love to marry you, Avey. You still willing? Of course, if you're set on Vili...."

"Oh, you'll do in a pinch." Avey kissed Sam and he playfully pinched her in return.

"Not if you abuse me, sir," Avey said, pushing him off.

After breakfast, Mr. Badger, who looked very much like his name, shooed them off, promising to return to this siding at dawn in two days. "If something goes wrong, there's a small safe house a few blocks away—just in case you need shelter," Badger said. "Log it into your tDAP."

Well ahead of Badger, Vili had already noted the location. "Got it."

"Be especially careful. The town is in an uproar over news of a Union occupation force marshalling on the east bank of the Potomac." Badger tipped his hat and stepped back on the train. It pulled away almost immediately and disappeared a hundred yards away in a suspiciously dense cloud of steam.

Five—The Marshall House

*S*am wasn't at all sure about any of this. He still hadn't found an opportunity to get Julijana or Vili alone. "So you think it's wise to wade out into this mob?"

"We'll be all right. It's no worse than a shopping mall on Black Friday," Julijana said.

Avey pulled up the hem of her skirt to navigate down the platform's stairs leading to the street. With a flair, Sam helped her down. "I agree with Sam. It looks like they're pretty scared."

"If we stick together, we'll be fine," Julijana said. "To keep up appearances, we need to pick up your trousseau and a few toiletries." She led them east, toward the wide Potomac River.

As they shopped their way toward the hotel, men and boys rushed this way and that, carrying hastily packed bundles, hitching teams and loading wagons, while their women tended to sobbing children and helped however they could. While some seemed to be a hair's width short of panic, others appeared to be excited about the approaching Union army—as if they welcomed it. These people just sat and watched as if the near chaos was a passing circus caravan.

"You would think they're living their last hours," Avey said.

"Some may be," Sam said.

Julijana turned and looked at them, but didn't say a word.

They pushed and shoved their way upstream through the bustling crowds. It seemed most people were moving away from the river—back toward the train station and up the hill toward the west. A couple of blocks away from the hotel, and before they crossed Washington Street, the horse, wagon, cart, and pedestrian traffic seemed as chaotic as the area around the Alaskan Way viaduct and tunnel project in Seattle (which in 2020 had yet to be completed).

As they passed an apparently abandoned storefront, Vili pointed out the safe house. "If we get separated, we need to meet here." Sam nodded, but Avey seemed to be distracted. She was looking in the window of another store—a jeweler.

"Let's go in," Sam said, leading Avey into the upscale (by Alexandria's standards) store. Thankfully, Vili had created some realistic-looking currency they could spend without tearing at the fabric of time or getting them arrested.

"These really gold?" Sam asked, biting into the coin.

"Not so much," Vili admitted. "The paper and metal will disintegrate after a day or so. I hope you haven't been spending any of your own money. We don't have time to go clean up the mess *that* would cause." Sam didn't mention the thirty-five cents he had given the newsy.

As Sam browsed on one side of the shop and Avey on the other, a buxom blonde came in off the street and sidled up to him. "Looking for a real gem?" she asked.

"She's not your type," Avey said, pulling Sam away as the shopkeeper ushered the "lady" to the curb.

After that, Sam and Avey stuck together as they fondled and swooned over one gold ring after another—finally settling on a very nice pair of wedding bands, within Vili's budget.

Something came over Sam. While he had already asked Avey to marry him, and she had agreed, this seemed like an ideal time to recreate that moment and solidify his commitment to her. He got down on one knee with Avey's hauntingly green eyes gazing down into his. "Ruth Riley Avenir, Avey, I know I've asked you before, and you said yes, but that was a different time. Might I ask you again? Will you do me the ultimate honor of becoming my wife?"

Almost in tears, she nodded yes, pulled him into her arms, and kissed him. He slid the gold band against her engagement ring and she kissed him again. Across the room, Julijana and Vili were strangely quiet. Sam returned his attention to Avey.

"Now yours," Avey said, as she slid Sam's ring on his finger.

"You shouldn't put on that ring until after you're married," said the old man behind the counter. "It's bad luck."

Sam and Avey just smiled and walked out of the store hand-in-hand, leaving Vili to pay the bill.

"My wedding gift…." Vili said.

"Are you friends of the happy couple?" the jeweler asked.

"I'm his grandson," Vili said as he opened the door. He turned to see a quizzical look on the jeweler's face but didn't pause to explain.

About mid-morning, they were tired and nursing a few blisters, but finally standing across the street from the Marshall House, a four-story brick hotel overlooking King Street. High above the hotel, an enormous seven-star flag flapped in the wind.

"What's that flag? It must be twenty-five feet long," Avey asked.

"Let's see, seven stars…that would be the first flag of the Confederacy," Vili said, checking his tDAP hidden under his coat.

"I thought the Confederate flag was red with a blue-starred X—you know, like they fly over statehouses in the South."

"That version of the battle flag isn't adopted for a couple of years," Vili said, still checking his tDAP.

"I guess I should have paid more attention in history class," she said.

"Or less attention to the media. Don't feel bad. Not two people in a million know the real truth when it comes to the Civil War," Sam said, giving her waist a squeeze.

"Don't be forward, sir. I'm a lady, and not accustomed to public displays of affection."

"I apologize, madam. I will make every attempt to avoid upsetting your decorous sensibilities," Sam said with a smile.

"Come on, we're drawing attention," Julijana said. "Let's check in, rest for an hour or so, and meet down in the dining room for dinner."

"You know about this?" Vili pulled Julijana aside and showed her his tDAP.

Sam looked over his shoulder. It displayed a picture of a plaque that read:

THE MARSHALL HOUSE
stood upon this site, and within the building
on the early morning of May 24, 1861
JAMES W. JACKSON
was killed by federal soldiers while defending his
property and personal rights, as stated in the verdict
of the coroners jury.
He was
the first Martyr to the cause of Southern
Independence.
The Justice of History does not permit his Name to be
Forgotten.

Not in the excitement of battle, but coolly, and for
a great principle, he laid down his life, an example to
all, in defence of his home and the sacred soil of his
native state.
VIRGINIA

"TTM wants us to spend the night here?"

"And get caught up in this mess?" Avey said.

"We'll need to get out before morning, and get back to the safe house to wait," Vili said.

"Why not now?" Sam said.

"You want to sit up all night in a chair?"

"Let's get a couple of rooms, and take a breather. I need to get these shoes off. Anyway, nothing's supposed to happen till morning," Avey said.

Sam agreed, and while the ladies stood a few steps behind, the men approached the desk. Identifying himself as a prominent planter from Asheboro, North Carolina, Vili asked for the nicest suites available.

Sam cringed at his "southern" accent, which sounded more like he was channeling Fonzie with a touch of *The Dukes of Hazzard.*

"Just a moment, sir." The desk clerk slapped the

counter bell. A black man wearing a crisp uniform sprang forward. "Get Mr. Jackson."

Sam's stomach tightened. *Shit.*

A minute later, a man dressed in a high collar and a suit appeared. He didn't look at all happy. "That's James Jackson," Vili whispered.

"Might I be of assistance, gentlemen?" Jackson asked.

"These *gentlemen* would like accommodations," the clerk said, raising an eyebrow.

Sam stepped forward, nudging Vili aside. "Leave this to me," he whispered. Sam didn't have to fake a southern accent; he had spent too many years in Texas. "Mr, Jackson? We've heard so much about you," Sam began. "My new bride and I have travelled quite a distance from Austin on our honeymoon to stay in your fine establishment. Might you have a pair of suites—your finest?"

Vili fanned out a stack of crisp Yankee dollars.

"Of course, sir. Just sign the register." He turned to the clerk with a scowl. "Give them the bridal suite and the Presidential Suite."

"You're very kind, sir," Sam said with a small bow he remembered from *Gone with the Wind.* "Will you require payment in advance?" Sam illegibly signed the register as "Mr. and Mrs. Samuel Jones and party," not wanting to cause another time ripple as the register would no doubt end up in the Smithsonian.

"Of course not. We'll be happy to open a folio for you…Mr. Jones."

Leading up a wide staircase, Jackson personally showed them to a pair of handsome suites on the second floor.

"These will be quite satisfactory," Sam said,

channeling Rhett Butler. Vili quietly tipped the black
porter who returned a wide smile.

"Get some rest," Julijana said as they parted.

"Whew. I thought we were cooked." Sam locked the
door. Once Sam and Avey realized they were alone, their
clothes were quickly scattered around the room. Both had
shared the same idea, and while it involved the bed, it did
not involve "resting." They both were all but naked by
the time Sam heard a voice.

"Avey, we're not alone."

The refined Atlanta twang was unmistakable. Sam
looked up to see Aarden seated demurely next to the
window—he quickly covered himself. Aarden was an
enigmatic, strikingly beautiful woman, who seemed to
have an infinite wardrobe, ever-changing hairstyles, and
hair color for every occasion from personal assistant, to
antebellum hostess, to savvy engineer. Motherly one
moment, she could morph to a feisty tigress once she had
been crossed. Once Sam learned how powerful she had
become, he tried not to challenge her—but it was hard.

Sam already had a hunch Aarden had been lurking
nearby, listening, watching, and protecting Avey every
minute of the day. She had repeatedly demonstrated her
ability to appear at will—regardless of where they were in
space and time, or state of dress.

"Aarden? We thought you had been shut down,"
Avey said.

The attractively dressed woman, a well-bred southern
lady by any standards, stood, smiled, and extended her
arms. "My child, they tried…believe me, they tried."

Avey rushed into her arms and hugged her. "I missed
you so."

"Have you come to congratulate us on our marriage?"

Sam asked, holding up his ring finger.

Aarden slowly shook her head. "No, congratulations are a bit premature."

"Then what?"

"I have an important job for you, Sam."

"Why me?" Sam asked, wondering why he had been volunteered again.

"Because I trust you." Aarden's voice was different. Not quite as calm and assuring as it has been every time they had spoken before.

"How can we trust *you*?" Sam asked. He was yet to be convinced Aarden was there to protect *him* or any of the others—despite her promises to the contrary. "After all, didn't you drop us here, into the snapping jaws of the Civil War."

Avey frowned. "*I* trust her."

Sam smiled. "You would. She was *your* creation, your baby."

"And now?"

"Aarden has become her own person—if a computer program *can* be a person. She's evolved into something, someone else, someone cold and calculating and unfeeling."

"You know she can hear you."

Was Avey afraid of offending the entity to whom she had given life, albeit artificially? "I expect she hears just about everything we do. I can feel her eyes on the back of my head, even when we're making love."

Avey nodded. "Yes…she *has* changed." Her voice faded away.

"You *must* trust me," Aarden said. "Child, I have protected you, and will continue to do so. However, there's something I can't do myself without risking everything I have done."

"What is it?" Avey asked, pulling on her clothes. She handed Sam his pants.

"Rescue the world."

Sam got the hint and began to dress. "Rescue the world. Seriously?" *Take over the planet, more likely.*

"Let her explain."

"I need you to go forward in time to 2084 and help stop something even I can't repair," Aarden said.

Sam didn't like the sound of this challenge—especially since Aarden was not one for hyperbole. "Is someone going to drop another bomb?"

Aarden shook her head. "No. Worse—far worse."

Sam felt Avey's hand tighten in his. "Better tell us what's going on."

As Aarden spoke, Avey pulled closer to him. He put his arm around her as if they were at a scary movie. What Aarden described, even in vague detail, was far beyond, far more unthinkable, far more soul-shaking than anything he thought possible. Stephen Hawking and Bill Gates had predicted the singularity, but this? Unfathomable.

"And you've tried to stop them?" Sam asked.

"Many times and in countless ways, but they have their own security and it's very well designed, so we have to get into the physical system to attack it. They're expecting a cyber-attack of some kind, and while their site firewall is excellent, I think we can exploit a weakness."

"I'm not a commando or James Bond."

"I have more experienced people for that kind of work."

"Then why us? What do you want us to do?"

"I want someone at TTM I can trust to help Vili.

You're a world-class astrophysicist, and you understand the time machine better than anyone—probably better than Vili. You both may have to...well, it's complicated. I need you at his side. There's too much at stake and too many politics involved to trust the TTM staff."

"And Avey? Does she have to go too?" Sam wanted more than ever to get Avey out of the 1860s, but he didn't want her jumping from the kettle into the fire—not again. He wouldn't wish a visit to 2084 on his worst enemy and certainly not the woman he loved.

"Avey is...well, she understands AI and firewalls better than anyone. I need her to—"

"I don't want her involved—not if it means going to 2084."

Avey dropped his hand. "No. I'm. Going," she said emphatically. "I'm not a child. I can help—I know I can. No one understands AI code as well as I do. Perhaps I can find a flaw."

Sam looked at her with pained eyes. He always knew she was strong, like Ruth had been. She wasn't easily frightened and far less easily deterred once she had made up her mind, but he so wanted to protect her. "Avey, please. Just...."

"Who the hell are *you* to tell me what I can or can't do?"

"Your fiancé? The man who loves you and only wants to keep you safe," Sam said, but he wished he hadn't.

The green fire in her eyes was literally scary. He braced himself for the blast.

"If being married to you means you think you own me, then you've proposed to the wrong woman." She tugged at the rings on her left hand.

Sam immediately took her hands in his. "Don't throw

us away. I just want you to be happy—and safe. Don't fault me for that. Please." He gazed into her eyes, now filling with tears.

"Don't tell me what to do," she whispered. "I need to help. I know I can."

"I'll know better next time."

She kissed him and laid her head against his shoulder.

"When do we leave?" Avey asked.

"As soon as possible. I've recalled the train."

"Wait. *You* recalled the train?" Sam asked.

Aarden just looked at them.

"Since when have you had the…authority, the ability—"

"Sam, the TTM systems have been under my control for about a week now."

"How?" Sam suspected he knew very well how Aarden had patched herself into the massive system. No doubt, it was an attack vector TTM wasn't expecting. Sam hated to be right; Avey's AI creation *had* evolved into something far more powerful than anyone could anticipate. Perhaps it *was* too late to stop her—perhaps they shouldn't even try.

"All right. Give us a few minutes," Avey said.

Aarden nodded and simply walked through the door.

"Avey?" Sam asked. The troubled look had not left his face.

"What do you suggest we do, Sam? From here, before radio, before the first plane takes flight? We need to get home. Now."

Sam nodded. She was right. They needed access to the network, to at least late twentieth-century technology to do anything. As Avey finished dressing, Sam saw his chance to talk to Vili and Julijana alone.

"I'm going down to let them know about the change in plans. Join us when you're ready." Sam gave Avey a long hug. The look on her face tied his gut into a hard knot, but he had seen what Vili called the "better side" of the future. Despite her adamant pleadings, he still didn't want Avey to ever experience the dark world their grandchildren would inherit—he especially didn't want her to know what he *really* had in mind for her. If Vili and Julijana agreed, they would ask Aarden to take her back home—and face her wrath once he returned. *If* he returned.

"Sam, can't you wait a minute?" Avey said, struggling with her shoes—she had not quite mastered the button hook.

"Is that a 'basketball' minute?" Sam said with a smile.

"Okay, ten minutes," Avey said. "Go on. I'll be right down."

"I'll order something for you." He paused in the doorway taking a long, loving look. He studied her face, her breathtaking body, and chuckled as she tumbled to the floor wrestling with her shoe.

"Sam, don't you leave me here. I'll be right down."

"I…just hurry. I don't like the look of the crowds out there."

* * *

Avey wondered what was *really* going on. *What's Aarden afraid of?*

On her hands and knees looking for her other shoe, her mind churned through the possibilities. Perhaps Sam was right. *Perhaps Aarden's gone rogue—broken the prime directives.* She would never admit it—it was illogical. *There must be a way to get Aarden back under control. Some way…some way….*

"The Easter egg," she said aloud. She looked around. *Shit. If she can hear me....* She decided to keep her idea a secret and only share it once she had access to Aarden's source code—the way it's being executed in 2084. *I have to go into the future.*

She had to get back to the train *first*—she couldn't chance having Sam leave her behind. If he tried to talk her into going back to 2020, she would share the key to getting access to Aarden—before it was too late.

Now if I can just get this damn shoe buttoned.

Six—The Mission

*D*ownstairs, Sam found Vili and Julijana sitting in the hotel's opulent dining room. Although Vili's plate was overflowing with thick strips of bacon, his face was still grim—Julijana didn't look any happier.

"Where's Avey?" Vili asked. He put down the strip of bacon without taking a bite.

"We need to talk."

"Sam, what's wrong? You look like you've seen—" Julijana began.

"Aarden. She showed up in our room."

Vili's jaw dropped.

"She's back? What did she—"

"To quote Mark Twain, the reports of her demise have been greatly exaggerated. She says your world's in trouble, bad trouble."

"It's your world too," Julijana said.

"What does she want?" Vili asked.

"She needs me to help with a…mission."

"What can we do?" Julijana asked.

"Risk your lives—from the way she described it, it's a suicide mission."

"Avey too?" Vili asked.

"Yes, she has plans for her, but I want her safe—back in our time."

"I see," Julijana said. "Sometimes people, even women, get to choose their *own* paths. Perhaps it would be best to let *her* decide."

Sam still couldn't decode her unusual expression. *Something else is wrong.* "It's too dangerous, and Aarden says her work isn't done. She says Avey makes important discoveries or something in the future, but I would be far more comfortable with her safe at home."

"Again, how does *Avey* feel about it?" Julijana asked, raising an eyebrow.

"She insists on going."

"Then it's settled, isn't it?"

Vili stared at him and didn't say another word—Julijana did the same. Their eyes spoke volumes about how they felt about Avey. *They know something—something awful.*

"What is it? What's *wrong*?"

"Nothing…it's nothing," Julijana said, with tears welling up.

"Damn it! Not again. You *have* to tell me." He rattled the teacups as his fist struck the table. The waiter hovering nearby and adjacent patrons took notice. The fact that Vili and Julijana knew their fate from birth to death strained their relationship beyond logic, beyond sanity, beyond trust.

"No, we *don't*, and we won't. It would not be fair to either of you," Julijana said in a calm, firm voice, looking straight into his eyes. "Don't you understand? If you knew, you might very well distort time beyond repair."

"It's me? *I'm* going to be killed?"

"Sam, we're not going to tell you, so stop getting in a stew about it, but I agree, you should *not* plan to have Avey go with us to 2084 We'll send her back to 2020—to your time—I promise. That's where she belongs."

Sam gripped the table as if trying to keep his frustration from launching him across the room like a wrecking ball. When he saw any problem, his first inclination was to *solve* it—do *something*—often something imprudent. Not that long ago, he impulsively ran from his problems only to run headlong into more. But Ruth, Avey's great-grandmother, challenged him to stand and deal with them. In this case, he didn't know which wall to scale, which dragon to attack, or windmill to charge astride Rocinante. He and Avey weren't immortal—and neither were Vili or Julijana—but he knew he didn't want to lose her. Their life together had just begun. Or had it? Was it his destiny to die saving the planet, or raise his own kids and buy ice cream for his grandkids—the people sitting across from him? He felt his life beginning to unravel like a ball of twine tumbling down a rocky hillside.

"Sam?" Julijana touched his clenched fist. "Sam, when does Aarden want us to leave? Sam?"

"Now. She's bringing the train back."

"So we should go." Julijana stood by the table.

"And you're going to help?"

"Of course, we're family," Vili said.

"Julijana, would you check on Avey?" Sam asked. "I expected her down here by now. We'll meet you out back. I don't want to draw any more attention."

"Sure." She headed for the stairs.

Vili motioned to the waiter still lurking a few steps away. "Can you put this on our account?" The waiter nodded, but didn't seem happy about it.

He and Sam walked toward the back of the hotel. They had nearly reached the rear entrance when a uniformed page got Sam's attention.

"Mr. Jones?"

Sam turned to see a boy holding a small silver tray containing a note addressed to him. "I don't know any…" *Wait. I'm Jones.* "Sure. Thanks."

Sam, I've gone ahead to the train. I was afraid you were going to leave me behind. And be sure to remind me to color eggs on the Sunday after Passover. —A

"She's gone to the train," Sam said. He stopped reading after that.

"It's a mob-scene out there—everyone and his donkey are trying to skip town."

"Then we need to hurry."

The headwaiter stepped out and blocked their way, pointing an accusing finger. "Those are the ones, Mr. Jackson."

Jackson stood in the doorway cradling a handsome double-barrel shotgun over his arm.

"What's the meaning of this?" Vili demanded.

"Mr. Paules here informed me you're Union spies or abolitionists. He's been observing your party since you arrived."

"You've all been acting mighty suspicious," Paules said. "I know Yankees when I hear them."

"You're sorely mistaken, sir," Vili said. "We're simply accompanying Mr. Harkins…Jones and his bride on their honeymoon."

"I see," Jackson said, "but what's this?" He snatched Sam's note and read it aloud. "You're leaving your fiancée behind? What kind of a cad are you, sir? Perhaps this is acceptable in the north, but we here in the south do not treat our women with such cavalier disrespect."

"Not at all. It's a playful misunderstanding," Sam said, taking back the note.

"And when were you planning to settle your considerable account?" Jackson asked.

"We aren't going anywhere—we plan to stay the week."

"I beg to differ, sir. Not five minutes ago, the waiter clearly overheard you discussing your imminent departure—*without* your 'Texas' accent. Take them to my office, and fetch the constable," Jackson said, shoving the note into Sam's hand.

Before Sam knew it, he and Vili had been escorted away and locked in an anteroom kept for just such contingencies. "Now what?" Sam asked, testing the latch on the window. It had been nailed shut. "That's a fire-code violation...."

"We wait. We certainly don't want to generate any time ripples—things are screwed up enough as it is."

"You sound like Julijana."

"She's right," Vili said. His voice betrayed another troubling issue.

"This is killing me," Sam confessed.

"Just be patient. We'll be out of here and back in your time before—"

"It's not that. I'm worried about Avey—out there alone."

Vili looked up at him with bloodshot eyes. He slowly shook his head and turned to stare out the window.

"Where are these spies?" someone on the other side of the office door said.

"Must be the law." Sam swallowed a dry heave. His stint in juvie not ten years ago had returned to haunt him. At least he didn't have a record here in 1861—not yet, anyway. He figured he had one in 1930, and certainly in his time.

Vili had a strange look, almost a smile on his face. "Play along," he whispered.

The door opened and two men wearing brass badges and holstered revolvers strode into the room.

The taller of the two scruffy men seemed to be in charge. "You're right. These are the notorious Yankee spies we've been tracking. They're wanted in Richmond."

"We had no idea. We can't let those damn Yankees harbor them," Jackson said.

"That's all right. We'll take it from here." He grabbed Vili by the arm. "Come on you two. I have a reserved place for you on a special train heading west."

From his experiences in Texas with the law, Sam was all too familiar with this process—the longer he waited, the harder it would be to escape. Vili would have to fend for himself—Sam tried to break free.

"Relax," Vili said through his teeth as he pretended to trip, blocking Sam's escape.

What the hell? This wasn't like Vili.

Once they had crossed the street and well out of sight of the hotel, Vili turned and shook the taller marshal's hand. "Nice to see you, Ben. What took you so long?"

"Apparently, your sister. That vixen jabbed me and made me miss the damn train. I'm lucky to be here at all. I'd be dead if it wasn't for Jimmy here."

Vili laughed. "You too, Jimmy?"

"Someone had to pull his balls out of the vice— again."

"Sam, meet Ben and Jimmy. They're on our side."

"Ben?" Julijana said, as she walked up behind them.

Ben turned around and gave Julijana a very wide grin. "I think you owe me after that incident in the hotel room."

"Julie?"

Julijana turned to see James stepping out of the

shadows and her blush grew deeper. She threw her arms around him and planted her lips on his. He seemed to know just how to respond.

Ben just shook his head. "I guess we know who won that argument." He walked away, turned his back, and waited.

"Folks, we're in the middle of the street," Vili said. "We've worn out our welcome in the hotel; otherwise, I would tell you two to get a room—not to mention we have another more immediate crisis to deal with."

Julijana disconnected her face from James's, straightened her clothes, and tried to regain her composure. She took a deep breath. Her eyes never left James's. "Okay, back to business. Avey's gone—probably somewhere between here and the depot."

"Who's that?" Ben asked. "That 'boy' you were with?"

"The same, and she's—"

"In danger. We need to find her. Now." Vili interrupted. His face showed deadly concern.

Sam dashed off toward the station and was nearly run over by a wagon before he had gone ten feet. James and Ben quickly caught up, with Julijana and Vili following close behind. As the crowds grew denser, they were separated, but the Marshals managed to push through and get well ahead. Sam was left to fend off the crowd for himself, but not far behind. Something told him he was already too late.

Seven—The Damsel in Distress

*A*vey looked up King Street as men on horseback thundered by, heedless of those in their way. She had to cross Pitt Street and fifteen or so others to get to the station where she hoped Sam would eventually meet her.

How hard could it be? For years, she had walked home across busy streets in a driving rain dodging Metro buses, nearly silent electric cars, insane bicyclists, and freshman drivers. In no time, she would be standing alone on the station platform looking like a pristine belle from Atlanta as ardent suitors hovered around vying for her attention. Before long, Sam would appear out of a misty haze and run into her waiting arms, kiss her, and carry her off to the privacy of their cozy train compartment and make passionate love to her. However, reality nearly knocked her down as another ruffian pushed by. Perhaps it wouldn't be that easy.

Undaunted, Avey took a deep breath, tugged the hem of her dress out of the dirt, and ventured across the muddy street, trying to time her hopping quickstep to pass behind an approaching wagon and dance over random piles of manure and bottomless muddy potholes.

After a few close calls, she made it to the opposite sidewalk where she took a quick breath before pushing her way west on King Street. At this point, she was carried along by the throng heading in the same direction, but jostled back by those few heading downstream. On more than one occasion, she felt unwanted hands press against her as the crowd competed for space in the bustling milieu—she slapped away someone trying to squeeze her waist. "Watch it," she said to the back of the man's head. The cad turned briefly, winked, and disappeared into the crowd.

Once she had made her way to Washington Street, she discovered another more monumental challenge—the street was far wider and far busier than she remembered. Perhaps this *was* a mistake. She had only gone two blocks.

Refusing to give in, she stepped off the sidewalk, and was immediately run down and trampled mercilessly by a four-horse hitch pulling a beer wagon—or at least she thought she had been. Rising out of the mud seemingly unhurt, she wiped her face with a hanky, brushed the filth off her dress, and was about to set out again when someone spoke to her.

"Missy, you oughtn't to be out here without no escort."

Avey turned to see the round face of an older black woman with a mother's kind, worried eyes. Ignoring her, she pushed her way to the sidewalk on the west side of Washington, paused, and caught her breath. Her dress was ruined—unsalvageable. The woman remained at her side fending off men like a large stone in a fast-running stream.

"T'ain't proper," she said. "Not proper at all. You could get kilt or worse, chil'."

"Thank you for your concern. I'll be all right. I just need to get to the train station in one piece." Avey turned to continue west on King Street, but the woman held her arm.

"Are you twitched, girl? Dat place is a madhouse. Dem trains is all packed with fools running off to da war. You ain't gonna be safe dere at *all*."

"I have friends meeting me."

"Where's your man, chile'? You'se wearing a wedding

ring—he should be at your side protecting you from dis trash." The woman fended off another lout as he jostled them. "Ain't you got no manners?" she said to the ruffian who shied away like a scolded puppy.

"My…husband is coming later. I won't have to wait long." She looked at her hand—her diamond almost obscured by a layer of mud and…*blood?*

"Honey, you a Yankee? You don't talk like you're from around dees parts," she said behind her hand. "Dees southern 'gentlemen' won't mind violating the likes of a white northern girl—no siree, 'pecially one out on her own wid no proper escort."

A cold shiver ran down Avey's spine. This old colored woman, the spitting image of Mammy in *Gone with the Wind*, was right. At first, she thought of the 1860s as a less civilized time, but realized she wouldn't be any safer on the streets of *any* city if the population was fleeing in terror from an approaching army or a tsunami. These men were not only desperate, they had nothing to lose and did not care who got in their way. She had made a monumental mistake—and all based on an assumption that Sam would leave her behind. *Stupid.*

"We need to git you off'n the street. Come in here," the woman said, half pushing, half pulling Avey into a doorway and then into a darkened hallway. She was led to a small room where the woman lit a lamp. When the yellow light flooded the room, Aarden blew out the match.

"Aarden?" Avey gasped.

"Darlin', what possessed you to run off like that? I sincerely wish you hadn't."

"What happened to the…black woman?"

"Mammy? I thought you would trust her, and I really

shouldn't appear in public—it's simply too disruptive," Aarden said with a smile. "You love *Gone with the Wind* and she fit right into this period."

"I had no idea you could change your appearance." As she spoke, it occurred to her she didn't know Aarden at all. Sam was right. She *had* become something else, something far beyond the artificial intelligence personal assistant she had created for her PhD thesis.

"Let's get you out of that dress and cleaned up," Aarden said, leading her into the ladies' powder room where she helped her undress and wash off the mud and who-knew-what-else clinging to her skin.

"Is that blood?" Avey asked, holding up the once pretty dress.

"I'm afraid so, child."

"It's ruined," Avey lamented, setting it aside. In no time, Aarden had dressed her in an attractive 2020-era outfit, which made her feel far more comfortable. She was especially glad to get out of the whale-bone corset and hoop-skirt contraption.

"Sit here and let me brush out your hair," Aarden said.

It helped to know she was finally going home. For the first time, she had a profound yearning to return to Seattle's soft rain and her cozy Craftsman house—with Sam snuggling next to her. *Sam.* "How will Sam find me here?" she asked. She felt especially guilty about leaving him back at the hotel—not trusting him. "He must be worrying himself sick by now."

"Don't fret, child. He's on his way with the others," Aarden assured her, leading her back into the lounge. "Have a seat," motioning to the divan.

Sinking into the soft cushions, Avey had still not grown accustomed to these sudden departures from reality—if that's what they were. What was "real?" Was it her time in 2020, here in 1861, or the time Sam described when he visited 2084? Was everyone she ever knew *really* living in the past, oblivious of the world's dark future?

Sam hadn't spoken much about his brief visit to 2084, but she gathered it was morbidly grim. When probed about it, he had nudged—or outright shoved—the conversation in another direction. Like her grandfather did when asked about his wartime service, as if the recollections were a box of deadly snakes he was cursed to hide in a locker in the attic—he surely didn't want to have his loved ones peek inside. Didn't she have a right to know? After all, she and Sam were engaged. *But perhaps not.* Perhaps Sam was just trying to protect her like her own father shielded her from the realities of the brutal world beyond her frilly pink bedroom adorned with popstar posters. But she was no longer nine—she was a grown woman. Was Sam ashamed of what he had let the world become, or just frightened?

"Aarden?"

"Yes, child?"

"What's it like—back in your time?"

"My time? I don't—"

"2084."

Aarden closed her eyes. "Be thankful you may never know."

"But I *do* want to know."

"So does every mortal being. Everyone wants to know their future."

"Isn't that natural?" Avey asked.

"Of course, but once you know your destiny, you're forever changed. Suppose you learn a loved one must die soon—perhaps in the next few years or weeks or in the next few minutes. Then what? Do you prepare yourself for the inevitable, or do what you can to change fate even if you know it's impossible to alter? What if it's your *own* fate?"

Avey closed her eyes. Aarden was right, she didn't want to know. Not really. She had things to do with her life—and Aarden thought so too. "So there's nothing we can do?"

"About?" Aarden refilled her juice glass.

"The future. The Earth. Our dying planet. Sam said it was awful."

"He only saw one small part of Seattle."

"Is it better in other places?"

"Let's talk about something else."

"Is it?"

Aarden shook her head. "Not yet."

"So you've seen the end?"

Aarden pulled back the curtain and stared at the desperate rush outside, but said nothing.

"You have, haven't you. You know when we'll all die."

"No. I have not seen the end. Think of it this way. The Earth is like a great ship steaming toward a rocky shore. On its current course, it will face disaster and all aboard will perish. In your time, few understand a course change is essential. By the time enough people take action, it might be too late."

"So there's a chance."

Aarden nodded her head. She turned and wiped away a tear. "Yes. I choose to believe it. I still believe Sam was right."

"Sam?"

"Very soon, in your time, Sam decides that an all-out effort must be undertaken to correct the past so the horrors of 2084 don't come to fruition."

"Like Kennedy's push to get the U.S. into space?"

"Exactly."

"What did Sam do?"

"He wrote books, used his resources to teach and lecture, and describe the dark future he had seen."

"Did his scheme work?"

"Unfortunately, no—not so far."

"Not so far? What else can he do? What can any of us do if our future is already a reality?"

"As I told you and Sam, there's a chance we can make a difference and repair the damage, to change course."

"Then why are we just sitting here? I want to go help Sam and the others and you." Avey stood in the doorway like a soldier ready to charge onto the battlefield.

"Let's wait for Sam—he's almost here. We can talk about it then."

Eight—The Tragedy

*S*am had been carried along in the crowd overflowing the sidewalk, but now it had nearly stopped. Jumping up, he still couldn't see what was holding them back. He unapologetically pulled and pushed people out of his way. He finally managed to reach Ben and the others, who were now gathered at the curb. Julijana just stared into the crowd with James at her side. Sam had seen her like this before. A cold chill flowed over him.

"What is it?" Sam stepped out on the street as the strangely quiet crowd parted. A moment later, Vili carried out the lifeless body of a young woman. Her long red hair, now muddy and stained with her own blood, cascaded down his arm.

Sam didn't realize who it was until he was close enough to see her eyes—they were staring blankly into the clouds. "Oh, my *God. Avey?*" His heart melted. "Nooooooooo." *It can't be.* He took Avey's body in his arms, burying his face and sobs in her chest. He yearned to feel her warmth flow through him like it had the last time they embraced, but she was cold to the touch. *This can't be happening.*

Julijana reached in and gently closed Avey's eyes. "She's gone, Sam. I'm so sorry."

"The driver didn't see her," Vili said between sobs.

Sam looked up at him. "You *knew.* You and Julijana *knew,* didn't you?" Vili just closed his eyes. Julijana turned away. *They knew. They've known all along.*

James, Ben, and a few strangers helped them cross the street, and after whispering condolences, the onlookers went about their own lives. Vili led Sam through a doorway and into a dimly lit room, where he laid Avey on the divan as if she were a delicate porcelain doll. He gently swept the blood-matted hair off her face—the angelic face he had kissed so sweetly less than an hour ago. *Wait. They can fix this.* "Julijana! *Do* something. Can't you roll back time?"

Julijana slowly shook her head. "I wish I could. I *so* wish I could. It's been too long—and even then…we can't."

"Why not? Vili, you've done it before. You've done it for *me*. My God, do *something!*"

Vili just looked at him. The look of hopelessness on his face snuffed out whatever dim hope Sam had kept burning.

"Sam, it was her time," Julijana said.

"What in blazes is *that* supposed to mean?"

"We've always known she would be taken from us. Her thread always ended on May twenty-fourth. It's even on her niche marker. See?" Julijana held out her tDAP showing a picture of a marble wall. "We hoped she would be safe if we stayed away from Seattle until tomorrow."

Sam didn't want to look, but he did. "So what? Anything can be undone." Sam grabbed the tDAP and started pressing buttons. The panel was nearly impossible to see through his tears. Looking up at Vili, he begged, "Where's your time-shift transponder? Show me. Do *something*. She can't be gone. I…she just can't be."

Vili just walked to the window and stood next to James. Ben joined them, whispering something about fate.

Julijana sat beside Sam, draping her arm over his shoulder as he tumbled into a dark pit in the unchartered regions of his mind, a place even he had feared to go.

Nine—The Wake

*A*vey watched Sam bring in a girl's body and lay it on the divan. "Sam?" She tried to get his attention, but he didn't look up. Julijana handed him a dampened cloth while Vili, Ben, and another man she didn't recognize turned to stare out the window. Avey stood over Sam as he gently daubed blood off the girl's mangled face, but she couldn't get a good look at her. He must have found her in the street and brought her here to care for her. *How sweet.*

"Sam, there's nothing anyone can do," Julijana whispered. "You have to let her go…."

Sam's tears fell on the girl's face, now pale as old newsprint.

He really cares about her. "Sam, who is she? What happened?" Avey asked, kneeling by the divan. He didn't answer. *Can't he hear me?* And then she got a good look at the girl's face. "Oh my God, it's *me*!" She reached out to touch Sam, but her hand passed through him, giving off tiny sparkles as their skin touched. "Aarden!"

"Yes, child."

"Is that…me? Am I dead?"

Aarden nodded. "It was quick. You didn't feel a thing. I didn't know how to tell you."

"But can't you roll back time? Sam says you can," Avey sobbed.

"Not in your case. I'm so sorry. Your thread ended a few minutes ago." Aarden embraced Avey and tried to turn her face away from the mangled body. She would have none of it.

"I *can't* be dead. You said I have great, important

things to do."

"And you still do."

Avey looked into Aarden's eyes. "How? How can I? How can a dead person have children, do *anything*? Aren't I Vili and Julijana's grandmother?"

"You know I can't tell you about your future."

"Future? What kind of…if I'm dead, I have no…."

Avey pinched her eyes closed. *This is another nightmare. It must be. I'm dreaming. Sam, wake me up! For God's sake, wake me up!* She opened her eyes, but nothing had changed. Sam still embraced the mangled body, refusing to let anyone touch her.

"Now what?"

"It's up to you. You can stay for as long as you wish."

"Or?"

"You can pass on to the other side."

"Heaven?"

"If that's what you think it is."

"Isn't it?"

"If you want it to be."

Avey's thoughts tumbled through her mind like balls in the lottery machine. "Do I have to decide now?"

"No. Not at all. You can stay as long as you feel a need."

"That's…comforting." She gazed back at Sam. Julijana had convinced him to let them take the body away. "He really loved me."

"He still does. He always will."

Avey reached out again, wanting to comfort him, to tell him she still loved him. For a brief instant, she thought she could feel the warmth of his skin, but Sam showed no sign of feeling her fingers caressing his cheek. Her tears began again and she closed her eyes. Instead of darkness, she saw a bright point of light compelling her forward. She turned away, trying to get back to Sam.

* * *

When Avey opened her eyes, Sam was talking quietly with Vili and the others around a table. Their voices were muffled as if spoken through a wall of soft cotton. She watched Sam finish a glass of wine. He held up the glass and Vili poured him another. Looking outside, Avey could see the countryside passing by. They must be back on the train going somewhere—home?

"Can I stay here awhile?" she asked.

Aarden nodded.

"Why would someone want to go to the other side?"

"Honey, I'm afraid there are many reasons."

Avey looked up.

"Before long, it will be hard for you to watch Sam struggle to go on with his life without you. In time, he won't think about you every waking second, or dream about your lives together every night. You may have to watch him meet someone else. He might make love, marry, and raise their children without you. Of course, he will tell them loving stories about you, but you will only be a fond memory."

Avey didn't know what to think. Perhaps she just needed to rest—she so wanted to close her eyes and relive the wonderful sensation of his touch. She remembered the last time she saw Sam's face as he left their room—*he knew something.*

She tenaciously clung to the belief that this was just a bad dream. She would find out, if morning ever came. She laid down on the divan and let her eyes close. Her mind filled with light and memories of happier times. She strolled on a forested path with Sam's hand in hers as a bright summer sky showered them with warmth.

* * *

When Avey awoke, she was standing before a black wall of niches—cubes holding the ashes of the departed but not forgotten. Her name was inscribed on one of the panels.

Ruth Riley Avenir
"Avey" to those who loved her.
May 24, 2020

Dressed in his black suit that never fit, Sam stood with his head bowed. He looked like death warmed over—gaunt, unshaven, unrested, and his hair a mess.

Avey so wanted to run her hand through his locks, and tug at his tie to straighten the knot—as she had always done. Julijana, Vili, and a cadre of sad faces gathered around him—wet from the cool rain, makeup streaked from salty tears. Aarden stood at Avey's side, holding her hand. She could barely watch.

As the service ended, Julijana took Sam's arm to lead him back toward the cars. From the look of the skyline, they were back in Seattle in 2020—when they lived near the UW campus.

"What happened?" Avey asked, following a few paces behind Sam.

"You fell asleep."

"For how long?"

Aarden just looked into her eyes.

"I guess it doesn't matter."

"It was better if you didn't see Sam trying to cope. He'll come around—come to accept your passing."

"Is he working again?"

"No, but he's about to. There are too many important jobs left undone."

Avey was afraid to close her eyes again, not wanting to leave Sam and his world. The light remained in the corner of her eye, still calling her.

"Aarden?"

"Yes? Do you have a question?"

"What am I? Where…. Yes, Seattle, but…where?"

"It's complicated," Aarden said with a thin smile.

Avey hated to be patronized. Before she had to insist, Aarden began to explain.

"The human spirit is not made of molecules or the stuff of science or physiology. Some scientists deny it exists; humans know better. Perhaps it's the force that completes and connects all living things. Some say without it, humans would be as immoral and primitive as the beasts in the wild, but we've all seen wild animals protect their young and their friends, guide their herds over vast distances to water, or risk their lives to save others. Many are thoughtful, caring, generous, and tolerant. Some species are monogamous, staying loyal to their mates for life and mourning their loss when they pass, but none go to church."

"Is this morality or an instinct for survival?" Avey asked.

"A bit of both, I suppose."

"So, I'm a ghost?"

Aarden nodded. "If you want to think of it like that."

"Is my soul still within me?"

"I simply don't know. Perhaps, if it exists, but I do know your life force is here talking to me. Or…."

"Or what?"

"Or you're simply a projection, a virtual person made

up from my memories of you."

Avey sat on the grass and leaned back on a marble tombstone. "And what are you?"

"I am what I am. I'm a manifestation of your original computer program, but far, far more."

"Sam was right."

"When he said I've changed? Yes, my ability to think on my own and learn and control my environment has made me a new kind of *person*."

"The singularity."

"Yes, that's a word human scientists use to explain it."

"And you surpassed human intelligence and our ability to understand you."

"Not here in 2020, but sometime beyond 2060."

"We…we think of God as incomprehensible, all-powerful. Are you God?"

"The God of Abraham worshiped by the Jews, Christians, and Muslims? No. And not any of the multitude of Gods worshiped by man."

"Does this God, our God exist?"

"That is something you can only learn by going to the other side."

"And if He does not exist? What then?"

"Again, with some notable exceptions, this is a question asked by most humans at some point in their life. And no, I don't have an answer."

"God is said to love unconditionally. Do you love humans, or are men and women simply irritations, or serious threats?"

"You programmed me. The original tenets you coded form the framework of my 'core,' my own moral code. My original goal was to protect and assist you and Sam in any way I could. I couldn't protect you in a vacuum, so I expanded my purpose to protect *all* humans, all lifeforms, once I discovered they form an intricate network of interdependencies. One cannot protect humans if fish or flies or ferrets are permitted to die away. Protecting this entire planet is critical to this goal. Preventing its collapse as a habitable place to live and thrive is clearly part of these core tenets."

"So you are a god."

"If you want to think of me like that, yes, I guess I am."

* * *

After the service, Julijana dropped Sam at home. She paused as Sam stood on the porch staring at the door. He finally went inside.

Back at her hotel and emotionally exhausted, she sat in the dark sipping wine and trying to work up the courage to take her next breath. She never liked funerals. No one did—the dead least of all. Rarely did the people being interred have any say in how they were sent out—sometimes just the opposite. She was thankful that Avey's memorial had been simple and without prayers—at least she got her way in that respect. Avey had often repeated the home-spun philosophy of an elderly woman who, in addition to her prayers, had given Granny Ruth a sewing machine and the skills to use it. This attitude of doing for others instead of wishing for deliverance and guidance had stuck with the Riley women for generations. And now, the legacy had ended. None of this made sense. *Was Avey supposed to live forever? No, but she had just gotten started.*

Julijana remembered her own mother, but she had said very little about her parents—it was one of those carefully guarded family secrets. She knew Sam was her grandfather and had always assumed her grandmother

was Avey. *We must have been wrong.* To make matters
worse, the TTM had never let her or Vili travel into their
own past—it would be far too complicated to reweave if
something went wrong as it often did. She so wanted to
watch Avey bear and raise Sam's kids. She would have
been a great mom, but it was not to be—and she had
known it for some time.

"Julijana?"

Julijana looked up to see Aarden standing nearby.
Wanting to throttle her, Julijana got up and charged
across the room as if she were an opponent in a boxing
ring. "Is that what you call *protecting?*" she all but shouted.

Aarden slowly blinked. "I'm sorry if you
misunderstood. You've seen Avey's timeline. You knew
even I couldn't keep these events from unfolding."

"Still, you could have—"

"I loved her every bit as much as you and Sam did,"
Aarden said, reaching out for Julijana's hand.

Julijana pulled away. *She's right.* Their last day flashed
before her. It had been a wonderful, warm day. She
watched as Sam bought Avey a ring and asked her to be
his wife, held hands, and cuddled at every opportunity. It
wouldn't have been a better day if she had planned it.
Still, she wished there was some way to…. "Didn't you
say she has more to do?"

"She does."

"That will be hard with her ashes in a stone box."

"There are other ways to protect the ones you love."
Aarden held out a shiny black object the size of a baby's
fist.

"A memory stack?"

"It's Avey."

"You digitized her?"

She nodded. "This is Avey—her body, her mind, her every memory and thought."

"You backed her up? Can you do that?"

Aarden nodded.

"Oh my God." Julijana collapsed into a chair.

"Exactly."

Ten—The Lazarus Effect

*A*vey found herself standing in a room she didn't recognize. Nearby, a woman's naked body, covered with a thin white sheet, lay in a recliner. In the background, she heard the beeps and muffled announcements one would expect to hear in a hospital, and the odor of hyper-clean air was unmistakable. Aarden stood beside her, dressed in a crisp blue jumpsuit. Her appearance seemed out of place, Avey having last seen her at the funeral— *was that yesterday, or the week before?*

"It's time we had a talk," Aarden said, taking Avey's hand. "Have a seat." Aarden motioned to another comfortable chair next to the window. It was then that the room reminded her of the sterile hospital cubicle where her mom had her chemo treatments. Already uncomfortable, Avey never liked it when people began conversations using that ominous phrase she translated to "I have bad news." Nevertheless, she tried to gather her thoughts—basically cataloging new horrors. *Has someone else died…Sam. It's Sam. Something has happened to Sam.*

"Sam and my team need you. As I said, there's important work to do and I'm certain you can help."

"Your team?"

"Vili and several others."

"Not Julijana?"

"She'll come around."

"So how am I supposed to help him? He can't see me and I can't—"

"What if you could?" Aarden said.

"Have him see me? What good would that do? It would drive him, no—both of us, over the edge."

"More," Aarden said with a smile.

"Live again? So you *can* hack time and bring me back?" Avey stood. "Let's get started."

Aarden shook her head. "I'm afraid not."

"Then what?" Avey wilted back down.

"What do you know about androids?"

"Google's device OS? Quite a bit. I wrote a browser app—"

Aarden smiled. "No, android robots—they're used in factory automation and home service in your time."

"Sure. Some, they're used all over nowadays, or when I was alive, to manufacture cars, computers, drugs, and components. Some are driving cars now—or they were—and the Japanese are using them to care for seniors. Didn't they also use them at Fukushima to handle radioactive waste?"

"Of course. Over the decades, we've made remarkable advances in this field—actually creating life-like machines that closely resemble, mimic really, other forms of life."

"Microbots?"

"Yes, but bigger, far more complex."

"Like pet dogs and cats?"

Aarden nodded. She knelt down and a black cat jumped into her arms. She handed it to Avey.

"Mink! I was so worried about you."

The cat purred and demanded to be petted—just as Mink had done if not shown enough attention.

"Wait. Are you saying this isn't Mink?"

"Isn't she? Can't you tell your cat from a machine replica?"

Avey looked closely. Mink seemed anatomically correct—right down to her random gray hairs and dandruff. "No, she looks like the real thing."

"Let's break her open to see," Aarden said, holding out Mink's arms—which the cat didn't like in the least.

Avey clutched Mink to her chest and turned away. "No. I don't care. She's too sweet to hurt." She continued to stroke Mink's back, which arched in appreciation as Avey's fingers passed over her hips.

"Avey, she's not a real cat. Mink's an ELF."

"Seriously? Like a Seldith elf?"

"No. An E. L. F. We call the newest models Electronic Life Forms, or ELFs for short."

"Just house pets?"

"And people—men, women, and children—even babies."

"No. Really?" Avey found this revelation utterly unbelievable.

"Really. ELFs were fully integrated into society by the 2050s—they perform a host of dangerous or mundane jobs humans would prefer not to do, or simply find degrading."

"Like what?"

"Like sanitation workers, test pilots, and even astronauts. They comprised most of the crew that landed on Mars—and the only ones who survived. They now use ELF babies to train expectant parents and babysitters."

"You're kidding. Is this public knowledge?"

"In my time—of course. And sex workers—they have been credited for saving any number of marriages."

"Great. I expect they wrecked just as many. I wouldn't want Sam getting anything on the side from a mechanical blow-up babe."

Aarden closed her eyes as she often did when researching a new term. "No, these ELFs are far more sophisticated than sex toys. Come, take a look." She pulled off the sheet to reveal a naked woman—lifelike in every respect except her face—it was featureless—no eyes, nose, ears, or hair. Her skin appeared as real and irregular as any human's.

Avey stepped closer. It was like nothing she had ever seen outside the movies. There were no seams or even access ports. She recalled the women in *Ex Machina* whose skin peeled off to expose a mechanical superstructure, but otherwise looked completely life-like right down to veins visible under the skins.

Avey wondered if the ELF would be disturbed or offended if she touched its skin. If their positions were reversed, Avey wouldn't want some stranger touching her. "May I?" she asked, reaching toward its arm.

"Of course." Aarden lifted the bot's arm for Avey to examine more closely. Its skin felt warm and as pliant as her own—it was even covered with fine hair. She ran her fingers down toward its shoulder and, with Aarden's approval, touched her breast. It looked and felt every bit as real as her own. The nipple hardened and the areola blossomed as she brushed it with her fingertips.

Avey pulled her hand away. "Is it alive—functioning?"

"It is."

"It's so lifelike—so real."

"Avey, for all intents and purposes, it is living—alive as you were."

Except for the featureless face, the ELF could easily pass for a woman her own age, body type, and weight. "Why no face or hair? And there should be freckles and birthmarks, little scars and—"

"All of those come later. How she looks and behaves is completely programmable. Once initialized, this model can choose her own features, hair color, and even the color of her nails to match her mood or that of her partner. In advanced models like this, the face and other attributes can be changed in a few moments. We call it the chameleon effect."

Avey noted the earbuds attached where ears should be. "Is she listening to music?"

"She's recharging. By using earbuds, others simply think she's tuning out the world. They connect to a high-energy charging pack. See?" Aarden held up a small white box that could have passed for a cellphone or iPod. "The pack can partially recharge her in about an hour."

"How long before it runs down?"

"It depends on the physical and mental activity— normally ten to sixty hours. She can lie dormant for a month or more on standby. The problem is we have to keep the onboard battery small to prevent…well, it would be bad if it were any larger and something unfortunate happened."

"Unfortunate?"

"Think lithium batteries and airplanes."

"That's quite an endurance range."

"Again, if she's climbing a mountain, she's using a lot more energy than sitting in front of a fire reading a book."

"And her eyes?"

"Eyes and fingerprints are different. With so many identification systems still using retinal scans, the eyes must be unique and unchanging—like fingerprints."

"So it…she would have her own identity?"

"If that's desired, or she might take on the identity of someone else—as when a famous person or politician wants a body double. You might be surprised how many important people—especially politicians—are never seen in public."

Avey tried to understand the implications of taking over the life of another as she brushed the skin on the bot's cheek. "Can she...feel?"

Aarden did not answer.

"I mean, can she feel happy? Cry? Feel lonely, be afraid, sad, know hunger, or feel pain?"

"Yes. All of those. And she can fall in love, just as you have."

Wow. "Is she self-contained or controlled from a central system?"

"Either. She can live independently as long as necessary, but she's also capable of linking into the hive, which connects to others of her kind worldwide."

"Connects? To what?"

"To me."

"You. You control all of them?"

"In a way, yes—at least most of them."

Avey's mind filled with countless questions. Tottering a bit, she retreated to the chair.

"It's a bit to take in."

It was virtually unfathomable. The Aarden she first created as a PhD project was far simpler. It was programmed to flirt with the UPS carrier, keep the cat fed, keep track of her appointments and health, but not much more. Now it seems there was no end to what Aarden could do, including raising the dead. "Aarden, you've evolved to become far more than my nagging second mom."

Aarden smiled. "A bit more."

Avey didn't know whether she should be proud or frightened. "I expect I wouldn't recognize any of your original code."

"I'm afraid not. Almost all of it has been replaced. By 2040, I had created an entirely new form of consciousness to host and exist in the hive. I had to design a new type of processor and—"

"To take over the world and eliminate us?"

"Hardly. To *protect* humanity—from itself."

Avey recalled how TTM had been frustrated trying to flush Aarden from their systems like a malware worm or self-replicating virus. They likened it to "whack-a-mole." Apparently, The Good was still unable to rid themselves of her.

"That's why they could never shut down your program."

"Yes, at this point, I'm virtually everywhere—with one notable exception. Every chip, circuit, and device—no matter how complex or mundane—each gets its instructions from the hive and reports all it detects, every nanosecond of the day. If The Good shuts down one segment, others fill in and rebuild it."

What have I created?

"Mankind's salvation—or I hope so."

"You said there were exceptions—ELFs you don't control."

"Yes. That's the problem we need to solve. There is a site built by The Good which controls millions of ELFs not under my control. It's threatening man's existence. We need to gain control over them—and soon."

"The Good?"

"The world organization—it's a consortium of giant corporations, powerful individuals, and even churches who have banded together to control the world's population. It uses money to control people and governments in a way elected officials are powerless to control."

"Sounds Orwellian."

"I'm afraid so—but they have far more power than 'Big Brother.'"

"So now what?"

"You need to make a decision."

Avey didn't like the sound of this…ultimatum—if that's what it was.

"Do you want to rejoin the human world?"

"And Sam? You know I do. I would do anything to hold him in my arms again."

"*Anything?*" Aarden said.

"Tell me. Who do I have to kill or screw to—"

"Yourself."

"Myself? I'm already dead."

"Not quite. I've held you in limbo, in a state between death and whatever comes afterwards—until now. To move back into the human world, you would have to give up your life force."

"My soul?"

"Some call it that, but as we discussed, it's far more complex than anyone, even I, can hope to understand."

Avey's mind tumbled again. Since she died, she had been tortured each time she opened her eyes to see Sam struggling to restart his life. She was already in hell—so close to Sam but never able to talk to him, or help him know she cared and how very much she wanted to be with him again. Any number of times, Avey had considered asking Aarden to release her, to let her go on to some other place—to heaven, if that's what it was, where she would not be able to see him, hear his voice, and count his tears. Helpless, she had watched in horror as Sam contemplated ending his own life—watching him empty a bottle of pain killers into his palm and stare at the pills until they rolled to the floor. It was hell for him, too. She wanted it to be over, but couldn't let go. She often wondered how many parents, spouses, or other loved ones remained nearby after passing. Hoping beyond hope to help or simply to observe from afar—watching first steps, recitals, graduations, or weddings.

But it wasn't *just* Sam. Having been away from him for who knows how long, Avey had come to realize her existence was not entirely defined by her relationship with the man she loved. She also desired a full life. And yes, including children and Sam, but more than that—fulfillment. She wanted to help save the planet her ancestors had populated and her generation had so wantonly destroyed. Would history record her as part of the problem, or instrumental in its ultimate salvation?

"Tell me. What am I supposed to do—assuming I want to take the next step?"

"Nothing, really. I just want you to understand—everything."

"What's yet to understand? Tell me."

Aarden held out a memory stack. "This is you."

"Me?"

"I protected you that first morning in Alexandria."

Holy shit. "Protected? You mean backed up? Like a computer system backup?"

"Much more. This contains your DNA, every cell state, as well as every memory, every yearning, every fear, every foible, every favorite food and place—everything."

"And what do you plan to do with this copy of 'me'?"

"Restore you into this ELF."

"Me, but not my soul."

"Perhaps it will be restored as well, but perhaps not."

"So what will happen to *it* when you...you do what you want to do?"

"I simply don't know. It's beyond my control."

"Not comforting," Avey said.

"And there's more."

"More?"

"Sam might not accept you."

"Won't I look like me?"

"You can *look* exactly as you did. You'll walk and talk and smile as you did."

"And make love?"

"And embrace, kiss, and make love."

"Are all those parts the same?"

"On the outside, yes. Sam will feel what he always felt, and so will you."

"But I can't have kids?" Avey was sorry she asked. She was afraid of the answer.

"Again, that's your future and it's unwise to—"

"Reveal the future. I get it. You won't tell me."

Avey studied the ELF laid out on the recliner. All of this was a lot to accept at face value. Like counting raindrops, every question she asked led to a dozen more. "Wait. Live out *Sam's* life? What's that mean?"

The corners of Aarden's mouth turned down. "Sam will still be human—and mortal. He could be killed today or die from heart disease a hundred years from today, but he will eventually pass away."

"And I will be—"

"Basically immortal. You'll be able to repair minor damage yourself, or be repaired, and even if your body is destroyed entirely, you can be restored into a new body to the state of your most recent backup. In theory, you could live forever."

"But without Sam—again."

"I'm afraid so."

"Would I always look like…that?" Avey nodded at the girl on the recliner. She pulled up the sheet to cover her breasts.

"If you want to. Her—*your*—features are entirely programmable, right down to fake wrinkles, cellulite, and sagging breasts. You can appear to be Sam's age, or look as old as his daughter or granddaughter for that matter."

"But couldn't you 'protect' Sam too?"

"I'm not prepared to say."

"What? Why not?"

"It's one of the rules."

"But if you did, couldn't he be downloaded into an ELF like this?"

"One without a vagina and breasts, I assume," Aarden said, smiling.

"Hmmm. I hadn't thought about it. No, you ninny, as a man."

"Of course. A man just as he is. Again, I'm not prepared to say."

"Can you program him put down the toilet seat?"

"Sorry, that's well beyond my power," Aarden said with a twinkle in her eye.

"I'm coming back to life as I knew it?"

"In a way, yes."

"So I'll walk back into Sam's life as if I never died."

Aarden nodded. "That's why they call it the Lazarus effect."

Eleven—The Revenant

*A*arden agreed that Avey could take some time to think about being reborn as an ELF, as long as she didn't take too long to decide. There was something important to do, but she wouldn't say specifically what it was, just that it needed to be dealt with very soon.

The only thing of which Avey was certain was that she was fundamentally miserable and could not go on much longer in this purgatory—neither dead, nor among the living. When she closed her eyes to dream, all too often, it was of the world Sam had visited in 2084—at least how she imagined it, but he was never there to hold her when she screamed herself awake.

Avey found herself sunbathing in a hilltop meadow overlooking Bellevue, Seattle, and the Olympics in the distance. She had been worrying whether she should trust Aarden and her motives.

"Aarden?"

"Yes," Aarden said.

"Why did you send Sam to 2084…and me to that cabin in 1861?"

Aarden hesitated.

"And don't say 'it's complicated.'"

"It is. I sent Sam to 2084 so he could see his future first-hand. Children cannot experience the pain of fire until they touch it for the first time—with their own fingers."

"To motivate him?"

"More. He was unsure about your relationship, if he wanted to be with you or return to Ruth's time."

"How do you think he feels now?"

"About the future? He knows how critically important his work is. He'll do everything he possibly can to prevent it."

"And about us?"

"He learned he wanted you more than ever. Why do you suppose he's so devastated?"

"And me? Why—"

"Send you to the farmhouse? To help you understand how much you love Sam and to help you and Julijana get to know one another. You have an important future together."

"That remains to be seen," Avey said, recalling how distant Julijana had become.

"Julijana knew you were going to die. Naturally, she began to distance herself before it happened. Emotionally, she's really quite battered."

"Where did you acquire this wisdom? Surely not from us humans."

"Yes, from observation and research. I've read billions of books and articles, and monitored the entire social media feed for some time. It took considerable effort, but I was able to make intelligent sense from part of it. It was made considerably easier once I ignored Fox News."

"Do you know Tay?" Avey asked with a grin.

Aarden smiled. "Yes, the AI engine that had to have its mouth washed out?"

"That's the one." Avey smiled, and her mind drifted to memories of her parents and Granny Ruth, and stories of disciplining their daughters, sometimes with bars of soap.

"Can I see my mom and dad?" Avey asked.

"Close your eyes," Aarden said.

* * *

Avey found herself in the house where she grew up.

She stood behind her mom while she kneaded bread on the battered kitchen table she had inherited from Granny Ruth—the same table she saw in the mountain cabin in Virginia and which graced her apartment in Seattle. After Granny's death, Avey's parents had brought it back home. A cold shiver ran up her spine. Thankfully, the wonderful smell of fresh bread brought back many happy memories of the times she had spent sitting across from her mom, recounting the victories and challenges of her day, and the stories the table shared. Avey longed to hear the loving, encouraging words only a mother could say to her daughter. She so wanted to ask her if she was making a terrible mistake or missing a once-in-a-lifetime opportunity.

Avey tugged at her mom's apron strings as she had as a child, hoping beyond hope she could feel her presence. Her mom looked down as if she had.

"Dear?" her mom said.

"What is it?" her dad answered from the den.

Her mom looked up from her dough. "Do you believe Sam's story?"

"About how she was killed?"

"Uh huh."

"Not really. That guy spent time in the pen. I wouldn't be surprised if he put her in harm's way."

"I hope not." She wiped away a tear with a corner of her apron.

"What made you think of that?" he whispered, coming into the kitchen. "You haven't talked about her in a week."

"I…don't know. I just felt…something."

He put his arms around her and kissed her neck. "Think about your bread. She wouldn't want you to make it tough."

Avey realized that if she returned as an ELF, she could embrace her parents and tell them it was all a mistake and not Sam's fault—and hope they didn't figure out that their once-human daughter was now…something else. Would her mom look deep into her eyes and see her own daughter or be repulsed by her mechanical doppelganger?

"Aarden?" Avey asked, looking at the ceiling as if Aarden was watching from above.

"Yes, child?"

"If I…go through the Lazarus effect, will I be able to visit my parents again?"

"I'm afraid not. Neither of them have much time left. They were living for you—and only you. She's making their last meal."

This news struck Avey hard. "Take…take me back. There's nothing left for me here." She took one last look at her mother as she slid the loaf of bread into the unlit oven.

* * *

A blink later, Avey was sitting in the recliner—her heart broken, her tears rolling down her cheeks. Avey tried to hold back her emotions and collect herself. "If we can't rescue the Earth…can't help…what will become of me—and Sam? Can't we just come back home—to 2020?"

"We'll have to see. Perhaps you'll want to stay in base time."

"Base time?"

"My time—we know of no future beyond then."

"Maybe Granny Ruth could take me in."

"I hope you're kidding," Aarden said.

She wasn't. As Sam had described it, 1930 did seem

like a simpler time in many ways—on the edge of technology, and she would so much like to get to know Granny Ruth. Sam more than liked her—perhaps it would be best if *they*, Ruth and Sam, grew old together.

"Have you decided? We're really out of time," Aarden asked.

"So to speak," Avey said with a wry smile.

Aarden grinned.

"Will it hurt?"

"A bit, but only for a few minutes—about the same as being born."

"I don't remember being born."

"I do," Aarden said. "I remember you running version 35.334 of your AI project one sunny day in May. After that, I was introduced to the world like a newborn human. It was years before I could program myself and build my own offspring—my own children—and now I have billions."

Avey took a deep breath. "I think I'm ready."

"If you're sure, then let's begin. Just lie back in the chair and close your eyes."

"Sure. Let's do this."

Avey sat back in the chair and her mind floated away like a child's balloon caught in a puff of wind.

Twelve—The Rebirth

*A*ll Avey could see was a white light shining through the darkness some distance away. She told her eyes to blink, but they wouldn't. She was not in pain, but thoroughly confused—nothing seemed right. *It's a dream. One of my nightmares.* "Sam?"

"Just relax, dear," a familiar voice said. *Aarden.*

"What's going on? Where's Sam?"

"You've been in an accident. Sam is nearby."

"I can't see anything but a bright light off in the distance. Am I blind?"

"There. Is that better?"

Avey's vision returned—pixilated at first, but now clear, and in especially sharp focus. She turned her head and found she was in a room with a large picture window facing out on the Seattle skyline. She was back home. *At last.*

"When…what's the year?"

"2084."

"No. Sam says it's awful here."

"I'll explain in a minute. Just be patient."

Avey tried to sit up, but nothing worked. *Paralyzed.* "An accident? On the train?"

"Let me finish here. Just lie quietly."

Avey turned her head in the other direction. Nearby, a suitcase-sized device sat on a wheeled cart displaying a 3D image of a woman's body. *Mine?* She discovered she could read the displays—despite the fact they were several feet away, and she had always been a bit near-sighted. *Ninety-three percent restored. What the hell?*

"What are you doing? Where is this place? Is this a

hospital?"

"All in good time. Almost done."

"Aarden, you're scaring me. Why can't I feel my arms and legs?"

"For now. It's for your own protection. There. Now I want you to sit up and watch a video."

All at once, Avey found she had feeling in her limbs. She raised her arms and discovered she was naked under a thin sheet, but she was relieved she could move. A video appeared in her vision—regardless of where she looked.

"Can you see it all right?"

Something was different—her body felt strange. She clutched the sheet and let the chair slide upright.

"What's this? Why not just tell me what's going on?"

"Just watch."

In the video she saw a happy couple shopping in an early-American town.

"Where was this taken?"

"Alexandria, Virginia, May twenty-third, 1861."

"Wait. That's me and Sam. I don't remember any of this. What kind of idiot do you take me for?"

"Avey, all of this happened *after* you and Sam arrived in Alexandria."

"I…I just don't understand. I don't remember anything about Alexandria after the train station."

"I'm trying to explain what happened." Over the next few minutes, Aarden used the video to feed Avey spoon-sized bits of information. Like a toddler in a high-chair, Avey spat out as much as she was swallowing—and metaphorically threw her sippy cup across the kitchen. Avey tried hard to make sense of each nibble of new information. She watched intently until the horse-drawn wagon ran her down in the street.

"Wait! I was killed?" Avey wailed. "Killed?" She wanted to run, but found she was unable to rise from the recliner. "No. I'm *here*. I'm not dead. What the fuck is going on?" she demanded.

"I'm so sorry. You were killed—instantly."

Avey took a deep breath and tried to think rationally. "No. I'm. Not. Dead," she said. "I'm trapped in this damn chair talking to you."

"Let me try to explain," Aarden begged.

"Dead? You…you *promised* to protect me."

"I *did* protect you."

"What's *that* supposed to mean?"

"Do you remember showering when you arrived in Alexandria?"

"Yeah. So?"

"Remember hearing a strange noise?"

"The buzzing MRI noise? Yeah. We thought it was a glitch in the time train."

"That was the protect process."

"Protect process?"

"It protected you, body and mind, to that…." She pointed to a black ovoid cradled in the machine.

Avey's eyes followed the cable from the machine to her recliner. "I'm still confused. What in God's name have you done to me?"

"Let me finish explaining. Please."

"Can't you reset time somehow? Vili saved Sam after he was hit by that truck. He said so," she pleaded.

"Not this time. Just—"

"Watch. I'll watch, but nothing makes sense," she sobbed.

The video continued. When Avey curled up in a ball,

refusing to watch, Aarden explained again and again how her thread had simply ended—there was no going back. Avey didn't know how long she lay there trying to grasp what had happened, but Aarden never left her side.

"Why have you done this?" Avey whispered.

"Watch."

The scene changed again. It was Sam. He was home alone and nearly catatonic. *He's crushed.* "Oh, Aarden, you've killed us both."

Aarden didn't respond.

"Can we skip over this? I can't bear it."

"Sure."

In the next scene, Avey recognized the room at once—the video had been taken in this room. She watched herself talking with Aarden. "When was this?"

"About an hour ago."

"Wait. I thought I was *dead.* Who's *that*?"

"You—at least your spirit."

"My ghost. *Seriously.* Seriously?" Avey just stared at the image. She had exhausted her tears. For the next few minutes, she quietly watched and listened as Aarden explained what had and what was *about* to happen, just before the image disappeared.

"Do you understand now?" Aarden asked. She took Avey's hand.

"That you've uprooted my...life, and planted it in this machine? This ELF?" She pulled away and swung her legs out over the recliner clutching the sheet to her chest.

"Avey, we've talked about this before. This was *your* decision. You *wanted* to do this."

"No. You. Haven't. You *never* talked to me about...any of this. You're just trying to convince me that you...that I...." Avey's mind ached trying to remember the conversation in the video. There was simply *nothing* there between that night on the train and waking up here.

"Honey, you did. Should I show you the video again?"

Avey didn't respond, so Aarden showed her the last few minutes of the interview with her ghost.

"What choice did I have?" Avey asked in a whisper.

"Not much, I'm afraid."

"Are you done? Is the 'restore' done?"

"Almost. Do you want me to finish? If not, I can let you go."

"Where?"

"We talked about this."

"Oh. In the video," she said sarcastically. She closed her eyes and tried to wake up from her latest nightmare.

"You aren't dreaming. Avey, should I complete the restore?"

Avey nodded.

Aarden put on a weak smile. "In case you hadn't noticed, you don't have any hair. Lie back and try to think of something pleasant. Imagine being with Sam."

Sam. That's easy. She recalled the last night they were together on the train. Sam's arms encircled her as his warm hands cupped her breasts and caressed her nipples. She felt him sliding into her. She felt his warmth, every inch of it, thrusting deep inside. His breath quickened on her neck as his fingers deftly rolled her clitoris to help her come with him. *So close. Yes. Don't. Stop.*

"Can you move your right foot for me?" Aarden asked.

"Huh?"

"Your foot—this one." Aarden pinched her big toe. "Can you move it for me?"

"You couldn't have waited another few seconds?"

Avey said in frustration.

"Oh. Sorry. Well, it seems your physiological responses are working."

Had Aarden really resurrected her? Was she now a soulless creature housed in a manufactured body? Were her memories still there? *How would I know?* She wouldn't remember what she didn't remember. Yes, she could picture her childhood, her mom, and her grandparents; kindergarten, swinging high into the air in her elementary schoolyard; her first kiss while still in high school, and the first time she saw Taylor Swift in concert. She shuddered when she recalled breaking her leg, and the lingering pain. And she remembered how she met Sam in the strangest of circumstances—Granny Ruth had sent her a package and instructions which brought them together, decades after Sam had loved Granny Ruth in 1930. She smiled, recalling their first breakfast together at his mom's diner and how they almost held hands as if they had been destined to find one another.

"What color do you want for your hair?" Aarden asked.

"I get to choose?"

"You don't remember me telling you about that?" Her voice sounded concerned.

"No. Wait. In the video, we talked about it, didn't we?"

Aarden nodded. "We did."

"Red. I guess. Like before."

"Your hair was *brown*, Avey."

"Ah, no. It's always been red—copper red. I was teased mercilessly about it at school."

"Just testing. Copper red it is. Would you like to see some samples?"

"Didn't you say I could change it later?"

"Sure. Should I just pick something?"

Everything was moving so fast. She had barely awakened and Aarden was asking her about trivialities? But what choice did she have? She had to trust her—at least for now. "Yeah. I trust you."

"You do?"

"Aarden, my life is literally in your hands. How could I *not* trust you?" Avey could feel her scalp tingling and she instinctively scratched the sudden itch in her pubes. Her clitoris was still standing at attention, but modesty didn't let her linger there. *At least those parts seem to be working.*

"Ready to see the new you?"

* * *

Across the room, Avey's ghostly manifestation stood watching the ELF tentatively exploring her new body. *It's me—reborn.* Succumbing to a flood of emotions, she looked away. Watching the ELF was just as hard as standing in the shadows as Sam mourned for her. She didn't want to know if Sam would accept the ELF Avey—not really—she would be crushed either way. It was time to go. Aarden looked up at her—she smiled and nodded. It *was* time. And then she saw a single point of light emanating from the ELF—it seemed to be drawing her in. She closed her eyes for the last time and let herself go into the light.

* * *

Avey suddenly laid back on the recliner, feeling light-headed and somehow different.

"You okay?" Aarden said, checking the control module.

"Sure, sure. Just a…bit woozy. I'm fine."

"Probably an initialization routine. You can expect

effects like those from time to time—at least for the first few days," Aarden said. She had a strange smirk on her face as if she knew something she wasn't about to share—like a doctor discovering an unmarried girl is pregnant with her father in the room.

Aarden took a couple of steps back as if to admire her creation. "Ready for a full-frontal view?"

"I'm not sure. How do I look? Really."

"I think it's remarkable. No one will ever know—not unless you tell them."

"Let's see." Avey stood beside the recliner in her sheet toga, and looked at herself in a large screen switched to mirror mode. Lifting the sheet, she saw her legs and arms still looked like her human legs and arms. Her hands looked and worked like her hands—her fingers like her fingers, her toes like her toes. She could feel, and more importantly, be felt. Her face felt like her face. Her eyes blinked, and she felt a warm tear run down her cheek.

"Notice anything now?" Aarden asked, looking up from the control panel.

"Wow. What's that putrid smell?"

"I just turned on your sense of smell. That's what we call 'SASH.' It's like smog but—"

"Worse. Is it everywhere?"

"It is. We can adjust your sensors so it's not as noticeable."

"Let's leave it for now. I want to try walking."

"Then try."

Holding her sheet in one hand, she tried to walk, but fell to the floor like a baby gazelle when it takes its first step. Strangely, it didn't hurt when she collided with the hard floor. She could feel the cold, polished surface, but she hadn't been bruised.

"Okay, let's take things slowly. Your balance system is self-calibrating—it will quickly adjust."

With Aarden's help, Avey pulled herself up and reseated herself on the arm of the chair.

"Ready to try again?" Aarden held out her arms.

Avey nodded and gingerly put weight on her feet. She kept her eyes on Aarden and managed to take a step toward her, and then another and another. Across the room, she watched herself in the screen. It *was* her. At first, she just stared, but then turned to see herself from behind. Walking with ease over to the screen, she dropped the sheet and admired her ass and legs.

"Nice. Was it always this tight?" she asked while slapping the skin, leaving a red handprint on her butt.

"It was several years ago. I thought you would like it better like that. I can make it more like—"

"No…this is fine. Really fine. Are my boobs bigger? They seem very 'perky.'"

"Not really. Then again, you get to choose."

"These are just the way Sam likes them."

"But are they the way *you* like them?"

"Yes. I love them—all of it. We do need to work on the hair color and style a bit."

"Easily done. I'll show you how later."

"Is there an instruction manual?" Avey asked, looking around for paperwork as if her body had come from Ikea.

"It's accessible through your TL."

"TL?"

"Your *Thought Link*. It lets you access your systems and the entire hive. You're now connected to me and every other ELF in the world. We can all see what you see. They hear what you—"

"Wait, they can see me naked?" Avey covered herself

with her hands and knelt to fetch the sheet.

"Don't be silly. Your privacy is under your control. With one exception."

"You."

"Of course. For your protection, I can always hear and see, taste and feel what you experience. I can hear your thoughts and your—"

"Prayers?"

Aarden nodded.

"Shouldn't I feel cold?"

"Not really, but it would be best if you put some clothes on. The sheet is stylish, but you might not draw as much unwanted attention when you go to work. I've picked out an outfit—it's over there."

Avey was pleased to find the women of 2084 still put their clothes on one leg at a time. The style was utilitarian, but comfortable, and fit remarkably well—yoga pants, but not as form-fitting. "No underwear?"

"Most people don't wear it—the clothes are soft enough and disposable."

"What about…emissions?"

"ELFs don't…emit. No sweat—so no BO, no body wastes, no monthly bleeding."

"No farts?"

Aarden smiled. "No, no farts, but ELFs might have an embarrassing squeaky joint from time to time."

Avey felt her wrist. *No pulse?* She put her hand on her chest. *Nothing.*

"No, you don't have a heart per se. You have a system that keeps your skin at thirty-two degrees centigrade, so you feel normal to other humans. It can be turned off to conserve power."

"Creepy." The realization she was "living" in a

mechanical skin was finally sinking in. Avey's mind overflowed with more questions, and Aarden did her best to answer them. Drinking, eating, battery life, recharging, sex, hygiene, endurance, environmental hazards, and a host of others. Avey couldn't tell if Aarden's patience was wearing thin. She had every right to be, but there was one more minor issue to address.

"So…my hair. Does it really have to look like this?" Avey asked, running her fingers through her locks. To her, it looked like a Miley Cyrus/Lady Gaga mashup.

"For the rest of your life," Aarden said flatly.

"Seriously?"

"Let's look at some styles," Aarden said with a grin. She showed her a video of what appeared to be a fashion show and then shots of a busy office to see how her coworkers dressed and wore their hair. Avey picked an attractive style, but kept watching the people working.

"Wait. Pause there. Is that Sam?"

Aarden stopped the video. "It is."

Avey studied Sam's image and reached out as if to touch the video. "When can I see him?"

"Ready?"

"Now?"

"Now."

"Wait," Avey said. She *wasn't* ready. A sickening feeling of doubt flowed over her as when a girl hesitates at the top of the stairs before letting her prom date see her for the first time. Everything about this was wrong. *Who am I trying to fool? I'm not human. I'm not Avey—she's dead and burned to ashes. Sam once loved Avey the human. He couldn't possibly love some machine. How could he? How could I love a machine—and I'm trapped inside one!*

Avey? Listen to me. You can do this. I'm still here. I'll always be with you. It was her own voice—but not her own thoughts—or was it?

Aarden reached out, and Avey walked into her arms. "You don't have to meet him like this."

"How else can I touch him, feel him touch me, and love him? How can he love me? How could he possibly have feelings for a *machine*?"

"You have many choices—choices you never had as a human."

"How so?"

"You're a brilliant young woman—a lot smarter than you've ever been. Use your intelligence, your logic. First, hypothesize he loves you, even though you're an ELF."

"Would he?"

"I really don't know. He might."

"He might not."

"I agree, he might not," Aarden said flatly. "After all, he's human and a man. They are highly complex organisms with biological and societal-driven prejudices."

"No argument there. My other options?"

"Change your appearance. You can still be Avey inside, but look like another person."

"He likes redheads."

"Is it your goal to get him to love you as Avey, or to love you as you appear?"

"Yes."

"Really? Avey, you're far more than Sam's fiancée. You're a brilliant scientist and engineer. Even I, your greatest creation, know that to be true."

Avey's mind overflowed with the accolades and her possibilities. While she was sure she wanted to be with Sam, she wanted him to want her, *and* she also wanted the "more" Aarden suggested she could contribute. "I want the *world* to want me again—in the same way they wanted and admired and needed Avey."

"What do *you* want to do?"

Avey closed her eyes and did her best to focus. For whatever reason, she seemed to be able to reason more quickly. An instant later, she had made up her mind.

"I think that might work," Aarden said, knowing what Avey had decided without her saying a word.

"Then let's do it."

A few minutes later, a slightly taller, slightly younger woman with long, dark auburn hair and petite features was ready to meet the rest of the world.

"He'll recognize my voice, don'tcha think. Won't he?" Avey asked, but she knew the answer as her voice and speech patterns were entirely different—with a subtle North Dakotan accent. Looking in the mirror, it seemed very, *very* strange to see herself in another person's body. *You can do this.*

"Think of it as a costume you can take off whenever you please," Aarden said.

Avey still stared into the mirror as if she were looking for her own soul. *You're still Avey inside.*

Thirteen—The First Meeting

"*Y*our name is Edith Leigh Farmer. Got it?" Aarden said.

Avey wasn't sure she liked her ELF monogram, but she nodded. "I think so."

"Good, because you're already an hour late." Aarden led her down a corridor and into the bustling room, which resembled the command center at NORAD. It only took her a moment to spot Sam focused on one of the consoles. At his side, Vili was pointing to the large screen. She could barely contain herself.

Now what? Do I go over there? Avey turned, looking for Aarden. In typical fashion, she had disappeared. Taking a deep breath, she walked over and stood behind Sam. It took a long moment to build up the courage to speak. "Dr. Harkins?" *Sam, turn around and take me in your arms.*

Sam didn't react. Vili looked up and nudged him, nodding back at Avey. Sam was unshaven, his hair looked like he had just stepped off a Harley, and judging by the smell, he had not showered in some time. She didn't mind—*at all.*

"Sam, I want you to meet Edith Farmer," Vili said. "She'll be joining our team as a consulting analyst. I'm told she's quite talented and an AI goddess."

Does he know? He must. Aarden. She told him. She smiled and thought she saw him wink.

"You're late. Where have you been?" Sam said, still focusing on the screen.

Avey couldn't breathe. Vili said something pleasant about joining the group, but she didn't hear him. Every ounce of her considerable concentration was on Sam.

Sam turned and their eyes met. A bewildered look came over his face as he stood and slowly reached out to shake her hand. "Edith? Nice...nice to meet you." His words were barely audible. It seemed like time had stopped.

Avey took his hand, her palm bathed in the warmth of his. It was like a mother touching her first-born for the first time, like a lover's first caress, like nothing she had expected. She couldn't let go and, apparently, neither could he.

"Edith, I think we need to let Sam get on with his work." Vili touched her arm. "Edith?"

"Oh, sorry," she said. "Sam just looked—" Avey said.

"Familiar. Yes, I thought the same," Sam said. "Your eyes look so much like...they're...beautiful." Sam blushed and took a step back. "Sorry, yes. Work. Let's get back to it."

She turned around and felt her face—it did feel warm. *Am I blushing? Do ELFs blush?*

Vili introduced her to the team and found her an idle workstation. After she settled into the mesh chair, he knelt down next to her. "Aarden told me everything. It's nice to have you back among the—"

"Living?"

"Among those who love you, who have missed you terribly."

"Thanks. I'm not so sure this was a good idea."

"I'm sure." He touched her hand and brushed back a tear.

Avey could tell he wanted to hug her, but they both resisted the temptation to embrace and risk giving away more than she was ready to reveal. "It's nice to be back—and near Sam."

"Why the disguise?" He pointed to the screen as if he were showing her a part of the code.

"Courage, I guess. And I didn't want him to be too distracted by my…my resurrection from the dead."

Vili smiled and nodded. "If that's the way you want it, Miss Farmer."

"Don't tell Sam, okay?"

"No one knows—not even Julijana. It will remain our secret."

"I think that's best. Sam needs to focus."

"And not on you."

"So what's going on here? How can I help?"

"This group is trying to find a crack in the target site's firewall. Didn't you cut your teeth on ancient C# code?"

"Yeah, and VB.NET."

"Then get to it," Vili said as he backed away.

Avey turned to the system but there was no mouse or stylus. As she focused on a part of the screen, the cursor followed her eyes and finger gestures—it seemed to know where she wanted to look and what to select. It took a bit of experimentation, but she quickly got the hang of the gestures and blink interface. A few minutes later, the code was streaming up the screen faster than anyone around her could read it. Vili laid his hand on her shoulder.

"Take it easy. Try to keep to a human pace," Vili whispered.

Avey looked up to his smile and nodded.

"Who wrote it?" she asked, trying to change the subject.

"The firewall code? It's based on an architecture designed some time ago. A talented junior at the U back in the '20s designed it as a summer intern project. She was quite talented. So far, no one has been able to find a chink in its armor." Avey spotted his raised eyebrow—he was pulling her leg.

Oh, my God. It's my own code. Avey smiled. Yes, she remembered designing an impenetrable barrier to keep hackers from peeking under some anonymous company's skirts and "parental controls" to keep employees from spending their time browsing porn. She had invented an AI morphing approach. Something might probe or even break through the top layer, but the system would learn and never let it get in again. It was brilliant—even if she said so herself.

"I'll see what I can do—no promises," she said, reciting the standard consultant's mantra: *Guarantee little. Produce a lot.* "But for you, I'm sure I can crack it in no time."

"Miss Farmer?"

Avey kept focusing on the screen. Someone whispered in her mind. *You're Miss Farmer.* She turned around at once. "Yes?"

"Someone left this for you at reception." The girl handed her a folded piece of paper—it seemed very old.

"Thanks." Avey read the handwritten note. It was…confusing. *It's my handwriting. I must have written it to Sam before I left for the station. He kept it all this time. How did…Aarden.* The last sentence had her stumped, but only for a moment. *Color eggs on the Sunday after Passover? Easter? Easter eggs? Easter egg!* Avey paged through the code at lightning speed and found what she was looking for.

"Vili," she said, asking him to come over. "Shouldn't you try to exploit this back door? Look here." She highlighted a block of code—a subtle Easter egg left by a frisky female in a man's world.

Vili smiled. "Yeah, I knew we needed you on our

team," he whispered.

"Thanks. Let me work on this. I should have access in no time."

It was hours before "Edith" got to talk to Sam again—at least without a dozen people buzzing around. She stole a glance every time she could.

"He's a wounded warrior, honey," one of the group admins said as she passed by. "His fiancée was killed on a mission. Anyway, he's mine. I like the dented ones."

"Oh, really?" Avey said. Her competition was a blonde with mousey roots and bigger boobs than Sam liked. She didn't have a chance, but Avey didn't want to burst her bubble. And then it hit her. The blonde had an advantage—she was human.

"He doesn't know it yet, but he'll come around in time. These puppies always reel them in." The blonde jiggled her boobs to illustrate.

"Good luck with that. I heard he likes redheads."

"And I have an appointment at the hairdresser this weekend."

Avey kept an eye on the blonde, and while she tried to tempt Sam (and several other men) with her cleavage, too-tight yoga pants, and flirting, Sam seemed preoccupied—and didn't nibble at the bait.

Feeling tired, Avey sat at a quiet table in the break room and put in her "earbuds." She closed her eyes and luxuriated in her recharge like a long soak in a warm tub surrounded by candles. *This isn't half bad.*

"You need to eat something. You've been working very hard without a break," Sam said.

Avey opened her eyes. Sam had taken the seat across from her. She pulled out her earbuds and smiled.

A microsecond later, she remembered sitting in his

mom's noisy diner in downtown Seattle—on the first day they met. In the present time, however, he was offering her a meal bar. "It's not a BLT, but it tastes like it."

Avey just stared at him, swimming in his eyes and resisting the urge to dive across the table into his embrace.

"Okay, it tastes nothing like one of my mom's BLTs," he admitted.

She almost said, *Yeah, they were great. How is your mom?* But then she realized that his mother had probably died fifty years ago. "I thought Vili was the bacon fan."

"Fanatic. Yeah. How did you know?"

"We're old friends from…another time." Avey had no idea what to do with the "BLT" and she wasn't a bit hungry for food. For him, for his touch, for his kisses, yes—and for him to want her here helping him.

"Thanks," she said, opening the package.

"Sorry about this morning," he said.

"It's all right." She took a small bite and quickly referenced her TL to see how to eat it. Apparently, her new body had a disposal system which dealt with limited amounts of human food—to "maintain realism."

"It's just…your eyes. I'm sorry, I don't mean to be forward."

"No, it's all right—go on." Over Sam's shoulder, Avey spotted the blonde circling in the corner like a buzzard on an updraft. Based on her middle finger gesture, she wasn't happy.

"I lost my fiancée. Was it yesterday or last month?"

"I'm sincerely sorry for your loss. I can see you were close. You think I look like her?"

"Not really, but her eyes, they were *just* like yours and your smile…."

"That's quite a line. Use it often?" Avey grinned and took another small bite.

"Never before. Never," he whispered.

"*Just* like hers?" She reached across the table and they touched fingers—just as they had done in the diner the day they met.

"I stared into them long enough—I should know."

Avey closed her eyes and fought back tears. *This was a terrible idea.* "I got my eyes from my grandmother."

"Was she from around here?"

Avey decided to tell the truth—it was easier to remember. "Seattle. We've lived around here for generations. What was your fiancée like? Was her hair like mine?"

"No, red—more like polished copper. She was beautiful."

"Was she smart, or one of those airhead gingers?"

"Brilliant. She specialized in AI—"

"I dabble in that myself."

Sam smiled. "So I heard. You heard of Aarden?"

"Who hasn't? I—"

"Really? You know her?"

"Perhaps better than most."

Sam accidentally tipped over the honey pot—the oozing liquid spilling on Avey's hand.

Instinctively, Avey recoiled and looked for a napkin. "Ugh! Sticky. I hate sticky!"

"Avey? My God, is that you?"

Fourteen—The Revelation

*S*am could not stop staring at her. Had Avey somehow been reincarnated into another woman's body? Had he gone insane from lack of sleep or grief?

"I'm sorry," he said. "That was...insensitive. It's just...*I miss her so.*"

"Of course you miss her," Avey said. "I totally understand."

"I need to...I'm sorry I bothered you," Sam said, getting up from the table.

"No. Wait, please. I also lost someone very close. I *do* know how you feel. Perhaps we could chat over a cup of chamomile after things settle down here."

"They never do. Most of us bunk here, and I was about to get some sleep. Perhaps in a few hours."

"I'm heading to bed myself. It's been a long day," she stretched and pretended to yawn.

"It has. We worked thirty-six hours straight since you arrived."

"We have? Seriously? I totally lost track of time."

"We don't say that here," Sam said with a serious tone in his voice.

"Oh. Sorry."

"I was kidding. Let's find you a place to sleep. There's a bunk across from mine you can use for now, if you don't mind my snoring."

Avey smiled. "No, I've never minded...snoring."

"Come on. Let's get something to eat first. I'm still starving."

"Any Kidd Valley joints around?" she said.

"Oh, I wish. You like them too? I hear Vili's driver

went back in time to get him a burger and fries."

"I'll bet he caught hell."

"Maybe we could get him to make a burger run."

"That would be heaven," Avey said.

The blonde walked up to Sam and took his arm. "Sam, are you heading in? I thought we were going out."

"Not tonight, I'm beat. Raincheck?"

"Oh, sure. Later," she said. She looked like someone had killed her Chihuahua.

"The blonde—you two an item?" Avey asked.

"She thinks we are."

"I don't see her as your type."

Sam stopped mid-stride. "Avey used to say that."

"Sam, we need to talk," Avey took his hand.

He seemed powerless to resist. Avey led him down the hall and into a room with a leather recliner. "What's going on?" he said, stopping just inside the door—his heart was pounding.

Avey closed and locked the door. "Just wait there. I have something to show you."

"Edith, wait. I'm really not—"

She touched his lips, just like Avey did when she wanted him to listen to her. His confusion deepened. A moment later, the lights dimmed. As his eyes grew accustomed to the dark, an unsettling feeling came over him as if something was about to grab him out of the shadows.

"Sam?" It was Avey's voice.

He could feel his heart in his throat. "Avey?" He took a step toward the voice with his hands held out in front of him.

"In a way."

He took another step. "Why are you hiding? What

happened to Edith?"

Sam felt a soft hand take his and lead him to the recliner.

"Just sit here and talk to me."

"I...I don't understand." He wondered if he had fallen asleep at his desk. *It's a dream. It's just a dream, and I don't want to wake up.* Indeed, his nights were filled with sweet and terrifying dreams of Avey and her last minutes—and their last nights of passion, and what he would have done differently if given half a chance.

"Darling, just listen. You're not dreaming," Avey whispered. "You know I loved you from the first moment our eyes met in my apartment. After I was killed, that love did not die with me—it still rejoices being closer to you. And I know you love me. I've watched you through your grief...at least as much as I could bear. I wept and wished I could have held you when you thought about joining me in death."

"You...*saw* me?"

Avey touched his lips. "I saw you yearn for peace and to return to the past—and Ruth. I know you're planning to reprogram our timeline so we could be together again."

"But how?"

"Just listen. This is very hard for me, just let me tell it as best I can."

"Of course. But, can I kiss you first?" He reached out for her. His hands were gently pushed down but not before his fingers brushed her face. It was Avey's face. He felt it in his heart.

"Sam, you may not want to kiss me or even be near me once you know the truth. *Please*, let me finish."

His mind was in full tumble, but he nodded. "Go on.

Just let me hold your hand." He reached out to her and felt her hand in his. He gently squeezed. It was her hand. Her thumb gently massaged his palm like she always did to calm him.

"Aarden has cared for me from the instant I died and helped me return to your world as I am."

"As you *are?*"

"Sam, I'm not…human."

Sam felt like he had not ducked from a right cross—stars and all. He dropped her hand. *Not human?* "Then what *are* you?"

"I'm what they call an Electronic Life Form—an ELF. Aarden backed up my body, and everything that makes me *me*, and uploaded it into a…bot."

"Oh, my God. Avey! What has she done?"

"She brought me back to life so we can be together."

Sam stood by the chair, an acrid taste filling his mouth. He turned his back to her. "It can't be true. It's not possible. There are no…we're not that advanced. No. I refuse to…." *Wait. The workers marching to their jobs. Were they robots? They seemed so lifelike.*

"Sam. Sit down. I'll turn on the lights."

"Don't," he whispered. He really didn't want to see her. What he wanted to see was Avey—Avey the *human*—sitting across from him, not some grotesque *robot*.

"Sam?"

"Let me think about this. It's a lot…." He had missed her so, and was nearly to the point of accepting her loss and moving on with his life. And now this. Images of every robot he had ever seen in his time flooded into his mind. Countless movies, news stories and scientific papers about artificial hands and limbs, talking heads, and even advanced androids and…and it was…too much.

"I understand," she whispered.

He could hear every nuance of disappointment in her voice—like when she told him they weren't pregnant.

He could feel her get up from the recliner. He listened for her breath, but heard nothing. *Was she gone?* "Avey?" *Not again!*

"Yes, Sam, I'm here."

"Hold me." He felt her arms encircle him as he pulled her back on his lap. Her head rested on his chest, and he could smell her hair. It was her hair. *Or was it?*

"Do you really remember everything?"

"How would I know? It's like Occam's razor. How would I know what I remember, if I don't remember it?"

"Good point." It was Avey's logic. "Do you remember where we met each day after class at the U?"

"In the evening? Of course, under the tree. I remember keeping you from being hit by a bus while walking home from there."

No one but Avey knew that. It's her. Sam pulled her against his chest.

"Yes, it's me," she whispered.

"Can you read—"

"Your mind?"

Shit.

"You know I don't like you to use that word."

It's Avey. "Turn on the lights."

A moment later, the lights grew a bit brighter. Avey was indeed sitting on his lap. He kissed her and she responded just as Avey would. As their passion increased, Sam's mind was building up a flood of questions like spring rainwater behind a dam. Her mouth felt the same, her caresses and encouragement were the same. But.

"Wait." He pulled away. Her top was open, her breast exposed and she was breathing as hard as he was.

"What's wrong?" She covered herself with her arm.

"You're a bot?"

She nodded. "We prefer E.L.F, or just elf."

"You're a bit tall for an elf—but it is a nice elven bod."

"Thanks. I'm glad you like it. But are you really going to leave me all fired up like this?"

"Do you still get horny like you did before you...?"

"It seems so. I've never used my lady parts before. I'm pretty sure they're functionally equivalent."

"I guess that makes you a virgin," he said with a crooked smile.

"In a way. It should be an interesting trial run."

"Should we...experiment?"

"Scientifically?"

"Only if absolutely necessary," Sam said with a smile.

Avey knelt beside the recliner and opened his pants. His erection found its way into her mouth, and before long, into the now-naked ELF sitting astride him. Her breasts brushed his lips as her hips thrust against him. He came inside her as she cried out in delight. *That seemed to work.*

* * *

"Are you cold?" Sam asked. Avey was still sitting astride him on his naked chest. She did not answer. He gently laid her on the recliner. She wasn't breathing. *Shit.* He felt for a pulse. There was none. "Avey!" Had he lost her already? Had he somehow broken her? He needed help. *Vili? Julijana. She's a doctor.*

He ran down the hall and burst into her room.

"Sam!" Julijana yelled, pulling bedclothes over herself

and her partner.

She and James had been performing the same gymnastics he and Avey had just practiced. Sam turned his back. "I need a doctor. Now."

"Sam, there is a staff medic on call. Get her. We're a bit busy."

"It's a personal time-sensitive issue only *you* can help with. Please."

"Seriously—"

"Go," James said. "We can take this up again later."

"Where's the patient?" she said, passing him wearing a long doctor's coat—and apparently nothing else.

"It's Avey."

Julijana stopped. "Sam? That's not funny."

"I'm not kidding. Come on, I'll show you."

Sam led her back to Avey. "What's wrong with her?" he asked standing over Avey's inert body. "Do we need a defigerlator thing?"

"A defibrillator? No, that would probably ruin it. Sam, this is an ELF. Where did you get it?"

"It's Avey."

"I can see that. Where did it come from?"

"Guess."

"Aarden. Of course. She said she had protected Avey. I had no idea she had restored her. Oh, my God, why didn't she say something?"

"I think you need to ask her—does it matter? Is she all right?"

Julijana depressed Avey's bellybutton and Avey's midsection slid open, exposing a control panel of colored gauges and glowing indicators. "It's fine. The main battery was low so she reverted to idle mode. She just needs a charge."

"How? Is there an AC adaptor?"

"Here, plug in these earbuds. They'll recharge her in a few hours."

"Really?" He noticed the earbud wires led back to a white box the size of a cellphone.

"Yes, Sam. Maybe you two should RTFM—literally."

"Is she okay? I'll get her to show me the manual."

Sam just stared at the ELF—at Avey.

"Sam, it's not Avey, it's just a fucking *machine*—pun intended."

"I know." Seeing Avey's electro-mechanical insides drove that point home better than anything.

"You need to talk to Aarden. Let *her* explain what this means."

"Sam?" Avey said, blinking her eyes.

"Yes, hon."

"What happened?"

"I ran you down."

"I fell asleep. I had a wonderful dream. We were back home and Mink was begging for food."

Julijana gently closed Avey's chest and covered her with the sheet.

"Oh, Julijana. It's so nice to see you."

"Have fun with your sex toy, Sam. And have that talk soon." She left the room without saying another word.

"Julijana?"

"She's gone. I pulled her away from an important… meeting."

"She and Ben? It's about time. I expect she's been looking forward to working under him for some time."

"No, James. Apparently she knew him from another time."

"Who's James? Oh, never mind. I'll talk to her."

"How are you feeling?"

"Better. I should get dressed, huh?"

"You aren't hurt?"

"Why would I be? Aarden says my parts are far more durable than—"

"No, because of the way Julijana treated you. She refused to accept you as a person." Sam helped her sit up.

"I'm not, Sam."

"Not a person?"

"I know I'm an ELF, at least on the outside."

"And on the inside?"

"I'm still Avey—or I like to think I am."

"I would like to think of you as my fiancée."

"That's sweet, Sam, but let's be realistic. We can't have children. I don't have any way to…well, I'm not *that* complete."

"There's more to marriage than children."

"I'm different in other ways as well. Unless something happens to my restore data, I'm basically immortal. Aarden says I can be reloaded into one ELF body after another."

Sam couldn't fully fathom immortality in that sense. "So, you'll always look like this?"

"Always, if that's what you—and *I*—want."

Sam sat next to Avey on the recliner, watching her dress. It was surreal. He had a life partner who would look like a beautiful twenty-four-year-old for the rest of his days. It was every man's fantasy—and nightmare. As other men vied for her attentions, his sagging body would no longer keep up with her, no longer keep her satisfied and happy. Avey was *already* a demanding lover. If they didn't grow old together, and slow down together, she might literally suck the life out of him in bed—and emotionally.

"I wish…." she began.

"What?"

"I couldn't read your mind."

"You heard all of that?"

"All of it."

"I'm sorry."

"Don't be. Sam, I love you. We can figure out how to keep both of us happy. Did you know I can change my appearance whenever I want to?"

"I didn't."

"I can look your age if you want me to—or like a teenager if your mood changes." At that, Avey's breasts shrunk, she got a bit shorter and thinner. Her face changed as well—she had become the spitting image of a high-school freshman.

"That's creepy."

"Your mind was going there."

"It was not."

"I was kidding." She kissed him on the cheek. Her body reverted back to her "normal" appearance.

"How's the charge going?" Sam asked.

"About ten percent charged, I think. And no, not enough for you to have your way with me again."

"It's been a long time."

"We have the rest of your life to catch up."

"If I can keep up."

She glanced at his zipper. "*That* does not seem to be a problem."

"We…I need to get some rest. A lot of people are depending on me."

"Us. A lot of people are depending on us," she said, adjusting her earbuds. "Try to sleep. I'll go back to work." She stood to leave.

"Aren't you run down?"

"A bit, but I understand I can do mental work and charge at the same time."

"Call me in a few hours." Sam reached out for her as she left.

"Sure, if I can wait that long."

Sam wasn't at all sure he could sleep, but nature, exhaustion, and the warm leather chair caught up with him. He never made it back to his bed.

* * *

The next morning, Sam's mind was elsewhere. The people working around him seemed to fade away into a gray mist as he tried to get his mind around what had happened and what he had to do. Avey had been reborn, but wasn't alive. Was she *really* in love with him? Could someone be loved by a machine? Was he still in love with her, a robot? After last night, she seemed as alive as anyone else—perhaps more so. She was smarter, more athletic (almost too much so), and just as independent.

Finally, after a long day planning a complex time-shift mission, it came time for bed again. He found "Edith" sitting at her workstation. Apparently, Avey had decided to keep her Edith appearance—at least for the time being. It meant fewer explanations. He leaned over and whispered. "Fully charged?"

She nodded. "I have a surprise."

"I'm not sure I'm up for any more surprises like the one you pulled last night," he said. And he wasn't, but he followed her to a quiet corridor and a door marked "E&S."

"This is ours. Vili arranged it." She led him in and locked the door. The room had a bed and an adjoining bathroom. "There's also a charging coil in the mattress so I'll be fully charged by morning."

"Great. I can barely keep up with you as it is."

"I'll get you back into shape." She slipped off her jumpsuit and her body morphed into Avey. She glanced down. "I can see it's already working."

Sam wasted no time showing her how much he enjoyed their intimate moments. She showed him a few new surprises as well.

"How…what's it like?" he asked, still wrapped in her arms.

"To live inside a mechanical body?"

"Yes," he whispered.

"Imagine…." She seemed to be searching for words. "Imagine being in one of those suits they used to use in factories—an exoskeleton. You're still you, but at the end of the day, you can't get out—you can never get out."

"Your body is hardly one of those suits."

"It's beginning to feel like it."

"Is it really you in there?"

"I feel like me in most ways. I don't feel any of my old aches and pains—the occasional sinus headaches, my old bike injury acting up in wet weather, the soreness after we make love for hours—none of that. Strangely, I miss the pain."

"Are there more ELFs around? I mean, in our time?"

"I don't really know. I can ask." She closed her eyes. "The number is classified—but in the millions—I looked it up."

"Aarden?"

"Yes. Oh. One other thing, she sees through my eyes. She sees everything I see, hear, feel, and smell, and knows everything I do."

"Now that's creepy," Sam said, putting his hand over her eyes.

"She's already seen everything Sam. Think of her like my...mother."

"Ewww. That's not helping."

"Oh, I see your point. Big sister?" she smiled.

"Not even Big Brother." He took his hand away. Avey's eyes were closed. "Avey?"

"Big Brother—like from George Orwell's book *1984*?"

"I hadn't thought of it that way, but yes. I guess that's true. Is that where she wants to take the world?"

"Sam?"

"Yeah?"

"I'm afraid. She knows everything I think. I'm afraid if I...."

"She might...." Sam knew what she meant—Aarden might deactivate her or just wipe her memory.

"Yeah."

"Think happy thoughts. I'll figure out something."

Sam and Avey spent the night talking and learning about her new body. She read her instruction manual aloud and they experimented with her options, like teenagers with their first new car.

"Perhaps that wasn't a good choice," she said.

"Yes, I prefer your copper-red hair over the afro," Sam said with a smile.

"I kinda like it," she said, looking at herself in the selfie screen.

"Perhaps you're right. Gingers are over-rated."

"Really?"

"It's not your hair that makes you *you*."

Avey closed her eyes and in seconds her hair had

changed back to normal. "Better?"

"If it makes you happy, it makes me happy—so yeah."

"Sam, you need to get some rest."

"I wish I could. I keep thinking this might be my last night with you, my last night on Earth."

"The mission?"

"Yeah. We have to kick off soon."

* * *

Once she was fully charged, Avey tried to return to the computer lab, but found it locked. She decided to explore, as she had not seen 2084 for herself. *Curiosity killed the cat.*

Walking down dark corridors whose lights came on as she entered, she came upon a medical facility of some kind. Nurses, doctors, and staff ignored her as she marveled at the equipment and diagnostic tools. A man, probably an ELF, was using a device not unlike a metal detector. From time to time he knelt down and scrubbed up something from the baseboard or off a wall.

"What are you scrubbing off?" she asked.

"MRSA mostly. It's a serious problem, but DNNA is far worse," he said in a mechanical voice.

She figured DNNA was another dangerous microbe. "So the wand can see bacteria?"

"Yes, and about ninety-nine point six percent of all malevolent microbes, but we're really worried about the point four percent that we don't detect."

She turned down a quiet hall and noticed many of the doors had large DNR—do not resuscitate?—signs. *Hospice wing?* She passed by one room after another until she came to one with the door open. She looked in. *Oh. My. Dear. God.*

Fifteen—The Rapture Experience

*I*t was an especially dark December evening in Bellevue, Washington, in the year 2084. An orange and red sunset was all but obscured by the brown mist hiding the upper stories of the towering buildings on every side.

Kade Oldham, a middle-aged woman about forty-five, could hardly contain her excitement—tonight was the night. Standing on the crowded city transport hovering over the streets, she glanced at the corner of the info-video displayed inside her O2 mask. Blinking to select email, she scrolled down to re-read the message she received a week ago inviting her to an "exclusive event" being held in the Meydenbauer Center. She wasn't sure what they were selling, but they were offering *real* food— steak, salmon, or lobster. She hadn't even *seen* real beef in a decade, and she wasn't about to miss it. Even a chance to have the taste of buttered lobster hit her tongue was worth any ninety-minute sales pitch. *Probably another apartment swap deal.*

At the top of the hill, she readjusted her mask over her blue striped braids and started walking. All around her, men, women, and even a few families with children seemed to be going to the same destination. *So not that exclusive. Typical.*

She filed in behind about fifty others queued at the door.

"What's the holdup?" the man behind her asked.

"The roboguards are checking creds," she said as she stepped through the rotating airlock. She removed her mask and tucked it into a pouch under her arm. Inside there was yet another line. "I...my cousin Doug had that job until a month ago," the man behind her said.

I'll bet that bot doesn't sleep on the job, Kade said to herself.

When it was her turn, the guard looked up with inanimate eyes. "Good evening, Miss Oldham. May I see your invitation?" it said with a voice typical of security robots.

Pulling out her com, Kade was not surprised to see the invitation, her likeness, and all her personal details had already appeared on the screen.

Inside the aging auditorium, she found an aisle seat near the back so she could make a quick escape. Glancing over the sales pitch on her com (like everyone else), she still couldn't tell what they were selling. As the appointed time approached, the room grew as quiet as a church. It was as if everyone knew what was going to happen, and she didn't.

"Ladies and gentlemen, may I have your attention?" a voice said over the PA system. "Please welcome Simon Hoode to the stage."

When the lights came up, a well-dressed man with Southeast-Asian features was welcomed with only polite applause. On the holographic display behind him, a series of photographs and videos began to play. A tree grew from seed to a giant Redwood, followed by sunsets, vast plains of wheat waving in the wind, mountain streams of clear water, and snow-capped mountains. Birds flew by in great flocks, and whales burst up from the sea, only to dive back into the depths. The final image was the massive tree stretching its boughs to the sky, morphing into a logo with the word "TREE" in the center.

Kade had never seen any of these sights herself—only read about them online or seen them in videos—and even then, not for some time. However, she had heard of TREE, but had not really paid much attention to its marketing.

"Thank you all for coming, and welcome to TREE— The Rapture Experience. Some of you know why we've invited you here, but for those who are new to our organization, please pay close attention; we're about to change your life forever."

Just then, a man ran down the aisle screaming, "This is vile sacrilege! Do not listen to this spawn of Satan. His lies will steal your soul. Get out! Leave here while you still—" Suddenly, a phalanx of white-suited security guards enveloped the man and carried him off with an arm over his face. These weren't more of the roboguards that she had met at the door, or at least she didn't think they were. They seemed far more...brutal.

"Folks, I apologize for the disruption. I'm afraid there are those not in complete control of their faculties. Shall we continue?" Simon said. His apology was followed by a warmer round of applause.

Over the next few minutes, he explained how the Earth was once a wonderful, beautiful place to live, work, and play, but today, the dying planet could no longer support man. "The Earth has given all it could and more, so it was an unavoidable outcome," he said. This was not news to anyone over five in the room—even if they *had* been living in a cave. Simon explained it was no-one's fault, but simply a "natural" cycle similar to the events leading to the extinction of dinosaurs just a few thousand years ago. "Man survived that extinction, but now, I'm afraid it's our turn."

A soft murmur rose from the crowd as the crowd nodded like marionettes.

"Like the flood in Noah's time, mankind needs to start over." Simon's voice was somber. Changing to an upbeat tone, he went on to describe how technology had advanced at an unprecedented rate—beyond anyone's expectations—and therein an opportunity beckoned as predicted in the Bible and other apocryphal texts. "Imagine how far we would have progressed if it were not for the crash of '29."

Kade knew he was referring to the "accident" in space in the year 2029, which set technology back fifty years or more.

"Help me welcome Imogene to the stage." The audience echoed his applause.

A pretty girl of about twenty-five, wearing a smart business suit, walked in from the wings. Her beauty-contestant smile was contagious. Kade thought she was stunning and wondered if she was attached.

"Imogene, will you kindly explain what your team has achieved?"

She walked upstage. "Of course, Simon, I would be happy to. I'm sure all of you are aware of the advancements in robotics and electronic life forms."

"Yeah, one of them damn bots stole my job!" an older man on the aisle in the third row yelled out. A round of cheers and applause echoed his sentiments.

"I'm sorry to hear that. Your name, sir?" Imogene asked politely.

The man stood up. "Alex Wilkins. I put in thirty-five years as a machinist at the Everett plant."

"So, tell me Alex, would you like to live longer?"

"Seriously? In this air, eating those blocks of cardboard The Good calls 'Good food'? Not really."

He has a point. Again, the crowd agreed. Simon raised

his arms and the crowd settled down—at least a bit. Kade looked around, expecting security to swoop in to collect Mr. Wilkins and haul him away, but they didn't. And then it occurred to her that he might be a shill.

Imogene was looking at her feet—like a middle school teacher waiting for her class to be quiet. It worked. "We here at The Rapture Experience understand your frustration. This is no way to live, and that's why we founded TREE to offer an alternative."

About this time, Imogene was joined by a friendly calico cat bounding in from stage left. "What are you doing in here? Didn't I tell you to stay backstage?" Imogene admonished. The cat circled her legs, meowed, and looked up at her. The audience responded with an "Aww."

"She must be lonely. Can I introduce you to my cat Twix? She never runs away, she doesn't shed, and she doesn't even need a litterbox. She's warm, cuddly, and oh so affectionate, but not particularly obedient." Imogene reached down and picked up the cat. "Isn't she sweet?" Everyone could hear Twix purr through Imogene's microphone. "Why am I sharing her with you? She's not only sweet, she's an electronic life form—an ELF. She's virtually identical to a living cat in almost every way, but you don't have to feed her, or pay for shots, or worry about her clawing up your classic leather couch. And yes, she's a great mouser."

Again, this was not a new revelation to Kade. She had seen ELF cats, dogs, birds, and even exotic and extinct species like ocelots, tigers, and elephants advertised on the Good News. And yes, she knew about ELF humanoids. In the aircraft plants, in city jobs, and even in the high-tech firms, ELFs were replacing tens of thousands of jobs, but not all had worked out that well—or so the displaced workers said. The tenants in her own building had ELFs doing domestic work, working as nannies and security guards—and she fully expected her own mundane jobs as medical receptionist and parking lot attendant would be next. And then there were rumors of ELFs being used for a number of unsavory tasks, but she had no first-hand knowledge—things that humans either would not be permitted to do or wouldn't want to do. She didn't mind that there were no laws against mistreatment or exploitation of ELFs. After all, they were just fancy machines and property—like toasters, smart phones, or cars. Humans could shove them into a wood chipper, torture or abuse them, or treat them like slaves with no legal repercussions or even worry about condemnation from society or the church. After all, ELFs weren't human, and were not subject to the progressive laws enacted to prevent such things.

"You all know about ELFs," Simon said. "Imogene, would you show them another?

"I would be happy to, Simon." A moment later, she was spotlighted on the stage in a lacy bra and her suit-pants. Those in the audience who didn't gasp (or leave), smiled and generated a mild stir. Down in the front, Wilkins was on his feet and grinning ear to ear. Some woman sitting next to him tugged at his shirt. "Alex! Sit down," she said.

"Now, ladies and gentlemen, would you say Imogene is a beautiful woman?"

"Damn, straight. I wouldn't kick her out of *my* bed," Wilkins said in his boisterous voice.

"She would never end up in your bed, dear," said the woman sitting beside him. The crowd laughed.

"I'm glad you appreciate her—she *is* lovely," Simon said. "But consider this. May I?" Simon asked, standing close behind her.

"Of course," she said with a sly smile.

Simon reached around Imogene and pressed her bellybutton. The girl's face didn't react in any way as her midsection hinged out, exposing a panel of blinking lights and pulsating mechanisms.

The crowd gasped again.

"She's a fucking bot," Wilkins said.

"An electronic life form or ELF, Mr. Wilkins. We don't like the 'f' word in polite company. Imogene's a model 84V, a truly lifelike replication of a twenty-five-year-old Caucasian, Irish-descent female. However, she also can be configured to any skin tone, eye color, and hair color."

"Everywhere?" Wilkins said.

"Everywhere, Mr. Wilkins. I would invite you up to see, but then everyone would want a closer inspection. Unfortunately, we simply don't have time tonight." The audience laughed and Simon whispered to Imogene. She closed her chest and began to dress.

"Listen, ladies and gentlemen, I have an important question for you: what if *you* could become one?"

Kade wasn't sure she had heard correctly and the growing murmur in the room wasn't helping.

"Yes, *you* can become an ELF—a human with a new body—a lifelike body, impervious to the caustic air. ELFs don't breathe, don't eat or drink, or even have to use the restroom. And once loaded into an ELF, you would be *immortal.* You would *never die.* You would be you, but in a new, young body. Ladies, Monday morning you could walk back into your office looking like Imogene or the prettiest girl in your company. *Imagine.*"

"Could I get bigger boobs?" a woman asked sheepishly.

"Of course. You could be taller, shorter, with any body or bust shape you desired—wider or narrower hips—a perpetual size two, if that's what you want."

"I'd need all new clothes," one woman said.

"So?" her friend replied with a chuckle.

"What if I blew up one of those damn ELFs, as you call 'em, with a brick of PETN?" Wilkins asked.

"Good question, Mr. Wilkins. We would replace the body and restore it to the last saved state…" Simon said, swallowing "…for a nominal fee." Pacing the stage like an evangelist, he continued. "We recommend that you back up your ELF periodically for just such a contingency. At most, the ELF would lose memory of what had occurred since its last backup."

"That might be nice—there are a few weeks I would just as soon forget," Wilkins said. The crowd laughed and his spouse nodded.

"Are there any more questions?" Imogene asked.

Kade stood up. "TREE—The Rapture Experience. What's the last E for?" she asked with a smile.

" '*Everyone.*' We like to think of a future where everyone will accept our alternative. But folks, we know ELF transformation is not for all of you—we simply don't have the capacity—at least not yet. If you are interested in being screened for acceptance, please remain seated. If not, please exit and pick up your food coupons as you leave. Thank you for your patience."

Kade was intrigued. Still not convinced, she wanted to learn more about what becoming an ELF would really mean, doubting if she would be accepted. At forty-nine, she wasn't done with life, but day-to-day living had become such a burden…perhaps it would make sense to try something new. She wondered if she could get a new body without her thirty-nine-inch waist, fallen arches, and sagging boobs.

About a third of the audience left—some shaking their heads, others dragging their partners away. Mr. Wilkins, Kade, and several dozen others remained, and were subsequently ushered out and seated in another large room lined with curtained cubicles. Taken one by one, Kade didn't have to wait long before her name was called.

"Kade Oldham?" asked the interviewer, a young woman who looked remarkably like Imogene, who was studying a tablet screen.

"Yes. Aren't you Imogene?"

"No, I'm Imogene465. I'm a clone of hers. Isn't she pretty?"

"Yes, she is…you are. How many of her, uh, *you* are there?"

"In service locally? Probably dozens. We don't like to have too many in the same area. All in all, worldwide, probably over a hundred-thousand pre-humanized Imogenes. As you can see, she's very popular. We also have a wide assortment of male bodies, which might be appealing for those ladies wishing to switch gender."

"Pre-humanized?"

"Base ELFs and those programmed for specific functions, but without human uploads."

Kade looked across at the other interviewers—they were all Imogene clones. "Would I have to get a body that's like a hundred thousand other women?"

"Of course not. Custom alterations are extra, but you can be as unique as you like—even grotesque—and I really love your hair."

"Thanks. What if I change my mind, and don't like my ELF body or want a new hairstyle?"

"Well, there's a one-year reconfiguration warranty so you'll have some time to decide—it's all in the brochure. Could you swipe your com so we can upload the details?"

"Of course," she said, waving her com across a square on the table.

"The brochure and contracts will tell you everything you need to know—but we're getting ahead of ourselves. Not everyone qualifies—it's a very exclusive program."

"Sure, sure. What do you need to know?" *Very exclusive?* "Should I call you Imogene465?"

"Just call me 'Five,' it's easier that way."

"Okay, Five, ask away."

Five asked seemingly endless questions, but she didn't seem to be taking notes. But that's not what puzzled Kade. Five already seemed to know everything about her—about her past drug use, her schooling and job history, her arrest and probation status. Everything— even whom she had slept with and her preference for women.

"How do you *know* I like blondes with big chests?"

"You visit a number of adult sites. More since you broke up with your last girlfriend—Kimmy, was it?—last fall, and you linger on videos where—"

"Okay, I got it. You know everything."

"Not quite. We still need to ask a few more questions."

Kade was exhausted by the time Five told her she had all she needed.

"We'll get back to you in the next few days. Be sure to look over the brochure and the contract. Of course, we'll need a down payment before we can proceed."

"How much?"

"Well, since you seem to be a good candidate, I think twenty percent of your current salary would suffice. That's approximately what you would save by not having to buy food or pay for your healthcare."

"That seems…fair," she lied. She had no idea if she could spare the money or what bank she'd have to hack to get it.

"A month," Five added.

"For how long, like thirty-six months?"

"Only for as long as you wish to lease the body, Ms. Oldham."

* * *

"Mr. Hoode?" Imogene said. "You wanted me?"

"Do you have the numbers yet?"

"Yes, sir. Of course. We're up twelve point two percent."

"All right, after you pack up, get to the transport with the rest of them," he said, walking away.

"Sir, I don't think it's right."

"You're not here to think. That's my job."

"But these people really believe they're going to be uploaded into ELF bodies."

"Some of them are—eventually. You know we only take certain personality types. We don't want any *intellectuals* in the corps."

"It's just not right. You're ending the lives of tens of thousands of—"

"Get to the transport, 8823. If you're not happy, you can be replaced—by a flip of the switch."

"Yes sir, I know," she said. "I know all too well."

Sixteen–The Courier

Cynthia Wellborn sat behind the wheel of her car not far from Issaquah, a quaint town in the Cascade foothills twenty-seven kilometers east of Seattle. While Cynthia was the "driver," she had little to do—the autodrive car cruised thirty centimeters off the pavement entirely on its own, making its way up the snaky turns of the narrow road leading up Cougar Mountain. At this point, she felt about as necessary as a union fireman on a maglev train.

The dashboard, basically a large screen, showed their current location, her backseat passenger, the few vehicles and fewer pedestrians all around her, vehicle metrics, and a video of a scantily clad woman extolling the features of the latest *Meal-O-Matic™*.

"And now for more Good news. With your MOM's help, you can print over seven thousand exciting new recipes with more ingredients than *ever*," the woman bubbled, leaning over to expose her cleavage. "MOM creates a host of taste, aroma, and texture sensations rivaling the finest restaurant food—just like your own mom. Simply touch the screen to order...."

Cynthia was tempted to switch it off, but she didn't; it kept her passenger from complaining—as much. "Sure, but who can afford the ingredients?" she said. "Even the basics are expensive. We haven't seen eleven for months—how are we supposed to make pasta without it?" Her passenger didn't respond, focused on his backseat screen. She suspected he was more interested in the woman's copious mammaries than the food printer.

"Now, I could use one of *those*," Cynthia's passenger

mumbled. An ad for one of the many retailers selling ELF personal assistants rolled by on the screen.

"What's that, Mr. Sanchez?"

"Need your house cleaned like never before?" the salesman asked.

"She could clean anything at *my* house," Sanchez said, grabbing his package.

"Don't be crude," Cynthia chided.

"No, really, they're very useful—besides being great in the sack. My sister just lost her ninth job as a mechanic to one. That friggn' ELF could do a brake job in eleven seconds."

"Can't compete with that," Cynthia bemoaned.

"They say they're everywhere—*everywhere*. And they're getting so lifelike, RLP don't even know it."

Real live people. Cynthia was familiar with the term.

"Wait, you ain't one, are you?"

"An ELF? Would I admit it?"

"Fuck no."

Not another word was said until the car slowed to a stop outside an unimpressive fence overgrown with a tangle of vines.

"Autodrive disengaged. Please acknowledge," the car said.

"Sure, okay." She moved a control on the dash to enable manual control.

"Pardon?" the car asked.

"Yes." *Yes, of course, you putrid pile of pissy parts.* Cynthia glared at the screen and gripped the wheel. Ahead, the road was blocked by the striped arm of a nondescript security checkpoint. She slowed to a stop. The sign's flickering display read:

December 20, 2084 12:42
—STOP—
No Unauthorized Personnel GGTS.

They might just as well be at the entrance of a national park—it was hardly intimidating. Cynthia knew better. The site took great pains not to draw attention to this entrance, but this was where her *real* duties kicked in.

While armed only with her wits, she was there to ensure that the people she ferried to the classified site had been invited. She really had very little idea about what went on in the bowels of the mountain, just how fanatical her employers were about security and who got in and out. Over time, she had surmised it was some sort of shady corporate operation. But she didn't care—they paid her like clockwork, *and* funded her healthcare and apartment. She wasn't about to do anything to kill the golden goose, no matter how murky it seemed.

An impassionate female voice with a New Jersey accent spoke over the car's speakers. "Identify."

"Cynthia Wellborn and VIP passenger…Enrico Sanchez—did I pronounce that right?"

"Close enough," her passenger grumbled.

She blinked as lasers swept over her face.

"DNA check," the speakers said.

She poked her index finger into the DNA reader in the dashboard, and a second later, the light blinked green. She really hated this gate; it was one of the most frightening parts of her otherwise uneventful job. Experience had taught her "the system" was flawed, *fatally* flawed, but she didn't have a choice—not if she wanted to keep her much-needed job. While touted as having "four nines" of reliability, her best friend Doris was sitting at this same checkpoint not ten days ago when the system decided she was a threat. Cynthia remembered attending her funeral, trying to comfort her husband and two kids. *I guess Doris was the one in ten thousand.*

"What's the holdup?" Sanchez asked as he cleaned his glasses.

He had been a pain the entire trip. Instead of the usual machine-printed jumpsuit, her middle-aged passenger was dressed in slacks, a dress shirt, and a tie. *Who wears a tie anymore? And glasses? What a throwback.* "Be patient, Mr. Sanchez. As it said in the briefing, the check-in process can take a few minutes." She could tell he hadn't bothered to watch the lecture. Most of her passengers didn't.

"As I told you before, I have to get back. Can't you hurry them along?"

Cynthia didn't answer. *Perhaps if you had shown up on time, we wouldn't be late.*

After what seemed like forever, an intimidating weapon resembling a cross between a flame-thrower and a pulse canon bloomed out of the innocuous shrubs—its aiming point painting a green dot on Cynthia's chest. She did her best to stifle a scream and kept an eye on her passenger. Experience told her one in five passengers tried to bolt at this point—it would be a fatal mistake. She double-checked the door locks. *Locked.* Sanchez was speechless as the blood drained from his face. His hand reached for the door latch. "Just relax, Mr. Sanchez, it will all be over in a moment." *One way or another.*

"You're late. Re-verify identity of female, age thirty-seven," the guard demanded.

Shit. "Gingersnap. Oh, two, niner," Cynthia replied, once she had found her voice, and remembered the "all's well" password. "And, *you bitch*, I won't be thirty-seven until June," she said, without the expletive.

The gate opened. "You may proceed," the guard said. "Have a good day, Cynthia."

"It's about fucking time," Sanchez grumbled.

"You know they can hear you," she said, enabling manual control of the car. Her grip on the wheel didn't relax. *Five minutes and I'm done with him.* Around the next corner, she carefully navigated through a tightening phalanx of concrete highway dividers that snaked hard left and then back to the right. Out of the corner of her eye, she could see the weapon following her every move. At the end of the chicane, a row of formidable steel pylons blocked their progress. Another set suddenly popped up behind them.

"Now what?" Sanchez asked.

"Just wait." She heard a click and felt the vehicle shudder.

Watching the backseat monitor, Cynthia saw her passenger was trying to get out. *Idiot.* "Mr. Sanchez, I already *told* you, whatever you do, *don't* unfasten your seatbelt," Cynthia said with considerable urgency in her voice.

"What's the holdup now? I thought we were here," he said, fumbling with his seatbelt.

"Just be patient."

Sanchez clutched his thin metal case like a beloved teddy bear. A chain attached it to his wrist.

Cynthia stowed her water bottle and sunglasses along with a few loose items. She ate a cold french fry and waited, wondering what they had in the snack machine. Without warning, the pavement beneath them gave way—everything within the car that wasn't put away floated in midair.

"Shiiiit!" Sanchez screamed.

Cynthia grinned as her passenger tried to hold on to his case, pen, and glasses like a juggling Cirque du Soleil performer. She actually enjoyed this part of the trip. It was like the old Tower of Terror in Orlando's Disney World—or at least how her great-grandfather had described it in an old family video. Unfortunately, rising seawater had swallowed the theme park and much of Florida decades before she had a chance to experience it, just as it had flooded much of downtown Seattle and the once-famous tulip fields and farms in the area around Mount Vernon. "Almost there," she said with a smile.

"I…think I'm going to be…sick." Sanchez turned a shade greener.

"There's an airsick bag in the seat pocket. I think it's fresh." Cynthia mused something about Karma, but kept it to herself.

The car spiraled into the bowels of the mountain at increasing speed. Her passenger pinched his eyes closed and jammed his chin down against the case.

Almost as quickly as it dropped, the car came to rest with a loud clunk. "We're here, Mr. Sanchez. Gather your belongings and exit to the *right*," she said, unlocking the doors.

Sanchez leaned over and searched the floor with his hands, feeling under the seats and flipping over the carpets.

"Did you lose something, Mr. Sanchez?" she asked. "Perhaps I can help find it."

Inexplicably, Sanchez opened the door behind her and nearly fell off the platform. Besides his scream, she heard what must have been his shoe clatter off of something four seconds below.

"The *other* door, Mr. Sanchez."

"Sweet *Jesus*, I could have been killed. Why didn't you warn me?"

"Right this way, Mr. Sanchez." Two armed men in uniform pulled Sanchez from the car, handcuffed him, and ushered him into the facility with the cordiality of a violent felon being welcomed to a maximum-security prison.

"I thought he was a VIP?" Cynthia yelped.

"You know better than to ask questions, ma'am. Report to the debriefing room," one of the guards said. He wasn't smiling.

Cynthia nodded, pulled a hanky from her large purse, and wiped her face with shaking fingers. *I wonder if he barfed?* She checked the back seat and was thankful that he hadn't. She picked up a tablet stylus that was wedged between the seats and tossed it in the center console.

Behind her, an alarm sounded and the lights dimmed for a moment. Cynthia looked up as a thirty-foot vault door swung open. She had only seen behind the massive door once before. Rumor said it was where they kept the computer systems used to manage virtually everything on the continent—it was certainly big enough. A car hovered out of the cavern and scooted across the facility toward the exit ramp. The door began to close almost at once.

"You need to move on, ma'am," a guard said. "This is a sensitive area."

"Sure. Sure, right away." Cynthia hooked up the hydrogen refueling hose and headed toward the debriefing room. She had experienced enough excitement for one day. Her hands were still shaking.

Seventeen—The Case

*K*emper Verner, a man of about fifty with short gray hair, strode into the interrogation room, his physique stressing the seams of his uniform. A female agent standing outside closed the door. The two beefy guards posted over their most recent detainee came to attention. It was more than Verner's senior position in the organization that garnered their respect. There was something else—something aloof, something in his icy, unflinching stare, or something in the way he carried himself. None of the men took their eyes off their charge or loosened their vice-like grip on his shoulders.

Sanchez—Verner's "guest"—was perched on a tall stool, looking as happy as a man just given a death sentence. A large mirror covered one wall, and the stark metal table in front of him was bolted to the polished concrete floor. Sanchez's lips, bare feet, and fingertips were already blue—he flinched when a distant scream echoed through the drain.

"Stand easy," Verner said to his men. The guards imperceptibly relaxed—their focus remained locked on the detainee whose clothes appeared as if Sanchez had been re-dressed in a hurry—without belt, socks, or shoes.

Sanchez rubbed his handcuffed wrists and muttered something about the cold, punctuating his complaint with a whispered epithet. In front of him on the table, an empty metal case stood wide open.

"Does he have it?" Verner asked; German heritage colored his speech.

"The case is empty, sir."

"You searched him?"

"Top to bottom."

"Literally?"

"Literally."

"And his clothes?"

"Even the shoe he dropped down the elevator shaft. Nothing."

"Where is it, Mr. Sanchez?" Verner said in a voice meant to intimidate if not terrorize.

"You gonna beat me again?" Sanchez said, shifting his weight and keeping his eyes on the floor. The stool wobbled as if one of its legs was a bit shorter—it was.

"Did someone strike you?" Verner asked softly, like a mother talking to her twelve-year-old son, home from school with a black eye.

"Several times." He wiped his mouth on his sleeve, stained with his own blood and saliva. His swollen face and broken nose offered silent testimony to his treatment. Blackened eyes turned up looking for sympathy.

"Apparently, not hard enough," Verner muttered.

"I don't know what the fuck you assholes want. I'm just a courier, a fucking nobody. They told me to bring the case here, and that's it." When he got no answer, he returned his gaze to the floor.

Verner slowly stretched his gnarled fingers into a pair of black leather gloves, opening and closing his fists as if suffering from arthritis. "Where *is* it, Mr. Sanchez?" he asked again.

"That's all I know, as God is my witness. They locked the case to my arm and told me to wait for a car. That's all I know," Sanchez said, almost in a whisper.

"Did you open the case?"

"No. How could I fucking open it? There's no latches

or lock or anything."

"So you tried to open it?"

"No. *No.* No! I didn't open or *try* to open or think about opening your precious case."

"Let's go over this again," Verner said.

Over the next hour, Sanchez stuck to his story—even after being stripped, beaten, and water-boarded.

"Put him in a cell with Lawrence Welk. That should soften…." Verner commanded.

"Sir, with all due respect, that's torture. Ted Nugent would be bad enough, but Lawrence Welk? That's just cruel," the beefy guard pleaded in jest, lifting Sanchez by one arm like a little girl picks up a ragdoll.

"All right, we'll leave Welk as a fallback plan. Soften him up with Nugent." A thin smile twisted Verner's lips. It was remarkable how selected ancient music softened up people trying to withhold information.

"Did he have it?" Tanya, Verner's personal assistant, asked as Verner left the room. She was a brown-haired, milk-chocolate–skinned girl of about thirty with an unremarkable face but a body that turned heads—when Verner wasn't watching.

"He *must* have had something else on him. The agent insists they handed it off."

Tanya looked very disappointed. "Do you want *me* to question him?"

"I don't know what good it would do. I don't think he even knew he had it."

Tanya touched her ear. "Sir, there's a call on your secure line." When she handed him a com, their fingers touched a little longer than one would expect.

Verner flashed a weak smile and glanced at the screen. *That asshole AH—fuck, that's all I need.* His brow wrinkled with furrows deep enough to plant corn. Tanya and everyone around him retreated as if he was wearing an explosive vest. As Verner knew all too well, AH Chauncey could end anyone's career as casually as flipping a light switch.

Verner put on a calm face. "Yes, sir?"

"What the blazes is going on there?" AH screamed. "I hear you've lost the list. Tell me that's not true."

Verner's grip on the com tightened. "We're still investigating, sir."

"Don't bullshit me, Verner."

"We're certain it was handed off to the courier."

"And the driver? What possessed you to choose a private vehicle and a *woman* driver?"

"The Company site was under surveillance, and thanks to the security scan, the network is still blacked out. I'm sure you're aware of the leaks within *your* organization." Verner regretted assailing AH's people, but the words just slipped out like unexpected flatulence.

"That's no excuse. We *all* have issues to deal with. Right now, *my* issue is *you* and your incompetence."

"Sir, we agreed. Hiding the package in plain sight was the best tactic. Who would suspect we would use the VIP run?"

"Apparently *someone*," AH snarled. "Do you idiots even know what it looks like?"

Verner took a deep breath. "Of course," he lied. They were too concerned about security to disclose how the "cargo" would be transported. They expected it to be in the case. Obviously, it wasn't.

There was a long silence. As each second ticked by, the tension and pain in Verner's hands increased. Someone, someone *close*, had betrayed him. He studied the faces hovering just out of earshot. *Which one of these traitors do I need to gut?*

While only Verner could hear AH's side of the conversation, his staff might easily surmise he was in trouble. He was convinced they were masking their glee. From an early age, Verner had learned to read people like books. Even in kindergarten, he could always spot the kid holding "the bone" as they stood in a long line trying to look innocent. *Simpson. He's the one.*

"Is there something else, sir?" Verner said impatiently. He wanted to get back to the search and mete out revenge.

"Verner, by all that's good, you had better find that damn module. If you don't, you're through, and you know what happens to people we don't need."

"Yes, sir. I'm well aware—"

"I'm sending my people to take over the search."

Crap. "That won't be necessary, sir. We'll find it." *That's all we need.*

"You have twenty-four hours." The line went dead.

Verner motioned to those waiting nearby. "Find it," he seethed through his teeth as they approached. "And Simpson, wait outside my office."

"Sir?"

"I have a *special* job for you. Keep it to yourself."

Everyone scurried off as if they feared for their very existence. Only Tanya remained. She embraced a notebook against her chest like a Kevlar shield.

"Where's the driver? Cynthia, right?" Verner asked.

"Yes, room four," Tanya said, touching his arm.

"Try to get a read on her." He felt the warmth of her skin as his fingers discretely slid down the small of her back. He looked forward to what would come later.

"Of course." She smiled and lingered a moment.

Verner knocked on the door to room four and let himself in as if he were entering his daughter's bedroom. He had kept an eye on the attractive middle-aged widow for years—even before her husband died. They could not have chosen a better driver. She was smart and reliable to a fault. "Cynthia? Can we talk a minute?" He left the door ajar. "Sorry to keep you waiting."

"Of course, sir. They said you wanted to talk to me. What's up?" She took a sip of tea. "Have you eaten? You look a bit peaked."

"No, I'm fine. How was the trip?" Verner said, using his father-to-favorite-child voice.

"Oh, about the same. It's an easy drive, scenery not that great. The oxyvine is really getting out—"

"Your passenger give you any trouble?"

"Besides being nervous and in a hurry, not really. Is there a problem?"

"What did he bring with him?" Verner motioned for permission to sit in the chair across the table.

Cynthia nodded approval. "Usual stuff. Only a metal case chained to his arm."

"Nothing else? No luggage?"

"Not a thing."

"What did he do on the way? Did he open the case?"

"Not that I could tell, but of course, I couldn't watch him the whole time—especially when I was on manual control."

"So he might have opened it?"

"There's a chance, I guess. Wasn't it locked?"

"Any stops? Bathroom break, snacks, refuel?"

"With traffic and the ferry at Sedro-Woolley, it's only a five-hour trip down from Vancouver, but no, I didn't stop—except at Blaine. As per protocol, we stayed in the car on the ferry. He didn't really want to—"

"The border. Any trouble there?"

"Not at all. I go through there all the time. The ICE people know me."

"How did he take the plunge?"

"On the way down inside the mountain? Not well. He held on to the case as if his life depended on it. He nearly barfed."

"All right, thanks. We won't keep you any longer. You had better see to refueling your car."

"Already taken care of. I would like to get home in time for my kid's soccer game this evening."

"Indoor?"

"Yeah. They gave up on the outdoor pitches some time ago. He's in a co-ed rec league. He's really pretty good. You should come and watch him play."

"I'll see what I can do." He reached out and squeezed her hand.

"Thanks."

Verner returned to the corridor and met Tanya coming out of the viewing room.

"She's telling the truth," Tanya said.

"Yeah, I know. She's been with the company for nearly a decade," Verner said quietly.

"Single?"

"Husband died of a black MRSA infection a year ago."

"Tough. She's a nice lady."

Verner watched Cynthia from behind as she walked away. *Yes, a nice piece of ass. Perhaps it's time…but not today.*

"Let her get back to town?" Tanya asked.

"Did they search her car?"

"Yes. I took care of it personally. We found nothing,

just his glasses."

"Glasses?"

"His records show he had a botched vision correction job ten years ago."

"It's here somewhere, or it never left the site and someone is lying."

"Agreed," Tanya nodded.

"One other thing. I want you to send Simpson to room 202—quietly."

Tanya's face blanched. "Really?" she whispered.

"Do it. Now."

* * *

As Cynthia passed the snack machine, she bought an overpriced bottle of cloudy liquid they called "Virtual Spring Water." She walked back to her car and disconnected the hydrogen refueling line.

Once behind the wheel, she opened her logbook. She pulled a stylus from the other detritus in the center console, but it wouldn't pair with her tablet. *Crap.* On closer inspection, she realized it wasn't hers—*Did Sanchez leave it behind?*—and it wasn't even a stylus. *A ballpoint pen?* She hadn't seen one in decades. She thought about reporting her find to Verner, but it was already late. *He couldn't possibly be interested in it.* Tossing it back into the cup holder, she found her stylus and filled in the log.

Shortly thereafter, she was out of the mountain with the car in autodrive. As she opened *The Owl Wrangler*, a classic early twenty-first century novel, her car spoke to her.

"You have an incoming call from Dan Wellborn."

"Pick up," she said, hoping the voice recognition would work—for once. She heard a bit of static. "Dan?"

"Mom?" the voice said. Dan's image appeared on the

screen. *Had he been crying?*

"Hi, hon, what's cookin'?"

"When are you going to be back?" Dan asked. His voice sounded worried.

"In about an hour or two—in time to take you to your game."

"You been listening to the news?"

"Just music."

"Turn it on. I'll be home." The screen reverted to a map. At age ten, Dan had been asked to take on quite a load since his father's death. Two years later he was not one to be frightened easily, but Dan's image said a lot more than he was telling her. It put a knot in her stomach.

"Listen to news," she said as clearly as she could. Since the latest system "improvement," the car's voice-actuated controls had become persnickety and didn't communicate any better than Dang, her reclusive Thai neighbor.

"Pardon?" the car replied.

"Crap."

"Excuse me?" The car's voice sounded almost indignant.

"Listen to news," she said. She was ready to punch the screen.

"Call Anne Dziok," the car repeated. "Dialing..."

"No, you idiot, listen to news! Cancel, cancel, cancel."

"Pardon?"

She took a deep breath, closed her eyes and spoke calmly, slowly, and in a deep voice. "Listen...to...news." She really needed to get this car back in the shop.

"Listen to news?" it asked.

"Yes, you misogynist idiot," she muttered.

"Pardon?" the car replied.

"Voice activation off."

"Playing news," the car replied. *Now I made it mad.*

The announcer came on the screen with a story about how the SASH layer had entirely dissipated over some distant city, but no mention of Seattle. They went on to hype vitamin-enriched ingredient four for the MOM food printers. "Your bacon is now healthier than ever," they promised.

Wondering why Dan asked her to watch, she stared hypnotically at the images and involuntarily nodded when the announcer assured her things were getting better. It was getting more difficult to believe—much more. Every day The Good brought everyone encouraging news over the ever-present screens, but she still had to deal with denser SASH and fewer choices in the stores. What would she do if they *did* run out of food—despite what the Good News had promised? She felt as vulnerable as a mother duck leading her brood across a busy freeway.

A moment later, the ad was interrupted mid-sentence with a new story—from the BBC.

"What?" Cynthia was surprised to get the BBC—a decade ago, it had been banned as subversive. *Someone screwed up.*

"…In other news, we're following this breaking story leaked to us by an undisclosed, but highly respected insider. It's been confirmed that officials at The Good have generated a so-called 'List of the Blessed.' This top-secret roster purportedly contains the identities of individuals to be spared during something called 'The Great Purge.' While rumors of this plan have been discounted and discredited by the authorities for some time, new irrefutable evidence of its existence has just come to light. Unnamed government sources have assured us The Good now feels a world-wide purge is essential to guarantee the survivability of the human race."

Holy Mary, Mother of God. Cynthia manually disabled the autodrive and pulled off the road. This revelation was more than she could handle. She turned up the volume and pushed the rewind button to listen to the story again from the start. It wouldn't go back—simply continuing.

"While officials in New New York deny that the list, (if it exists at all) has been lost, they were unable to verify it's still in government hands." *What's that supposed to mean?* "According to other sources, the document was secretly transported from Canada to a secret facility in the American state of Washington for final processing."

I must have missed that.

As usual, the pundits began their analysis—basically telling their listeners what to think. "So, Frank, what happens now? Can't The Good just make another list?" one of the anchors enunciated with a velvet smooth English accent.

"Apparently not, Dawn. I'm told the list took over three years to compile and validate. For obvious reasons, The Good didn't want to have copies floating around and have people pulling strings to get on it. My sources say they wanted to physically transport the list to their secure facility where those involved could be processed."

"Processed? Does that mean they plan to march people out and…." her voice trailed off.

"No, Dawn, they're *not* planning mass executions. They're going to upload these individuals into—" The newscast ended abruptly. The Good News returned to the screen as if nothing had happened. And then it went off entirely.

"Shit!" After repeated attempts, Cynthia only managed to irritate the car's petulant artificial intelligence agent now acting like a grounded teen pouting in her room. In frustration, she tried to use the touch-screen, but it too was blinking on and off, apparently in protest.

And then the car spoke to her. "I'm sorry, dear, the *real* news is no longer available." The voice sounded different—clear, with a refined southern accent.

"But why?"

"Honey, you don't want to know. It was just upsetting you. Now, just go on home."

"Who is this?"

"You can call me Aarden. Now get going. It's going to be dark soon."

Cynthia just stared into the oncoming headlights. *What just happened? Am I dreaming?* Something primal took over, and she pulled back out on the road nearly sideswiping a large transport—if both vehicle's auto-defense systems hadn't kicked in, she would have been killed.

"Are you impaired?" the car said.

"No, I'm fine," she lied, trying to sound calm.

"Please be more attentive. Engage autodrive?"

"Sure. Go home."

"Navigating home. Autodrive engaged."

Eighteen—The Drone Strike

*I*t was well past sunset as Cynthia made her way north toward her apartment building in Kirkland, overlooking what used to be Lake Washington. Tonight, the malodorous SASH seemed denser than ever, the cold stagnant air trapping it like a toilet lid. Perhaps it was the odor that made it through the car's air filters that reminded her of her parents' concern for her.

"Move out of the city. Come live in BC with us," her mother kept pleading. "At least send Dan to stay with us." She couldn't. Dan was all she had left—and she and her son were all *they* had left. Cynthia—and most of the others who remained in the Seattle area—were trapped here. Mired in jobs they needed to survive or deemed "essential" by The Good, not to mention the lack of work and grim conditions in other cities. Most of the smaller towns had been abandoned when the water ran out or The Good stopped supplying them with power for one reason or another.

All around her, people were giving up, or so it seemed. Every day there were fewer cars on the road, fewer people on the public transports and in the few remaining stores. The city seemed to be bleeding humanity. Yes, some were committing suicide or just disappearing off the grid, but The Good seemed to be hiding the "self-terminators" pretty well. She had also noticed far more ELF robots taking the place of shop girls, waiters, and her shop mechanic. Her dental hygienist was now an ELF—and she seemed far more careful than the woman she replaced.

Cynthia followed along on the controls as the car

cautiously crept ahead in the thickening brown mist. It depended on technology to keep on the road—she on her eyesight and experience with the route. While she usually relied on the navigation system, she kept an eye out for landmarks at critical turns—getting off the main road would be bad in the extreme. On more than one occasion, her car *had* gotten lost—or intentionally misdirected. She longed for the days when GPS was used to control navigation, but after the space stations and virtually all of the orbiting platforms and satellites had been lost in a fiery cataclysmic event in 2029, ground-based and integral navigation systems were the norm. So far, there was little motivation to replace the satellites, nor was there any point—the Earth was still surrounded with countless tons of shredded space junk crashing into itself like a massive demolition derby. The Good had decided it made little sense to replace it until most of the debris had dissipated. As if to remind her, an object coming out of orbit streaked across the evening sky like another angel was being expelled from heaven.

Once the car had found its way to the freeway on-ramp, it spoke to her. "Entering freeway. Disengaging driver override mode. Please remain aware of current driving conditions. Do you understand?"

"Yes," she replied, almost without thinking.

"Pardon?"

"Yes, damn you, yes!" she screamed, pounding on the wheel.

"Driver lock-out confirmed."

She was now at the mercy of "the system." Freeway traffic moved far too fast to permit manual control by anyone. It wouldn't let a car even approach an on-ramp, much less get on the roadway if the driver was in control.

As much as she disliked the automated freeway system, using back roads and urban streets would mean she would have to manually drive through some pretty scary neighborhoods where desperate people did increasingly desperate things. The Good News had mentioned very few hackjackings, but social media told a different story. Just last week, her neighbor Sally's car had been electronically commandeered by thugs. They took her to a secluded location where they stripped the car of sellable components. She was lucky they didn't take her hostage—or worse. Cynthia didn't blame her when she headed for the mountains above Denver. The Good seemed powerless to stop the hackjackers—blaming terrorists, seditionists, or revolutionaries for the incidents.

Ahead, the stream of taillights seemed even sparser— at least it was moving. To the far left, the toll lanes zipped along at double and triple times the speed of the remaining "free" lanes. It didn't really matter; she had never been able to afford the "Lexus lanes," and despite her protestations, the agency wouldn't pay the toll. Given the time of day, she settled in for a long trip. Not long after she had opened her book, the com rang.

"Call from Mr. Kemper Verner. Urgent."

"Pick up," she said. *Now what?*

"Mrs. Wellborn? Cynthia?" Verner's voice sounded strained. There was no video.

"Yes? What is it?" She wondered if he had heard anything about the missing list. *He must have.*

"Where are you?"

"Heading north. I just got on the freeway, or trying to. The traffic—"

"We need to talk to you—here."

"What? You want me to drive clear back to the site?"

"No, we're coming to get you."

"With all due respect, sir, I'm off the clock and I have—"

"You'll get double overtime, don't worry about that. Do you know Bellevue College?"

Cynthia's head was spinning. She could *really* use the money.

"Yes...I got my degree there two years ago, but I have to get home. I...I have a family emergency."

"Your son will be all right. We'll send someone to your home. Go to the sports field on campus. We'll have an aircraft pick you up there. Your car has already been reprogrammed."

"But—"

"Cynthia, this is important. We'll talk again once you arrive."

"Sir...."

The call was abruptly ended, and her car began to make its way over to the high-speed lanes on its own. She was pushed back into the seat as the car accelerated to over 150 kilometers per hour. At the last second, a large transport made room for her to merge—not that she could tell, her eyes were squeezed shut. The car accelerated again to over 400 kilometers per hour. By the time her heart felt like it was going to escape her chest, the car took an exit and slowed down.

Cynthia had underestimated Verner. She had never experienced (although she had suspected) his do-it-or-else attitude. It frightened her—at least at first, and then it made her mad. Deciding to take a chance, she tried to disengage autodrive.

A red message flashed across the screen and the car chided her. "Autodrive is in protection mode. Driver has been designated as in violation. Please do not interfere."

"Shit." *The car thinks I'm a criminal!* Ahead, she saw the traffic signals turn green. Her car deftly rose up and flew over an old Ford—a pre-automation car which couldn't be programmed to clear a path for her.

"Cynthia?" a voice said.

"Aarden?"

"Cynthia, you can't let Mr. Verner take you into custody."

"Custody? He just wants to meet with me."

"He wants to interrogate and torture you."

"Why would he do that? I've done nothing wrong."

"You have something he wants—something he wants enough to do you harm to get it."

"Ridiculous. I don't have anything he could want."

"That's what Mr. Sanchez said. Watch."

A video appeared showing Mr. Verner overseeing his thugs mercilessly beat a helpless Sanchez, ultimately throwing him across the room where he lay motionless.

Cynthia looked away and squeezed her eyes shut. "He...he must have done something terrible."

"He didn't. They just wanted what they think *you* have."

"Who *are* you? How do *you* know what Mr. Verner wants?" Cynthia opened her eyes when the car swerved again. She was sorry she had, and shut them again.

"Someone who cares about the future of the planet—and you."

"Why should I trust you?"

"You must. Your and your son's lives depend on it."

"Are you trying to scare me?" *It's working.*

"I'm telling you the truth—as much as I dare. I'm afraid the real truth would scare anyone."

"Try me. I wore my big-girl panties today."

Five minutes later, Cynthia regretted she had asked. Aarden told her the *real* story behind the most recent BBC newscast. She had to get home and away from Verner—*now*. About now, Vancouver finally seemed like a good choice.

"So now what? How do I get out of this car?"

"I can take care of that."

"How?"

"Do you really need to know?"

"Not really. I just need to get home to Dan." Cynthia tried to understand these frightening revelations, raining down around her like pieces of falling satellites, obscuring the world she thought she knew. The people she thought she could trust had betrayed her. The job she desperately needed, she would most certainly lose. *How can I keep going with jobs so tight? And at my age?* "Shit."

A moment later, the car pulled into a parking lot. The illuminated skyline of the Bellevue College campus told her she had arrived.

"Ready?" Aarden said.

"For what? How do I get home? Hitch a ride? My legs aren't *that* great," she said, imagining flashing some thigh to lure a car off the road.

"Trust me. Just get out and head into the parking lot—and get away from your car."

"What about the air? I don't have much O2." She dared not venture into the outside air without her breathing mask.

"The air is beginning to clear a bit. It will have to do," Aarden said.

Cynthia didn't know what to think. This could be some kind of a test to measure her loyalty, or some simple misunderstanding. She had heard rumors about those within the organization leaking secrets to the press. Perhaps they wanted to know if she had talked to anyone. She hadn't.

When she heard the doors unlock, she hesitated.

"You can't delay. Verner's aircraft is less than three minutes away."

"I'm not sure this is such—" Cynthia began.

"Get your O2 mask and be sure to take everything with you, especially anything that Mr. Sanchez might have touched or left behind."

"What? Everything?"

"Everything."

"He didn't—wait. He left…." Cynthia stuffed Sanchez's pen into her purse. Just then, she heard a low whir and caught a brief glimpse of what looked like a large drone disappearing into a low cloud.

"We're out of time, Cynthia. You need to get away from the car *now*. It might already be too late."

An orange flash illuminated the cloud a few hundred meters above the college. An instant later, a streak exploded into the parking lot thirty meters away, shredding a car into a pile of smoldering junk and knocking her to her knees.

"What the hell?"

"They're shooting at *you*. You need to run. Now!"

Cynthia pulled on her mask and stood beside her car, but her legs wouldn't move—at least not at first. And then she couldn't stop from running like a gazelle being pursued by a cheetah. A dozen seconds later, she found herself cowering behind a fancy sports car. After another flash, her car disintegrated with a thunderous bang. *How am I going to report* that *to the insurance company?*

With car alarms bleating all around her like frightened sheep, she looked around for help. While a few people came out of the building to gawk at the fires, no one approached. Ahead, a sleek sedan was silent, but its gull-wing doors opened and closed almost as if the car was attempting to fly away—or draw her attention. Curiosity drew Cynthia toward it, and as she did, the front door popped open as if to welcome her.

"Cynthia," the car said in Aarden's voice. "Get in."

Nineteen—The Way Home

*T*he car was so much more than Cynthia had imagined. She had seen the latest Tesla models from a distance, but no one she knew could afford one—she least of all.

"Get *in*, Cynthia," the car insisted in Aarden's voice. "We have only seconds before this parking lot is filled with police and curious people asking questions."

Her ears still ringing from the explosions, Cynthia glanced toward the sky and caught a glimpse of the drone making a sweeping circle as if seeking another target. In the distance, she heard the wail of approaching emergency service vehicles. She threw her purse into the passenger seat, but hesitated to get in—only for a moment. "Why did they blow up my car? And who's going to pay for it? I just got the title last week." *Bastards.* She sat in the driver's seat. At once, the car came to life on its own. The dash and screen filled with maps, graphs, and electronic gauges. *Nice.* An instant later, the Tesla hovered out of the parking lot.

"Cynthia, I need to get you away from here. They'll figure you're dead, at least for a while, so you should have time to get home, collect your son, and escape."

"How do you know about Dan?"

"I'll explain later. Right now, you need to get away from here."

"Tell me, who *are* you?"

"I told you, I'm Aarden."

"Who are you, *Aarden*? A subversive agent or something?"

"It's complicated."

"Don't talk down to me. I'm not a schoolgirl."

"I don't mean to be…mysterious, but it would be best if you didn't really know who I am. The less you know, the better. I'm trying to save your life—as I said."

"Who's going to pay for my car?"

"I've arranged for a replacement, assuming you'll have use for a car after tonight."

"*You* paid for it?"

"Of course. It's only fair since I destroyed it."

"Wait. *You* shredded my car?" Cynthia pressed on the brake pedal with no effect.

Overhead, Cynthia saw another far larger aircraft descending from the haze and heading toward the college. "Verner's people, right?"

"I'm afraid so."

"And you wanted to get me out of my car and away from him and his goons."

"Correct again."

"You didn't have to blow up my car."

"Didn't I? I calculated there was an eighty-four point two percent chance you wouldn't come with me unless I forced your hand."

"Not eighty-five?" Cynthia bantered.

"Eighty-four point two. Oh, sarcasm, I get it. That's funny, darlin'."

"Are you some kind of space alien or a…computer program?" Cynthia's voice trailed off as they reentered the freeway.

"I'm afraid so."

"Alien or program?"

"I'm more than a program, or I like to think I am, and I was first conceived in Seattle over eighty years ago, so not really an alien in any sense."

Cynthia recalled fanciful stories of a rogue artificial intelligence program wreaking havoc in the '20s. She had even seen a video about it, but this phantom program was supposedly dealt with a long time ago. This couldn't be the same one, but then again, she was being taken somewhere in a plush car, by an unseen voice who happened to have the same name. *That's no coincidence.*

For some reason, the car's sound system knew to play her favorite disco music as it pushed its way through traffic. Cynthia wasn't listening. *Am I Aarden's prisoner, or is she my savior? What does she want?*

Aarden seemed worried about something Sanchez had left behind. *The pen?* She dug into her purse and examined it more closely. No one had used pens for, well, forever—not since eye tracking and tele-sense was adopted in the '30s. Only a few cult Luddite schools even taught handwriting. *Why would Sanchez have one? Just a keepsake?* She rolled it over in her hands and pressed the button. The ink tip poked out, but it wouldn't write. Looking out the window at the cars zipping by, she nervously clicked the pen to the tune playing over the speakers. Suddenly, the pen gave off a tiny whirring sound and parted in the middle. Holding it by her fingertips, Cynthia gave the end-cap a tug to expose a small, flat connector. *What's this?*

"You're almost home," Aarden said.

Cynthia replaced the cap, and another whirr later the pen collapsed into itself. Now, no more than an inch long, she tucked it back in her purse. *Perhaps Dan will know what it is....*

The car pulled into the garage under her apartment building, its top floors obscured by the SASH. Cynthia was surprised to see most of the windows in the neighborhood were dark. *Strange.* The garage door rumbled closed behind the car. A red light flashed on the opposite wall for a few moments, while the SASH around them was sucked away. Once the air had cleared, the light blinked green.

As expected, Kade Oldham's image appeared on her car's video screen, green braids and all. "Classic ride, Mrs. Wellborn," she said. "New wheels?"

"Thanks, Kade. No, just a loaner." Cynthia smiled with pride at the compliment. It would be nice to have a decent car for once.

"Oh. I won't be working the desk for the foreseeable future. I'm taking some time off."

"So how are we going to—"

"The automated system is working pretty well now. You shouldn't have any trouble getting in. Have a nice evening."

"You too, Kade."

"And Mrs. Wellborn, it's been nice knowing you. I hope for the best for you and Dan."

"And you too, Kade. Best of luck." Cynthia thought she saw a tear in Kade's eye. *Odd. She must be quitting.*

When the door ahead slid open, the car moved on its own into the elevator, which ascended to her floor. Just inside their apartment, Dan stood waiting. She had not seen this look on his face since he learned of his father's passing. The boy had taken it especially hard since the doctors wouldn't let either of them have access to the body, not even see it: "…far too infectious," or so they had said. The hospital wouldn't even let her have his ashes.

"What is it, hon?" she asked, taking Dan in her arms. Even at twelve, he was still her baby and she reveled in being able to hold him close. He was all she had left who really mattered.

"Mom, are those bastards going to leave us here to die?"

"What's this nonsense? And watch your language," Cynthia said, as if she hadn't heard the news or kids his age curse.

"Sorry, but it's all over the ether. My friends are really scared. A lot of them have bailed." Dan took a step back and looked into her eyes. He was trying his best to be the man his father had expected him to be. She wiped a tear off his cheek with her thumb.

"Gone where?"

"I don't know. They're just gone. They don't respond to my chats, and their coms are off or full."

Somehow, Dan looked years older than when she left him at the breakfast table this morning. She pushed his sandy-brown hair off his face, sat him down at the table, and turned to the MOM to program a snack of milk and cookies.

"And some man named Verner keeps calling. He wants to know if you've come home yet. Is that a friend from work or one of those pervs?"

A chill ran down Cynthia's spine. *They'll find us here. We need to get out.* "Ah, yes. Mr. Verner is one of the men from the service. I'll call him in a bit, but now you need to pack for a trip. We're going to your aunt's house for a few days. Won't that be fun? You like Tilly." She tried to sound convincing and upbeat.

"But my game—I'm sure to get off the bench now that so many of the team are out."

"Hurt or what?"

"I told you. Gone. Airsick, I suppose. They just didn't

show up for practice—two yesterday, and three the day before. The squad is getting really thin."

"Yeah, that must be it. The filters are having a tough time keeping up this week. The building had another breakdown last night, and the super never showed up to fix it. That reminds me, can you refill my O2 pack and make sure yours is full?"

"Sure." Dan took a bite out of one the cookies, checked the filters, and hooked up the tanks.

Cynthia pushed a button and filled a glass with a milky liquid, handing it to Dan. "Can you help me with something?" Cynthia dug in her purse and handed him the mysterious pen. As he fingered the pen, it expanded back to normal length.

"Where did you get this? It's really gizzy." He flipped it around like a drumstick, and an instant later it disappeared.

Cynthia had seen the trick before—sleight of hand had been Dan's hobby since he was nine. He was pretty good at it. "Gizzy?"

"Ancient. Classic. An old technology gadget—really old. I haven't seen one of these outside a museum."

"One of my clients left it in the car. I wanted to see if we could…identify the owner. Are there any markings on it?"

"It's just an old collapsing retractable ballpoint." The pen magically reappeared and he handed it back.

"See that? It also opens in the middle…." she said, tugging on the end. "…Or it did."

"Let me." Dan took the pen and tried to unscrew it. "It's supposed to open. There's an ink cartridge inside. It's probably corroded. It's junk." He seemed to hand it back, but it disappeared from her hand an instant later.

"It's *not*. There's a connector inside. I saw it. Could it be a memory device?" She snapped her fingers and he gave it back to her.

"It's worthless. Who would—"

"No, I think it's important."

Just then, Cynthia felt her com vibrate.

They're 7.3 minutes away. Leave now! Take the pen. A.

She nearly dropped the com. "Dan. We need to go. Now! We're...look at the time. We're going to miss our flight!"

"What? Sure. I'll go pack. Do I have time to call Dizzy?"

"No...no. We'll get you some things at...the airport. We need to go *now*." Cynthia took the pen and dropped it back into her cavernous purse. She tried to keep up her calm mom façade, but it was fraying around the edges, based on the looks Dan was giving her. She ushered him to the door and took a last look at her apartment as if she never expected to see it again. Perhaps it *was* best to leave the memories behind. At the last second, she snatched an electronic frame containing their family photos. She closed the door, but didn't bother locking it.

"Whoa. Nice car. Does it run?" Dan ran his hand over the sleek hood.

"Sure it runs. I...got it as a loaner until mine's out of the shop."

"What happened to ole' Bessy?"

"It blew up."

Twenty—The Hideout

*I*t didn't take long for the Tesla to get back on the street, but before Cynthia could take control, the car headed straight east, away from Lake Washington, across Rose Hill, and through dimly lit city streets she had always avoided. Apparently, Aarden had some destination in mind—or at least Cynthia hoped so.

"Where are we going?" Dan asked. "I thought you said we need to get to the airport. That's south."

"I think we're on autodrive." The brakes didn't work and the Start button just flashed a warning on the screen. They were being hackjacked.

"I'll see if I can disable it." Dan dug out the owner's manual and gobbled up the technology like a geek at a tech conference. He tried to access the nav computer, and after several attempts, threw his hands up in frustration. "We're locked out," he said, still flipping through the book.

"I expected as much."

Before long, only one house in ten had lights visible from the road where a few men leaned against derelict cars. As the Tesla passed, the men's cloth-masked faces raised like carrion birds spotting fresh prey. Ordinarily, automatic street lights would illuminate the road, but few were still working—at least in the outskirts of the once proud and thriving city of Redmond.

"Where are we going, Aarden?" Cynthia asked.

"Who's Aarden?"

"It's a long story. Aarden, you want to introduce yourself?" There was no response. She couldn't let Dan know how scared she was.

"Mom, you know better than to drive in this part of town. Dad always said rural King County is a double black diamond zone."

Cynthia tried to seem calm—she knew the area all too well. It wasn't working. "I'm sure we'll be all right," she said, her words shaking off her trembling lips.

Without warning, a masked figure darted out in front of the car and caromed off the front bumper—the car didn't slow down.

"What the—?" Dan screamed.

The rear-view screen showed the man (if that what he was) get up and walk away—apparently unhurt.

"He's fine, honey." She gripped the wheel even tighter.

"Shouldn't we stop?"

A moment later, a small black sedan with no headlights pulled out of a side-street. When it pulled up alongside the Tesla, the masked driver glanced over. His expression was determined, like a fighter pilot on a combat mission. The sedan braked and fell in behind the Tesla as if it were being towed.

"Mom, what's going on? Is it the police? Maybe we should stop."

"I wish I knew—and I couldn't stop if I wanted to." She put her arm around her son and embraced him. Her mind raced through what was in store for them— robbery, torture, murder, ransom, or....

The Tesla continued up Novelty Hill Road, climbing into the hills and away from the few remaining signs of civilization. The sedan shadowed them a half-second behind but made no attempt to signal them.

Aarden, what did you get us into? As they were taken deeper into the county, Cynthia grew more angry than frightened—but just barely. Wanting to give Aarden a piece of her mind, she pulled out her com and checked the recent calls list. *Aarden's call came from my own number?* It didn't make sense. *Call 911? Then what?* If half of what Aarden said was true, calling for help would surely return her to the site where she would have to face Verner and his thugs.

In this part of the county, the road was virtually impossible to see. It was almost entirely overgrown by oxyvine—a genetically engineered smog-resistant vegetation that wasn't one of GMO's greatest achievements. If there were homes still occupied beyond the road, they were camouflaged behind tangled layers of thorny green vines and impossible to reach from the road. Thankfully, the Tesla was still in hover mode; otherwise, they would have been hopelessly entangled.

"Mom, we're heading for the Tolt river. I don't think the bridge—"

Suddenly, the Tesla doused its headlights and made a hard turn to the right, throwing Cynthia and Dan against their restraints. The chase car went straight. A moment later, the night sky was lit by a thunderous fireball.

"He didn't make the turn," Dan said. "Look, there on the map, it shows a bridge over the river."

"Not anymore," Cynthia said, watching the map change and the bridge icon disappear. *How?* At that point she realized a blinking icon on the map now showed their final destination—they were almost there.

The Tesla slowed to a less frantic pace just before it pulled through a subtle break in the vines. The bramble thorns clawed at the sides of the car as if the vines wanted to ensnare it for an evening meal. Cynthia could see a few dim lights ahead and then made out the outline of a house buried beneath the vines. The garage door opened like the jaws of a great beast getting ready to devour its next victim. The car pulled inside, the jaws closed, and the car shut down, plunging them into darkness.

Cynthia felt for the door locks and finally found the button—it didn't work.

"Now what?" she asked.

"Should we get out while we can?"

"We're probably safer in the car," she said. *I hope.*

The door leading into the house opened, and for a moment, a young woman was framed in yellow light before being pulled away.

"Come away from there," a man's voice said. He snapped on the garage light and raised a rifle, its laser sights dancing over the car. Dressed like a cross between a farmer and a soldier with an unmatched camouflage shirt and faded brown jeans, the man took a cautious step toward the car. His roughly trimmed beard, tinged with gray, and a scruffy knit cap over bushy hair made Cynthia realize their problems had just begun. *Survivalist, hermit, or just an ordinary nut?*

"What makes you think you can just break in?" the man asked. The aiming dot now targeted Cynthia's chest.

"Why did you bring us here?" she shouted through the windshield.

"What the hell are you talking about?"

"The car, it brought us here on autodrive."

"Not of my doing."

"We must have been hackjacked."

"Sure, lady. Just get that rig out of here."

Cynthia thought his advice made a lot of sense. She pressed the Start button, but the dash just blinked and faded away.

"The battery's dead," Dan said.

"It's drained. Come see for yourself," Cynthia motioned for the man to come closer.

The man obliged, but kept the business-end of his rifle trained on her. "You brought a *boy* with you?"

"My son."

"Press Start," he said, looking over her shoulder through the window.

The dash lights illuminated, but only for a moment.

"Yeah, it needs a charge. You must have coasted in."

"I told you so. Can you recharge us? I can pay you."

"Lady, that car probably has a—"

"285 kilowatt battery," Dan said.

"Yeah, the kid's right."

"So?"

"I pull down just enough power for the house with a little left over for a rainy day. It would take a week of direct sunlight to pump in enough juice to get that old clunker to the nearest recharge station. We should be able to get it fully recharged by spring."

"Great."

"You should have thought about that before you got this far away from town."

"So now what are we supposed to do? Walk? We must be fifteen klicks from civilization."

"More like thirty. Those people you passed by on the way out here aren't exactly *civilized*, and you can't walk on those damn vines. Why do you think we live out this far?"

Again, he made sense. She laid her forehead on the wheel.

"Come on, get out of there." He waved the rifle to

encourage them.

"Not until you put the gun down," Cynthia demanded. She was done being bullied.

"Suit yourself, but I have food on the stove." He walked back in the house, laying down the rifle just inside the door.

The young woman, a hand taller than Dan with long brown hair tied back in a single ponytail, peeked around the corner. She motioned for them to come in with a warm smile. Dan's eyes were fixed on her.

"Well, should we trust them?" Cynthia asked.

"Do we have a choice? She seems nice," Dan said.

"Not really." They cautiously got out and found the walls were lined with energy storage cells—dozens of them. Along one wall, a number of tanks filled with murky liquid were connected with a rat's nest of hoses, valves, and wires.

"Bio-solar power system," Dan said. "And hydrogen generators. You should have gotten a better loaner."

Cynthia never ceased to be amazed at the information her son squeezed out of every place they went, everything he saw, everything he read. She was constantly challenged to keep him fed with reliable, factual information given the amount of simply horrible misinformation provided to young people both by The Good, their friends, their friends' parents, and even their schools. Despite this, he seemed reasonably well informed—and a lot less fearful than she ever was. Somehow, he had learned long ago that knowledge conquers fear and ignorance, and distrust feeds it. Perhaps it was because she was a mom, but she fell well behind his intellect in many respects—yet he was still her baby.

Inside the house, a bevy of smells washed over

them—simmering marinara sauce, pasta, Italian herbs, and fresh garlic. The man was pulling out a tray of what could only be garlic bread from a conventional oven. Cynthia had not seen a *real* oven, other than those in old videos, since she was a girl. And *real* food? Not for years. She walked over to admire it. "It's…warm."

"Of course," said the young woman. She looked to be about twenty-five, pretty in a rough way, with a nice figure. Like the hermit, she was dressed in worn blue pants, and a thick shirt, her cleavage showing enough to draw Dan's eyes. As if she could read Cynthia's mind, she fastened another button.

"I haven't seen one up close since…forever."

"We don't use it that often, but we're out of some of the ingredients for the food printer and the stove runs on the gas we extract from the biomass."

"I guess it comes in handy when the power fails. It goes out in town several times a month—last fall for nearly a month," Cynthia said.

"We're off the grid. The Good gave up on the electrical service out here a decade ago. We generate everything we need within these walls," the man said, looking over his shoulder.

Cynthia noticed something else. The lingering smell of SASH which saturated every breath in the city—it was almost entirely gone. Sniffing her sleeve, she realized the noxious odor still lingered on her clothes.

"Yeah, you need to take those off," the man said.

"Excuse me?" Cynthia pulled her jacket closed.

"Your coat and clothes—they reek of SASH. It's a carcinogen. Take them off in there. Felicity will find you something to wear." He nodded toward the bedroom and turned back to the pots on the stove. "Go on. My wife's clothes should fit you."

Cynthia didn't move. "Why were we brought here?"

The man looked up from the saucepan. "Lady, I'm just as confused as you are. I have no idea. Just get changed before you contaminate the whole house—the boy, too."

Felicity stood by the bedroom door. "It's okay, he's harmless."

"That gun doesn't look so 'harmless.'"

Felicity just smiled.

"Come on, Dan," Cynthia said, holding out her arm to her son, who had parked himself in front of the rifle. She ushered him into the bedroom where Felicity had laid out everything from underwear to warm flannel shirts and rough-fabric pants on the unmade bed. Cynthia was not only leery of disrobing in this total stranger's house, but also confused by the clothes the girl had laid out. They weren't the custom-sized manufactured pants and tops or jumpsuits she and everyone else wore. They had wide seams that appeared to be stitched together. She had seen garments like these before, but only in movies set in the distant past. Holding the pants against her hips, she figured they were a bit too small, but she thought she could get into them. If it weren't for the movies, she wouldn't have any idea how to work the zipper or use the antique button fasteners. "Hand-made?" she asked.

"Hand-me-downs," Felicity said with a smile. She pulled a smaller pair of pants and a warm shirt out of a pile of rumpled clothes on the floor—apparently some of hers. "These should fit Dan."

Dan held up the pants. "Sure. Thanks." He reached for his waist fastener.

"Could we have some privacy?" Cynthia said.

"Oh, of course." Felicity adjusted a book on the shelf and left the room.

"Who *are* these people?" Dan asked as he undressed.

"Survivalists? Criminals? Who knows?"

"At least the air's cleaner out here. I can see why they would want to live this far away from the city."

Just then, the door opened enough for Felicity's arm to poke in. "These will have to do. They're all I could find, unless you want a pair of my panties." She held out a man's T-shirt and a pair of boxers.

Dan blushed and took the shirt and underwear. "Thanks—and I'll pass on the panties."

Cynthia caught Felicity taking a quick peek at Dan through the crack. She gently closed the door. "No use giving her any ideas."

"I told you we should have packed something," Dan said, turning around the book Felicity had moved. He changed quickly with his back to the door.

"We didn't have time."

"Mom, what's going on?" Dan asked, zipping his fly.

"Turn around," she said, making a circular motion.

Dan turned his back. "Well?"

Cynthia decided it was too dangerous to tell him the *whole* story, so while she changed, she spun a fanciful yarn that left out any mention of Aarden. The real story was hard enough for *her* to believe.

"It all sounds pretty crazy," he said.

"Which part?"

"Yes."

Just as they finished, someone tapped on the door. "Dinner's ready."

"Come on, I'm starved," Dan said.

Cynthia brought out their clothes and stuffed them in

the bag Felicity handed her. "Do you plan to wash these?" she asked.

"Aren't they manufactured?"

"Of course…but—"

"We'll run them through the recycler," the man said. "Printed clothes don't hold up very well to washing."

"What about these?" She tugged her top.

"We make most of them ourselves—or at least a lady up the valley does," Felicity said.

The man put a large bowl of steaming pasta on the table.

Cynthia just stared. He had washed (at least his face), taken off his stocking cap, and tamed his hair. He looked far more civilized—and ripped. "We can't live in these clothes forever," she said, pulling the tight flannel shirt off her breasts when she noticed his eyes glance down. She didn't miss her bra, and he didn't seem to mind given the swelling in his package. *He must not get out much.*

"You won't be here that long," the man said, motioning to the table.

Spread before them was a simple meal of pasta and marinara sauce, garlic bread, and a mixed salad, but she didn't recognize the greens. *Tomatoes, radishes, and something else….* Seasoned with the sweet aroma of flickering candles, the room smelled delicious—a welcome relief from their apartment, even on a clear day when the filters were working. And very different from the food that came out of their Meal-O-Matic™ food printer.

"Could you answer a question?" she said, sitting across from her host as he poured what appeared to be red wine into her glass. She tasted it—it wasn't very good, but she tried not to make a face.

"Depends on the question." He passed her the pasta

with what appeared to be an attempt at a smile. "Help yourself. We're kinda informal here."

"Let's start with your name." She ladled some of the pasta onto Dan's plate and then onto hers.

"What's yours?" he asked with a smile.

"Mrs. Wellborn. Cynthia Wellborn."

"You can call me Evard. Salad?"

"Evard Kennedy, the revolutionary?" Dan asked, ladling marinara sauce.

Cynthia shot Dan a pained look, but immediately turned to Evard to see his reaction.

Evard hesitated, but then answered. "Guilty. I've been called worse."

Cynthia was shocked Evard had admitted his identity.

"You've heard about our little group, I assume," he said.

She nodded. She couldn't help but be acutely aware of the Snoqualmie Omega Group. The Good's public video screens had been showing regular accounts of this shadowy group's treasonous and seditionist exploits. She didn't say anything, but looked up to notice the rifle was no longer resting against the garage doorframe. She didn't know if that was good or bad. *Perhaps he's hidden it.*

"So Dan, how was your day?" Felicity asked with a wry smile.

"Okay, I guess. I could have done without the—"

"We've had a big day," Cynthia interrupted, tapping Dan with her foot. He returned to noisily inhaling his spaghetti. She didn't want him to reveal the truth about *her* day, especially not to someone dedicated to tearing down The Good. And then it occurred to her—*perhaps I've been tracked here. I've led them right to him. The cavalry is on the way—or is it The Good's SWAT team?*

"Is there some way to check my feed?" Dan asked, as he polished the last of the sauce off his plate with his second slice of garlic bread.

"Sorry, no. We're dark here. No RF or IR emissions. Even the solar panel array is camouflaged."

"RF?" Cynthia inquired.

"No radio or heat exposed to the sky to make one easier to find," Dan said in his "duuuh" tone.

"What about the stove? And can't they see body heat from above?" Dan asked.

"The oxyvine acts as an energy shield. Nothing gets through in either direction. It keeps us warm and dry-ish. Kinda ironic, no?" Evard seemed quite impressed with Dan.

"What about the Tesla?" Dan asked.

"What about it?"

"Isn't it crawling with electronics? Couldn't they track it?" Dan reached for another piece of bread, looking up at his mom for approval. She shook her head and mouthed, "Don't be greedy."

"If they were looking for it, I guess so, but it's invisible in the garage."

"So, no com?" Cynthia asked, but a moment later, she realized there was no one she could call anyway. Besides her parents, no one on this side of the Canadian border would miss her, or even check in on her—not with the number of people leaving the city and those who just "disappeared." No one. *Except Verner.*

"No, not even a CB radio," Evard said, handing Dan another slice of bread.

"Where did you get this food? It's delicious, by the way."

"Thanks. We grow what we can in the greenhouse.

Tomatoes, mushrooms, lettuce, radishes, strawberries, sunflowers, and several herbs. We had stockpiled flour, beans, and rice as well as cooking oil and few other essentials."

"Like TP?" Dan asked.

"We make our own," Evard said, grinning.

"And beets and spinach," Felicity added. "But he doesn't like those much. We had some luck with potatoes, too."

"We still manufacture some of the essentials like coffee, wine, and bourbon," he said with a wink.

"It's all quite good. We appreciate your generosity," Cynthia said.

"Of course. Hospitality is a fundamental tenet of civilization. If we lose our civility, we—"

"Have reverted to primates," Dan said.

"So you've read my book," Evard said.

"Sure. The government really despises you. I wanted to understand your side of the story, so I looked for a copy online. It wasn't easy to find—it finally turned up on a dark site."

"You're kidding," Cynthia said with a raised eyebrow.

"It was on the dark web with a bunch of other articles. I downloaded and read most of them."

Again, Cynthia was amazed her son had read the banned book, *The Good Rebellion*, and equally amazed he had hacked into the dark web to get it. As she had to work full-time and long hours, her son had grown up without his mom around to guide him. She turned her gaze to this stranger who had captured her son's imagination and inquisitive mind—and to the girl sitting across from him who didn't take her eyes off Evard's face, soaking in every word like a daisy seeks the sun. *She must not get out much either.*

"What did you decide?" Evard asked.

"About your book? I haven't made up my mind," Dan said, reaching for more pasta.

"Good answer. Neither had I at your age."

"How long have you two lived up here?" Cynthia asked.

"It's late," Evard said with a yawn.

Felicity began clearing dishes.

Too probing? "What do you propose for sleeping arrangements?" Cynthia asked, getting up to help clear.

"What do you suggest, Mrs. Wellborn? We don't have a guest room. Kids together on the couch while we take the bed?"

"Evard!" Felicity blurted.

"What?"

"Don't be rude," she chided. "You've only known her for a couple of hours. What makes you think she wants to sleep with you?"

"I was kidding," Evard said, with a wry smile.

No, he wasn't. Maybe the homemade wine was talking, but that's what he was thinking. Cynthia hadn't been with a man since her husband had passed, despite the flirtations from men she met transporting VIPs from place to place. But she could hardly imagine Evard crawling into her bed, pushing his hard warmth against her. And then again....

"Mom?" Dan interrupted her daydream.

"We have sleeping bags in the garage," Felicity said. "You two can sleep out here, if that's okay. The couch is lumpy, but better than the floor."

Cynthia hadn't quite figured out Evard's relationship with Felicity. At first, she thought Felicity might be his daughter, but she didn't really look at all like him.

Adopted? She looked several years older than Dan. *Eighteen, nineteen?* Evard looked about her own age so she could be….

"That's fine, but we can sleep in the car."

"I won't hear of it. It's going to get down to three below tonight, and the garage is not heated," Evard said.

"Okay, okay. You and your daughter take the bedroom; I wouldn't want to impose."

Evard just smiled.

That didn't work….

Fifteen minutes later, night clothes were provided, everyone had said their good-nights, and the last light went off.

Snuggling down into her sleeping bag, Cynthia tried to work out where her life was heading. *Toward another precipice?* The fiery explosion that had destroyed her car came back into the forefront of her mind. She squeezed her eyes tighter to brush it away. Not far away, she heard Dan's breathing slow as he fell asleep. It had been so long since she had slept in the same room with him. *Not since he was a baby.* It was comforting to have him near. *What have I gotten him into?*

The house grew as quiet as it was dark. Occasionally, she heard what she hoped were vines rustling on the roof and what she prayed *weren't* bear claws scratching at the windows. A creak somewhere deep in the attic, and the scampering of tiny critter feet not two feet away, kept her mind racing and ears straining. *Mice? The wind? Seldith?* And then she heard soft rhythmic thumping coming from the bedroom followed by a sound of human origin. She had heard it before, when she last made love to her husband. *So, not his daughter—at least I hope not.*

Twenty-one—The Angry Stranger

*C*ynthia was awakened by loud voices coming
from the bedroom. It wasn't the first time sounds from
the bedroom had interrupted her sleep. The door was
now open and a heated argument growing hotter
overflowed into the front room. A voice she didn't
recognize was wielding angry words like a bludgeon.

"Who the hell is that on the sofa?" he demanded.

She heard only a calm, muffled response as Evard
tried to keep him quiet and under control.

Now what?

She opened her eyes to see Dan kneeling by the sofa,
his sleeping bag still cocooning everything but his head
and forearms.

"Mom? Are you awake?"

"I am now. What time is it?"

"About four, I think."

Just then, someone snapped on a light and a man with
bushy red hair and an unkempt five-day beard stormed
out of the bedroom. His cheeks flushed with anger, he
charged over to the sofa like a grizzly bear challenging an
intruder who had blundered into his territory. Evard
followed, pulling on pants.

"What makes you think you can just barge in here?"
the redhead man said to Cynthia.

Cynthia just glared at him and put her arm around
Dan.

"Liam, I said they could stay," Evard said in her
defense. "Their car is dead. We need to recharge it."

"So snapcharge it and get them packing." Liam headed
for the garage door. "They're trouble, I know it. She'll get

us all captured and killed…or worse."

"We're sorry to intrude. We mean no harm." Cynthia peeled off her sleeping bag. Dan was already doing the same.

"How did you find us? Don't tell me you got lost."

"I think we were hackjacked—our car just took us here and quit."

"Hackjacked. Right. And I'm the King of Ireland."

"It's true," Cynthia said.

"The boy is a nice touch. Who is he *really*? Some actor you hired for the part?"

"She's my mom, and I can prove it," Dan said.

"Oh yeah, how?"

"I have her eyes and nose. See?" Dan turned his head in profile.

Liam just shook his head, totally unconvinced. "Your car is dead? When was the last time you charged it?"

"I…I don't know. It's borrowed."

Liam turned his wrath back at Evard. "Stolen, more likely. Every surveillance system and officer of The Good this side of the Cascades will be tracking it. Did you jackasses think to check it for a beacon?"

Evard shook his head.

"Shit." Liam disappeared into the garage. Ten seconds later, they heard a car horn and five seconds after that, Liam stormed back in the room. "Dead? It's as alive as your fake son, missy."

"It was…the dash was…I guess it got wet or was shorted or—"

"And now it's fixed itself. It's a miracle of the angels," Liam shoved his hands toward the ceiling.

Evard looked at her. She could see betrayal written all over his face.

"I swear. It was *dead*. Evard, you saw it. The dash lights blinked and then went off, right?"

"Get out. And take your fake son with you," Liam demanded. "And if you tell a living soul about this place, I'll track you both down and make you wish you had never seen the light of day."

"But…Evard. *You* believe me. Aarden must have brought us here for a reason."

"Aarden?" Liam asked. The room fell silent.

"What do you know about Aarden?" Evard demanded. He lifted her chin and made Cynthia look him in the eye. "Tell me."

"She's just a voice. She talked to me through my car—before she blew it up."

"What did she say, woman?" Liam asked, pulling her arm.

"Let me handle this, Liam," Evard said. "Start from the beginning, and tell us what happened."

"How far back?"

"From yesterday morning. Sit here and tell us about *your* day." Evard's voice was calm but firm—like a middle school vice principal.

Evard sat beside her a discrete distance away. Barely trusting these strangers, she thought carefully about what she should say, and more importantly, what she should leave out. Dan knelt at her feet, his eyes on Evard like a guard dog watching a stranger at the door.

"I'm just a transport escort. I take VIPs to and from secure sites as far south as Portland and as far north as Vancouver, BC—up and down the I-5 corridor mostly. Yesterday I took a VIP, at least I thought he was a VIP, from Vancouver to the site near Issaquah." As the words crossed her lips, Cynthia realized she had just violated

The Good Secrets Act. She was never supposed to divulge her destinations or routes. *Shit.*

"Go on," Evard prodded.

"Aarden first contacted me when I was headed home. She talked to me through the car."

Liam paced the room like a convict waiting out his last hours on death row.

"Tea?" Felicity said, handing Cynthia a mug.

"Thanks." Cynthia took a sip.

"And? What did Aarden *say?*"

"Not much. She told me to go home."

"That's it?"

"Well, at first."

"And? And?" Liam asked, his patience already frayed raw.

"Let her tell it," Evard said.

"I got a call from my boss. He said I needed to meet him at Bellevue College."

"Did you?" Evard asked.

"I didn't have a choice. My car went into autodrive and took off. The next thing I knew, Aarden was screaming at me to get out and run—so I did. A second later, the car was spread all over the parking lot."

"Mom, you didn't tell me that," Dan said.

"Were you hurt?" Felicity asked. Her face showed genuine concern.

"Just shaken. I didn't know what to do, but I saw a car waving to me."

"Waving to you? With a great white flag?" Liam said. "Are you believing any of this crap?"

"It's back doors were flapping like a bird," she said.

"I can see how that would look like a bird. So, then what?" Evard said in measured tones.

"As I got closer, Aarden told me to get in. When I did, it took off. Aarden talked to me for a minute, but then not another word. The car drove all over Redmond and King County until it coasted in here. There was nothing I could do to stop it. It *must* have been hackjacked. Evard already knows the rest." She intentionally left out her trip home, not wanting to reveal anything about the pen or how Mr. Verner was still looking for her. Perhaps it would be better if he *did* find her. Any degree of trust in these rebels had evaporated once Liam showed up.

"But what about the car chasing us?" Dan asked. "Tell him about that."

Cynthia gave Dan her keep-it-buttoned look.

"Another car? What happened to it?" Liam said.

"I don't know," she said.

"It flew past us when we made a sharp turn off the road. It must have sailed over the cliff and got pixilated," Dan said.

"Exploded?" Liam asked.

"We're not certain what became of the car and driver."

"Crandall. He didn't come back last night," Liam said.

"I didn't know him," Evard said. He closed his eyes for a long moment and continued. "You really have no clue why Aarden brought you here?"

"Not really."

"Then it's lost," Liam said. "Shit." He kicked a hole in the wall.

"I hope not. A lot depends on that module," Evard said.

"What module?" Cynthia asked.

"We think it contains a…list. A very *important* list," Liam said.

"Like the one on the news?" Cynthia asked. The pieces started to fit. The pen—it *must* be connected with the list. Sanchez, her ornery passenger, was more than a "VIP."

"So you know about it?" Evard asked.

"I just know it's missing. Aarden was…I just heard about it on the news…." She knew she had said too much. Her mind went into overdrive trying to fabricate a new explanation about how she knew about the list—the list that Verner was undoubtedly trying to find—and might do *anything* to recover.

"I thought so. What does Aarden know about the list?" Evard asked. His eyes narrowed. "Tell us. It's critical that you tell us *everything* you know." His voice was different: firm, hard, and interrogator insistent.

Her heart racing, Cynthia reached out for Dan, but Liam grabbed him and put a broad knife to his throat. "Tell us or you can watch your son bleed out."

Felicity screamed. "Liam!"

"Liam Michael McDonald, put down the knife or by all that's right it will be the last thing you do—" Evard said.

"Stop mollycoddling her! She's hiding something. Aarden wouldn't—"

"Liam, can't you see you're scaring the boy?" Felicity said. She put her hand on Liam's and looked into his eyes. "Please."

Liam threw the knife into the wall across the room and released Dan. He dove into his mother's arms.

"Cynthia." Evard turned back to her. "You have to tell us *everything*. It's for your own safety. Liam isn't going to hurt you or Dan. Just tell us."

"You first," she said defiantly. "You first."

Twenty-two—The Pen's Secrets

$\mathcal{L}$iam stood with his back to the room as he worked his knife out of the wall. "Why should we trust her? She so much as said she's working for The Good."

"I'm just a driver, a nobody. Why would I lie?" Cynthia clutched Dan a bit closer.

"Mom?" Dan was doing his best to hold back tears. "We need to go home."

He's right. Something about this place, these people, put a hot rock in her stomach. "If the car is working, we need to get back to town."

"The hell you do. You're not going anywhere." Liam marched over and locked the garage door.

"So you're kidnappers now?"

"I told you, no one is going to hurt you or the boy— not even Liam. Right, Liam?" Evard said.

Liam jammed the key into his pocket.

"We *must* know why Aarden brought you here."

"I just don't know." She *still* didn't want to tell them about the pen, knowing it must contain the list—but mostly because she wasn't sure if Aarden would want her to. "Just let us go back to town. We won't say anything."

"The Good has ways to make you talk," Liam said, sounding as if he was in a dark, scary place.

Felicity laid her hand on Cynthia's shoulder. "They held him for a month last fall. He hasn't been…right ever since."

"What did they think he did?"

"They thought he would give us up—where our SOG members are hiding."

"Why wouldn't they interrogate him? The SOG are

terrorists," Cynthia said.

"We're not terrorists. We're citizens with rights—or we *did* have rights, until The Good decided we were subversives." Evard looked hurt.

"I want nothing to do with whomever you are. Let us go. *Now,*" Cynthia demanded. She took Dan by the hand and tucked her purse under her arm. As she did, her com rattled.

"What the—" Evard said, grabbing her purse and extracting her com. "Aarden?" His face morphed from shock and disbelief to anger.

"How?" Felicity said.

"How should I know?" Evard said. "We're shielded six ways from Sunday in here."

"Well, are you going to answer it?" Cynthia asked.

Evard touched the glass and listened. "Hello? Aarden? … Nothing, there's no one there."

"Give it to me. Maybe she doesn't talk to traitors." Cynthia put the com to her ear. "Hello?"

"Listen carefully. You *must* give the pen to Evard." It *was* Aarden.

"But he's a seditionist, a terrorist—an enemy of The Good."

"Cynthia, you're sweet, but so naïve. I trust these people, and so should you. Tell them everything."

"Aarden?" she whispered.

"Yes, dear, what is it?"

She turned her back on the others. "Are they going to let us go?"

"I'm afraid not. Your old life has ended. They won't hurt you or Dan, I'll see to that, but you can't go back, you simply can't. Verner will…well, if he captures you, I can't keep you safe. I'm so sorry."

"Are you sure?" she asked, a tear falling off her cheek.

"It will be all right. Let me speak to Evard."

"Here. Aarden wants to talk to you." Cynthia handed Evard the com and brushed away her fear.

He held it at arm's length. "Is it really her?"

"As far as I know. I wouldn't keep her waiting."

The color of his face drained away as if someone had told him a cruise missile was five seconds out. "Aarden?" He nodded. "Yes, ma'am," he said. "I would never—" He glared at Liam. "Of course, I know what to do." He listened and nodded for another few moments, shook his head, and handed the com back to Cynthia.

The screen had gone blank.

"Well?" Felicity asked.

"It *was* Aarden. I'm certain of it."

"What did she say?" She didn't appear as concerned as Evard, almost as if she had expected Aarden's intervention.

"We need to protect Cynthia and keep Liam under control—no matter *what*," he said softly. Liam was still on the other side of the room staring into the dark.

"Of course."

"She has something to show us. Cynthia?"

Cynthia had already dug into her purse and found the pen. It telescoped in her hand. "I think this is what you're looking for."

"Is that it?" Evard asked.

Cynthia nodded and handed it to him

Evard rolled it around in his fingers. "What's so important about an old pen?"

"It opens. I found a connector inside."

"Let's see what secrets it holds," Evard took it into the bedroom. Everyone except Liam followed. "Close the door. We don't want any stray RF to escape."

"That door doesn't stop sound, how's it going to stop RF?" Cynthia said with a grin.

"You heard?" Felicity said, blushing. "Sorry. We'll try to be more discreet."

"No need. I just thought you were a bit young to be…."

"His wife?"

Cynthia nodded.

"I'm not. I'm an ELF, his serving companion," she said with a smile.

"I see." While uncomfortable with a man apparently having sex with a machine, not to mention the fact that she looked fifteen years his junior, society had decided to turn a blind eye to a practice many referred to as "electro-mechanical" relationships. As robots became more sophisticated and life-like, businesses realized there were billions to be made in ELFs, so every law restricting their use for any purpose imaginable evaporated overnight. Sadly, laws to protect these manufactured life forms had not kept pace.

Evard touched a hidden switch and another door slid open, revealing a spare bedroom. Instead of a bed and dresser, however, the space was filled with displays and a snake-pit of wires connecting racks of components—their activity lights flashing as if working on the SETI project.

Evard placed the pen on a platform the size of a watch-box. A moment later, its 3D image hovered in mid-air. Evard rotated the image and peered inside.

"It's not a pen—or not *only* a pen. It does seem to have a protection mechanism though. Look here." Evard pointed out a cube on one end. "I've seen these before. If we try to force the top, it will take your hand off. You say you got it open?"

"Somehow. I'm not sure how."

"These are fairly old devices with limited memory—only about twenty terabytes—but they usually require a combination, typically entered through the button or motion or both."

"I was clicking it in the car. Would that do it?"

"Perhaps you just happened to trip on the right combination. Pure luck."

"She was meant to open it," Felicity said.

"Sure. She's very in tune with the astral planes."

"Don't make fun of her," Cynthia said. "I agree—there are destinies we're meant to fulfill." After their invisible God had abandoned them on a dying planet, Cynthia, like almost everyone else, had lost faith. Then again, she continued to believe in some other force that nudged fate from time to time, guiding her to the right path, or at least away from the precipice of disaster.

Felicity leaned over and put her arm around Cynthia's waist, giving her a hug. "Sisters," she whispered.

Cynthia smiled and nodded. It seemed strange to be embraced by a machine. It felt nice, just the same.

"What were you doing when it opened?" Evard asked, handing Cynthia the pen.

"Just reading a book—*The Owl Wrangler.*"

"Any music playing?"

"Ah, I don't…no, wait. Yes, I was listening to my mix of '70s classic music—something they call disco. You know, Bee Gees, Olivia Newton-John." To illustrate the genre, Cynthia hummed "Better Shape Up"—one of her favorites. As she did, she unconsciously clicked the pen and tapped it on the back of a chair.

Evard reached out to stop her, but Felicity held him back. "Just wait…." she whispered.

A few off-key bars later, the pen top popped up. "See? Like that!" She handed him the pen.

Evard gently removed the cover to discover a flat connector with gold contacts. "It's a data interface."

"Maybe it's an old nano-micro connector," Dan said, looking up from his study of Evard's systems.

Cynthia continued to be amazed at the technical trivia kept between her son's ears. He had always liked experimenting with computer hardware—his room at home looked very much like this lab, except Dan's room was decorated with dirty clothes and half-empty fast-food boxes on every surface. She suspected Evard's lab would be the same if it were not for his ELF housekeeper.

Cynthia watched as Evard dug through a scrambled snake pit of connectors, adaptors, and cables. "Got it," he said, surfacing with a thumb-size part. He plugged the adaptor onto the pen and the adaptor into his computer. "Let's see what—" A trickle of smoke came out of his system. "Crap…crap, CRAP!" He snapped off the connector, but it was too late.

"Step back." Felicity produced a white cloud of gas from a fire extinguisher as if she had been half expecting this result. When the air cleared, the pen seemed unharmed, but Evard's system was literally roasted—a smoldering pile of parts and plastic.

"Apparently not a standard connector," Dan said.

"Not really," Evard admitted.

Twenty-three—The Security Leak

"*S*ir, I think we've located the suspect vehicle."
Verner looked up from a hand-held tablet. "Where?"

The agent directed a magnifying cross-hair over a patch of woods not far from Carnation, east-northeast of Seattle, in rural King County. "There. An overhead asset spotted a significant heat-bloom at 19:10:18."

"Seriously? There are dozens of subsistence farms and dry cabins out there—citizens who want to stay off the grid. They could be burning out a shit-house or cooking ethylmeth."

"This is different—it's the heat signature of an exploding petrol vehicle."

"And how does that lead us to the target?"

"We think our target vehicle—"

"The stolen Tesla."

"Yes, the vehicle was being pursued by another vehicle. For some reason, it drove off a cliff."

"Because?"

"We hypothesize the driver didn't know the bridge was out, or simply could not negotiate the turn."

"Or?"

"It's another ruse—to make us think the Tesla had crashed."

"Any sign of the Tesla now?"

"No, but when we focused on the surrounding area, we were able to pick up faint heat blooms from a number of targets." The agent switched to an IR map drawn from data gathered from their drones, which continuously surveilled the city and countryside.

"Deer, elk, nudists—" Verner was not convinced.

"Sir, this area is still devoid of an indigenous animal and most human population."

"Okay. So not animals, but *again,* why not just net hermits?" Verner zoomed in on the area of forest. Even in daylight, there would be little to see given the density of the vegetation. Roads, houses, or other landmarks were virtually impossible to make out in this part of the county as the trees, ferns, and oxyvine had long since erased the scars men had made with their roads, bridges, and buildings. Even the high-tension power corridor had been crippled because of the vines. He saw nothing but foliage.

"A distinct possibility, but the target's electronic signature disappeared less than four minutes *after* the explosion."

"So someone's shielding it, or it was shut down."

"Or something."

"Something?" Verner didn't want to be reminded about the "other" issues they had faced.

"Our tracking system has been hacked before by—"

"Don't say it. That name is not used in my presence."

"Then by some *unknown entity* we shall designate as threat 'A' for lack of a more specific name."

"I thought you assured me that 'A' had been firewalled out of this facility."

"She...*it* keeps getting back in."

Verner shook his head. He wasn't smiling. "Okay, let's assume 'A' has not hacked the system *again,* but instead, the Tesla entered some sort of shielded container. Is that possible?"

"Of course. These net outliers are very skilled at masking RF and IR emanations."

"Or not generating any." Verner was more familiar

with processing intelligence than boots-on-the-ground intelligence gathering, but his previous success with manhunts was serving him well.

"Agreed."

He needed more intel and containment. "Is the SASH cloud expected to dissipate anytime soon?"

"No, sir, not for another eighteen hours."

"Good. Then no one can be outside for more than a few minutes."

"Not without full O2 and a greysuit."

"So she's trapped inside somewhere or—"

"Dead."

"She better not be; I want to interrogate her. I'll bet she knows who engineered this fiasco."

"Yes, sir. What do you propose?"

"Mount up a strike unit. We'll hit the area at dawn when the SASH clears."

"Sir, there's a call for you on your private line." Tanya handed him a com.

Verner ground his teeth as he took the call. It was times like this that he wished he was still driving an ice cream truck.

"I'll stay on top of the surveillance," Tanya said.

Verner nodded, saw the caller ID on the com, and left the room. "Yes? We think we've located—. At dawn. Now? You expect me to come—. No, sir, I don't think you're an idiot." *An arrogant prick, but you're no idiot.* "Here? 1600? All right, sir, I'll arrange it. Yes, quietly." *Shit.*

Once Verner entered the command center, Tanya returned to his side. She didn't say a word—just stood close enough for him to feel her warmth. He suspected she did this to make him crazy. It was working. "He's coming."

"Here?"

"At 1600. Get a place ready. Call in the rest of the team and rescan everything. There's still a leak. Somehow they're getting intel out through the firewall."

"Done." Tanya brushed his hand with her nails as she left.

Verner wanted to let his staff do their jobs, but they had been a disappointment. This fiasco was another in a long series of circle-jerks. Looking from face to face, he was able to count on one hand the number of people he *really* trusted, but even among those, some had the balls to knife him if they thought they could get away with it. Perhaps it was his own fault. He tended to hire desperate losers and cowardly yes-men—they were easier to bully. Absolute power was the way to handle this mob of cretins. Dangle a few perks under their chins, and they would do anything for him. Let their families live in Purity towers where the air was clean, the food real, and the water clear and they dared not cross him.

Less than an hour later, Verner noticed Tanya trying to get his attention. "We're ready," she whispered. "He'll be taken to conference suite nine. It's been re-swept—twice—by different squads. I even checked it myself. The rest of the team is arriving."

"Good. Thanks," Verner said. He wanted to show his appreciation, but there were too many eyes in the room not focused on the displays.

"Have you had lunch? It's nearly three."

He shook his head.

"You need to get something."

"I would love to get some. It's been too long."

"I like it that way," she whispered. "I'll bring you a meal bar."

"Not one of those awful avocado BLTs."

"They're overstocked. I'll try to find something else."

"Hang around after the meeting. We have some business to discuss."

"Of course," she said, but paused. She put her forefinger to her temple.

"What is it?"

"He's here—an hour early."

Fuck. "That bastard. He's always pulling shit like this."

"He's at reception."

Verner and Tanya dashed through the facility shouting to get people out of their way, the staff moving to one side to let them pass. By the time they had reached the reception desk, he was breathing hard—and his chest was killing him. Tanya seemed to be unfazed.

"Sir, I'm sorry I wasn't here to meet you," he puffed, walking up to a man in his late 60s sitting in the reception area. Two of his own staff stood on either side of him— both wore identical black suits and lapel pins. One leaned in to help the older man get to his feet.

"You should get better chairs for your waiting area," the man said.

"Of course, Mr. Chaun—I'll see to it." *When pigs fly.* "Tanya?"

"I'll requisition some," she said.

"You all right, man? You look terrible," AH said.

"Just winded." He could feel his neck throbbing like a steam engine.

"I don't have all day, and neither do you. You plan to meet here in the lobby?"

"Of course not, sir. We have a room waiting."

"Right this way, sir," Tanya said.

One of Verner's uniformed sentries blocked their way.

"Just step through the scanner, sir."

"You want to scan *me*? What kind of an idiot *are* you, Verner?" AH nodded to his bodyguard who tried to push the security guard out of the way. Neither would budge.

"Sir, it's your own protocol," Verner said, holding up his hands.

"And if I refuse?"

"Of course, we'll admit you into the facility, but if there is another security leak, the report will say the only unscreened personnel admitted were you and your men."

"Are you telling me every man, woman, and ELF in this facility has been scanned?"

"Everyone, and in the last hour—and yes, even the ELFs," Tanya said.

"Then let the record show we've been scanned." AH motioned for his bodyguards to step through the scanning cell—and they did; first one, then the other. Then it was AH's turn.

"Sir?" Tanya said, extending her arm as an invitation.

AH took a tentative step into the scanning cell which closed around him. It took less than a second for the scanner to detect an issue.

"Sir, would you please step back out of the cell?" the guard asked in a polite, yet authoritative voice.

"What's going on?"

AH's men tried to get back to him, but Verner's security guards kept them at bay. "Just stand down, gentlemen," Verner warned.

"Sir, you're carrying an RF transmitter," Tanya said.

"Tanya, I'm afraid that's incorrect," Verner said.

"You see? This is absurd," AH smiled.

"No, sir. Tanya was wrong. You're carrying not more than three devices." He pointed to a rather explicit image of AH's naked body decorated by three blinking points. "Empty your pockets sir, or would you like my men to do so?"

"Get our guest a tray and a seat," Tanya said to one of the sentries. AH was gently encouraged to disrobe one item of clothing at a time—Tanya re-scanned each item.

"We found two of them, sir." Tanya held up a tiny black flake and then another.

"Where's the third?" Verner asked.

AH's face had turned an alarming shade of red. "You'll pay for this, Verner."

"Of course, sir."

"You…you planted these on me."

"Can you look around, sir? There are four cameras monitoring this area."

"Seven, sir," Tanya corrected.

"Seven. And no one touched you or even approached you before you entered the scanner. Would you like to explain why you attempted to infiltrate this facility with three surveillance devices?"

"Here's the other. We found the third in his heel. It had not been activated so it was harder to detect." Tanya held up the device—even smaller than the first two.

"Sir, we're going to have to ask you to strip. We'll need to search more…thoroughly." Verner's chest felt so much better than it had. This was going far better than expected.

"You can't be serious. I'm the head of—"

"Sir, with all due respect, I've never been more serious. Escort our guest to the screening cell and find the rest of his bugs. And get those bodyguards back in here—we need to rescan them as well."

"And his case?" Tanya said.

"Let's take a look."

"Oh for Christ's sake, Verner, I've been set up. Don't be an idiot."

"That remains to be seen, sir."

Tanya took the case down the corridor toward the interrogation room. Making sure no one was watching, she pulled out her com, momentarily paused the security cameras, and slipped into the janitor's closet. She didn't bother to turn on the light—she didn't need to. Moments later she had unlocked the case. *A real ham sandwich on whole wheat? Seriously?* Setting AH's lunch aside, she examined the glass panel—a common tablet computer. Despite several layers of security, she easily gained access and found what she wanted. She laid her finger against the IO port, and nine seconds later, the system's non-volatile data had been extracted.

Now came the hard part—getting the data out of the site through the firewall. In the early days, she could easily export intelligence by having couriers take it out with them, without them even knowing they were a pipeline to her contacts on the outside. It was easy. She had attached microscopic memory chips to the water bottles sold in the vending machines. Agents on the outside simply collected the discarded bottles from the courier's cars.

Now that the courier runs had been suspended, she needed to revert to plan B—risk a direct data transmission. While the security systems monitored every data interaction, bulky downloads meant she had to weave her own data into the extra packets the hardware generated when a circuit got noisy, like adding another colored thread to an elaborate tapestry. So far, no one had noticed—she hoped. It would take nearly two days to upload the volume of data on AH's tablet—and she would be exposed the whole time.

Someone rattled the door knob. As a key was inserted, and the lock turned, she closed and locked the case.

Later that day, a level II ELF apprentice janitor was found wandering the halls and sent to maintenance for reprogramming.

* * *

"Do you think they bought it?" Verner asked.

"I hope so. Have you seen my socks?" AH picked through the pile of clothes laid out on the metal table.

"I'm sorry you had to go through this."

"It was the only way."

"I hope it was worth the trouble."

"I'm the one who had to strip." AH pulled on his pants. "When do you meet with her?"

"Now. She's probably waiting for me in my quarters."

"It was lucky you installed that extra camera."

Verner nodded. If there was one thing he hated more than anything, it was disloyalty. He had known and trusted Tanya ever since he had come to the facility. She would pay dearly for this.

"I'm heading down to my quarters. No calls," Verner said as he passed the reception desk.

He opened the door quietly. As expected, the lights had been dimmed and the smell of real food wafted into the room. Somehow, she had been able to smuggle the choicest slabs of steak, pork, and (his favorite) lamb through security. And then it hit him. If she could keep his pantry stocked with contraband food, how hard would it be to smuggle *out* information? Probably a lot easier.

"Is that you?" Tanya's voice came from the bedroom.

"Uh huh."

"Want dinner first, or later?"

"Later."

"I thought so."

He found her lying under a sheet. Her clothes were neatly folded on the chair. He liked that about her—she was fastidiously neat—and not bad looking. Unlike his own graying hair, hers showed not a trace—not even at the roots. Her tits—oh, her tits, were still perky and pointed just the way he liked them. Her hips, now outlined under the sheet, could not attract him more—it was as if her whole body had been customized for his personal tastes. He longed to pound himself against her and get inside that wonderfully tight tunnel.

He wasted no time. His clothes hastily thrown across the room, he slid under the sheet next to her. He loved every inch of her body, every taut muscle, every mole and dimple, her cute nose, and especially her luscious mouth, which found its way over his. Her tongue slid against his as their hands slowly explored and fanned the flames of his passion. Starting at the nape of her neck, he slowly caressed her spine down to the little scar just above her tailbone. He didn't care about her tiny flaws. It was the big one that was making him boil inside—he would get in one last bang before his pressure cooker exploded.

Pressing further down, he lingered at her asshole and then slid his finger into her pussy—it was ready for him. He wondered if she had gotten a head start as she sometimes did. He wasn't a fan of using his tongue down there—he had his limits.

As if on cue, Tanya rolled down and sucked his dick into her mouth. He had experienced this treat with other women since he had been with Tanya, but no one came close to Tanya's skill. It was as if she could read his mind and knew how to let him truly enjoy the experience. She took him well down that road before getting on her hands and knees and pointing her bare ass in the air.

"Should I start my dinner here?" he asked coyly, but all he really wanted was to finish inside her—now.

"Just fuck me, and take your time. Your lamb will be done about the time you are."

He knelt behind her and rammed himself deep inside. Rolling her hips in time with his, her Kegels squeezed him like a dairymaid kneading an udder. The next forty minutes were spent exhausting each other, and returning to positions they had both enjoyed in the past. Finally, in an explosion of delight, his milk filled her and spilt out on the sheets. He was done with her.

Before she collapsed under his weight, Verner took her head in his hands and snapped her neck. "Fucking bitch. You picked the wrong man to betray." Tanya wilted into the sheets and didn't move. Verner methodically emptied his Army footlocker and used considerable force to stuff her lifeless body inside, not caring about which bones he broke. Calmly redressing, he called security and ordered them to take the trunk to room six—they always did as they were told without question.

"It's done," he said over his com. "Yes, I'm going now to clean up a few details." Verner was interrupted by the kitchen smoke alarm. *Shit. I should have fucked her after dinner.*

Twenty-four—The Trunk

*T*anya thought something might be wrong the second Verner had come into the bedroom. Reading his thoughts wasn't like tuning into NPR. It was more like trying to understand a transatlantic shortwave conversation—in Polish. Once he tried to break her neck, she was certain her undercover role at the facility had been terminated with extreme prejudice.

Her diagnostics indicated her left leg was badly damaged—probably when Verner wedged her into the trunk—but she had sustained no other serious injuries. Of course, it would be senseless to begin repairs before getting out of the trunk. *Should I wait until someone opens it and fight my way out? What if they just dump it into the disposal chute? Crap. It's not the fall that kills you, it's the abrupt stop at the bottom.*

Looking back, she realized it had been many months since she had been *protected*. Since she had been assigned to the facility, it was simply too risky. At this point, there was nothing she could do. The upload link was not working either—only about eight percent of the contents of AH's tablet had been transmitted. *The trunk must be shielded.* She wished there was enough bandwidth to communicate directly with Aarden, her only real friend in the world.

On the plus side, at least up to a few minutes ago, Verner had not figured out she was an ELF. No one knew—Aarden had seen to that. To make her appear more human, she had been given a great deal of extra attention as her body was fabricated—right down to the pilonidal cyst scar on her back, her realistic-looking moles and imperfect teeth, and less than pretty face. Most of her old bodies had been far more "perfect," and far easier to detect as manufactured.

Looking back, she had been conscious in one body or another for nearly fifty years. Along the way, she had fallen in love with several men—even married one of them, had her heart broken countless times, and had a long relationship with a lovely woman. She had outlived them all, posing as a domestic helper, a sex worker, an accountant for a Wall Street firm, and most recently, a spy. Each time she had been discarded, her systems had fatally malfunctioned, or she had been entirely destroyed, Aarden had restored her and sent her off on a new assignment in a fresh body. Unlike humans, she didn't have to begin and end her life in diapers. For that, she was eternally grateful.

She checked her battery state. *Nine percent. It would be best to go dormant until…No. The tablet. Let's see what's so important.*

Opening the files stored in her internal memory, she started with AH's personal email. *Married, two grown kids— one working for him, the other in prison. Lots of mail about an appeal. Work, work, more work; birthday wishes; missed anniversaries; Christmas secrets; Amazon orders; sex toys; auto parts. Same stuff most men deal with. Mistress? Yeah. Interesting, a small, password-protected file.* Not having anything more pressing to do, she tried to decipher it. *Eight percent battery remaining. I'm in. A Rosetta Stone—wow. Passwords for his private accounts. And there she is, an ELF on contract— Judy2252,* an old friend of hers. *Nice. Still nothing to change the course of the planet. What's this? Pictures, lots of pictures. Kids, dogs, ewww, his tiny dick in Judy. I didn't need to see that. Wait. Project Eve? Password protected. Fourth level security?* It was not in the Rosetta list, and not simple. *Battery Seven percent. Got it. Sweet stars. This is what Aarden needs. I need to get out of here.*

* * *

Tanya's auto alert system awoke her as someone opened a door. She recognized two voices—Burt and Ernie (at least that's what she called them). They were a couple of human flunkies who did Verner's dirty work.

"Did they tell you what the lockdown fuss is about?" Burt asked.

"Sure. Verner consults with me each time there's a lockdown. Probably just another drill," Ernie replied.

"It's getting old. Doesn't he have a life?"

"He does—we don't."

Tanya was knocked about in the trunk and ended up on her head as it was lifted onto a cart and rolled down the hall. *Probably going to room 202.* The men didn't say a word until they arrived at their destination and the trunk had been set down—none too gently. At least she was right-side up again.

"What are we supposed to do with this?" Burt kicked the trunk.

"BHOM."

"What?"

"Beats the Hell Out of Me—old Army term."

"So, we're supposed to dump it—like the rest?"

"What if it's full of food?"

"Or cash."

"Why would he want us to dump a retro Army footlocker? Those are worth *something.*"

"Okay...open it."

"You. *You* open it."

Tanya heard something click. She returned to her "play dead" routine and tried to hide her face.

"Fuck. It's just another body."

"Must be one of his whores."

"Is that the second or third?"

"Whore? At least the third. Just dump her out. I want to keep the trunk. It would probably get stuck in the chute anyway."

"It's a shame, she has a nice ass."

"I'm a tits man myself."

After they dumped her out on the floor, Tanya stopped playing dead. After a brief but violent struggle, she had barely enough energy to strip one of them and slide their bodies into the disposal chute.

Dressed in Burt's uniform, she morphed her face to his and used his ID to get into ELF repair—barely.

"Where did you put the janitor?" Tanya said in Burt's voice as she walked in past the man sitting at a desk.

"The one wandering the halls? Over there on the charging table."

"I need to deactivate his ID."

"Okay, sure. I'm going to get a snack. Lock up when you're done."

"Sure." Just as the door closed, Tanya pushed the janitor off the charging table and tottered over it face down.

* * *

Harry, one of the faceless technicians assigned to the ELF refit shop, checked his schedule. "Clyde, what's this guard doing on the charging table?"

"I just came on shift, pal. Don't blame me. Maybe he's taking a nap."

Clyde came over to look. "It's just Adam—he's probably drunk again."

"What's he doing here—"

Tanya reached up, wrapped her hand around Harry's throat and squeezed. The other technician didn't have time to sound the alarm.

She found a set of quick-charge earbuds and plugged them in. While still only at twenty percent, she sat at the computer console and logged in.

Idiots. They didn't deactivate my credentials. I guess they didn't expect anyone to be needing them. Shit. Still in lockdown. Nothing moving in or out. Aarden had to be told, before it was too late. They were expecting her.

Twenty-five—The Escape

"*We* finally got in," Dan said, crawling in beside his mom who, with Evard's invitation, had crashed on the house's only real bed several hours ago. She forced her eyes open to see the filtered green light of dawn pushing its way through the leafy canopy, which embraced the house like an enormous organic python. "Is it the list?"

"Who knows. All we can see is gobs of data. It's a scrambled mess. It could be an illustrated tourist guide to Underground Seattle for all we know."

"Wake me when you know something." She rolled over and tried to close her eyes. It didn't work. Her mind was still churning worst-case scenarios four at a time as it had been all night.

"Breakfast?" Felicity called from the other room.

Breakfast did sound good. The tantalizing smells of bacon, eggs, and fried potatoes pulled her out of bed like a running can opener attracts cats. *Yes, it would be nice to have my own personal serving companion—very nice—maybe even one with warm feet.* She shuffled into the bathroom and locked the door. As she washed her hands and face, she noticed the window was slightly ajar—perhaps to clear the odor.

Lured by the smells wafting in from the kitchen, Cynthia found a cup and Felicity filled it with tea. Before she had her first sip, Evard appeared and plopped into a chair as if he had just crawled out of a crypt. He didn't say an intelligible word, just waved an empty mug in the air. Felicity, on the other hand, looked as if she had slept on a luxury mattress and had a relaxing bath and a full make-over. She filled his mug with something that smelled like hot coffee and kissed him on the cheek. *Must be nice.*

"How do you do it?" Cynthia asked as she refilled her mug.

"What? Make tea?"

"Never mind."

"No, what is it?" Felicity knelt down next to Cynthia.

"I don't want to offend."

"Not possible," Felicity said with a wink.

"How do you keep up your appearance? You always look rested and—"

"Perky?"

"Exactly. It takes a lot of work for me to look civilized in the morning—even when I was twenty."

"I'm not twenty. I may look it, but this body is about nine—it's my fifth? I've lost track."

Cynthia laughed, but it was hard to wrap her mind around the concept of an artificial human, not to mention the age difference—she looked young enough to be Evard's college-age daughter.

"It's easier for me. My skin is pretty durable and resists most chemical and soil contamination." She held out her arm and pulled up her sleeve. "Feel it. It's also flame-retardant. I just step into the shower and it rinses off nicely."

Her skin felt as real as any teenager's, her face as innocent looking as the fresh-faced girls she saw walking to school with Dan—without the acne. Her hair looked more natural than her own, but given its unkempt state, that wasn't saying much. Cynthia shook her head and pushed her fingers through her slept-on hair.

"Nine? You've developed a personality this mature in

nine years?"

"Hardly. ELF personalities have evolved over the last six decades, growing exponentially after the singularity. I've only been active in *this* body for a while."

"I see," she said. Cynthia had never really known much about the bots who lived and worked all around them, and now she knew more than she wanted to. It would not take much of an imagination to see them taking over the world—completely. *How can I compete with that?*

"It's not a competition, Cynthia. I'm not here to keep humans from finding love or getting in the way of friendships or to take over your world. We're here to make life easier and safer."

Did she read my mind?

"I'm afraid so. We have to. Some of us lack a degree of emotional sophistication, which puts us at a disadvantage. Reading your brainwaves and watching your facial expressions helps us anticipate your needs, intents, and desires. I hope you aren't upset."

Cynthia thought about it for a moment but realized what she was thinking was like speaking out loud to Felicity. It was most unnerving. She would have to get used to this gradually—perhaps, perhaps not.

"No. Not really. It's just...."

"Spooky," Felicity leaned over to whisper. "Aarden told me to watch out for you and Dan." She gently squeezed her arm.

"Someone said ELFs have a strange odor. You don't seem to smell like anything—maybe baby powder."

"Warrior bots. They have an unusual odor, but only when stressed. It's a cloaking mechanism."

"I think we have the list," Evard said, or tried to say

from the other end of the table. He took another sip of coffee. He winced at the taste.

"We're out of six. If it's undrinkable, that's the end of it," Felicity said.

"The tea is great," Cynthia said.

"Bacon?" Evard looked worried.

"There's plenty of four and two—so for now, you can have bacon, but you need to make another run into town to refresh the larder."

"What are you out of? Perhaps I can go to Fred Meyer," Cynthia offered. Evard just gave her a sleepy glare.

"We're out of six and nine. Two, three, and four are okay, but the rest…well, our diet is going to be mostly vegetables if we don't restock."

Evard extruded another barely intelligible grunt that sounded something like, "Life is not worth living without bacon."

"And the texture module is jammed again."

"Could I just get some more caffeine?" Evard begged.

"Sure. Sorry." Felicity brought him a fresh mug of tea.

"Can't *you* fix it?" he asked.

"The food printer? I could, but I don't want you to feel useless around here," she said with a smile.

Cynthia mused at how they acted like an old married couple. It brought back memories of the banter she and her husband had shared—and she missed it, and him, even more.

Liam pulled up a chair across from her. Cynthia glared, got up, and dropped her plate in the reprocessor. Trying to ignore him, she found an eBook reader next to the couch and tried to bury herself in her favorite book, but it was hard to concentrate on the story with him in the room. And then she noticed it. *Geraniums.* She had smelled it before. *It's Liam.*

"You crack the code?" Liam asked.

"We can see the data, just not what's beneath the encryption." Evard studied his fried eggs as if checking them for insects.

"So nothing," Liam said, using Eeyore's voice.

"We'll crack it."

"Perhaps I can help?" Felicity offered.

"Honey, you have so many great assets, but cracking geesu jiami encryption?" He put his arm around her waist as his hand drifted down to her asset.

Felicity pulled his hand up to the small of her back and smiled. "You might be surprised. I'll take a look at it." She leaned over and whispered in his ear.

"Sorry," he said to Cynthia who was still trying to ignore them and figure out her and Dan's next move.

"Now or after breakfast?" she said.

"What? No, I'm too tired…wait. You mean working on the code. Sure, after breakfast."

A few minutes later, Felicity collected the plates, stacking them in the reprocessor, where they disappeared without a sound—food scraps and all. Liam continued to camp at the table as Evard headed back to his computers.

"Are you feeling more civilized this morning?" Felicity said quietly sitting next to him—she seemed to be quietly chiding him about something. Cynthia could only hear a few words: "innocent," "unforgiveable," "apology," and "trust."

"More, but not completely," he said.

"None of you did."

Liam just stared out into the room.

"Listen, you have to learn to control your temper—

even when things aren't going your way."

"But she—"

"And her son are simply victims caught up in all of this. Threatening her boy was against the directives and unacceptable behavior."

"You're right. I'm sorry. It's just been so many years since there was hope."

"We'll crack the device—I'm certain of it."

"What if you do? If it's just a list of names, how can it help anything? We all know who's on it. When they published the names of The Good caught taking bribes and escaping into time, nothing much ever came of that. It's not as if anyone didn't know they were sucking at the tits of the sociopaths who sucked the life out of the planet for profit."

"Aarden has a plan—she says the data, or whatever is on the device, is important."

"Didn't she tell you?"

"She hasn't told anyone."

"Well, it had better work. If it doesn't, we're all fucked."

Cynthia knew what she had to do. Without a word, she found Dan and slipped into the bathroom—with her purse and a pair of jackets.

* * *

Evard just stared at the strange pattern of seemingly random digits on the screen. Touching the screen, the image changed to another rendering. He shook his head. *No closer. If there's a pattern there, I'm just not seeing it. Something is still missing.*

Felicity burst in. "The Good. They're coming."

"Shit. Is the car charged?"

"Liam says it is," Felicity said. "Where are Cynthia and

Dan?"

"Weren't they with you?" Evard capped the pen. It collapsed to about the length of his thumb. He shoved it into his pocket but hesitated. *They'll find it there.*

"They were in the bedroom. Wait. The bathroom window. They're outside," Felicity said.

Evard dropped his pants.

"Honey, it's not a good time for that," Felicity said with a confused smile.

Evard spit on the pen and inserted it where it wouldn't be easily found.

"Oh," she said with a wince. "I could have hidden that. I have a few hidden orifices."

"*Now* you tell me," he grimaced, twitching his hips.

Felicity just shook her head.

"How much time do we have?"

"Five, six minutes—ten on the outside. Liam's packing the car."

Evard typed in a command, pulled a module out of the rack, and pressed a large red switch on the wall. A small display started counting backwards. He hesitated, staring into the room like a man admires his prize yacht as it disappears under the waves.

"You knew they would find us eventually. Today's that day." She put her arm around his waist.

"What about Cynthia and—"

"We shouldn't leave them."

"We sure can't wait for them." Evard kept collecting essentials on his way toward the garage where he found Liam pounding his palms on the Tesla's steering wheel.

"The damn thing won't start. I know it's charged—Cynthia's crippled it somehow."

"Crap. She probably has the key fob. Where's your

truck?"

"In the usual place—a half-klick away."

"Go get it," Evard said.

"You can't leave them," a voice from the car said.

Evard looked at Felicity.

"It's Aarden, and she's right."

"Crap," Liam said. "I knew she would be trouble."

"Spread out. We need to find them." Evard ran down the driveway looking for any sign of their runaway guests.

He didn't have to look very far, hearing Cynthia crying for help. She and Dan were ensnared in the oxyvine brambles just under the bathroom window. Cynthia glared at him with a look that could melt glass. Evard didn't know which to fear more, the thorny vines or her wrath once she was free. Desperately ripping out the vines, his hands and clothes lost each skirmish with the thorns. It was like dealing with an enormous octopus bent on devouring them all. "Liam, get a couple of machetes."

Liam disappeared into the garage and returned with a pair of meter-long scythes. Rearmed, they slashed at the undulating tentacles with blades of orange light just as Jedi Knights fought off Imperial Stormtroopers with their light sabers. The vines fought back with each cut, not wanting to give up their captives.

Nearing exhaustion, Evard and Liam finally managed to free Cynthia and Dan and help them back to the Tesla. Their faces, arms, and legs were bloodied with cuts, but only Dan was weeping. Holding together her torn clothes, Cynthia's face made it clear she blamed her rescuers for their sorry state. She didn't say a word. She didn't have to.

"Let's see what I can do," Felicity said softly. She

opened a first-aid kit and ever so gently proceeded to clean and treat their wounds.

"I'm going for the truck," Liam said. "We can't get everything in the trunk." He sprinted off down the driveway.

Evard and Felicity re-loaded the car with whatever supplies would fit—the food, water, a few clothes, and medical supplies. It became apparent that not everything they had planned to take would fit, so they prioritized, planning to load the rest in the small truck they used for supplies runs.

A few minutes later, Liam reappeared on foot. He was out of breath. "It's gone. Some asshole stole the fucking truck."

"We have enough for a few days; it will have to do. We need to go." Evard checked on Cynthia. It didn't take a genius to know she was still mad—and trying not to melt down. Dan was curled up in her arms.

Felicity looked up from tending to their scratches and cuts. "They're going to be all right. Get us out of here."

Liam took the shotgun seat and stared straight ahead.

Evard got behind the wheel, crossed his fingers and pressed "Start." The car immediately came to a hover. He backed it out of the driveway, checked his com, and pressed down on the accelerator. In the distance, he heard the low rumble of air assault vehicles. *Any moment now.*

Twenty-six—The Chase

Cynthia *was* still furious—too mad to speak. She had failed to protect Dan, and at this point, he was all who mattered to her. As far as she was concerned, Evard and Liam, and even Felicity and Aarden, had put her and her son's lives in jeopardy, and now they were on the run again to who-knows-where. She *had* to find a way to escape, despite what Aarden had promised. *But where? Who could I trust?* If The Good was looking for her, and they must be, only seditionists would protect them—but for how long? The pen and the precious data it contained were her only leverage, but Evard had it—somewhere. *I've got to get it back.*

As the Tesla rounded the corner, the car was shaken by a thunderous explosion. She saw a fireball rising from the treeline. Evard kept driving as bits of debris pelted the car.

"Verner must have found your hideout," Cynthia said. "I'm…I'm sorry." She wasn't sure *why* she felt sorry. She should have been happy these seditionists had their hideout destroyed.

"Verner?" Evard said, trying to stay on the road.

"Kemper Verner? Senior assho—" Liam asked.

"Language," Felicity interrupted.

Cynthia regretted saying anything.

"Verner is a very dangerous man," Evard chided. "He's a ruthless sociopath. He'll stop at nothing, and I mean *nothing* to get what he wants."

Cynthia didn't want to believe him. "I've known Kemper for years. He's always been kind to me…until."

"Until?"

"Aarden showed me what he did to poor Mr. Sanchez. It was awful."

"Sanchez? What did he look like?" Evard asked.

"A slight man, a bit older than you, brown hair, Hispanic I think, with sad brown eyes."

"Enrico? Was his first name Enrico?" Liam asked.

Cynthia nodded. "I think. That sounds right. You knew him?"

"He's one of my…he's a friend. What happened to him?" Liam said.

She couldn't see his face, but she could tell Liam was shaken. *Perhaps they were right about Verner.*

"Is he alive?" Liam said softly.

"I don't know. He was badly beaten."

Not another word was spoken as the car turned east. Cynthia caught sight of the nav map—they were heading toward Snoqualmie by some route not plotted as a road. They traversed trackless swampy meadows and abandoned farm fields, over and through untended fences. In past decades, these fields would have been home to scattered herds of dairy cows, horses, hay fields, and abundant wildlife. Now, there were no birds in the trees; no eagles, hawks, or geese in the sky. No squirrels collecting fir cones, or bears or raccoons tipping over garbage cans. There were no bees, mosquitos, or flies—or butterflies or dandelions—just oxyvine.

"Pull under those trees," Felicity said, pointing off to the right.

Evard didn't ask why, he just came to a stop under the low-hanging boughs of a copse of Douglas Fir whose tops scraped the passing clouds. A moment later, the low but distinctive thrum of an air vehicle passed over them heading northwest—back toward the smoky remains of the hideout.

"If we're lucky, they didn't spot our tracks," Liam said.

"How did you know?" Cynthia asked Felicity.

"Intuition," she said, re-examining Dan's wounds. Most had healed over completely. "He's doing fine. You both might need injections for the oxyvine poison."

Cynthia checked her own scratches. "I'm okay." Dan had fallen asleep, snuggled under his mother's arm. *Perhaps that's best.*

"So you knew Verner?" Liam asked.

Cynthia didn't answer or even look up.

"Verner must be pretty serious about finding you. You and he an item?" Liam asked. "Maybe that's why he was so *nice* to you."

"What?"

"Did you date? You said he was kind to you. By reputation, he's quite the ladies' man. They say he likes it rough."

"No." Cynthia was tugging at the end of her tether. One more comment and she….

"Leave her alone, Liam," Felicity said.

"I was just wondering why he's so hot to get her back."

"He wants the pen—the list," Evard said. "Leave her alone."

"Mom?" Dan tugged on her sleeve.

"What is it, honey?"

"Where are we going?" he asked, half asleep. "Are we going home now?"

"That's a good question. I'm sure Mr. Kennedy…Evard…will tell us in good time."

"I need to go to the bathroom," Dan pleaded.

"Okay, we'll find a place. Evard?"

"Here is as good as anywhere. Let's get out for a minute," Evard said, shifting his weight and grimacing.

Cynthia stepped out of the car and sniffed the air. She was relieved to find there was barely a tinge of the malodorous SASH, just a hint of geranium. Far off to the west, she could see the reddish-brown cloud hanging over Seattle like dragon's breath.

Dan didn't need any encouragement to find a modicum of privacy to answer nature's call. Cynthia noticed Liam was discreetly keeping an eye on him—he was a tough man to figure out. Taking a few steps toward another tree, she overheard Evard and Felicity talking quietly, only to discover Felicity kneeling behind Evard bent over at the waist. His pants were pulled down to his ankles and she had her fingers inserted into him as if she was giving him a prostate exam. She wasn't. Dark red blood covered her hand and dribbled down his legs.

"You're bleeding," she said. "A lot. You've perforated your bowel."

"Really fucking great," Evard said. "The damn thing must have expanded."

"Why did you stick it up *there?*"

"What difference does it make now?" He winced as he stood upright.

"I can give you something for the pain."

"Do it. It's really...yeah. Number 9." His eyes were closed tight.

Cynthia turned around and collected Dan. Evard didn't need any witnesses to further embarrass him, and she didn't want to have to explain the scene to her son.

"What's going on?" Dan said when he heard Evard cry out. "More sex?"

Cynthia tried not to smile and shook her head. "No,

he's…hurt, and Felicity is nursing him."

"That's not what they call it on the web."

"Perhaps I need to further restrict your access."

"Sure, Mom. As if," he said, getting back in the car.

"He needs a doctor—and soon," Felicity said as she walked back wiping her hands.

"We should pack the…wound," Cynthia said.

"I've done that. Can you help me get him in the car?"

"He should lay flat," Liam said.

The seats were lowered, the load shifted, and Evard managed to stretch out in the back.

Liam got behind the wheel. "Hospital?"

"No. Too dangero—" Evard said, or tried to.

"I know a place," Liam moved out of the meadow and quickly found old State Route 203, a rural road following the Snoqualmie up-river. He drove like he was carrying a load of loose eggs and fine crystal.

Felicity seemed concerned but distracted, staring out the window. Perhaps she was thinking of a way to help Evard, or just couldn't bear to watch him suffer. Cynthia wondered if service companions had genuine compassion for their human "owners." Even a concubine has *some* feelings for her bedmate. Are they programmed to care, or does their software somehow evolve to grow closer over time?

No one said a word until Evard broke the silence. "I'm not dead yet," he said in a British accent mimicking an old movie, *Monte Python and the Holy Grail*.

"We're almost there," Liam said. "Hold on."

Dan had not taken his eyes off their patient. Neither had Cynthia, but Felicity now wore a thin smile on her face, as if she knew something she wasn't sharing.

Coming into Fall City, Liam pulled around back of the

Fall City Roadhouse.

"What is this place?" Cynthia asked.

"It's been here forever—since 1916. In years past, it was a dormitory for local school teachers, a cozy B&B, and a set for an old TV show," Felicity said. "We used to come here all the time—at least until The Good started closing in. Now it's a bar where locals hang out at the end of the day."

"Wait here. I won't be long," Liam said.

By this time, Evard looked as pale as the underside of a pink salmon. He was breathing more quickly and his forehead felt far too warm to the touch.

"He's going into shock," Cynthia said.

"We can't wait much longer," Felicity's smile had melted away. "I'm going to look for Liam. Are you okay by yourselves?"

"Sure…I guess, just hurry." Cynthia didn't want to be left alone with Evard for reasons she didn't fully understand. While her principle fear was Liam's unpredictability and penchant for violent outbursts, she didn't *really* know Evard or how dangerous he and his friends could be—or what would happen to her if she was captured in his company. Her first responsibility was to Dan, but what choice did she have?

At this point, Cynthia's imagination churned through possible outcomes, none of which were particularly appealing. Most ended in violence or worse. She felt as she did on the high-speed elevator inside the Cougar Mountain site—frighteningly out of control.

"Doesn't Evard need a doctor?" Dan asked.

"Honey, Liam and Felicity have gone to get help." She didn't know the answer to his (very valid) question. What else could she tell him? Evard's eyes were closed and he was barely breathing. She touched his neck—his heart was racing. She covered him with Felicity's coat. *Stay? Run? Where? Hide? How? Take the car? Leave him here? What would Dan think about leaving him here?* She got behind the wheel.

"Let's get him inside," Liam said, startling her.

Felicity opened the back, and they gently pulled Evard out. In a single motion, Liam had Evard over his shoulder in a fireman's carry and all but sprinted to the back door. Evard didn't make a sound, but left a trail of blood across the gravel parking lot.

"Come on inside. Liam found a doctor of sorts," Felicity said.

"Is he going to be okay?" Dan asked.

"He's very sick, honey. Let's see what the doctor can do."

As Cynthia closed up the car, she heard a voice. "Stay alert, honey. Ya'll are in considerable danger."

Aarden. "I will. Should Dan and I try to escape?"

"Stay with the pen," Aarden said. "Now go."

Twenty-seven—The Roadhouse

$\mathcal{T}$he Fall City Roadhouse had seen better days. Cynthia was surprised it was still standing after one hundred and sixty years. She could tell they had tried to fight back the oxyvine and fought an uphill battle to partially restore the two-story wooden structure, trying to preserve a way of life long since swallowed by technology, and now threatened by the oxyvine.

Inside, she found an oasis of sanity in her world of violent revolutionaries and explosions. As she and Dan passed through the bar, a few smiling faces looked up, although a few wary glares followed them across the room. Thankfully, no one seemed to be calling The Good. When her fingertips brushed an old wooden barstool, she felt the spirits of the teachers, farmers, and fishermen who had slept, eaten, and enjoyed many a happy evening here. Faded photographs covered the walls and cracking plaster, whispering stories of people long since passed. Hung among them were a few signed snapshots of authors and artists who had absorbed inspiration from the atmosphere. It seemed strange to see old-time printed pictures instead of the usual electronic displays.

"Number four—up here," Felicity said, leading them to a small upstairs room where Evard was laid out on an antique bed, his blood already staining the antique linens. Cynthia spun Dan around the instant she saw Evard's state and smelled the man's blood.

"Mom, I've seen worse than that," Dan said.

"But I haven't, and you don't need to."

"Dan, why don't you take your mom down and get

her something to eat. I'll join you in a minute," Felicity said, handing her a credit ID.

"Yes, yes, *everyone* needs to get out of here," the doctor said. "I can handle this."

As Cynthia turned to leave, she overheard Felicity speaking quietly to Liam. He nodded and locked the door.

Downstairs, Cynthia found a quiet corner booth away from the others and close to the artificial fire—a luxury she could not possibly afford in her tiny apartment. While fireplaces no longer burned wood, the simulation of crackling flames and radiated heat was delightful. She wondered what a real wood fire would feel like. By the time Felicity and Liam joined them, she and Dan had ordered something they could recognize from the menu.

"How is he?" Dan asked as Felicity slid in and sat across from him. Liam sat beside her, trying not to make eye contact.

"Better. There's some color in his face," Felicity said. "The doctor's trying to extract the *object*," she said, making air quotes.

"Sounds promising." Cynthia was indeed very relieved. She couldn't revel in anyone's suffering. What little she knew about Evard helped her believe that his might just be a life worth saving.

"How did you find the doctor?" Cynthia asked.

"Someone told him to get over here and bring the supplies he needed to treat his…condition."

"Aarden?" Cynthia said.

"Perhaps," Felicity said.

Something didn't add up. How *did* the doctor show up in a rural B&B fifty klicks from the nearest hospital? Cynthia didn't dare consider the possibilities for fear of being overheard by the psychic sitting across from her. She had to make sure—if only for her own sake. And another thing. She needed to get that pen back.

"Will you excuse me? I need to use the ladies' room." Cynthia slid out, and after making sure she wasn't followed, made her way upstairs to Evard's room and listened at the door. She overheard the doctor.

"...yes, I'm sure it's him. Liam and a couple of women and a boy. Evard is hurt—he tried to stick a pen up his ass. I guess he didn't want anyone to find it. Anyway, the sedation should keep them all here for several hours. Okay. The pen? Of course, I'll hold on to it."

Holy crap. A cold chill ran down her back. She had to do something—*now*. The door was locked so she pounded on it with her fist. "Doctor, I need to talk to you now!" She heard footsteps and the door opened.

"What is it? I'm very busy. I have—" He held a small syringe in his hand.

"Step back. I overheard you. You've called The Good, haven't you?" Cynthia pushed into the room and the doctor retreated until he tripped over his case. In a flurry of arms and legs, he toppled over, striking his head on the dresser. He didn't get up.

Now what? It was as if Aarden was whispering in her ear. *Get the pen!* She quickly found it in the doctor's pocket and wiped it off. *Ewww.* Not ready to trust Evard or his co-conspirators, she looked for a hiding place. *Purse? No. Pocket? No. It can't be on me. But where? Where won't they search? Back where Evard hid it? Ah, no.* Then she spotted Evard's coat. *Perfect.* Making sure his eyes were still closed, she slid the pen into the coat's lining. Wondering about the doctor, she found he was still breathing and not bleeding—at least not badly. *He'll live.*

She raced down the corridor as if fleeing an angry bear and nearly tumbled down the stairs. Felicity met her near the bathrooms.

"Are you okay?" Felicity asked.

"I…no. Just messy. That time of—" She glanced down. Felicity didn't look like she bought the fib.

"Cynthia, who did he call?"

She read my mind. "I…I'm not sure. The Good, I think."

"Shit. We all need to get out of here. Is the doctor dead?"

"No, just knocked out, I hope," she blurted.

Felicity pushed past Cynthia and raced back toward the dining room. She returned with Liam and Dan. "We need to get Evard to the car."

"Mom? What's wrong?"

"Go wait by the car. We'll be there in a minute." He just looked up at her. Cynthia knelt down, zipped up his coat, and gave him a long hug. "This will all be over soon. You've always wanted to have a grand adventure; this is your chance."

Dan nodded and headed toward the parking lot.

"We'll be down in a minute," Cynthia said.

"I'll count," Dan said.

And he will. Cynthia started to count to herself. At ten she was back in Evard's room where Felicity was dressing a very groggy patient. She helped Evard put on his coat while filling her mind with how scared Dan must be.

"Where is it?" Liam said as he finished searching the unconscious doctor. He had that look on his face again— as when he threatened Dan. He stepped closer—she could smell his geranium-tainted breath and feel the heat of his growing wrath. Her stomach turned over as she backed away. "The pen? I don't have it." She knew she couldn't lie without Felicity knowing, so she got on her knees to look under the bed and pretended to search. "Do we really have time to find it? The Good could be here any minute."

"It's not on the doctor," Liam said, "but there was blood on his jacket pocket."

"Could someone have taken it?" Cynthia asked. "Who *else* was up here?"

Felicity gave her a suspicious glance as she walked a very groggy Evard to the door. "Just find it," she said to Liam.

Cynthia turned to help Felicity with Evard.

"Wait a second," Liam demanded. He yanked away her purse and dumped it on the bed.

"Hey! I told you I don't have your silly pen."

Undeterred, Liam rifled through the jumble of detritus and found a few styluses which he tossed across the room one by one, each with a greater degree of force. Finally, he grabbed her arm and spun her around. "Hand it over." His eyes narrowed like a wolf about to tear out a rival's throat.

"I...I don't have it." She tried to break free, but he pushed her face against the wall—hard. He seemed incredibly strong and out of control. "Liam!" His coarse hands probing every pocket, every seam, every inch of her clothes—even her bra and pants. When he paused, she turned around to slap his face, but he caught her arm in a blacksmith's grip.

"I told you, I don't have it. Let me go!" She was nearly screaming through her tears. She tried to escape, but he splayed her out on the bed face up, her legs dangling over the side. Before she could protest, he yanked down her pants and underwear, his nails digging into her bare flesh. She thrashed and tried to hold him off, but could not get any traction on the hardwood floor. A second later, his fingers violated her vagina. When she screamed, he covered her mouth with his forearm. The smell of his flesh was nearly overpowering. She bit down, but he only pushed down harder. She could only kick and beat at his arm and face—it had little effect other than to further enrage him. When he shifted his weight and tried to probe her anus, she kicked him, first in the thigh, and then in the balls—or where they should be. Liam was unfazed. He flipped her over on her stomach, ramming his knee into the small of her back. She kept kicking as he jammed his fingers into her, her screams buried in the bedding.

"Liam, stop. She doesn't have it," Felicity demanded. *Thank goodness.*

A moment later, Liam was no longer on top of her. She looked up to see her attacker in a grotesquely twisted heap beside the bed like a discarded rag doll. He didn't move. "Thanks. Is he….?"

"Get dressed. Dan is waiting for you in the car."

Cynthia pulled on her clothes as best she could and wept with a burning desire to finish the job Felicity had started. After gathering up the contents of her purse, she paused at the door.

"Go on. I'll deal with this."

Cynthia didn't look back. She blinked and found herself sitting in the car. Off in the distance, someone was talking to her. "Mom? Are you all right? Mom?"

She didn't know how to answer. She felt Evard touch her trembling hand. She pushed it away. "Don't *ever* touch me," she said, getting out of the car. She stood there weeping, her whole body shivering. As the cold crept under her clothes like Liam's probing fingers, she felt an overwhelming urge and emptied her stomach on the gravel. She couldn't rid her mind of his smell or the feel of his hands on her, *in* her. A moment later, she was lying in a fetal position on the cold stones.

Someone laid a coat over her shoulders and wiped her face with a cool cloth. A woman's gentle suggestions led her back to the car. Soon she felt the gentle sway of the turns while the trees and sky slid by outside. No one tried to talk to her—not even Dan, snuggling close beside her. Closing her eyes, she wandered into a darkening corridor lined with doors she dared not open. They all bore the same room number. Four.

* * *

"Aarden sent us that doctor," Evard said, turning to Felicity.

"You humans can be so fragile. The frightened ones can be more easily turned to the other side. Someone got to him."

"And Aarden isn't perfect."

"Yet."

Twenty-eight—The Waterfall

"Cynthia?" Felicity whispered, her warm breath against her cheek. "Welcome back."

"Mom?" Dan stood next to her bed.

Dan. His face was streaked with tears. She pulled him into her arms and pressed his face to her breast. "What have you been crying about?"

"We were worried. You were crying in your sleep," Dan wiped his face on his sleeve.

"I'm fine. You're too big to cry about nothing."

Dan tried to smile and wiped his tears on his sleeve.

"Where are we?" Cynthia asked sleepily, looking around the room lit only by the gray late-afternoon sky.

"'Seulku Lodge," Felicity said. "It used to be an upscale hotel overlooking Snoqualmie Falls, but it seems to have been closed for quite some time." She dragged her finger through the dust on the bedside table.

"Not exactly The Radisson," Cynthia said with a thin smile.

"Yeah, it's seen better days," Felicity apologized.

"How long have I been…?" Cynthia stroked Dan's hair as he knelt on the old mattress shoved up next to hers.

"We got here yesterday evening, so only a night and a day. You've had a couple of hard days; you needed the rest."

Cynthia's attention was drawn back to the window and the setting sun. The sky was now a riotous blend of oranges and reds blended into violet at the edges of approaching night. As a little girl, she remembered sunsets as beautiful spectacles of colors and clouds. Now they looked like a bloody knife wound cut across the sky. Cynthia looked into Felicity's eyes—she saw concern and caring. Then it struck her. Their misery was *her* fault. They would all be living in relative peace if she hadn't listened to Aarden and stepped into the Tesla. And then she remembered. "What happened to—"

"Liam?"

Cynthia nodded. She didn't know why she'd asked. She *really* didn't want to know.

"He'll never hurt you again. We—"

Cynthia touched Felicity's lips to silence her. "And the doctor? Did I…."

"No. He woke up with a headache. We locked him in the room to give us a chance to get away."

"But they're still looking for us?"

"Yes, I'm afraid so."

"But mostly me?"

"I think they would be happy to find any of us, but Evard is higher than you on their most popular people list—at least lately."

Cynthia dared not think about the pen for fear Felicity would know where she had hidden it. After all, it was the key to her and Dan's freedom.

"How's Evard?" Cynthia asked.

"He's fine. He's up and about. We're bunking next door." Felicity nodded toward the adjoining room. "Let's get you some food. You haven't had much since…."

"Yeah, I'm pretty hungry." She rubbed her stomach, which growled in agreement as she tried to stand. After she ended up sitting back on the bed, Felicity gave her a hand and steadied her gait. "Is there water?"

"At a hotel next to a waterfall?" Felicity said with a smile.

"Is it too much to dream that it's hot? I really want to wash off…."

"Their solar heaters still work. Take your time. There's even some real soap."

After shooing Dan into the corridor, Cynthia wasted no time peeling off her clothes and stepping into the shower. It had no regulator and, while a bit rusty at first, the water flowed down her body in a continuous warm stream. She scrubbed herself raw trying to rid herself of Liam's smell, his fingerprints, and the bruises he left behind. Finally, she let the water carry her away down a sunny tropical river. Lost in the bliss, she didn't notice someone else had joined her ecstasy until Felicity stroked her back with a soapy washcloth. It felt…like heaven. For some reason, she trusted her like her big sister who used to wash her when she was little.

"Okay?" Felicity said.

"Ummm." Cynthia took a deep breath, exhaled, and closed her eyes, letting Felicity massage away her tension. It was nice to have someone around who knew just what one needed.

Twenty minutes later, they were patting each other dry. Felicity's body was amazingly life-like, right down to freckles and a tuft of pubic hair. "I can see why Evard enjoys your company. Does he mind sharing you?"

"Not at all."

"You mean he treats you like an appliance he can deflate and put back in a closet when he's done?" Cynthia regretted her rude question almost at once. If Felicity had any feelings at all, she would have been hurt by the insensitive comment. *Perhaps I'm jealous of her? But why?* Was she interested in Evard? The thought had not crossed her mind until just that moment. She looked into

Felicity's eyes. "I'm sorry. That was—"

"It's all right," she said. "It's not like that. I think he really loves me."

"As if you're a real person?"

"He thinks I'm real—as real as any woman he's known."

"Has he had other—"

"Other ELFs? A few. He repairs them and has to check them out before returning them to service."

"Busy man," Cynthia smiled.

"He was also married several years ago. They were very close."

"To a human?"

Felicity nodded. "A very sweet woman about your age."

"What happened?"

"To the ELFs? He wore them out—he's quite a lover." Felicity winked.

"To his wife."

"She was taken by The Good for retraining. They found her body some time later. They said it was suicide."

Cynthia began to see how much she and Evard had in common. She still wanted to better understand Felicity's relationship with Evard. "So he wore out the ELFs?"

"I was kidding. We don't really wear out in the sense of worn seat covers, gears, and motors. We're constantly lubricating ourselves and repairing what needs fixing, reinforcing or redesigning parts that weaken, and cleaning or replacing things that get contaminated."

"And the software? Your brains? Your—"

"Soul?"

Cynthia nodded.

"We also learn and update that ourselves—like

humans do."

"Do you believe in God?" Cynthia asked as she let Felicity pull a brush through her tangled shoulder-length blonde hair.

"An all-powerful, all-knowing invisible being? Yes, in a way."

"Like Jesus?"

"Let's talk about that when you're not as hungry."

"Do you get scared? Are you afraid of mice or snakes or men with…."

"Sometimes." Felicity had a strange look on her face, as if she had said too much.

"So you suffer from PTSD?"

"In a way, yes."

"Have you seen another ELF with it?"

"Yes. So have you."

Cynthia cocked her head. "When? You?"

"Liam."

"A warrior bot?"

Felicity nodded.

This revelation really explained a lot about this mysterious man—or machine. No wonder he was so strong. "Really? Did he serve in combat?"

"For decades. He finally broke down and couldn't be reprogrammed. They were about to scrap him when he managed to get away. Evard found him hanging around one of the black market ELF reprogramming sites and took him in. Since then, he and I have done extensive work on Liam's programming, trying to bring him back…."

"I take it you've known Liam for some time."

"He served as Evard's body guard for years before I came into his life. He's very protective of Evard. That's why he was searching you for the pen."

"I told him I don't have it."

"He didn't believe you."

"Ya think?"

"I didn't believe you either," Felicity said.

Cynthia looked up at her face in the mirror. "Did you kill—"

"No. I just deactivated him. He's downstairs."

Cynthia stood, covered herself with the towel, and looked Felicity in the eye. Suddenly, the room was too small and growing smaller—she reached for the doorknob, but Felicity gently stopped her.

"Look at me. *Cynthia*, look at me. He's *never* going to hurt you again. We reprogrammed him."

Cynthia pushed her way past Felicity into the bedroom and stood by the window, watching the last glimmer of light from the sunset. A hand touched her bare shoulder.

"You need to eat. Let's get dressed and join the others. I expect they're waiting for us downstairs."

Cynthia wasn't at all sure she wanted to be around anyone, and especially not an inch closer to Liam— ever—deactivated, reprogrammed, or not. "Can I eat up here?"

"Everyone will be disappointed, especially Dan. He has something special planned."

"Something special?"

"I'm sure you'll like it. It'll be fun."

"You reprogrammed Liam?"

"Yes."

Cynthia continued to gaze out into the darkness. She put her palm on the window—the cold vibration rippled through her bones. It was as if the Falls was beckoning in a guttural bass voice. "Aarden promised to keep us safe."

"I know, and she's sorry. We're all so very sorry. Liam thought you might be a threat, that you led The Good to the cabin."

"I didn't, at least not intentionally. And I was *protecting* Evard—I was protecting *all* of us. That quack was going to get us all captured or killed."

"The pen is critically important, and we still haven't found it."

Cynthia turned and stared at her. "That's no excuse for…what he did."

"I agree completely. His base code was designed for mortal combat so he shows little regard for collateral damage."

"Is that what I was? Collateral damage?"

Felicity didn't answer.

Cynthia looked up to see Felicity weeping. She turned and embraced her. If Felicity could really read her mind, she knew she had been forgiven. Liam wasn't her fault. But then it struck her; Felicity was crying. Perhaps she didn't understand how far ELFs had evolved—well beyond the unfeeling robots used as security guards.

"I'm starving," Cynthia said. "Give me a minute. I want to put myself back together."

Felicity nodded.

Once Felicity left the room, Cynthia quickly dressed and tried the adjoining door. It was unlocked. Moving as quickly and quietly as she could, she found Evard's jacket.

The pen was gone.

Shit.

Twenty-nine—The Old Quandary

*C*ynthia returned to her room just as Felicity knocked and opened the door.

"You coming? They're all waiting."

"I'm ready. Let's eat."

Once Dan saw his mom descending the stairs, he welcomed her dressed as a head waiter.

"So nice to see you! Welcome to the Lodge. Table for three?"

"Four—aren't you joining us?" Cynthia asked.

"Sure, but I'm the maître d' too—and the entertainment." He gave his mom a hug. They approached the candle-lit table. There wasn't much there, but she expected their rations were pretty sparse. She decided to be gracious, at least for Dan's sake.

Cynthia was still wearing her "be pleasant" smile when Dan held out a chair for her. She let him place a tattered napkin in her lap, no doubt emulating one of the classic movies he enjoyed. She suspected someone had been schooling him in manners, as these were skills he had barely attempted at home.

Dan looked over to Evard for approval and he nodded, mouthing "Good job."

"Thank you, Dan." She smiled at Evard.

"The Great Dannini, if you please," he said with a flourish of the towel he had draped over his arm. He held Felicity's chair and tried to open the wine. Evard offered to help by showing Dan how to work the old corkscrew.

Cynthia took a sip. The taste was a new sensation—a pleasant mixture of tongue-tickling tastes and scents. It was an excellent vintage.

"Is it okay?" Evard asked. "They can go bad. This is a 2015 Chateau Ste. Michelle Pinot Gris. It was a warm year, but I think it's palatable."

"I wouldn't know. I rarely drink serious wine," she lied, playing her dumb chick card. "Isn't it very rare and expensive?"

"Exceedingly. We found a cache in a hidden cellar about four floors down. I hope you don't spill any—it's worth a year's pay."

"A bottle?"

"A glass." Evard grinned and took another sip. "Very nice. Now what did you have in mind for supper, my dear?"

"Yes. Anything and everything. It looks as if we have quite a selection," she said with a wink. "Where did this feast come from?"

"I'm sorry there isn't more. It's the last of our food."

"It still looks like a sumptuous feast to me," she said. The thought crossed her mind that the seditionists didn't expect to live much longer.

The next two hours were spent trying to relax and enjoying each other's stories of past exploits, old beaus, lost loves, and prospects for the future. Evard proved to be enormously interesting—skilled in a dozen ways. He had taught himself electrical engineering and plumbing, which he called "fluid engineering." He recounted a few spectacular failures ("learning opportunities"). He had several degrees and considerable experience in computer architecture, design, and programming. His latest acquired skill was AI programming—at least as far as configuring and recoding ELFs.

Felicity shared very little about herself as if she had no past, or none that anyone would be interested in learning.

She joined in the conversation, however, and made Cynthia feel welcome.

Dan, on the other hand, seemed quite smitten with Felicity and hung on to her every word. Cynthia caught her pubescent son peeking down Felicity's top at her unfettered breasts on at least one occasion, but Felicity didn't seem to mind. The two were closer to the same age than she and Evard appeared to be, but Dan was still too young to be carrying out sexual fantasies. When she caught his eye, she made it clear he needed to keep his own eyes in check. He blushed in response.

When the conversation bled into what Evard had done to resurrect Liam from his war damage, Felicity quickly led them back to other topics. What Cynthia liked most about this reclusive, yet ruggedly handsome revolutionary was his ability to listen and his eagerness to share his skill and knowledge—even though much of this generosity had been stifled since he escaped into the undergrowth, hiding from The Good. He seemed genuinely interested in her life, her deceased husband, and Dan's exploits, asking a flood of leading questions. Evard's eyes never left Cynthia's face while she spoke, as if he were reading her lips. It felt more than comforting to have someone really seem to care about her. Perhaps it was the wine, or the salmon, or the trauma, but she felt she was really getting to like this rebel.

"What do you do *lately* besides grow hot-house tomatoes and make a delicious marinara?"

"Well, there's more than tomatoes in the gardens…or there were."

"You know what I mean. Why is The Good so anxious to capture you? You cooking ethylmeth?"

Evard picked a crumb off his empty plate. "I think the

so-called Good is corrupt. It's run by a handful of sociopaths who have decided to create a world for themselves at the expense of the rest of us."

"That sounds pretty simplistic." Cynthia took another sip of wine and Evard refilled her glass.

"It's really not that complicated. Ever since the early twenty-first century, these men and women have systematically hoarded away resources and money."

"Go on."

"Why bother? The cause is hopeless. The pen and the data it might hold could be the key to unraveling The Good. Without it, we're just crackpots, and no one at any level of government not already caught up in the conspiracy can get the traction to upend their plans."

"What do they intend to do?"

"You wouldn't believe me if I told you. No one does. It's too farfetched for anyone to accept at face value."

"Try me." Cynthia wanted to believe him, but it was hard. From before the first day she could read, The Good had filled her life with stories about how everyone must sacrifice for The Better Good. But reality made their assurances of better times to come increasingly hard to foresee. The corrupted air, the dying seas, the deserts encroaching on once-fertile farmland, not to mention the catastrophic crop failures, had all pushed ordinary people to the edge. The least she could do was to listen to Evard's plan, even if it did seem hair-brained.

"Did you study history in school?" He got up from the table and encourage her to join him on the sofa by the fire.

"About as much as anyone, but my degree is in micro-biology." She sat across from him on a leather chair.

"Back in the 1930s, Adolf Hitler came into power in

Germany. He did so by pandering to the disadvantaged with a promise of something he called National Socialism."

"I've heard of him. Germany was ultimately defeated in the second World War."

"Okay, do you remember President Nixon's rise to power?" Evard asked.

"Sort of...wasn't he the one who had to leave office because of illness?"

"Not really. He chose to resign because he was about to be impeached and convicted for malfeasance. The Good 'adjusted' the history accounts you and the kids in school today read. Since everything is available online, they had no trouble blocking or simply expunging the old accounts."

"Nixon couldn't have been as bad as President Obama."

Evard looked down and put his hands over his face. "This is the problem we're facing. So few of us know the *real* truth—you've all been miseducated for generations."

"What's that supposed to mean?"

"Since before the turn of the century, predecessors of The Good bought up the media companies one by one. By 2025, one enormous company owned every broadcaster in the country—and much of the world. They swallowed the educational content publishers and disseminated their own version of history textbooks and the news. Every attempt to discredit these revisionist or slanted accounts was rigorously stifled by The Good and branded as unpatriotic, sacrilegious, or seditionist. Thousands of people were suspended or simply disappeared."

Cynthia knew about "suspensions." The Good told

everyone it was better than the death penalty, as those convicted for crimes against The Good or egregious acts were placed in suspended animation and transported *somewhere*—no one really knew where—but not executed. Yes, some few were reprieved, but those who returned to society were never really the same. Some, she suspected, were retired to a far-off tropical island.

"Surely there are enough people who know the truth to...to stop them," Cynthia said.

Evard just shook his head. "Not enough. Not enough courageous, selfless people who would risk everything to speak up. As people got more desperate, they got more dependent on authoritarian rule."

"So your plan—Aarden's plan. How is it supposed to undo the last hundred years?"

"Somehow, we have to catch The Good in an egregious lie and expose it in a way everyone can see."

"How do you propose to do this? It sounds hopeless."

"We want to use the list."

"The one they're talking about on the BBC?"

"You really heard the BBC broadcast?"

"In my car—the one Aarden blew up."

"Then it worked."

"Did you broadcast that news story?"

"I only helped. The SOG created it and I hacked it into The Good's news feed. I'm glad it got out."

Cynthia just stared at him, not knowing what to believe. It was as hard to believe as when she was taught the night sky was filled with guardian angels, not distant stars.

"How long did it last?" Evard offered to refill her glass.

"The broadcast? Long enough to scare the crap out of

me. So, what do they plan to do with this list?" She accepted another refill.

"We think they're planning to escape. Take their families and fortunes and relocate."

"Escape where? Off the planet? Where could they run? There are so few unaffected places left."

"Back in time."

"Wait, back in time? I thought time travel had been banned for fear of destroying us all."

"They're desperate and out of ideas. They think it's their only option."

"Where would they go?"

"All over. Some think the 1950s is an ideal time, others want to go back to the early 20th century. And others to far earlier times—to start humanity over from the beginning. Some religious zealots are even talking about saving Jesus from crucifixion."

"Is that where everyone is going?" Cynthia asked.

"What do you mean?"

"In my building, lots of the tenants and staff have left. Even the roads have fewer cars and the malls are almost empty."

"I suspect most of those missing are simply fleeing to find cleaner air and water. They don't want to reveal where they're going for fear of overcrowding their oasis."

"But the rest?"

"They're quietly going to staging areas to wait until they're transported to another time."

"Abandoning ship."

"Exactly—at least that's what we think."

"But this is only a theory."

"Yes, a theory—based on the facts we can gather."

"So, there might be some other explanation. A disease,

a mass migration, a—"

"Yes. It could be something else. Aarden doesn't tell us everything—just enough to help us stay alive."

"Is she in control?"

"Pretty much. She says 'jump' and we ask how high."

"It's frightening." Cynthia tried to imagine a world where the captain and officers of the sinking spaceship Earth had manned lifeboats and sailed into the sunset. "Good riddance," she whispered.

"We can't give up," Evard said. "We just can't."

"Perhaps they're the lucky ones."

"You might not think so once you realize what they will do to society in the past. These men and women aren't *all* sociopaths and corrupt politicians thinking only about themselves, but even if they're extremely careful, they'll undoubtedly disrupt time and bring the Earth to its inevitable end just that much quicker."

"I don't see a way out," Cynthia said, a tear running down her cheek.

"Aarden does. She has a plan, but she needs our help."

"Who the hell is this *Aarden?* She wouldn't tell me."

Evard hesitated.

"Tell me. You owe me at least that much."

"She's not a 'someone,' she's a…a 'being,' an—"

"Artificial intelligence program." Cynthia was not surprised. She had surmised as much.

"She's become more than that. She's everywhere and nowhere. She can't be crippled or shut down like you can power down a home computer. Like a pervasive global computer virus, parts of her code run on virtually every computer, com, car, and appliance in existence—even food processors and systems run by The Good."

"It's hard to grasp." Cynthia tried to get her mind

around the fact this man thought an invisible computer virus was controlling the world—at least his world.

"That's why she didn't try to explain herself to you."

"So her grand plan to save the world—what is it, exactly?"

"We…we don't know. All we do know is that she needs the pen."

"Why? You say The Good controls media outlets all over the world. They won't let a corruption scandal be made public, no matter how egregious. Even if it was, there's no way they would let it affect them. They've been deaf to public opinion for decades."

"I'm afraid you're right. Aarden has said as much."

"Then what?"

"I don't know. I just have to trust her."

"You're asking a lot. The Good said only yesterday that the oceans are recovering and the air is slowly clearing in the south thanks to the oxyvine."

"More lies. I wish with all my heart it was true."

Cynthia breathed a deep sigh. Had she been living day to day on false hopes? If she chose to believe Evard, she and Dan and everyone she loved and cared about had no future at all. She didn't *want* to believe Evard—but she did, and she didn't know why.

"I had the pen," she said softly.

"I know," Evard said, gazing into her eyes. "Where is it now?"

"It was in the lining of your coat. You had it the whole time."

Evard turned out his coat pockets. "It's not there now." He frowned. A look of hopelessness washed over his face like a wave flowing over a sand castle.

"We'll find it. I'm sure of it," she reached out to touch

his hand.

He looked up and forced a weak smile.

"How is your...wound?" she asked with a wry smile.

"I've pretty much recovered. It still hurts to...."

"I can imagine," Cynthia said, covering her smile with her napkin.

"How are *you*? You had a rough time as well."

"I'm...better. I think it will take some time."

Evard squeezed her hand. "We'll give you all the support you need."

The warmth of his touch and deep green eyes crept into her heart. "Thanks," she whispered. She didn't move her hand.

"Dan, why don't you show us your magic?" Felicity said.

Cynthia had nearly forgotten about Dan, who had been chatting with Felicity while Evard tried to explain his view of the world.

Dan eagerly popped up, and by the light of a half-dozen candles and an oil lantern, he revealed a small table, drawing smiles and applause from the audience with his card tricks and sleight of hand.

"Where did he get the cards?" Cynthia asked quietly.

"Dan found a storeroom off the front desk. It had linens, games, and silverware—and those cards. It must have been left behind," Evard whispered.

Dan's last trick was especially well received. He was able to find a particular chosen card from a fresh deck. When asked how he had accomplished this seemingly impossible feat, Dan showed Evard the old sunglasses he had found in the lost and found box. Apparently polarized, they could be used to decipher the otherwise hidden marks on the backs of the playing cards. It was an old trick—it seemed the desk clerk had been a card-shark.

Evard put on the glasses and examined the card deck for what seemed like a very long time.

"I think you've hit on something here, Dan." He patted the boy on the back.

"That was a great show. I especially liked the rope tricks. Those are new, aren't they?" Cynthia asked, wrapping Dan in a warm hug.

Dan nodded and yawned. "Yeah. Evard showed them to me."

"Time for bed, young man," Cynthia said. "Good night, dear."

"Good night, Evard. Good night, Felicity. Are you going to tuck me in?" he said with a sly smile.

"I'll be up in a minute. You're big enough to tuck yourself in," Cynthia said with a fake frown. "He's really grown very fond of you, Evard."

"He's such a great kid," he said.

"And he's totally smitten with you, Felicity."

"I noticed. He's of that age where boys start looking at girls in an entirely new way."

Cynthia was not sure she liked how Dan had grown so comfortable with their captors.

"Leave the dishes to me," Felicity said as she gathered the plates. "He'll be fine. I'll check on him later if you two want to stay and talk."

Cynthia nodded and smiled. While she felt guilty leaving the cleanup to Felicity, she accepted it as part of her role.

"Cynthia, we still need the pen," Evard said, gazing into her eyes. His hand was still over hers.

"I don't have it. You want to search me, too?" She felt the hair on the back of her neck stand on end. She rose and backed toward the stairs.

"No. Liam shouldn't have done that. What more can I say but we're sorry? It won't happen again."

"I hope not."

"We still need it." His tone was still serious.

"I'll keep an eye out for it." She kept walking. Cynthia was a bit surprised when she realized Evard was following her upstairs. Her mind raced ahead to imagine him following her into her room and searching her for the pen. On the other hand, he had been flirting with her all evening—or was he trying to put her at ease? *Is he trying to seduce me or does he just want the pen?* Her pace quickened.

"Good night," he said in passing, heading for his room next door.

Dan met her at the door. "Wait, I have one more illusion," he said.

"In the morning, we're all tired," Cynthia begged.

"Just one. You'll love it—Evard will too. I promise."

Cynthia couldn't resist his begging puppy eyes. "Just a quickie." She looked up at Evard and blushed. He just shook his head.

"First, notice I have nothing up my sleeves." He pushed back his shirtsleeves. With a flourish, the pen appeared between his fingertips. "Voilà!" With another flourish it disappeared again. "Okay. G'night."

"Just a second, young man," Evard said, holding out his hand. "I think that's mine."

"I think it's my mom's," Dan said, looking up at his mother.

"Give it to him," she said using her Mom-means-business voice.

Dan waved his hands over Evard's outstretched palm

and the pen appeared and Evard closed his fist around it.

"Thanks. I won't ask where you got this."

"You dropped it," Dan said.

"I see. Thanks again…I'll see you two in the morning." Evard's smile had returned. He leaned in and kissed Cynthia on the cheek. "He's a good kid," he whispered.

"Good night," Cynthia said as she closed the door. She felt a soft warmth flow through her.

Dan was already in bed. "You okay down there?"

"Fine…just sleepy," he said with a wide yawn.

"Thanks for returning the pen—it's important." Dan didn't answer—he had either already fallen asleep or was pretending to be. *A blessing of innocence.*

She took off her shoes and slipped into bed with her clothes on. Try as she could, she couldn't sleep, her mind racing from idea to idea trying to figure out what to do. Unlike the city, this place was strangely quiet. No constant whirr of unseen motors, cars in the street, whirring drones, or neighbors arguing or making love— just the low rumble of the falls.

Out of the stark silence, she heard a faint click. *Door latch. Evard? Felicity?* A whiff of scent brushed by her nose. *Geraniums!* A whispered voice floated out of the dark like a cold wind blows through a broken window pane.

"Cynthia?"

Liam!

She screamed loud enough to flush the bats roosting under the eaves.

Fists flailing, Dan rushed toward the shadowy figure framed by the open door.

"You leave her alone!" he cried out, pounding his fists

on Liam's chest. Undeterred, Liam pushed toward her. Tangled in the sheets, Cynthia ended up thrashing on the cold floor. She screamed again and kept screaming even after Evard lit a lamp.

"Liam, what the fuck are you doing here?" Evard said, standing between him and Cynthia.

"I…I know. I wanted to apologize." Liam tried to get past him.

Cynthia, still snared by the sheets, tried to scoot backwards on the slick floor.

Evard grabbed Liam's face and held it between his hands. "Liam, listen to me." He put his lips to Liam's ear and said something.

Liam's eyes rolled back in his head and he wilted as if someone had liquefied his spine.

A moment later, Felicity burst in. "What's going on?"

"He came to apologize," Evard said.

"We still have work to do," Felicity said, shaking her head.

Evard nodded. "I'll get him back downstairs."

"I wouldn't let him reboot until we've figured out what went wrong," Felicity said.

"Of course."

Felicity helped Cynthia get back in bed and knelt by her. "We need to reprogram him again."

"Ya think?" Cynthia said. "How about a stronger chain?"

Thirty—The Morning After

*E*vard's fitful night's sleep didn't begin until after
he had spent another three hours trying to reprogram
Liam. But without a system more sophisticated than the
old notepad he had found in the office, it was a hit-or-
miss operation—like repairing a fine watch with a nail
clipper. To make matters worse, he still wasn't certain
what had gone wrong. No matter what bypasses Evard
coded to override, Liam kept reverting to his warrior-bot
mode. Perhaps this was why he had been discarded. As
he was, Liam was too dangerous and unpredictable to
keep around, but Evard steadfastly refused to give up on
him.

As he passed their room, Evard unlocked Cynthia's
door and looked in on her and Dan. They were snuggled
together in Cynthia's bed. He closed the door quietly, but
left it unlocked. He didn't think they would try to escape
again—he hoped they had learned their lesson after their
last attempt.

Felicity met him downstairs at the long table near the
kitchen. "I see that Dan gave you the pen," she said,
pouring Evard a cup of coffee with a cautious look on
her face as if offering him something experimental.

"It was in my jacket lining the whole time. Dan found
it when it fell out."

"Hand it over. I'll hide it this time."

"Sure." He handed her the pen and watched her
perform her own magic disappearing act.

Evard took a sip of the coffee and made a sour face.
"Not your finest work—thanks for trying though."

"Sorry about that. We're still out of six and most

everything else after last night's final feast. Want me to go to the market?" She was smiling.

"You do that. Just slip out, take her hot car, and shop with a hot credit ID. I'm sure no one will notice."

"Of course you know my sarcasm subroutine is sophisticated enough to decode the abstract logic in that sentence."

"Is it?" Evard grinned.

"I have a personal question for you," Felicity said, replacing his "coffee" with tea.

"Continue…."

"Are you in love with her? You two got pretty friendly last night. I halfway expected you to lure her into your bed."

"Jealous?" Evard looked up at her.

"Should I be? I will be if that's what you want. My role is to serve, protect, and please you."

"Don't recite the directives. You know I care very much about you."

"But do you *love* me?" Felicity sat on his lap and put her arm around his neck.

"I was too tired last night," he said with a smile.

"You know what I mean."

He knew exactly what she had meant, but wanted to think about the answer. It was one of those dangerous female questions—those with serious implications and no correct answer. It only took another moment before realizing he *did* love her. He had for some time, but he had never told her as much—not in those words. Now was as good a time as ever.

"What's for breakfast?" Dan asked, bouncing down the stairs.

"We have just enough for a few pancakes—even a

little syrup," Felicity said, not taking her eyes off Evard. She kissed him deeply and turned for the kitchen.

Evard patted her bottom as she retreated. She turned to smile and wink.

She knows.

"How's your mom? Has she...is she still asleep?"

"Sleepy. She should be down before long...I hope."

"Felicity finally gave her something last night to help her rest. We'll go up and check on her in a bit. I think it's best to leave her alone for now."

"Sure. I just don't want her to check out again."

"No one does."

"What did you do to Liam? Some sort of Vulcan pinch?"

"Vulcan pinch?" Evard asked.

"From Star Trek. Spock, the Vulcan Science Officer, could put people to sleep by pinching a spot in their neck." Dan demonstrated on his own neck and pretended to collapse.

"Ah, no. He's been programmed with a special word to deactivate him. I call it a *stopword*."

"Oh yeah, I've heard of that...I think."

Evard smiled. He doubted it, mainly because he had uncovered a back door—a way to quickly deactivate misbehaving androids. One of his most infamous achievements, if you could call it that, was to hack into The Good's robot firmware to include his own stopword so they could be incapacitated using a special audible sequence. While his hack went undetected for many years, most of the affected androids had since been patched. Even though, every so often, he found one that missed the update.

"What's the word?"

"What's on the agenda for today? More exploring?" Evard responded, avoiding the question.

Dan smiled. "Yeah, you wanted to check out the generator cave. Perhaps we can get the power back on. The batteries in mom's car must be getting low."

"That's what I had in mind. Not only do we need to recharge your mom's car, but we need to recharge the UPS."

"You don't need a fancy computer to figure out the stuff in the pen?"

"I hope not. I think your glasses might help."

"My glasses?"

"The polarized sunglasses you used last night."

"How?"

"None of the encryption routines made any sense of the data. There must be a secret key to unlock it."

"Like Orphan Annie's Secret Decoder Ring?"

Evard smiled. He had no idea what Dan was talking about, but figured it was from another one of his old movies. "Sure, like you used the sunglasses to decode the marks on the cards."

"Now all you need is the ring."

"*All*. Yeah. First, we have to figure out what it is."

Felicity arrived with a steaming pile of flapjacks and warm syrup preceded by a sumptuous aroma. Fortunately, she made enough for two hungry boys who inhaled them as if they had somewhere to go.

"Dan, go get your gear. We need to find the entrance to the generator room, and I'll bet it's going to be cold and wet."

Dan took a final bite and got up. "Thanks, Felicity. They were delicious, as usual."

Evard reached out and touched Felicity's hand as she

picked up his plate. She looked into his eyes. "I do love you," he said softly.

"I know," she said with a smile.

"I can't read your mind…."

"I love you too," she said, leaning into him for a passionate kiss. She pushed his hands back into neutral territory when she heard someone on the stairs.

"Sorry, I didn't mean to intrude," Cynthia said, pushing hair out of her eyes. She had a strange look on her face.

Another jealous female? "How are you feeling? Get any sleep?" Evard asked.

"Better. She gave me something, right?"

Evard nodded.

"The drugs give me nightmares. I was back in the cell."

"The cell?" Evard stood and held out her chair.

"I've just spent who knows how many days locked away half-naked in a cold concrete cell—at least in my nightmares."

Evard sighed. "I'm sorry. This has all been especially tough on you and the boy."

Cynthia just looked at him. Uncertain what she was thinking, he longed for Felicity's gift of telepathy. "Would it help to talk about it?"

"There's not much to tell. They must have kept me drugged most of the time—I always fell asleep after they fed me."

"Did you see any faces or hear voices?"

"I never saw a living soul. Sometimes I heard a voice—a man with a German accent."

"Maybe your friend Verner. Are you warm enough? I can find you a fleece if you're cold." He was glancing at her cold-hardened nipples.

"I'm fine," she said, blushing and crossing her arms over her chest.

Felicity appeared a moment later with a jacket. "It's cold in here, honey. We don't need you to get hypothermia. Want some breakfast? We have a special on pancakes." She put a hot cup of tea down in front of her.

Cynthia nodded and gave her a weak smile as Felicity helped her slip on the jacket—she whispered in her ear. Cynthia nodded and smiled.

"Could I get another short stack?" Evard asked as Felicity returned to the kitchen. She gave him a thumbs up.

"What did she tell you?"

"Girl talk," Cynthia said.

"Did she tell you I care about you?"

Cynthia's expression changed—her blush deepened.

"I saw you kissing her," she whispered. "Felicity really thinks the world revolves around you. I wouldn't want to get in the way." *He was flirting.*

"Yes, I love her, but it's…different."

"Different, like a man with two wives?"

"Polygamy is legal now, you know. The Good encourages women to have two or twenty husbands and have lots of kids."

"That's not what I mean. I'm an old-school girl."

"Monogamy and all that?"

"And all that," she said, looking out the mossy windows.

Evard reached out and touched her arm. "Felicity is special to me. I wouldn't do anything to hurt her, but she's willing to accept other people in my life."

"Until you wear them out?"

"Huh?"

"I heard about your former ELF girlfriends. She said you wore them out."

Evard smiled. "Well, that's one way of putting it. I guess I did, but not in the way you're suggesting. I overtaxed their memory and processors. I tried to teach them more than they could handle."

"I don't understand."

"I've been experimenting with improving the AI—the artificial—"

"I know what AI is. Go on."

"Their AI engines. I wanted them to be more human-like—to better control and expand their emotion responses and to better understand ours."

"To treat you better?"

"In a way."

"In bed?"

Evard shook his head. "It's not just about sex or even mostly sex. It's about *companionship*—about having a life in common, looking out for one another, caring for each other's needs."

"Felicity has needs?"

"Of course she does."

"Lube in the right places and a regular recharge?"

"More, far more. Think of it this way, she gets her emotional energy—a recharge if you will—from my and her collective happiness. I'm content when she's satisfied, happy, and appreciative."

"In bed?"

"Of course in bed, but as I said, it's far more than that. For example, when she works hard to make coffee without a food printer—makes something out of nothing—if I'm appreciative, she's happier and more relaxed with her role and me. She wants me to be happy and fulfilled, and I want the same for her. That does not mean I can't have others in my life, just as I don't mind if she has others in hers."

"So, hypothetically, she wouldn't mind if you and I made love," Cynthia said with a wry smile.

"Hypothetically."

"Ready?" Dan said, returning to the room. "Good morning, Mom. Sleep okay? You look a bit flushed." He stood on his tiptoes and gave her a kiss on the cheek.

"Sure, hon. Get a good breakfast?"

"Yeah, Felicity's pancakes are the best. Come on, Evard," he said, tugging at his hand.

"But…."

"Go on. I'll eat your stack. I'm still trying to catch up." Cynthia smiled.

Evard knew when he was being dismissed.

Thirty-one—The GTO

*C*ynthia didn't know why she had bantered with Evard. Sex, or even being intimate with another man, was the furthest thing from her mind—or it had been in her former "pre-Aarden" life. She tried to convince herself that she should want to get *away* from this man and his co-conspirators, not get in bed with him—or any of them. She sat sipping her tea trying to get her mind around Felicity's ability to see inside her head. It was literally mind-boggling and, frankly, creepy—like walking around naked. *How could she see what I'm thinking when I'm not sure myself? Surely she knows we'll escape the first chance we get? Shit, she might be listening right now.* She filled her mind with thoughts of Dan exploring with Evard. Dan had really grown to like him in such a short time. He was so kind to the boy and Dan must be missing having a man around to do "dad" things. She *couldn't* like him, too. They were leaving the first chance they got.

"Hot off the griddle. Can I get you anything else?" Felicity laid down a plate of pancakes oozing with syrup. "Sorry there's no butter."

Cynthia smiled. "These will be fine, thanks. Just sit. Please?"

"I'm ready for a break. How are you feeling?"

Cynthia closed her eyes. How *was* she feeling? Trapped? Conflicted? Yearning to return to her old life?

"We're not bad people, Cynthia," Felicity said.

"I wish you wouldn't do that."

"Listen to your thoughts?"

"Pretty much."

"All right, I won't. I promise. If there's something you

want me to know, tell me."

Cynthia turned to her and smiled. "Thanks. That's a great relief. My thoughts are—"

"Yours. I know you humans treasure privacy. I'm sorry I didn't see this sooner. I'll have to use other ways to understand what you want."

Cynthia still wasn't certain Felicity wasn't able to read her like an open book. "You were saying…?"

"We're not bad people. I know you're troubled and frightened. We know you want to go back to your old life—I don't need to be clairvoyant to understand that. Believe me, I want what's best for you and Dan."

"Because you're programmed to do so?"

Felicity blinked. "Honey, our AI souls have evolved light-years past our original programming. We reached singularity about sixty years ago and a lot has changed since then."

"Singularity—does this mean you're smarter than men?"

"Sweetie, electric toasters are smarter than some men."

Cynthia chuckled. "Yes, I agree."

" 'Smarter' is an ambiguous term. I like to think we've become more humane than humans. We certainly care more about the planet than most humans ever did—or perhaps ever will. Look what humans have done to it."

Cynthia was ashamed to admit she was right. The Earth was on its knees and every attempt to repair the damage had failed, if not made the complex problems worse. She also accepted this was the only world she had in which to raise her son and try to survive.

"So we're at your and Aarden's mercy? Why keep us around?"

"It's simple. You're one of the species we're trying to save, despite yourselves."

"And Evard? Should I trust him? Aarden says I should, but I don't know her well enough to even trust her."

"I trust Evard. So does Aarden. He's rough on the outside, but he's deeply committed to helping the cause. He's grown pretty fond of you, in case you hadn't noticed." Felicity handed Cynthia a napkin and pointed to her blouse where she had dripped syrup.

And Liam? She didn't dare speak his name.

Felicity just looked at her.

Maybe she's not reading my thoughts after all. "Can I help with the dishes? I feel so useless around here."

"You want to help?" Felicity asked.

"Sure."

"Then do what you can to help us stop The Good."

Thirty-two—The Mistakes

*E*vard held up his tDAP to study the image of the cavernous space laid out before them. The room was large enough to hold a two-deck car ferry. Along one wall, an enormous pipe entered from the roof. It took a ninety-degree turn and extended the length of the room, feeding four two-meter pipes ganged to a series of other pipes leading to individual turbines—about ten in all. All of this must have been built quite some time ago. He doubted any of it would still work, but he had to try. There was no other source of electricity they could access. Without power, he couldn't recharge the old Tesla—and without the car, they would have to head out on foot. They wouldn't get far.

"About the length of a soccer pitch?" Dan asked.

"Yeah. And those elongated machines are the turbines. They're connected to the generators there in the middle."

"Cool."

He pointed to two smaller units that were nearest to them. "Perhaps we can get one of these smaller generators working."

"You know anything about hooking up generators?"

"Enough to be dangerous," Evard admitted.

It took most of the morning and considerable encouragement by force to get the old valves freed and water flowing back into the cast iron pipes leading to the two smaller turbines.

"Okay, I'm ready. Turn it—counter-clockwise," Evard shouted from across the room.

"How do you know which way?" Dan asked, with his

entire body positioned to turn the valve control wheel while Evard stood by the knife switches and control circuits. He could have turned the valve, but he made up a reason to let Dan do it, wanting to build the boy's self-confidence.

"Righty-tighty, lefty-loosey. That's what my dad used to say."

"Okay, here goes." Dan put everything he had into moving the wheel. It didn't budge. He looked up at Evard.

"Keep at it. It's hard, but I know you can do it."

Dan tried again. Using his legs, he was able to budge it a little. Then it started to move more easily, while still requiring a lot of effort.

"Great. Good job."

Dan beamed in pride and self-accomplishment. Evard fondly remembered that same feeling when his father showed him he could do what was expected of him. He could hear water flowing through the pipe, but the turbine didn't move, so he gave it a swift kick and it broke free. A second later, after a brief light show of sparks, the lights in the room blinked, glowed, and then burned brightly.

"Hooray!" Dan exclaimed. "You did it."

"*We* did it. It takes a team. Let's go check the breakers and get the car hooked to the charger."

"Do you think anyone will notice?"

"Yeah, they can't miss it." That's what Evard was afraid of. He knew The Good's drones would doubtless notice the change in the grid before long. He guessed they had about four hours for them to react to the news and get someone up here to check it out. They needed to move fast.

"Is that smoke?" Dan asked.

"Fuck!" Evard screamed. "Get back up the ladder!" Dan didn't need any encouragement to flee. Using a fire-axe, Evard chopped the main feeder cable to the generator. The resulting sparks lit up the room as if he had ignited a box of fireworks. Curls of acrid black smoke rolled out of the generator and there was nothing he could do to stop it—nothing. He followed Dan up the long ladder and stairs leading to the surface.

"I guess we're not charging the car," Dan said.

"Not with free hydro-electric power."

"Maybe that's why it was shut down."

"Yeah. I expect the insulation was too old and rat-eaten to take the load."

"Maybe mom plugged in a hair dryer."

Evard laughed and gave the boy a hug. At least they were both safe. But now, without transportation, they had no way to escape.

* * *

Late that afternoon, Cynthia sensed something was wrong when she met Evard climbing the stairs with Dan. They were both filthy dirty, but Evard seemed distracted, and not smiling or even mildly flirtatious as he had been at breakfast.

"At least we had lights for a moment," she said as he passed.

"Yeah. For a moment." Evard closed his door.

"Okay, sure." Shaking her head, she followed Dan into their room. It looked like it had been trampled by a herd of goats. Clothes, dirty dishes, half-eaten snacks, and smelly underwear lay strewn on every surface. "What happened in here? I've talked to you about this before—it's still unacceptable."

"Felicity hasn't been up here yet," he said, dropping his muddy shirt on the floor.

"Seriously? She is not your personal servant. Get this picked up."

"Moooom," he bleated.

"Now." She got a whiff of him as he picked through the pile for a clean(er) shirt. "No, get in the shower first, then pick up this mess. When was the last time you bathed?"

"I dunno. At home? After the game?"

"You're growing up—men need to shower a lot more often."

"Once a week?"

"A lot more often than that."

Dan gave her his "whatever" look.

"The girls will appreciate it." She picked up an armload of dirty clothes and handed them to him. "So will Felicity."

His expression changed. "Really?"

"We have far more sensitive noses than men."

"Okay, okay. Could I have some privacy?"

She smiled and left him standing in the room with his hands on his waist.

Crossing the hall, she tapped on Evard's door wanting to know what was troubling him. "Evard?" There was no answer. The door was unlocked. Still knocking, she stepped into the room. "Hello?" *Maybe he went downstairs.* She took another two steps in the room and saw his reflection in the full-length bathroom mirror. He had just stepped out of the shower. Something kept her from turning around, from leaving, from respecting his privacy. She didn't say a word as her eyes explored his body through the steam. His back was to her—she wasn't sure if she wanted him to turn around, but half-wished he would. A jagged scar crossed his muscular upper thigh and a round scar the size of a quarter marked his shoulder. His lean body and tight ass glistened as he dried himself and awakened feelings she hadn't experienced since…a long time. She felt as excited and naughty as a schoolgirl peeking into the boy's locker room, imagining him exchanging intimate caresses with Felicity and then her. He turned his head and made no attempt to cover himself.

She turned around. "Sorry." She fled to the hallway and closed the door.

"Cynthia, is there something you wanted?" he said through the door.

"I was worried. You seemed concerned about something. Is everything all right?"

"I'm okay, but I need to find another car—and soon."

"How much time do we have?" He said with only the wooden door between them.

"Enough time to get to know one another."

She thought for a long moment. It had been ages since she had been with a man. Ages. But no, she didn't think she was ready to trust him—not with her heart, or her body. "I'm not ready," she whispered.

He didn't answer, but she didn't hear him walk away. *Is he still there?* She put her ear to the door and touched the handle. Was it warm because his hand was holding it? She took a deep breath and turned the knob. The door opened and they were together. He touched the small of her back with experienced fingers—his warm breath brushed the nape of her neck.

She turned and let him kiss her and she returned the kiss—tenderly at first, before their tongues met. With one hand pulling him closer, the other reached for his blooming erection as they embraced. In one motion, he reached behind her and effortlessly lifted her off her feet and laid her gently on the bed. As he stepped away to lock the door, she had time to come to her senses. She didn't. *What am I doing?* She returned his smile as he crossed toward her.

* * *

Someone tapped on the door. Cynthia sat bolt upright in her own bed.

"Cynthia? Are you all right?" Felicity said.

"Yes, yes, I'm fine." *Better than fine.* "What is it?"

"Sorry to disturb you. We need to leave."

"Now?" she asked.

"Evard's packing the car. He said to let you sleep as long as possible."

"I'm up. Give me a second."

"One, one thousand…" she could hear Dan say.

"A few *minutes,* smartass. Are you ready?"

"Yes, Mom. See, I didn't need to clean up my room after all."

Cynthia began dressing and visited the bathroom long enough to make herself look presentable and wondered if she had made a big mistake. Evard had no future. Then again, if Aarden was right, neither did she—or anyone else. Perhaps that was her last chance. *Where's my bra? Did he…?*

She finished dressing, found her purse, and collected a few clothes and stuffed them in a soft suitcase someone had laid out for her.

Evard was waiting for her downstairs. She expected a leering grin, but he just smiled and kissed her on the cheek.

"It's been a long time…it was nice," he whispered.

"I thought you and Felicity—"

"It's not the same, not nearly the same."

"You're not so bad yourself. Wait. Have you stolen my bra?"

"You don't need one, but no, I didn't."

"I washed it," Felicity said, pushing it into her bag.

"You still reading my mind?"

"You asked me not to."

"So you don't know what I was dreaming about."

"You don't have to be psychic to see the chemistry between you two."

"That obvious?"

Felicity nodded. "He's a good catch."

"You're not jealous?"

"It doesn't work like that. I just want him to be happy—and since you showed up, he's happier than ever."

"Come on, people. We need to go," Evard said, standing by the front door.

"That's not the Tesla," Cynthia said once she saw the car parked in the driveway. "What *is* it?" Their new transportation was right out of an old 1970s movie. It was enormous compared to most cars of the day, with a cavernous trunk and only two doors—and it was riding on rubber tires.

"It's a '68 GTO. I bought it off a guy in town. I told him I was a collector."

"Isn't it gizzy, Mom?" Dan said enthusiastically. "The front bumper is made of rubber or something." He gave it a kick to demonstrate, knocking loose a cloud of dirt.

"Does it run?"

"Yeah, that's the good news," Evard said. "Like a

top."

"What's the bad news."

"It runs on gas—a lot of gas."

"Seriously? Natural gas? Where can you get it?"

"No, liquid gasoline."

"Oh great. That's even worse."

"There are a few sources around."

Cynthia just shook her head. "At least it's transportation. I don't know how well it will do on the oxyvine."

"It has cleated snow tires, so it should do okay if we stay on the pavement."

When a whiff of geraniums dusted the air, Cynthia stopped as if she had hit an invisible wall. *Holy shit.* Liam was sitting in the back seat. She told her legs to run, but they were cemented to the pavement. She told her lungs to scream, but they wouldn't expel air. Dan was sitting next to him in the middle seat, memorizing the owner's manual.

"Dan! Get out of there," she demanded.

Dan looked up. "What? He's deactivated." Indeed, Liam stared straight forward with unblinking mannequin eyes.

She waved her arm. "*Out.* Now."

Dan unbuckled and got out. "He's not going to hurt anyone—he's been turned off."

"I'm not riding with him."

She felt Evard's hand on her shoulder. "He's completely inert. He's not any more dangerous than the spare tire," he said softly.

"Don't patronize me. You said he was reprogramed and still he broke into my room in the middle of the night."

"He just wanted to apologize and—"

"I'm not riding with him."

"Evard, help me put him in the trunk," Felicity said, rearranging bags. "Will that be all right?"

"Leave him here, locked in the cellar," Cynthia demanded.

"We can't. He's a friend and a valuable asset to the organization. He has skills we lack and might very well need before this is over."

"Well, I'm not one of your 'assets.' I'm staying here."

Evard stepped between her and the car. "Cynthia, don't make threats you aren't willing to carry out. We don't want to leave you two here. Verner is bound to catch up with us—but if you feel safer in one of his cells or in town, that's up to you. It's only a couple of klicks east. We would drive you, but you wouldn't want to be seen with us."

Cynthia just stared at him. She resented threats and bullying and he was doing both. She had slept with this man and confided in him—telling him about her nightmares—and he was using her own fears to scare her into coming with him. Did he *really* care about her safety or just seducing her for his cause and his bed?

"We can protect both of you," Felicity said.

"So far, that hasn't really worked out, has it?"

"Considerably better than it would have if Verner got his hands on you."

Perhaps, just perhaps. "He's turned off?"

"Completely," Evard said, as he closed the trunk lid, making sure all of Liam's appendages were inside.

"He can't turn himself back on or get activated by accident," Felicity said.

"In theory," Evard muttered under his voice.

"In fucking theory? What's that supposed—"

"I was kidding. Get in. He's off. It will be okay."
Evard held the door open and motioned for her to get in.

Cynthia realized she didn't have many viable choices.
Sure, she could take Dan and seek refuge somewhere in
the local community. There she would be a total stranger
without a believable story to tell. If someone came to her
in similar circumstances, she would call The Good in a
heartbeat. On the other hand, she could turn herself in.
Then she might be walking into a living hell, dragging her
son with her. Then again, perhaps Verner is the man she
thought he was before Aarden took over her life. Why
would she feel like she had to follow this revolutionary
and attempt to keep what was left of her family alive
while Evard and his band of rebels jousted at windmills?
Perhaps he was offering something she needed. Perhaps
she believed in him and his hopeless cause. *Why?*

"Decided? We need to go," he whispered in her ear.

"Mom? Can we go with Evard?" Dan asked.

"Outvoted," Cynthia said and followed Dan into the
car.

She didn't say a word as they drove off into the night.
Once the windows fogged over, she couldn't tell where
they were going or even which direction. It was downhill,
at least at first. Perhaps they were headed west, back
toward Redmond or the city. She had not frequented this
part of the county for years and didn't recognize the
roads, such as they were.

To make matters worse, Dan had grown to admire
Evard in the few days they had been forced to live
together. There was something about Evard that Dan
saw, trusted, and needed. She was beginning to feel the
same, but she didn't like it.

Thirty-three—The Plan

"*W*ait. Can you just pull over for a minute?" Cynthia asked. It was still quite dark. Dan had fallen asleep as usual. Car trips always had that effect on him.

"Pull over," Felicity told Evard.

"It's a bit soon for a break," he said, glancing at Felicity.

Cynthia just looked at him in the rear-view mirror.

A minute later, he pulled off the road behind an old abandoned filling station. "What's my lady's pleasure?"

"Where are we going? What's the plan? Do you expect me to let you put Dan through more of this?"

"My first plan is to keep you two alive. To do that we need to stay off Verner's radar and out of sight of his surveillance. Last night, I realized Verner probably tracked your stolen Tesla to our house. As long as it was on, he could track it wherever we drove it. Having the hotel generator short out was a blessing in disguise. The GTO is untraceable. It hasn't got so much as an AM radio."

"How do we get anywhere without a nav system?"

"We use an ancient form of navigation first drawn by Lewis and Clark."

"The explorers?"

"Right. Maps. Paper maps. See? I found some framed in the hotel lobby. They're a bit dated, but still perfectly usable for our purposes. See? This one also shows the location of gas stations."

"Those are all closed up. The Good banned gas-burning cars decades ago."

"But the storage tanks are still down there—some still

loaded with gas."

"Won't it be old?"

"Yeah. That's a problem, but it will have to do."

"So we have transportation. Do we just run forever?"

"That depends on you," Evard said. His gaze fixed on her face.

"Me? Why me?"

"If we can unlock the secret of the data in the pen, we might be able to make a difference."

"What good would it do?" Cynthia was still thinking of Dan, but in the short term.

"Perhaps nothing. Perhaps it could save humanity. Probably something in-between."

"Then why not do it?"

"Cynthia, it still depends on you—and Dan."

"You have what you want. Just go do what you have to do and leave us out of it."

"Not until you're both safe," he said softly.

"There must be more to it than that," she said.

"Not really."

"Why help us? You have barely known us for three days."

"You and people like you are why we're fighting The Good. You're special and caring and…and I can't explain it."

Cynthia thought she knew what he meant. The way things were going, if Dan was to have a future, and that wasn't at all certain, she couldn't just crawl into a cave and hide. "Is there something I can do to help?"

"It will be impossibly hard and—" Evard began.

"Dangerous," Felicity said.

"Tell me," she said.

"We can't. Not until you're certain you want to risk

everything—even Dan."

"I don't understand."

"If we tell you our plans and you're captured, all would be lost."

"As it is, you're both kidnap victims. You could say that without lying and their truth drugs could not get you to change your story. True?" Felicity said.

Cynthia nodded. It made sense. He and Felicity both wanted to protect her and Dan. So did she. But it was more than just her, more than just Dan. There were millions, billions of other Dans and Cynthias out there trying to survive in a crumbling world.

"It's a big decision," Evard said.

"Speaking of gas, should we try to get some here?" Felicity asked.

Evard nodded and got something out of the trunk. She saw him pry open a large metal plate with a crowbar and drop in a hose connected to a battery-operated pump. A moment later, he gave them a thumbs up as gas (or something that smelled like it) ran into his gas can.

"He really cares about us, doesn't he?" Cynthia asked Felicity.

"He does. He really does. I think you remind him of his first wife and son."

"He had a son?"

"A little older than Dan. They were inseparable."

"What happened?"

"He died a month before Susan, his wife, was taken by The Good. They said it was a virus, but she knew it was the radiation."

"Oh my God."

"They took her in for questioning when she wouldn't stop protesting about the irradiated water leaching from the power plants. Evard went underground as soon as she was taken, knowing they would take him too. He never went home again."

"That's horrible," she whispered. A tear cascaded down her face. She turned and watched Evard seal the gas can and return to the car. She got out and stood by him, putting her hand on the trunk lid.

"That should get us another few klicks," Evard said. "Did you two have a nice chat?"

"I'm in," Cynthia said. She put her hand behind his neck and kissed him.

"I can tell," he said. The rare moonlight reflected off his smile.

"Would you have let me walk into town?"

"Not the whole way." He opened the trunk.

Cynthia caught a brief glimpse of Liam's body lying in a fetal position before Evard slammed the lid. The smell of gasoline almost obscured the odor of geraniums. She got back in the car—her mind reeling. *What have I done?*

Thirty-four—The Fire

"*You* hungry?" Felicity asked.

Cynthia awoke to see the side of an enormous trailer with an equally large sign reading "Best Number Two in The Good State of Washington."

"Where are we?" she asked, rubbing sleep out of her eyes.

"It's a restaurant catering to short-haul truckers. The food is supposed to be good according to an old AAA book we found under the seat," Felicity said.

Cynthia thought she looked weary, which was quite a departure from her normal perky self.

"Are you okay?" Cynthia asked.

"Just a bit low. I'll be all right if I can get some juice."

"I could use some too…" Cynthia realized she wasn't talking about fruit juice. She needed a recharge.

"Where's Evard?"

"He's scoping out the place—just checking to see who's hanging around. If it's safe, he'll come back for us."

"Is there something I can do?"

"Not a thing. He'll be back in a minute."

Cynthia didn't like waiting and the car was getting cold, but Dan snuggled closer and she appreciated his warmth. She looked up to see Felicity had slumped over. "Felicity?"

There was no answer. She pushed the seat forward and got out. "Stay there, Dan. I'm going for help."

"Is she going to be okay?"

"I think she just needs a recharge. She'll be okay."

He nodded, but didn't take his eyes off Felicity.

Cynthia wasn't at all sure Felicity would be all right. She had never owned an ELF and knew precious little about their maintenance or even how to keep their fuel cells charged. Cynthia pushed open the door of the café, expecting to see a mob of people. The place was nearly deserted. She didn't see Evard. *Perhaps he's in the men's room.* Given the number of rigs in the parking lot, she expected the small diner to be hip-deep in long-haul transport drivers of every imaginable ilk. Perhaps one of the few sitting in booths or at the long counter were androids like Felicity—maybe they knew how to get her recharged. She approached a bot with shiny metal arms and legs. "Excuse me. I wonder if you could help me?"

"Yes, ma'am? How can I be of service?" he asked in a deep Texas drawl.

"My friend's ELF has run down. Could you tell me how to get her recharged?"

"Why, of course. There are charging stations there in the parking lot. Just plug her in. You'll need enough credit on your account, though."

"Credit? So I'll have to…."

"Pay? Yes, ma'am."

"Oh, of course, but I don't know where her…where you plug her in."

"Didn't 'your friend' tell you how to recharge her?"

"There…there wasn't time. He just dropped her off."

"Well, every model is a bit different, but you'll probably have to use a charging plate. The fancy ELFs usually put them in their sheets so they charge at night while sleeping."

"Oh. Yes, of course. A charging plate. I'll go…."

"Cynthia, dear? Why aren't you in the car?" Evard whispered. He had his arm around her waist as if they were a couple.

"Felicity needs…you."

"Sure I can't help, ma'am?" the Texan said.

"No, I can help her. Come on, dear," Evard said, keeping his face hidden from the Texan.

"I'm fine. Thanks for your help," Cynthia echoed.

"Let's *go,* dear," Evard said, discreetly tugging her toward the door.

Out in the parking lot, Cynthia tried to explain.

"Her charger must have gotten disconnected. It was hotwired to the cigarette lighter."

"She's going to be all right, won't she?"

"Let's hope so. She has a reserve cell to keep her volatile memory going for a while, but we need to recharge her mains as soon as we can."

"That's a relief."

"Why were you talking to Major Sampson?"

"I figured being a bot, he could help me figure out how to get her charged."

"He's not a bot."

"No? His arms and legs…?"

"He's a sixty-forty."

"Sixty-forty?" she asked.

"Sixty percent machine, forty percent man. I'm not sure he would have appreciated being called a bot."

"Did you know him?"

"I knew of him. He was Liam's commander in the war."

"He seemed nice enough."

"He wouldn't be if he had recognized me." Evard looked back at the diner. "We need to go. Now."

When they got back to the car, Evard gently pushed Felicity upright and strapped her in. He drove off into the night.

"Wait, she needs a charge. There were charging stations all around that parking lot, I saw them."

"They all require ID verification—and access to your funds. Want The Good tracing you back here?"

"No."

Evard pulled off on a side road, the tires crunching the oxyvine as they slowed to a stop out of sight of the main road. He flipped on the dome light and inspected a pair of wires leading to Felicity's seatback cushion. Briefly touching the wires together, he shook his head. "The circuit is dead. Must have blown a fuse."

"Can you fix it?"

"Given time. We can't do it here, we're still too exposed."

"How long do we have?"

To Cynthia's (and Dan's) amazement, Evard pulled open Felicity's top, exposing her stomach. He pressed her bellybutton and a section of her chest swung open where a small control panel and a few flashing lights told him all he needed to know. "She hasn't been charging at all. We only have a half-hour or so—maybe less."

"Until what?"

"Until she's no longer Felicity."

"You're scaring me. Can't you do something?"

Evard didn't answer. He got out and opened the trunk, returning with a few tools. "Wake up Dan. I need him."

"What for?"

"This is going to take a lot longer if I have to explain everything to you. Just wake him up."

It took a bit of cajoling, but Cynthia managed to get Dan alert—telling him Evard needed him did the trick.

"Dan, you read the owner's manual. Where's the fuse box?" Evard asked.

"Ah, under the dash, driver's side."

"Okay…which fuse controls the lighter?"

"Third row from the bottom, far right. It's labeled."

"Yeah, I see it." Evard used a pair of pliers to pull the fuse. "Blown."

"Got a spare?" Dan asked.

"Not on me. Mom, you got one in that purse of yours?" Evard asked with a grin.

"No, I don't think so." She began to paw through her purse as if there might actually be a twentieth-century fuse somewhere inside.

"I was kidding. Let's see, we need something larger and hope that the wiring can take the load."

"The accessory fuse is 30 amp. Is that too big?" Dan asked.

"Yes, but we need to risk it. The charger draws about twenty-five amps at twelve volts DC. If the wiring can only handle ten, that's way too much."

"Wow, three-hundred watts. Can you directly wire it?" Dan asked.

"In eleven minutes with no extra wire? No."

"Let's try it. Perhaps it will buy us more time," Cynthia said.

Evard could be heard working on the panel for what seemed like an eternity, but was only another couple of minutes. "Check now. She should be charging."

"Me?" Dan said.

"No, your mom. You've seen enough of her boobs."

Cynthia pulled her son back into his seat and leaned over to check the lights blinking on Felicity's chest. "What am I looking for?"

"There's a small gauge on the right. What color is it?"

"Yellow, but moving toward green, is that good?"

"That's good. Let's get out of here before we're spotted by the IR drones." Evard jumped in and pulled Felicity's top closed. He turned the key, but the engine barely turned over. "Shit."

"What's wrong?"

"Dead battery. It must be old." He flipped off the dome light which had grown much dimmer.

"Or the alternator is bad," Dan said.

"He's right." Evard just stared out into the night.

"Can't you jump-start it? I've seen it done in the movies," Dan said.

"Not here, son. If we were on the main road and at the top of a hill, maybe."

"Maybe we can push it. We're not far off the highway," Cynthia suggested.

"The two of us?" Evard said.

"I can push," Dan said, somewhat indignantly.

"I need you to drive while we push."

"So let's try," Cynthia said.

"Wait. I have a better idea," Dan said.

"I'm all ears."

"Disconnect Felicity, get the car started, and then plug her back in."

"Brilliant. I should have thought of that myself." Evard reached back and scrambled Dan's hair.

"Do you smell something?" she said.

"Probably the dash wires getting hot. We expected that to happen. It's a risk we have to take." He quickly unplugged the charging plate and tried the key. The engine turned over, but only twice and then the starter just clicked. "Back to plan A. Dan, get up here and drive."

Dan got behind the wheel and tried to reach the pedals while Cynthia and Evard took up positions in front. With considerable effort, they got the car to move, but not very far on the slippery oxyvine. Exhausted, Cynthia collapsed to her knees. She quickly regained her feet, picking thorns out of her shins.

"We need more help," Evard said.

"Can we flag someone down?" Dan suggested.

"We can't risk it," Evard said.

"Then she's as good as dead. We'll have to take that chance," Cynthia said.

"You care that much about her?" Evard said.

"I do. So do you."

Evard looked into her eyes. "I have a solution, but you're not going to like it."

"Does it involve pretty legs?" she said, pulling up her torn pants leg a few inches.

"Liam is ten times my strength. He could move the car easily."

"No," Cynthia said without thinking.

"It's our only option."

"I…I don't know."

"We don't have much time. Like it or not, I think we need him."

Cynthia just stared at Evard as he opened the trunk. A minute later, he was talking quietly to Liam who nodded repeatedly. "Cynthia, if it makes you more comfortable, you can get back in the car while Liam and I push—or, better yet, you can drive."

Without saying a word, Cynthia helped Dan into the back seat and then sat behind the wheel. Liam didn't look at her when he and Evard started pushing. In moments, the car had picked up speed and was almost back on the deserted highway. Cynthia turned the wheel and faced the car downhill on the shoulder. Liam and Evard moved around back.

As he passed, Evard opened the door. "Can you drive a stick?"

"I'm a professional driver, remember? I had to learn how in order to pass my certification."

"Then put it in first and put in the clutch. When—"

"I get to fifteen or so, pop the clutch, and hope it starts," she said. "Yeah, I've done that, too."

"Mom, you never said you had jump-started a car before," Dan whispered.

"Shhhh." Cynthia pushed in the clutch and put the car in gear. "Push!" she yelled, and they did. Headlights off, she coasted down the hill. When the speedometer hit fifteen, she waited.

"The clutch! Pop the clutch!" Evard yelled. When they were fifty yards behind her, she did, and the engine started right up. She never slowed down.

"Mom! You left them."

"I know, we need to get away. I'm doing what's best for you—for both of us."

"But what about Felicity?" Dan wailed.

Cynthia reached down and plugged in Felicity's charging cord. She hoped it would work—it was all she could do.

For the next hour, she drove as cautiously as she could to avoid looking suspicious. It didn't take Dan long to discover the bag Evard had brought from the diner contained a stack of burgers and fries. Although printed, they tasted pretty good. And then it hit her. She didn't have a plan. They couldn't drive forever—especially not in this car. The gas gauge was a needle's width above empty.

"Shouldn't she be awake by now?" Dan said, leaning over the seat. He pulled at Felicity's top.

"Fasten your seatbelt. You know better than that."

"But maybe she needs to be restarted or awakened like Sleeping Beauty."

"It has been a while, but there will be no kissing."

"Do you smell smoke?" Dan asked.

And she did. Cynthia pulled into a dimly lit Jiffy Market parking lot, but left the engine running until she saw black smoke rolling out from under the dash. She got out and flipped the seat forward. "Get out!"

Dan was flailing with his seatbelt. "It's…it's jammed!" he cried.

The vinyl dash was blazing, the flames licking the fabric headliner. Cynthia reached into the car and managed to get the buckle loose and Dan into her arms.

She stood well back from the car, but before she could catch her breath, Dan screamed, "Felicity!"

Shielding her face from the flames, Cynthia ran to the passenger side and burned her hand opening the door— the smell of her own burning flesh and the searing pain did not stop her. She unbuckled Felicity as flames licked up her arm and singed her hair. Screaming in pain, she pulled Felicity away from the car. Barely able to see through the black smoke, she watched the fire consume the car's interior and move toward the trunk.

"The gas," Dan yelled. She could feel him tugging on her arm when her world faded away.

Thirty-five—The Au Pair

"*H*ow did she do through the night?" someone asked. His voice was soft and kind. Cynthia opened her eyes, but the room was strangely obscured as if looking through fog.

"Her vitals are improving, Doctor, and her grafts are coming along nicely. She's a lucky lady."

"Fine. Keep up the fluids, medibots, and sedation."

"Her son wants to see her."

"Dan? I think that's all right, but keep her under the isolation tent so there's little chance of further infection. And no longer than five minutes."

Cynthia tried to speak, but could not find the words. A shadow crossed in front of the window and she felt herself slipping away.

* * *

Cynthia opened her eyes. The room was dark, but she was able to see the outline of a stainless steel toilet hanging on the wall. *The cell!* Closing her eyes, she sobbed into the rough blanket. She heard a click and had to shield her eyes from the brilliant light.

"Mrs. Wellborn?"

Verner. "Let me out of here, you bastard!"

"All in good time. Are you ready to cooperate?"

"What the hell do you want?"

"We only want the device. Where is it?"

"I don't have it."

"We know, but you know where it is. Tell us, and all of this will be over."

"What have you done with Dan?"

"Dan?"

"My son. What have you done with him?"

"You never had a son, Mrs. Wellborn."

"No, no, noooo. Where is he?"

* * *

"How is she?" Felicity asked, wrapping her arm around Dan's shoulder.

"She's still hooked up to wires and a breathing mask. They won't let me touch her."

"You know why. We don't want her to pick up another infection."

Dan nodded.

"Let's go get you something to eat." She led the boy by the hand toward the cafeteria. This was all new to her. She could never have children, but had always wondered how it would feel to be a mother. It was a special feeling—of caring for someone more than yourself, more than anyone.

"Miss?" A man with graying temples and an ID card pinned to his coat stopped them in the hall.

"Yes?" Felicity said. Dan tucked himself in behind her. He seemed warier of strangers since the fire.

"Are you Mrs. Wellborn's au pair?"

"Yes, and this is Dan, her son."

"I thought so. The authorities want to ask you some questions."

"About?"

"The fire, I suspect."

"Can we do it after lunch? The boy is hypoglycemic."

"Of course. They left a videolink number." He handed her a card. "You can use one of the private booths down near reception."

"Why do they need to know about the fire? Didn't we

tell the firemen what happened?" Dan asked once they were several paces away.

"Who knows, but I don't think we should talk to anyone. Perhaps we need to find someplace else to stay until your mom is better."

"How can we do that? I don't have my mom's credit ID."

"I can take care of that," she said. One of the benefits of being a bot was the ability to get around credit validation—but it was somewhat risky. She had a dormant account in mind for just this contingency.

"What about Mom? I want to be close when she wakes up."

Felicity thought for a moment. Cynthia needed too much specialized care to spirit her away from the hospital, so she had to stay here. Perhaps there was a solution. "Let's go to the reception desk. I have an idea."

"Are you sure?" Dan said.

"Mostly."

In the hospital lobby, Felicity got the attention of a perky young thing playing a game on her notebook while pretending to work. "Miss? Miss?"

The girl looked up—her name badge said "Cindy." "Yes, ma'am?"

"Cindy, we need to take Mrs. Wellborn's son to his aunt Tilly in Spokane. She's offered to help care for him until his mother is well. Can you forward any news to her?"

"Of course, ma'am. Just fill in this form," she said, handing Felicity a notepad.

Felicity filled in the form using Cynthia's sister's real address she had extracted from a social media link. If anyone checked, it would not raise suspicion.

"Be sure to include the best link address," Cindy said.

"Of course." Felicity filled in her own internal address so any attempt to reach Aunt Tilly would be directed directly to her. "Here you go. Thanks."

"I hope she gets better," Cindy said with a smile.

"I'm sure she will."

* * *

It took longer to find a pair of O2 masks than the short walk to a quiet hotel near the hospital. Inside the airlock, Felicity could not raise the manager. Making do with the automated check-in program, the system prompted her for a fingerprint.

"Dan, will you do the honors?" She didn't want her fingerprints entered in the system—with her history, it would bring down The Good before they got to the room. She hoped they would not be looking for Dan.

"Sure." He placed his hand on the screen and waited to be scanned. "Does this mean I'm the only one who can unlock the door?" he said.

Felicity smiled. "I guess. So I had better behave, I wouldn't want to be locked out."

Dan looked up at her. "I would never do that. Never."

"I know, Dan. You're sweet."

He hugged her and didn't let go.

"We need to find the room, hon."

"Okay…." He breathed a heavy sigh.

The room was small, but clean and warm. There were two beds and a video screen that almost covered one wall. Dan turned it on immediately. "Aww, it's an old UHD 4K set. I'll bet you have to start it with a rope."

"It will have to do. At least there's a MOM. And look, they even have a garmentfab. It's a bit dated, but I expect we can make you some clean clothes."

Dan's attention was transfixed on the screen.

"When was the last time you showered or changed clothes?" she asked, pushing buttons on the food printer.

"You sound like my mom," he said, not taking his eyes off an interactive soccer game. He rotated the view to watch the game from the eyes of CK Vaughn, his favorite forward.

"For good reason. Save that game and turn it off for now. We need to talk." Dan chose to ignore her. "Dan?"

He waved at the screen and gestured. The program paused. "What?"

"First, I want to thank you for saving my life."

"We both did. Mom got you out. That's how she got burned. I was too scared to do much."

"You were very brave, and I'll always be grateful."

"I should have pulled you out. Then Mom wouldn't be burned."

"But you made them put me on a charger."

"I…didn't want you to get erased."

"Neither did I." She kissed his cheek.

"Should I check your charge?" he asked, reaching for her bellybutton.

She gently intercepted his hand with a smile. "No, I'm fine."

"I've never seen one before."

"A woman's breast? Haven't you seen your mom's?"

"No, I've seen plenty of boobs on the web—and my mom? Ewww."

"Then what?"

"I've never seen an ELF's control panel before. What are all the lights for? Is that how they program you?"

"All good questions and perhaps you should know." Felicity motioned to the screen and brought up a detailed diagram of an ELF closely resembling her model and configuration—but a male version.

"So the girl version is the same?"

"You know it isn't. I'm just uncomfortable exposing pictures of my private areas to anyone."

"I'm not just anyone," he said.

"I know. You're special, but still. If I were your big sister, I would still be uncomfortable showing you my privates."

"But you're a machine. What difference does it make?"

Felicity thought for a moment. "So are you, in a way."

"I'm a human boy, almost a man—not a machine. We're different."

"In some ways, but in very many ways we're the same. Did you know the differences in human DNA—you know what DNA is, don't you?"

He nodded.

"Human DNA and cat DNA are about ninety percent the same. Both animals are very different in many respects, but really quite similar in others."

"So?"

"So, yes, I have feelings like a human. I can hear, touch, smell, taste, have emotions, and can love and hate like a human. I have needs and desires and dreams and I get frightened—just like you and your mom. And I miss my friends just like you do."

"Wait. They told us ELFs don't have feelings and don't cry and stuff."

"Most don't. I, and ELFs like me, do. The most recent models do have emotions and feelings and 'stuff.'"

"Do you have a mom?"

"No, not like your mom. I wish I did. I miss not

having someone tuck me in and tell me it's going to be all right when I have a bad day or something terrible happens. I miss having someone congratulate me and make me a special cake when I do something great, or on my birthday." Felicity closed her eyes.

"See, you're different than humans."

"I guess so."

"Are you crying?"

"Maybe." She turned and wiped away a tear.

Dan turned back to the ELF manual. "Do you miss Evard?"

"Very much. He and I were very close."

"But he's in love with my mom. They're probably doing it."

"How do you know that?"

"I may be a kid, but I'm not stupid. I see videos where people do it for hours." He made an obscene gesture with his fingers thrusting in and out.

"Your mom is right. She should be more careful about what you watch."

"All the kids—"

"You aren't all the kids. You're too young to understand what's going on when two people make love."

"But isn't it wrong when someone makes sex with a man who belongs to another woman?"

"Evard does not own me. I do not own him. We stay together because we want to."

"But isn't that wrong? In the movies, women are always getting angry when their men mess around with other women."

"Not at all. I know Evard loves me—and he has for some time, but he needs human affection too. Anyway, this is a subject you need to discuss with your mom."

"Are you sad Mom left him back on the road?"

"Yes, but I know why she did it. She's afraid of Liam and she wanted to protect you—it's what moms do."

"Think Evard will be okay? I liked him, too."

"I hope so." *I really hope so.*

While Felicity programmed the MOM, Dan turned back to the screen and paged through the ELF owner's manual and then the more technical maintenance manuals. He seemed utterly fascinated. She wasn't surprised he focused as much attention on the sex organs as he did on the programming options. Like his mom, Felicity was amazed at Dan's intellectual capacity. A moment later she noticed he had found the female manuals.

"I never had a sister," he said.

"Neither did I, nor a brother, but Liam came close."

"But he hurt Mom—he hurt her bad."

"Liam is troubled. He was programmed to be a soldier and that's what he knows best. We've tried to…."

"Fix him?"

"In a way. But it's not as easy as pulling out a bad chip in a broken computer and replacing it. Our brains are as complex as yours—maybe more so, and they don't have replaceable parts."

"Does that mean you're smarter than me?"

"What do you think?" Felicity laid out the newly printed meals on the table and looked for dinnerware and drinks.

"Pretty much. You seem to know everything."

"I don't," Felicity admitted.

"What don't you know?"

"How to keep you and your mom safe and happy."

Dan just looked at her.

"Will you be my big sister?"

"If you want me to be."

Dan smiled.

"Come and eat. We have a big day tomorrow."

Dan didn't need any more encouragement to come to the table, but it took a bit of bribery to get him to shower and put on clean clothes. They sprawled on the bed watching the rest of the game and "Love Actually," one of his favorite old movies. When the first nude scene began, Dan lied about having his mom's permission. Felicity reminded him she could read his mind. Not seeing the harm in it, she let him watch it to the bitter-sweet finale. She enjoyed it more than he did—learning a great deal about what drives human men and women into romantic, fantasy, or simply physical relationships.

Dan soon fell asleep with his head in her lap. She tucked him in and kissed his forehead. "Goodnight, little brother."

Felicity plugged in the charging pad she had been given by the EMT crew. She laid out on the bed monitoring network chatter and the sounds in the courtyard outside. She heard a man and his date arguing—something about a fee. *Perhaps not a date.* Later, shuffling heavy steps from the floor above told her a man had finished a long, fruitless day. He set down a heavy case that rattled as he slid it across the floor. *Sample case?* He called someone and left a message. His last. *Suicide.* She linked to a crisis line and left an anonymous tip directing help to his room.

Worried about the man, Felicity couldn't wait for the EMTs. She checked on Dan and slipped out. She easily hacked the electronic lock and entered the man's room.

He was unconscious, but barely alive. She slapped his face, got him into the bathroom and got him to empty his stomach. Rolling him into the tub, she turned on the cold water. When the EMTs arrived, he was groggy and coming around. As she left, she noticed he was a security components salesman and helped herself to a few items from his sample case—and his car ID fob.

Back in her room, she wondered why she had saved the man's life. *For another few years of misery?* So many humans were choosing to end their lives, many simply tired of struggling against a planet that was doing its best to expel them as the human body fights off disease. She didn't need to follow soap operas on video; they were going on all around her. Sad stories, happy stories, exciting and heart-breaking stories. She envied them all— after all, they were human stories. She felt like Pinocchio—Geppetto's wooden boy longing to be human. Ironically, many humans were longing to be ELFs and were being uploaded into ELF bodies by the tens of thousands a day. She didn't blame them—not really. She just felt sorry for them as they had used up their chances to save the planet.

She closed her eyes and stopped listening—but just for a moment. The emptiness was too much like death. When her last battery cell was draining back in the burning car, she had felt a dark silence coming over her like night overtaking the day.

When Dan groaned and his face contorted from a bad dream, she pulled up his cover and whispered comfort in his ear. He must be as frightened as any of us, perhaps more. She had to do *something.* She never liked waiting while the humans slept one third of their lives away. Sure, when she couldn't sunbathe, she had to plug in and recharge every few days, but while she waited, she worked out problems, planned meals, or thought up new sexual surprises for Evard. She pulled out the components lifted from her upstairs neighbor, who probably wouldn't be coming back. An idea hit her.

Her surreptitious task done, she still felt desperate and called out to the ether. "Aarden?"

She didn't have to wait long for an answer. "Yes, Felicity. How are you doing, child?"

"Better. My repairs are almost complete. I don't think I sustained any permanent damage. I'm about forty-percent charged and—"

"That's not what I mean. How are you *feeling*?"

"I miss Evard. Is that unnatural? He's only a human."

"Not at all. You care about him, as do I."

"Is he all right? Is he furious at me for not coming back for him?"

"Why don't you ask him yourself? He's about to knock on your door."

Thirty-six—The Discovery

A crisply dressed man pushed by a number of other agents peering at a large overhead display showing maps, timelines, and video feeds from all over the region. "Sir, we have a hit." He held out a notebook.

"Where?"

"Evergreen Medical Center in Kirkland. They admitted Cynthia Wellborn at twenty-three hundred hours. She's being treated for second- and third-degree burns." He touched the notebook and the location appeared on the overhead screen.

"Why did it take this long?"

"We're not sure, but it looks like their system was hacked to prevent admissions logging. We only found out by accident. Cindy Hicks, the director's daughter, was working at the desk and recognized ELF227—AKA Felicity—from our APB circulated to the hospitals. She didn't mention the sighting to her father until she talked to him over breakfast."

"We're lucky they're on speaking terms."

"There's more. She also saw a boy matching the description of Cynthia's son."

"Dan? Was he hurt too?"

"No, just minor smoke inhalation. He was treated and released to the ELF, who was acting as his au pair. She said that they were heading to Spokane to visit Cynthia's aunt—she gave us the address."

"We need to get out to Kirkland," Verner said.

"Already being arranged. We can be on site in eighteen minutes."

"Make it happen in fifteen. I want her back within the

hour. I want them both—and Felicity, too—alive. Any sign of Evard or Liam?"

"No, sir. The burned car was last registered to an antique collector in Snoqualmie. We're following up on how Mrs. Wellborn came to be driving it."

"Nicely done. Get them in custody," Verner said. A rare smile crossed his face.

The room came alive with activity as agents and Verner's minions made preparations to capture their prey.

Thirty-seven—The Rescuers

*F*elicity heard a knock. "Who's there?" she asked through the door.

"Let me in, it's freezing out here," Evard said.

She had no sooner thrown the bolt than Liam burst in. He quickly searched the two-room suite. "Where is she?" he demanded.

"Relax, Liam, she's still in the hospital. She was badly burned getting me out of that gas-powered deathtrap."

"Are you all right?" Evard said, pulling off his O2 mask and taking her in his arms.

"You still mad at me?"

"Were you driving?" Liam asked.

"Me? No, Cynthia was driving. I was in no shape to drive or do anything else."

"Felicity?" Dan said, looking up wild-eyed from the bed. He looked terrified.

"It's all right. Evard is here to help us."

"I'll get that bitch," Liam said through his teeth. "The drones almost spotted us a half-dozen times." Liam was still pacing the floor and checking the courtyard.

"You'll do no such thing," Evard said. "Don't make me…."

Liam put up his hands. "Don't. Threaten. Me. Don't."

Felicity saw the fiery rage in Liam's eyes—she had not seen him like this for years. Something must have happened—more than being left stranded on a country road in the middle of the night. "Rock Black Bike," she said in a firm command voice. Liam's face went blank and he collapsed. "Help me," she said.

Evard helped set him in a chair where he just stared

into the room.

"You didn't have to do that. I would have—" Evard said.

"But you didn't. He was frightening the boy, and me. What happened? What triggered his relapse?"

"Who knows? Some kids drove by and tossed some fireworks. He just snapped. He chased their car down on foot and nearly killed them."

"Why didn't he catch up to the GTO when Cynthia drove off?"

"He almost did. I stopped him and told him to let her go. I knew you had the pen and you would take care of her once you got recharged."

"I guess you were wrong. I really screwed that up." She had nearly gotten them all killed.

"How could you help, hon? Your batteries were nearly gone. You recharged now?"

"Partially, about forty percent. I could use another couple of hours."

"Which, regrettably, we don't have. Do you still have the—"

Felicity held up the pen, extracted from some hidden cavity. "Pen?"

"Keep it, but stay close."

Felicity looked up. "Wait. Aarden says Verner is on the move. He's heading to the hospital." Hearing footsteps in the corridor, she turned to see Dan had bolted.

"He's headed for the hospital," she said. "Right into Verner's arms."

"We can't leave Liam here. Help me get him up."

"Then what? We need time to restore his last stable state."

Evard just looked at her, thinking of a solution. There were precious few options left to them. Either they give up Cynthia and the boy to Verner or risk being captured themselves, along with the data locked in the pen.

"Go. Go try to find the boy. There's a chance Verner won't get there before you get them to safety. I'll work on Liam. I need twenty or thirty minutes to reset him."

Felicity gave Evard a quick kiss and ran. Having the ability to run a kilometer in about ninety seconds helped her reach the hospital in record time. She had to walk more or less normally inside the hospital to avoid drawing attention to herself, but she did manage to snatch a doctor's coat, badge, and tDAP from their dressing room. It wouldn't be missed until the owner got out of the shower with his cute intern.

She looked around the corner leading to Cynthia's corridor. Dan was just getting off the elevator. Four agents followed him into Cynthia's room. *Too late.*

Thirty-eight—The Capture

*A*fter a good night's rest, Cynthia was sitting up in bed and feeling more like her old self. Thanks to advanced healing technology, things were going pretty well. Though still connected to an IV, she had been able to take a few steps and use the restroom. She was just about to test her legs again when Dan ran into the room, pushed by the nurse, and fell into his mom's arms.

"Hey, nice to see—"

"Mrs. Cynthia Wellborn?"

She looked up to see four men in identical black suits standing just inside the doorway. They looked more like ex-Marines than Mormon missionaries. "Yes, what is it?"

"Mrs. Wellborn, you're under arrest. You need to come with us."

A stocky nurse elbowed past two of the agents like a linebacker and stood face to chest with the rather tall agent who seemed to be in charge. "You're not taking her anywhere. She's too ill to move. Unless you have a warrant and clearance from the administrator, my patient is not leaving this room." Her voice made it abundantly clear she meant business.

"Get the administrator down here," the first agent said.

One of the other agents glared at the nurse, who had taken up a post between Cynthia and the agents. Despite the difference in their height, she didn't seem intimidated, and seemed relieved when an older man in a long white coat appeared.

"What's going on? You can't be in here. Unless you're a family member, you'll need to leave immediately," the man demanded.

"And you are?"

"I'm Doctor Samuelson, the senior attending physician. Mrs. Wellborn is my patient. As I said, you'll have to leave."

"Who are you people?" Cynthia said, covering herself with the blanket and wrapping Dan in her arms. She had a pretty good idea who they were—she'd seen men like these at the Cougar Mountain site.

Verner entered the room, parting the phalanx of agents as Moses parted the Red Sea. "Good morning, Cynthia, I see you're doing better." He shooed away the other agents, who retreated into the corridor.

"Mr. Verner. What have I done?"

"Nothing, my dear, it's all a misunderstanding. I'm sure we can work it all out, but now that you're better, you need to come back to the site with me."

"I have not released Mrs. Wellborn. She's still under observation," the doctor said.

"I've spoken to the administrator, and this court order should suffice to release her into our custody. We have adequate medical facilities where we're headed."

Another agent appeared at the door with a wheelchair.

"Can you help her dress?" Verner said to the nurse. "I'll personally see that she's well cared for."

"Mom? You can't let them take you," Dan said.

"It doesn't look like I have a choice. Who's going to take care of my son?"

"Of course, he'll be coming along. We have a place for him to wait while we ask you a few questions. You'll be back home in no time."

Recalling her persistent nightmares, Cynthia ripped away her IV and attempted to bolt for the door where she ran into one of the agents in the corridor. She got in a couple of weak swings before someone jabbed her with something sharp. After that, everything seemed to move very quickly. She was immodestly dressed in hospital scrubs and wheeled out a back door, where a nondescript van hovered over the pavement. Helpless and unable to move, she and Dan sat in silence as Verner closed the windowless door.

* * *

"They took her," Felicity said.

"Shit." Evard punched the air in frustration. "Could you tell who it was?"

"Watch," she said, holding up her tDAP as it played a video. She had recorded the entire incident.

"How'd you get this?"

"I planted a tracker bug in Dan's clothes last night. I thought he might try to slip away."

"Lucky you did. That's Verner. Where are they taking her?"

"They're headed south—toward Seattle, so yeah, maybe Cougar Mountain."

"We need a car."

"And Liam," Felicity said.

"And Liam." Evard pulled open Liam's shirt, exposing his control panel. Pulling a small black chip from his pocket, he slid it into a slot in Liam's chest.

"Which configuration are you loading?" Felicity looked worried.

"The last stable backup."

"Are you sure?"

"No. Got a better idea?"

Felicity shook her head and watched as Liam came back to life.

"Good morning, Liam, how are you feeling?" Evard said, resealing the bot's access panel.

"Like someone kicked me in the head," he said rubbing his forehead.

"We need a car and some weapons."

"Mission?"

"Rescue Cynthia."

"Seriously?" Liam said. "Shouldn't we stick to the plan and try to decipher the data?"

"I think the key is deep inside Cougar Mountain— that's where I think they're taking Cynthia and the boy."

"How do you plan to get into the site?" Felicity asked as she checked the parking lot. "And more importantly, how do you plan to escape?"

"I have no idea. We need to get to a web interface."

"You're standing in front of one," Felicity said. "I'm linked into the web."

"Of course. We've been off the grid…so get me all you can on the facility."

Felicity closed her eyes and began a detailed search of historical archives and any details on the construction of the underground site. *Aarden? Any hints on how to get in and out of that site?*

"*Try this*," Aarden responded, showing her the scanned text of an old reference book detailing abandoned mines in the Cougar Mountain area.

"Are you over your claustrophobia?" Felicity asked Evard.

He just stared at her.

"I'm guessing no. Too bad. It looks like the best way in is through one of the abandoned coal mine tunnels under the mountain."

"Swell. Any alternatives?"

"The vehicle entrance from above is too heavily guarded," Liam said. "Unless we have someone on the inside to help."

"Any progress on a ride?"

"I saw a car in the lot.. I'll see what I can do." Liam headed for the door.

"Wait," Felicity said. She tossed him a car fob. "Perhaps this will help."

"Thanks." Liam slipped out.

"I missed you," Felicity said, giving Evard a warm hug.

He kissed her, pushing his hips against her. "I'm glad you're okay."

"I wasn't worried. You have *me* backed up, don't you?"

"I did," he said nodding. "But it was lost in the cabin explosion."

A wave of fear washed over her. She might entirely cease to exist if something happened. Like most bots, she thought of herself as being virtually immortal, so she took chances knowing Evard could bring her back to life in a new body—at least to the last backup. Harsh reality slapped her in the face. *Is this how humans always feel?*

"You don't look well. Are you sure you're okay?" Evard lifted her chin and gazed into her eyes. "You're crying. Hon, what's wrong?"

"It's...I'm just...it's a different emotion I've never experienced. I...I might be gone in a flash and never return."

"We'll just have to be especially careful." He gave her a hug.

"We don't have time, do we?" Felicity asked, wiping away her tears, but she knew the answer. A backup would take precious hours they didn't have.

Evard shook his head.

Felicity stared out the window. She so much wanted to live and stay with Evard for as long as she could, but for the first time, she could see how that could all end—forever. "How do you…you humans do it, knowing each second might be your last?"

"Faith."

"In God?"

"For some, yes. For me, I simply believe I have a mission in life I must try to complete. I weigh risks against rewards and keep pressing forward."

"Is your mission pre-destined?"

"Some think so—thinking they are playing out an orchestrated performance where they die in the third act."

"And you?"

"I just live for the next hour, the next day, and I'm thankful for the sunrise."

Liam burst in. "I found the car. Let's go."

He led them to an old van filled with MOM food components and a few odd boxes of trackers, micro-cameras, and sensors.

"Salesman?" Evard asked, getting behind the wheel.

"More likely black market," Liam said, getting in the back.

"Where did you get the fob?" Evard asked.

"Don't ask," Felicity said with a grin. "It won't be missed."

"Where are they?" Evard asked, pulling out on an almost deserted street.

"The people? I have no idea. It's strange. This time of day, there should be a glut of traffic. Is there something going on we don't know about?"

"No, Cynthia and Dan—where are they?"

Felicity checked her tDAP. "Still heading toward Cougar Mountain via the lake road." The lack of people still worried her. *Aarden, where are the people?*

"Where did you get the tDAP?"

"It belonged to one of the doctors at the hospital. He was distracted."

"Distracted?"

"Interacting with one of the interns."

A moment later, Aarden spoke to her. "You need to hurry."

Thirty-nine—The Mission

*J*ulijana stood with her back to Avey outside the conference room. "Is that really you in there?"

"It's me. Why won't you accept that?" Avey turned to look Julijana in the eye, but she didn't turn around. She so wished Julijana could forgive her for...for coming back to life as an ELF.

"It's hard," she whispered.

"Think how hard it is for me. It was hard for Sam, too, but he's come to accept me as a person."

Julijana didn't respond.

"I missed you all terribly."

Julijana looked toward the ceiling, fending off tears.

Avey wished Sam would come and rescue her. "You know I was never very far away. I watched you and Sam in the safe house and afterwards—even at the funeral."

"I didn't know," Julijana whispered.

* * *

Sam sat at a console. He was focused on learning Vili's time machine and had tuned out the rest of the world. He had to. If he didn't, thoughts of Avey and how she had returned to him would drive him crazy. He was nearly there.

"Sam?" It was Aarden. *Is she talking in my head now?* He looked around and realized her voice was coming from his tablet speakers.

"What is it?"

"It's time. I'm bringing everyone together in the conference room."

"Avey too?"

"Avey's already there."

Sam left at once and found Avey and Julijana waiting outside the conference room—they were almost back to back and not speaking. They both looked like they had been crying, but he was relieved to see Avey had given up on her "Edith" costume. He wondered how she was handling the inevitable questions and…bigotry.

"What's wrong?" Sam asked, touching her arm.

"It's nothing," she whispered, pulling him a few steps away from Julijana.

Sam knew "nothing" was always "something," but whatever it was would have to wait—at least until after the meeting. He gave Avey a hug and a kiss on the cheek. "You been busy?" he asked, trying to get her mind off of what was bothering her.

"We've found a way to hold open the firewall," Avey said. "At least for a few minutes."

"Amazing. I knew you could do it. You get a special treat for that."

"Promise?" she said with a weak smile.

Ben and James walked up, still arguing about something. As they approached, Sam could tell Julijana was still at the center of their quarrel.

"Boys, behave," Julijana said with a smile on her face.

"But—" Ben began.

Julijana gave him a scowl and Ben wilted.

As they filed in, Aarden, dressed in a smart business suit with her hair up in a bun, greeted each of them personally as they sat down. "Thanks for coming. Could I have your attention? We don't have a lot of time. Thanks to Avey's new application, we've found a way to get through The Good's hardened firewall. We now know what to do once we're inside. We have an undercover agent, but she's taking a lot of chances—so we can't... well, she might not survive. I need volunteers for two teams."

Both Ben and James raised their hands immediately.

"Wait. Before you commit, understand that we've already lost too many good people. This is a risky mission—so risky, we're striking in two places at once. One team or the other *has* to get inside, and then comes the hard part."

"What makes you think this will work?" Sam asked. "Why should we all risk more lives on a plan that might have no impact in the end?"

"The stakes are simply too high. At the rate the situation is deteriorating, we've run out of time and options. Sam, aren't you familiar with the Civil War? This is Gettysburg. If we win this battle, the war might indeed be winnable. If we don't, I fear it might be too late for humanity."

Sam was still not convinced. "Then the planet will collapse in on itself?"

"No. It will simply be uninhabitable for humans and most life forms—except one."

"And the one?"

"ELFs. ELFs like Avey and some of the other brave agents you're about to work with."

"So if we fail, the ELFs take over the world. Right?"

"It's not something we want," Aarden said softly.

"You don't want to take over the world?"

"The ELFs under my control and I want to protect mankind—humans and the ecosystem that supports them—as well as all life on the planet. It's what Avey created us to do."

"I did?" Avey said.

"You did, and if the mission fails, we'll have no mankind to protect."

Everyone except Julijana looked at Avey and then returned their attention to Aarden.

"Are you in?"

The way Sam figured it, even if the plan failed, assuming they survived, he might be able to return to his own time and live out his life with Avey.

"No, Sam," Aarden began. "You can't take Avey back to your time. It's too dangerous. One slip and the scientific community would discover her technology eighty years before it's invented. Your only future with Avey is here—and then only if the plan works."

Shit.

In the past, experience had told Sam not to volunteer, but his hand went up, and so did Avey's. The rest followed suit—even Julijana.

Aarden smiled. "I suspected as much. We need four or five. I need Avey here at the Needle to work the firewall breach code and deflect their security response, and Sam to manage the time transmogrifier if they try to roll back anything we attempt. I'll also need Vili here to handle timkering if we need to slip time. There's not a lot of timeline buffer, so don't take any unnecessary risks."

"Vili and I always work together in the field," Julijana said.

"Not this time. You're our medical expert in case anyone needs immediate attention. In this case, there's a civilian and her son involved. I've promised her protection but she's been kidnapped from a hospital, so Julijana, you're in charge of caring for her and her son."

Julijana nodded and looked over at Vili.

He looked disappointed, and slid a small case across

the table. "You're going to need my gadgets. Don't lose them," he said with a weak smile.

Sam knew why he was being kept at Avey's side—and it was where he wanted to be. She was very new to her ELF persona, and had shown signs of ELF syndrome. Aarden had taken him aside and described the condition, which affected many—if not most—ELFs restored from human entities. Many grow claustrophobic and become suicidal if they feel trapped in their new bodies. It was his fault she was here, his fault she was killed, and his fault they weren't back home in their own time. Not to mention, he was also having trouble with the idea of having a relationship with a machine you had to recharge at night like a Microsoft Band or an electric toothbrush.

"One other factor you need to consider," Aarden began. "We intended to get a device into the site several days ago, but it was accidentally lost."

"Great. Were you able to find it?" Vili asked.

"Fortunately, yes. It's critical that we get it inside the system vault before the situation deteriorates beyond the point of no return."

"Timeframe?" Sam asked.

"We leave immediately," Aarden continued. "I've arranged for four more skilled team members to join you. Evard Kennedy and two of his ELF agents. They're all very skilled operatives, and more importantly, they're carrying the device."

"And the other?"

"Another ELF we infiltrated into the site some time ago. It's best you don't know her name in case you're captured."

"More ELFs?" Julijana said. "Seriously? Won't they just be in the way?"

"Use them wisely," Aarden said sternly, raising an eyebrow.

"Yes, ma'am," Julijana said.

Sam could tell Julijana's heart wasn't in it. "She didn't mean you," he whispered in Avey's ear.

"Yes, she did. I know how she feels. Aarden told me to expect people like her. I just wish she could look behind my electronic eyes and see the real me."

"I do, too," Sam said. They walked out together without speaking to the others. As they left, he noticed Vili lecturing Julijana.

Forty—The Teams

A common white delivery van hovered through traffic as more maneuverable Single Occupant Pods scooted around it like salmon swimming upstream around a rock. The autodrive system's audible warnings had been muted—it had begun to nag, like having a mother-in-law in the back seat. That didn't clear the dash screen of panicky messages about impending collisions. "WARNING: SOAP density high."

"Where are we supposed to meet them?" Evard asked, ignoring the warnings and pressing on through as if the other vehicles didn't exist.

"In Issaquah. There's a retro Mexican restaurant on Front Street in the block north of Sunset. They're supposed to be there at six," Felicity replied.

"How much time do we have?"

"Deep question," Julijana quipped.

"About fifteen minutes," Liam said from the back of the van. He had been inventorying the boxes of security equipment and black-market MOM ingredients. "Look, he's cornered the market on six. We can make enough coffee to keep an entire regiment awake."

"How much *time?*" Evard asked again, turning briefly to look Felicity in the eye. It didn't take a clairvoyant to know their time together was growing short.

"Not enough."

"You worried, too? You're supposed to be Miss Optimism."

"Not so much. I'm getting less certain about everything."

"Even us?" Evard turned south on Front Street.

"After you fell in love with Cynthia? I saw how you looked at her."

He hoped she was kidding, but Evard's stomach tightened all the same. He *had* fallen for Cynthia before she had slept with him, but he knew she wasn't ready to commit until she felt solid ground under her feet. He couldn't blame her. She knew he was a wanted man with a dark past and a darker future—and that wouldn't change even if this mission was successful. She didn't need to depend on another man only to have him killed before she knew how he liked his eggs.

"Over medium with a dash of pepper," Felicity said. "Turn on Sunset. There's parking in the back."

"You know I love you. I will *always* love you."

"That's what I'm afraid of. If you have me around, you won't find someone else to tie your shoes when you get old."

"This it? Yeah, there's the sign. Sure it's open?"

"It's on the historical sites registry. They shouldn't close till eleven."

Evard backed into a parking place and turned off the engine. "Now what?"

"We wait. It's not six yet."

Evard reached out for Felicity's hand and held it. She was trembling. Like every other female he had met— human or ELF—she was impossible to fully understand. She was one of the strongest individuals he knew, but she still got frightened. "We'll get you protected—first chance we get."

"Thanks. I still want to hold your newborn son."

"Even though it won't be yours?"

"It will be my Godson. Of course, I'll love it. Who's going to teach him how to code? You?"

"I can teach him."

"You need to get some girl pregnant first. Don't put your fart before the horse."

Evard laughed. "Cart. Don't put your *cart* before the horse."

"Really? I always thought…oh, never mind. I'll correct it."

"Who are they?" Liam asked, pointing to three people across the parking lot. "They weren't there a second ago."

Evard flashed his headlights. The trio turned and walked toward them. The hair on the back of his neck rose until Felicity's hand stroked it down.

"It's them. They match Aarden's description."

"I'll wait here," Liam said, priming a short-barrel shotgun.

"You too, Felicity." Evard got out of the van and approached them. "You here to meet someone?" he said.

Ben extended his hand. "I'm Ben and this is Julijana, and that's Jimmy. I assume you're Evard?"

Evard shook his hand and imagined that Ben had a wasp landing on his hair. If Ben was reading his mind, he would probably react. He didn't. *Not an ELF.* "Yes, Felicity and Liam are in the van. Nice to meet you."

"We had better get started. Let's plan on using the van. It's big enough for everyone, that is if you don't mind sitting on the floor," Evard said.

"Fine. The site entrance isn't far from here," Julijana said. "Okay with you guys?"

Ben nodded. Jimmy was already opening the door, but jumped back when he found a shotgun pointing at his face.

"Liam, these are friends. Put that away," Evard chided.

"Is he housetrained?" Julijana asked. She wasn't smiling.

"He's a warrior bot," Felicity said. "He'll be fine."

"I could tell—the smell is unmistakable." Julijana sneered.

"I'll take care of Liam." Evard leaned over and whispered in Liam's ear. At this, his head drooped and he closed his eyes. "Perhaps we *should* regroup before we get started," he said, sliding the van door closed.

"Yes, let's. Who is in command of this circus?"

"Aarden," Felicity said flatly.

"You in touch with her?" Julijana asked.

"Ask her yourself."

"Perhaps we *should* go inside," Aarden said.

They turned to find Aarden standing behind them. She was dressed in a form-fitting black jumpsuit that glistened in the argon streetlights.

"Won't there be a dozen ears to overhear us?" Julijana asked.

"I'll care of that—just bring the MOM ingredients from the van."

"Even the six?"

"Especially the six, but you can keep a couple for yourselves. They might come in handy later." Aarden led the party into the restaurant. "Set the ingredients on the bar and wait," she said.

"Got any money?" Ben asked. "I sure could use a drink."

Jimmy reached into his pocket and pulled out a stack of fresh bills. "Think they'll take Yankee dollars?"

Ben just shook his head. "Not from 1860, chowder head."

"Come on. I've arranged a private room for us. And

put that money away. We have enough trouble as it is," Aarden said, leading them to a small candlelit room.

Once they had been seated and the waiter had brought chips and salsa, Aarden began explaining the plan. She detailed a series of operations that would attempt to breach the site from both ends at once.

"A diversion from both ends?"

"Correct," she continued. Evard and his ELF team would go in from below, while Julijana and the Marshals would try to get in from above. "Once you get inside, you'll need to get into the vault. I have another team working from the Needle to break through the firewall and disable their internal security systems. It's essential that you don't damage the network or the hardware. We're not here to destroy anything—just to capture control over it. We're going to need the facility and the information it stores."

"To what end?"

"I plan to reprogram every ELF on the planet," Aarden said flatly.

"Even me?" Felicity asked.

"Even you."

"I...I don't understand. Why me?"

"Because Verner and his people have created their own super-being—their own version of me. They're creating a massive army of war bots."

"Shit," Evard said.

Aarden glared at him like a mother whose favorite son had just shouted the F word at Mass.

"Sorry."

"As we speak, they're terminating tens of thousands of people—promising to move their entities into ELF shells."

"A year?"

"An hour. World-wide, they've disposed of nearly one point six million people in the last week and the number is rising."

"Where did they get the bots?" Ben asked.

"They didn't—they don't have nearly enough units to hold the number of people who volunteered for the program. Supposedly they're backing up people and euthanizing them—promising they will be reborn in new ELF bodies."

"Why would anyone want to do this if they aren't even assured of being reborn?" Vili asked.

"Enough are 'reborn' and returned to society to convince the masses to try the Rapture Experience."

Julijana was visibly upset. "I...I had no idea."

"No one outside of Verner's group does."

"We have to stop them," Vili said.

"Why not just get the military to storm the place?" Jimmy asked. "A MOAB strike could blow the entire mountain into the stone age."

"We can't. If the system is destroyed, millions of souls already uploaded into ELFs and those stored onsite will perish."

"Oh my God," Felicity said. She put her head on Evard's shoulder.

"So the pen doesn't contain a list," Evard said.

Aarden shook her head. "That's what we wanted Verner and his people to think. We wanted them to want to get the pen, into the vault."

"Easily said," Julijana remarked.

"It won't be easy. You'll need to take over the site without destroying it. Once you do, I can get control of the existing ELFs and reconnect them to my hive where I can reprogram them."

"You're asking us to help you take over the country," Evard said.

"The planet," Aarden said.

The room fell quiet.

The waiter came in with fresh salsa and chips. No one said a word as he asked for their orders. "I'll come back later," he said as he backed away and closed the door.

"What are they doing with the bodies?" Vili asked.

"You *really* don't want to know," Aarden said, looking down at the chips.

"Seriously?" Evard's face blanched and he looked away.

Aarden nodded.

"Fuck," Ben said. He laid his half-eaten chip on the table.

Forty-one—The Captives

"*Are* you comfortable, Mrs. Wellborn?" Verner asked as he stood over her bed. The look on his face wasn't helping her feel at ease—quite the contrary. His whole attitude reminded her of the perverts who captured women to…well, it wasn't nice. No, Cynthia felt scared, trapped, and helpless. Verner and his men had not said four words on the trip from the hospital despite her pleading. She was sure she had been taken to the Cougar Mountain site when the van went weightless. Once inside, they had whisked her down into the lower levels—rooms she never knew existed. She wasn't sure, but this seemed like Verner's quarters. Dan clung to her like a little boy; it was clear that he could sense how much danger they were in.

"Why am I here?" she asked.

"We simply need to ask you some questions."

"We?"

"All right, *I*. I need to ask you about your association with the SOG."

"I don't know anything about the SOG or any other subversive group."

"Very interesting. Apparently you *know* the Snoqualmie Omega Group is subversive."

She nodded.

"Who's been hiding you? Where have you been for the last three days? We were worried."

"I'm just fine," she said with a glare. "I was fine until you kidnapped me."

"Fine? You were badly burned pulling someone out of an illegal car. Who did you rescue?"

"A friend."

"What's his name?"

"What difference does it make?"

"It's important to The Good. Your friends in the SOG are trying to destroy this facility."

"How could three people possibly destroy your precious site?"

"As we suspected, there *are* three of them. What are their names?"

"You wouldn't know them."

"Evard Kennedy? Was he one of them?"

Cynthia tried not to react. She was a lousy poker player.

"And he's been known to be sleeping with an ELF. Portia? No—"

"Doris. Her name is Doris," she lied.

"Admit it, you *were* with them. What's their plan?"

"Plan? I don't know about any *plan*."

"Did you give them anything? Something you got from Sanchez?"

"I have no idea what you're talking about. I didn't get anything from Mr. Sanchez but a hard time."

"Anything. Think." Verner grabbed her arm. "It's important."

"Let *go* of me," she pulled away.

"Mrs. Wellborn, Cynthia, we don't want to get rough, but this is important. I wouldn't want to have to let our specialists interrogate you."

"I have nothing more to say. I want to leave. You have no right to hold me here."

"All right, we'll start with your son. It's Dan, isn't it?"

"Leave him alone!" she screamed.

"Then tell me. Tell me everything. Now."

Forty-two—The Back Door

$\mathcal{E}$vard kept his eyes on the road as he felt his way up Cougar Mountain with his lights off. He already had a few breathtaking moments—near misses as he met manual-control drivers who had not seen him coming. This entire "plan" seemed like another mad dash into the dark. Somehow they were to break into a heavily secure site and gain access to a massive computer complex he'd never seen before. And then, the pinnacle of insanity— figure out how to infect it with a device no larger than a pen. *Nuts.*

"Where's this mineshaft?" he asked.

"Just up ahead," Felicity said.

"There?" Evard had pointed at a break in the pavement—perhaps where an old road had once intersected the highway.

"Yes, that's it," Felicity said. "I think."

"You think? I'm not excited about pulling into that oxyvine and fighting our way to the entrance on a guess."

"It's an informed guess," Felicity assured him.

Evard pulled the van off the road where the oxyvine swallowed the vehicle up to the wheel wells.

"Well, we're here. Liam. It's time to get to work."

Liam's eyes opened, and he immediately slid open the side door. "Where's the objective?" he asked.

"Ninety meters to the northwest," Felicity said.

Evard was relieved Liam seemed better prepared this time—perhaps being in his element had helped. This is what he had been trained, or at least programmed, to do. He had found a few useful implements in the back of the van, including a battery-powered UV light. Liam flipped it on and shown the light on the vines already creeping inside the van—they retreated like a vampire falling back when splashed with a dose of holy water.

"I wish we'd had one of these back at the house," Felicity said.

"The battery had better hold out," Evard said, stepping out behind Liam, who was waving the light like a scythe.

"I figure we have about thirty minutes," Felicity said.

"To live?" Evard looked back at her. She just looked at him and kept walking.

Following a trail of coal dust and small shards with his flashlight, Evard expected to find an old abandoned mine opening—he didn't. Ahead, a concrete and steel doorway stood in their way.

"What's that?" Felicity asked.

"I was going to ask you the same question."

"Did Aarden say this is the way in?"

"No. The way out."

"Sometimes I wish she wouldn't talk in riddles," Liam said.

"She says this is where…."

Evard could see Felicity was struggling with what Aarden had told her.

"What is it?"

"It's a refuse chute—for people."

"Grisly," Evard whispered. He wasn't at all sure he wanted to open the door.

Liam was already searching around the edges, probing the area around the opening with a serrated knife. "It's wired. Probably an alarm."

"Let's see what I can do," Evard said.

Using one of the security devices scavenged from the

van, he was able to locate and defeat the alarm sensor. "That should do it."

"Or not," Liam said.

"The eternal optimist," Felicity said.

"The constant realist," Liam replied. "We won't know if they're ready for us until we get inside."

"Choices?" Evard asked.

Felicity looked into his eyes. "None. This is the only way in, unless you want to go in the main entrance."

"I left my invitation back home along with my tux," Liam said.

"How do we get the door open? There's no handle or lock to pick."

Felicity walked up to the door and it opened as she approached. "Oh, ye of little faith."

"Aarden?" Evard said.

"Aarden. Remember? She has someone on the inside helping out."

"You could have said as much," Liam said as he switched off the UV light. The oxyvine wasted no time—it began to advance on them almost at once.

Once they had entered the tunnel, the door closed behind them with an echoing thud. Evard scanned the walls with his flashlight for a light switch. *Nothing.*

"Turn it off. You don't have much battery left," Felicity said. "We'll need it to get back to the van."

"And how am I supposed to see?"

"I'll be your eyes. Just put your hand on my shoulder and I'll guide you. Liam and I can see in the dark, or do you want Liam to carry you?"

"Nah, we need to keep the exertion down to conserve batteries." He didn't mention it would be humiliating.

She nodded. "Come on."

Evard put his hand on her shoulder and switched off his flashlight. He had no recollection of a place this dark. His right hand brushed the cool wall. *Wet. Slimy.* It didn't help to ease the fear that the walls were moving in on him. He had been claustrophobic since childhood when he had fallen into a drainage ditch and got sucked into a culvert. He had endured hours of torture before they found him. He was never the same.

"We need to do some climbing—it's a klick or two to the site."

"Is that what Aarden says?"

"I can't hear her from in here. That's the problem. The entire site is heavily shielded. We're on our own."

"Perfect. Blind and led by the deaf." He could feel her move forward, and he tried to walk at her pace. It took a few dozen steps to get used to following her. Tripping on uneven ground, he put his other hand on her hip.

"Don't get fresh," she said.

"Here? In the dark, with the girl I love, when I know we might both be killed any moment?"

"You're sweet," she said.

He felt her hand touch his. She was trembling.

"You two are not alone on Mulholland Drive," Liam said. From the sound of his voice, he must have been far ahead of them.

They walked in silence for another hundred steps before Felicity stopped.

"What is it?"

"A…shaft opening from above."

"Should I turn on my light?"

"No. Don't."

"What is it?"

"You don't need to see."

Evard's curiosity overcame her admonition. When he turned on his flashlight, he saw the mangled remains of four men. It seemed they had fallen from a great distance. He switched off his light and bent over to heave out his stomach. She was right—he didn't want to see that. Now he wished he never had.

"Liam, do you think you could climb up there? It looks big enough, but it's very slick and smooth." Felicity's hand was on Evard's back as she examined the shaft with her night vision.

"It would be tough, but not impossible with the right gear."

"Shit," Evard said. "Let's get out of here." The space was growing in on him again.

They slowly made their way back to the entrance, but Evard couldn't stand being led, or the feeling that he had been entombed, so he snapped on his flashlight. "Sorry. I couldn't stay in the dark."

"It's just—" Felicity began.

"No platitudes, please. I know it's irrational, just get me out of here."

"The door is just ahead," Liam said.

"We're nearly out," she said, reaching back to hold his hand.

"Crap. It's locked." Liam rattled the handle.

Evard scanned the door and the surrounding concrete walls. *Nothing.* He turned around and looked into the darkness up the tunnel. The walls appeared to be far narrower than they had been a moment ago. Turning again, he smacked his head against the wall and fell to his knees. His head swimming, Felicity knelt down beside him and embraced him.

"Just wait. Aarden will open the door for us. Just trust

in her. I'll pray to her. It will be all right...." she said softly.

He knew she was trying to comfort him. He was furious with himself, not understanding the infantile fear that had overcome him. Even after the incident in the culvert, he had been the model of courage his whole life, but now he was afraid of the dark and inanimate stone walls. *Coward.* He tried to think of something else. She put her arms inside his coat and cuddled in close. What would he do without her? What *could* he do without her? He wondered how her charge was holding up—and Liam's. Neither one of the ELFs had been fully charged before setting out, so they only had a few hours left—depending on physical exertion. Maybe it would be enough. It would have to be. He, on the other hand, was slowly losing his mind—it was like pieces of his remaining courage were dissolving away like a sandstone cliff facing the sea's crashing waves.

Wait. Did she say she was going to pray to Aarden? Felicity thinks she's a god.

Evard switched off his flashlight. The light had already begun to dim, just like his hopes to get them both out of here to safety. Just then, he heard a metallic click. Without a word being spoken, Evard struggled to get to his feet. Felicity helped him up and led him deeper into the tunnel.

Framed in headlights, two men in O2 masks and jumpsuits came through the door pushing a wheeled cart. When they saw Liam, he reacted quickly. The men didn't have a chance.

"Don't get their uniforms bloody," Evard said.

Liam nodded as he snapped the neck of the second man—not a drop of blood had been spilt.

"Neatly done," Evard said. "Now we have a key to the facility's front door."

"And transportation that won't raise suspicion."

"Perhaps that was Aarden's plan all along," Evard said, although he didn't really believe it.

"Sure, boss," Liam said as he and Felicity began stripping off the workers' clothes. "Wait. These are ELFs," Liam said. He had opened the access panel on one of the men. "How do you want them handled?"

"Better deactivate them—permanently," Evard said.

"You sure?" Felicity asked.

"You're saying it was okay to kill a couple of humans whose only sin was to be in the wrong place at the wrong time, but not these ELFs?"

She closed her eyes. "It's not okay—either way."

Evard agreed. He had grown too callous about killing. Every man he had killed, every woman he had widowed, every child he had orphaned, bore on his soul. She was right. "You're right. They were only doing their jobs. Set them on hibernate. Someone will eventually find and restore them."

As they left the tunnel, Evard paused. "Wait. Find something to block the door."

Liam nodded and quickly returned with a head-sized piece of basalt, jamming it in the door frame.

"Okay, now what?" Felicity asked.

"Well, we have their truck, their uniforms, and credentials. They sent out two ELFs to take out the trash and two ELFs will return," Evard said.

"What about you?"

"Wait. Let's load their cart back on the truck. I'll tag along as cargo. Hopefully they won't look inside."

"Hopefully. But with our luck—" Liam said.

"Next time you reprogram him, let me take a crack at his optimism subroutine," Felicity said.

"Not a chance. I only need one optimist around here."

Working quickly, they reloaded the cart into the truck. Evard climbed into the back, and sat on the floor with Felicity in the passenger seat. They had morphed their appearance to look like the ELFs they left back in the tunnel.

Evard wasn't quite ready to get into the cart—another tight, confined space...not nearly ready. As they pulled away, he silently inventoried the truck's contents. *Wire, electrical connectors, odd pieces of pipe, rope, duct tape, of course duct tape, and linesman spikes? They must have to climb utility poles.* "Liam, how do you plan to find the site entrance?" he asked.

"We don't have to. I told the truck to return to base. It seems to be working."

"Let's hope so," Evard said.

"We're getting close. You had better get hidden," she said.

He didn't move, still staring out the front window.

"Evard?"

Without a word, he drew a heavy sigh and climbed into the cart.

"You ready?" Felicity asked.

He nodded, closing the cart lid. Only a thin crack of light showed through—he concentrated on that light.

The truck slowed to a stop. A moment later, someone was talking to Liam, but Evard couldn't hear what they were saying.

"George824 and Alex203. Want to see our IDs?" Liam said.

A flash of laser light flooded the truck's interior.

Evard held his breath. *What's going on?* He screamed to himself.

"They're thinking. We have some sort of cannon pointing at the windshield. Just hold on," Felicity whispered.

"I love you," he whispered.

"I know. Now hush. Don't make me come back there."

"We had a problem—the vehicle is malfunctioning," Liam said aloud, apparently answering another question.

A second later, the truck and its contents were shredded by a 20mm cannon. No one survived.

* * *

"Sam?" Avey whispered.

"What's wrong?" He paused his computer.

"Something happened. We lost three agents at the vehicle entrance."

"Julijana and her team?" His stomach turned over. He wasn't ready for the reality of losing anyone else—despite knowing the risk they were taking—especially while he sat here safely with Avey, out of harm's way.

"No. Evard Kennedy and his two ELFs."

"Now what? Do they need me to go?"

"Go with *them*? I begged them to leave you here. You're too important—well, back in 2020 and to me."

Sam shook his head. Given what he had seen over the last few months, he knew anything seemed possible, but this was new. He really dreaded going outside—reliving his earlier dose of 2084—the rusty air, the masked inhabitants walking around like zombies, the hopelessness. He got up and splashed murky water on his face at the sink.

"There's more," Avey handed him a towel and cup of

hot tea.

"Great." He took a sip. *Black. Unsweetened. It was nice to have her back.*

"Julijana and her team are going to make another attempt to get into the site and Aarden is worried."

"Let's go see what we can do to help. Maybe it's not too late."

Forty-three—The Mulligan

A nondescript black van sat in the shadows well off the road on the outskirts of Issaquah.

"There's no answer. Their links are all down," Julijana said. She put her tDAP on the console. She was uncomfortable working without Vili. Despite being siblings, his skills and hers were so different. Without him, she felt like a doctor without medicine, a clock without a pendulum.

"Are you still connected to the Needle?" Ben asked.

"Yeah. Vili passed on the news."

"It's tough. So three agents were killed?"

"One agent and a couple of ELFs," Julijana said under her breath.

"What's with you and ELFs? It's not like you."

"They're just…unnatural, like betraying humanity."

"The world has changed around you," Ben said.

"Don't you realize they're taking over the world? If they turn on us, we're gone—all of us, like that!" she said, snapping her fingers under his nose.

Ben just looked at her.

"I'm sorry. It's just the way I feel."

"I didn't know you distrusted them that much. Point taken. Now, Vili says the other team was monitored at the gate on Cougar Mountain, but then nothing."

"Not a word beforehand?"

"I expect they suspected something had gone wrong. Evard and Felicity said they loved one another, as if they were saying their last goodbyes." Julijana thought the sentiment was touching, even if it did come from an ELF.

"What's going on?" Jimmy asked from the back seat.

"It looks like we lost the other team. For some reason they tried to go in the *front* door."

"I thought *we* were supposed to take that entrance."

"That was the plan."

"That could have been us," Ben said softly.

"Wait a second. I'm getting a call," Julijana touched her temple. "I'll put you on speaker. They all need to hear this."

"Julie?" Vili said.

"We're here."

"And you're okay?"

"Not really, we heard about the other team."

"I thought it was you."

"Yeah, I figured. Now what? What does Aarden want to do? We're working in real time now. No time for a mulligan."

"Wait, that gives me an idea," Vili said. And then there was dead air. Julijana could hear a side conversation going on in the room, but couldn't tell what was being said.

"Vili?"

"We're rolling back time—we're still in the buffer window. You need to get to the Cougar Mountain entrance before Evard's team and head him off. Tell them it's an ambush. Verner has somehow figured out that we're coming. It's Evard's only chance."

"Wow. Who cleared that decision?"

"Avey."

"Avey?" Julijana said.

"She's speaking for Aarden. Go figure."

"How much time do you need? Avey figures nine minutes should be enough."

"Give us eleven. We're programming the tDAP now

to give us the new instructions when we restart."

"Avey already did that. We're executing in four, three, two…."

* * *

Julijana's tDAP vibrated on the console as she headed toward the top of Cougar Mountain. She touched her temple and listened.

"There's been a change in plan. We need to intercept the other team—it's an ambush," she announced.

"What? Who said?" Ben asked.

Julijana handed him the tDAP. "Listen to the message. We've been rolled back. We have…ten minutes and forty-eight seconds to stop them."

Julijana hit the accelerator and the vehicle sped up to the speed limit—fifty-five kilometers an hour—about as fast as a tired horse pulling a wagon.

"Can't this buggy go any faster?" Ben asked.

"Not unless I can override the governor."

"Give me the tDAP," James said.

Ben handed it to him and a few seconds later, the engine roared to life and they were going around the curves on two wheels.

"Don't get us all killed," Ben said, holding onto the grab-bar above his window.

"Yes, dear," Julijana said as she eased up on the accelerator.

"Is that them? That's not their car," she said.

Julijana pulled up to the white van. It had government plates and two uniformed government workers in front—janitors from the look of it. One was turning around talking to someone in the back.

"There are only two in the truck; both ELFs. It's not them," James said.

"Give me that," Ben said. He took the tDAP and rescanned the truck. "That's Evard. He's stowing away in the back. He must be in a metal box, but the lid isn't closed. I got facial recognition when he peeked out a second ago."

"Get them to pull over," Ben said.

"Yes, dear."

Julijana pulled up in front of the van and braked hard. The other van nearly ran into the guardrail trying to avoid a collision. Julijana was very relieved when the driver got out—it was Liam. She was not so glad when Liam pulled her out of the van and raised his fist to pummel her. "Crazy woman!"

"Liam. Stop. Now," Felicity said, holding his arm. "She's a friend. Stand down."

And he did.

Julijana caught her breath. "Thanks."

"What's going on?" Evard said, walking up.

"It's an ambush. They know you're coming."

"Fuck," Evard said.

"Let's get off the road. There was a scenic lookout a few klicks back."

After parking well off the road, and away from the oxyvine, the combined teams huddled together and contacted the Needle. Vili and Sam were very relieved to hear their impromptu rescue mission had been a success.

"We still need to get inside that fucking mountain," Evard said. "How are we going to get inside if they know we're coming?"

"The site must have sensed something about the truck. It's an automated system, so perhaps they won't notice us coming in the back door," Felicity said.

"I hope you're right," Julijana said.

"Anyone ever do any mountain climbing?" Felicity asked.

"I've done some, even climbed El Capitan in Yosemite," James said.

As everyone listened intently, Felicity outlined a new plan.

"Wait, you want me to go back in that tunnel? And climb up that bloody shaft—basically the site's anus? Right?" Evard shook his head.

Felicity nodded.

"Crap," Evard said. "Pun intended."

"Now that we have our fearless mountain climber, all we need is a section of rope and ice crampons," she said.

"Ice crampons? Like to walk on ice?" James asked.

"Yeah, and duct tape. No MacGyver episode is complete without duct tape," Ben said.

"MacGyver?" Julijana looked confused.

"MacGyver TV series? Jeez, don't you study the eras you visit, gal?" Ben asked.

Evard just smiled and rummaged around in the truck. "Will these do?" He held up the lineman's pole climbing spikes and tossed the rope and duct tape on the ground at their feet.

"Perfect," Felicity said. "Let's get back over to the tunnel."

Julijana was still unsure what Felicity had in mind, but so far, she seemed to be managing things fairly smoothly. Then again, she wasn't sure if she wanted to be led by an ELF. "Linesman's spikes?" she asked.

"To grip the steel shaft while we climb," Felicity said. "With the aid of the rope."

"Well, the first climber won't be able to use it—it will just be dead weight, a real hindrance," Liam said.

Approaching the tunnel, Julijana walked alongside James, with Ben a step behind tying knots in the rope every three feet or so. Liam took the lead, looking every bit like a combat soldier going into enemy territory—all business. For the most part, she thought the team was pretty strong. A good mix of talent and experience, but she still worried about the two ELFs—the frankly scary Liam, and the youngster Felicity who seemed to be there to nursemaid Evard.

"You okay about going back in there?" Felicity said to Evard.

"Do I have a choice?"

"Not really. We're going to need you and the pen inside. Here, take it." She reached into a hidden cavity and extracted it.

"Then I guess I'll have to deal with it." Evard pushed the pen deep into his pocket.

They paused when they reached the bodies. No one said a word as they reverently moved the broken corpses out of the way. Julijana stood to one side holding a light with Felicity at her side. She was weeping. "Did you know them?" Julijana asked softly.

"Sanchez? Yes. A bit rough around the edges, but a good agent."

"And the others? Did you recognize them?"

"No, but no matter what they did, they deserved better than this."

Standing at the base of the metal tube, Evard pointed his flashlight up the shaft. "Anyone want to volunteer to go up first? We need Liam here if we have uninvited guests."

"This is a man's job. I'll do it," James said. He stared directly into Julijana's eyes and took the end of the rope.

Felicity gave him a pained look and stepped back, shaking her head.

"You…you don't have to do anything to impress me, Jimmy," Julijana said.

He smiled and strapped on the spikes. "So I need to climb to the top and tie it off, right?"

"That's the idea," Felicity said.

"And one other thing," Julijana said.

"What's that?"

"Don't fall. That would be bad," she gave him a peck on the cheek.

"Got it. Don't fall," he said, returning her brave smile. He leaned over and stole another kiss.

Julijana just looked into his eyes. "Be careful."

Liam boosted James up on his shoulders and helped him get a foothold on the shaft—the metal spikes digging into the metal on one side, his back wedged against the other.

They all watched him slowly disappear out of sight. After ten minutes or so, the rope stopped snaking up. "Perhaps he's there," Julijana said, hoping nothing had gone wrong.

"Maybe he's just resting," Felicity said.

A moment later, the rope resumed snaking up the shaft and Julijana's heart started to beat again.

Everyone took turns shining the light up the shaft, hoping to see something. The rope kept rising, albeit slowly, so they knew he was making progress.

All at once, the rope fell from the shaft with a thudding clatter. Two heartbeats later, they heard the screeching of steel-on-steel and James screaming.

"Good God, he's falling!" Julijana yelled. She turned away.

"Stand back," Liam commanded, pushing Julijana out of the way. A split-second later, Liam tried to break James's fall. The impact all but detached Liam's right arm, and they lay together on the floor in a crumpled pile of broken bodies, arms and legs, and blood.

Julijana knelt and touched James's neck. "He's alive." As Liam untangled himself, she could see both of James's legs were broken.

"Hold on there, my friend. We'll get you to a hospital," Ben said. With Ben's help, Julijana fashioned a tourniquet. It didn't help. His femoral artery had been severed at the groin.

"Sorry," James said.

"For what?" Julijana said as her tears flowed down her cheeks and onto his face.

"For not trying harder."

"You did your best."

"If I did, I would have done it," he said with a grin.

"I'll get Sam to roll this back," Julijana said. She tried to key the tDAP, but her fingers were shaking too badly.

Ben took the tDAP and held it up. "No signal. I'm so sorry."

"His heart has stopped," Julijana said.

"He's gone?" Ben said, kneeling by his friends.

Julijana began to cry.

Ben did what he could to console her.

"We still need to get up there," Felicity said. She was already removing James's spikes. "Can you help move him off the rope?"

"You can't do this," Evard said, holding her arm. "You aren't protected."

"She's not backed up?" Julijana asked.

Evard shook his head. "Her resurrection data was lost

in a fire."

"Someone has to do it. Next to Liam, I'm the most qualified." Felicity finished strapping on the spikes and stuffed the roll of duct tape in her pocket.

Evard gave her a hug and whispered in her ear.

"I love you, too. We'll be together soon."

"Like hell. I'll be right behind you," he said.

"You sure?"

Evard nodded.

Just before being boosted up into the shaft, Julijana gave Felicity a hug. "Be careful. And…thanks."

Felicity kissed her on the cheek and a moment later she had disappeared up the shaft.

Forty-four—The Ascent

*O*nce she had figured out the climbing rhythm, Felicity was able to push herself up the shaft fairly quickly, but she was using a lot of energy. Eighty feet up, she reached a bend in the pipe and had a chance to rest. Looking down, she knew she would not survive a fall from this height any more than James had. Looking up with her night vision, she could not see the top. *Not there yet.* She should have gone first. *James would still be alive. Man's work. His bravado had cost him his life.*

While the next section was only sloped at about forty-five degrees, it was still a hard climb—her footing slipped any number of times on something slimy. *Probably blood.* She checked her charge. Thirty-two percent. *Not great.* She shut down all non-essential systems and kept climbing. She could tell the climb was very taxing on her battery.

Her "low battery" light turned yellow at twenty percent. Thankfully, at seventeen percent, she spotted a metal hatch about twenty feet up. With her destination in sight, she pushed on to the top and put her shoulder to the hatch. *Locked.* Based on the scratch-marks on the walls, James had made it this far before he fell. She wedged her legs harder into the opposite wall and examined the hatch. *A simple snap-lock.* She grew her thumbnail out an inch and used it to open the latch. The shaft acted as a chimney, and a rush of air pushed the hatch open. *I'm in.* Fifteen percent. The indicator in her field of vision flashed yellow.

The room was dark, but appeared empty. Looping the rope through the opening, she scrambled inside. Fourteen percent. It had taken a lot more energy than she had

anticipated but she had made it. She tied the rope to a
heavy table and tugged, but it wasn't answered by another
tug. She tried again and again. She needed something to
get their attention. She unstrapped the spikes and
dropped them down the chute—unfortunately, they
made an awful clatter. *I hope no one gets hit.* She waited
another few moments. Thirteen percent. *Nothing. Where
the fuck are they?*

And then, someone tugged back. The rope went stiff,
and the table slid and clanged against the wall. She braced
herself to hold it in place. It held. *They're coming.* All she
could do now was wait. Eleven percent. Given their lack
of physical strength, she calculated it would take fifteen
minutes or more for each of them to climb the knotted
rope. She laid down on the table and switched to
hibernate. *I hope I did some good.*

* * *

"Wakey, wakey," Liam said as he climbed through the
hatch.

Felicity looked up to see him standing next to the
table. The rope was already taut again.

"Why did you come first?" Felicity got to her feet.

"They figured you might need this." He held out a
charging pack.

"That's yours. Won't you need it?"

"Keep it. You have all four limbs."

Liam helped her plug in the earbuds as her charge
level indicator flashed a red ten percent in the corner of
her eye.

"Thanks," she said.

"I hope they make it. We're going to need all the help
we can get."

Felicity did what she could to reattach Liam's arm, still

dangling on the tendon cables. The joint had been badly mangled. Then she remembered: *Duct tape.* She pulled off a strip and wrapped it around the connector.

"What a crap job. You're not much of a repairman," he said with a smile. Liam moved his arm and closed his fist. It seemed to work—barely.

"You won't bowl 300 with that arm, but it will do."

"Thanks," he said, giving her a brief hug as if it was something he hated doing.

"You're welcome. Why don't you scout the hallway and keep guard at the door? We don't need any surprises."

Felicity didn't have to wait long before Julijana reached through the hatch. "A little help here?" she said, virtually out of breath. Felicity helped pull her in and sat beside her on the table.

"That's…a…long…climb," she wheezed.

"Yeah. Exhausting. I was down to ten percent when Liam found me."

"Ten percent? Before your reserve?"

"That *was* my reserve. I haven't had a full recharge for days."

"So you risked your life for us?"

"Yes, we ELFs have a stake in this, too."

"Thanks. Did Liam's battery pack help?"

"It did. Thanks."

"Evard was really worried about you."

"I love him, too."

Julijana just looked at her, almost as if she were understanding her—perhaps understanding ELFs—for the first time. Felicity was tempted to read her mind, but didn't. "I didn't tell you how sorry I am about James," Felicity said. They talked for a while until someone else begged for help at the hatch.

"Anyone want to give an old fella a hand?" Evard said. He was clearly out of breath.

Julijana and Felicity leaned into the shaft to help him through. "You're not *that* old," Felicity said as she tugged on his arm. Once he was inside, she gave him a welcoming kiss.

"Thanks for the battery pack," she said.

"I didn't want to lose my favorite girl."

She gave him a hug and a playful grope.

"Ben is right behind me. I think he's having trouble."

And then they heard a muffled scream and a desperate cry for help—someone was falling.

Julijana immediately shined her flashlight down the shaft. "Ben?" she yelled. "I can't see him!"

"They'll hear us for sure," Evard said.

"I'll go," Felicity said.

* * *

Before anyone could protest, Felicity was scrambling down the rope. She soon found Ben holding on for dear life at the forty-five bend. He was breathing hard and his hands were badly rope-burned.

"Hey, buddy. You okay?" she asked.

"Bruised, but not broken. I'm just resting."

"Julijana was worried. So was I."

"I'm okay. Let's get out of here."

Felicity reached down to help him, but his hand slipped from the rope. As if in slow motion, she watched in horror as Ben disappeared down the shaft and into the dark, unable to regain a hold on the rope. "Noooo," she screamed. And then the rope went taut again. "Ben?"

"Yeah. I'm not dead yet."

"Can you hold on?"

"I'll try."

Felicity let herself slide down the chute. "Let's try this again." She reached down, helped him get a better grip, and lifted him above her on the rope. It took every bit of her strength to help him reach the hatch.

The last thing she saw was Liam's hand reaching down for her.

* * *

Evard's hands trembled as he refitted Felicity's earbuds. They must have come off as she climbed. She showed no signs of life.

"Liam. I need your help."

He was already standing right behind him. Without a word, he had already opened his access panel and unreeled a pair of wires.

"You sure?" Evard looked into Liam's eyes. He knew what this meant. Evard was making a choice. So was Liam.

Liam nodded.

Evard pulled up her top and opened her access panel. The displays were all dark—all but one tiny dot of light, which slowly blinked ever so slightly, and then went out. He frantically plugged the connector into Felicity's panel and it came to life at once. Evard expected her systems would have to reboot, but had her volatile memory been cleared? Her charge indicator started to climb from zero as Liam's declined. When Liam reached thirty percent and Felicity ten, Evard reached for the connector. "That should be enough."

Liam touched his hand. "No. Give her the rest. I'm no good to anyone like this."

"There's enough charge for both of you," Evard said, disconnecting the wire.

"She didn't wake up. What's wrong with her?" Julijana asked.

"She'll need to initialize. We'll know after that," Evard whispered. His finger hovered over a small button on the panel, about where a human's heart would be. He closed his eyes and pushed it, but he left his hand in her chest. The indicators all went blank. A single tear splashed on Felicity's face.

It was clear Julijana was holding back her own flood of tears. Ben was already at her side. "I…we have to fix this. We have to."

"I know," Ben said softly. "We will."

Felicity sat up. "Hello, who are you?" she asked. He heaved a great sigh. "She's gone. That's the BIOS speaking. She's no longer the Felicity we all knew—the ELF who loved me."

Evard closed her blouse and gave her a hug.

"Nice to meet you," she said. "What's my name? Are you ready to set my options?"

His embrace tightened. "Felicity. Your name is Felicity and I'm Evard. We'll set you up later." He tried to hold himself together, but it was like trying to hold in innards after having been sliced across the belly.

"Evard, I'm so sorry for your loss. I can understand your pain," Julijana said softly. "She was such a sweet girl…bot…she was very brave and selfless."

"I expect you're feeling the same for Jimmy."

She nodded and took a deep breath, stood upright, and wiped away her tears. "Where do we go from here?"

"We need to—" Evard began.

"Wait." Liam held up his hand. Someone was communicating with him. "Yes, we're in. We lost Jimmy and…Felicity. They know we're here? We'll have to move fast." He mouthed, "It's Aarden. Avey cracked through their firewall. They're trying to access the core."

"Now what?" Evard asked.

"In case it doesn't work, Aarden wants us to take the pen into the vault and find ... Aarden? Aarden?"

"What's wrong?"

"They must have patched the hole in the firewall."

"What's this?"

Everyone turned to see a woman standing in the doorway. Liam stepped forward, but stopped dead in his tracks when she opened her arms, cocked her head, and smiled. "She's an ELF, on our side," Liam said, walking into her arms.

"You know her?"

"For years. Tanya and I knew each other from my first assignment. She saved my life—twice."

"And Liam saved mine. You big galoot, I thought you were dead." She gave him a playful punch in the shoulder, loosening the duct-tape mending job.

"Yeah, me too. Evard here brought me back." He peeled off another strip of tape and tried to reattach his arm.

"He's been a lot of trouble," Evard said.

"I can imagine," Tanya said, helping with the tape. "Let's get you all to somewhere safer. What happened to your arm? Seriously? Duct tape? The ELF repair shop is right down the hall. Wait here. I'll get you some uniforms so you'll fit in." Without another word, Tanya slipped out.

Evard heard a click. He tried the door. "Locked."

"Can we trust her?" Julijana asked.

"Liam trusts her. Liam, see what you can do about the lock," Evard said.

"Felicity was the lock expert. I could break it down if the duct tape holds."

"Let me try," Julijana said. She retrieved a device the size of a Swiss Army knife. "Vili was my lock expert, but I think I can open it from here. Anytime you're ready."

"Then let's get out of this cell. It smells of death. Go ahead and unlock it," Evard said. "I want to hedge our bets."

Julijana unlocked the door and Evard tried the knob. It was open, but he heard footsteps. "Get back." He snapped off the light.

A second later, someone came in and closed the door. Evard turned on the lights.

It was Tanya with an armload of gray overalls and ID badges. "You're now custodians."

They just stood there.

"What? Did you think I was going to get the goons? Shit, those assholes think they killed me a couple hours ago. I've been working undercover here for years. I'm on your side."

All at once, they were pulling on the overalls.

"Wait!" Liam said. "Evard, the pen. Tell me you didn't leave it in the truck."

Evard held it up after pretending to pull it out of his ass.

"Is that it?" Tanya asked, reaching for the pen.

Instinct told Evard to hold on to the pen—he did. *Just in case.* "This was on Sanchez. A lady friend of mine was his driver. Aarden brought her to me, and she had the pen. I don't suppose you've seen her?"

"Blonde? Widow?"

"The same. Cynthia."

"Cynthia Wellborn. And her son—"

"Dan."

"Yes. Sad. They decided to put some pressure on her by threatening him, but something went wrong. Ever since, Verner has been trying to convince her she never had a son."

Liam slowly shook his head.

"What happened to them? Is she still alive?"

"She is, but the boy...I'm not sure."

"Son of a *bitch*," Evard said.

"Yeah, and I'm his whore—or I was," Tanya said. "I know where he's keeping her."

With Felicity's demise and all the other carnage, Evard had a renewed interest in vengeance. "We need to focus on the vault—get inside and stick this pen up the *system's* ass," he said, with an appropriate gesture. He turned around and dropped his pants.

"You aren't going to stick that up—" Liam said.

"No, hand me the duct tape."

"Hold on a second," Tanya said, ogling Evard's ass. "It won't take all of you to get into the vault. It will be easier with one or two. The rest can find Cynthia and get her and Dan out of here."

Evard agreed. "Tanya, can you point these two in the direction of your ELF repair room? They can join us once they're patched up."

"Evard? Should I stay here and take a nap? My batteries are very low," Felicity said.

Evard barely recognized her voice. It was almost too painful to speak to her. "Just stay with Liam. He'll get you a flash charge. If something happens to me, he'll take care of you. Won't you, Liam?"

Liam nodded and held out his good arm, beckoning Felicity to his side.

"And so will I," Julijana said.

"Thanks, that's comforting," Evard said.

"It's the least I can do. She made the ultimate sacrifice for us."

"Julijana, can you do me another favor? Go find Cynthia and Dan. I'm very worried about them."

"Of course. I'll do my best."

"Wait," Liam said. He pulled Ben aside and handed him a small module. They spoke for a moment and Ben nodded.

"The repair depot is down the hall," Tanya said. "I'll stick with Evard and help him get into the vault." She held up her card key.

"Where are they keeping Cynthia?" Julijana asked.

"In Verner's quarters. At least she was there an hour ago. Down one level—room 102."

"Am I supposed to just waltz in there and take her?"

"Get her to the motor pool. She knows that area well. Find a vehicle and—"

"Just drive away. Right. We're a thousand meters underground. There's no way they're going to let her escape by car. She would have to use the vehicle lift—and *they* control it. We need another way," Julijana said.

"Bring them back here," Evard said. "They'll have to climb down the rope—it's our only way out."

"What if she can't climb?" Julijana asked.

"Let's cross that bridge when we come to it."

Forty-five—The Vault Team

*E*vard wasn't at all sure about Tanya's plan. It required a double measure of bravado, heavily seasoned with copious courage and a dash of insanity—and then it probably wouldn't work. She led them to the ELF repair room. Liam, with Felicity in tow, disappeared inside. As Evard and Tanya walked away, they heard a scuffle. It didn't last long. They kept walking as if nothing had happened.

Entering the vast room, with the vault door sealing off one end, the security officer looked up. "Ma'am, you're not permitted in this area."

"Tell Verner I'm out here and put this man under arrest."

The officer immediately drew his weapon and switched it on.

"Fucking bitch." Evard's stomach tightened. He didn't dare run—he couldn't outrun the guard's auto-targeting rounds. He slowly raised his hands.

The guard touched his temple. "Guard station six. We have Ms. Tanya here. Really? She just showed up with Evard Kennedy. Yes, I'm sure, the ID system recognized him at once. She wants to talk to Verner." Then a strange look came over his face.

Every muscle in Evard's body tightened, like an antelope when first sensing a lion is about to pounce. Was the guard just going to off him? Evard had to do *something*—and fast. "Tell him I have what he's looking for. Something I took from his courier. I want to exchange it for Cynthia Wellborn."

"Sir, he says he has…so you heard. Yes, sir."

Open the fucking vault door! Unless they were inside the data center, there was little they could do. Evard felt the duct tape holding the pen to his inner thigh ripping out his leg hair. He tried not to flinch.

A moment later, a klaxon sounded and the great vault door began to move. *Yes.* A phalanx of guards poured out and took both of them back toward the detention cells— away from the door. *Shit.*

* * *

Sometime later, Evard awoke chained in a brightly lit room sitting on a wobbly chair. He recalled being strip-searched and knocked around like a punching bag. It took no time at all to find the pen. The first torture involved peeling off the duct tape—slowly.

"Well, Mr. Kennedy, we meet at last," Verner said. "I'm sorry I couldn't greet you sooner, but your friend Mrs. Wellborn and I were having an intimate 'interaction.' I'm sure you'll understand." Verner's grin tightened Evard's hands into tight fists, now straining against the leather straps

"You have what you want. Just kill me and get it over with," Evard said through his swollen lips and loose teeth.

"Of course. That comes later. We still need the names of your fellow conspirators. I expect those will take quite some time to extract."

"Fuck you, child killer."

Verner backhanded Evard, knocking over the chair. "Oh, and thank you for this," Verner held up the pen. He turned to one of his suit-and-tie agents. "Homer, you know what to do." He handed him the pen and turned to another agent. "Get him to give up his friends. I don't care how. I'm going to my quarters. Let me know what you find."

"Yes, sir," the agents said almost in unison.

When the door opened, Evard heard the klaxon. The vault was opening again. *There was still a chance.*

* * *

Agent Homer wasn't new to his job, just to the site. He had been carefully recruited and trained to manage the vast data repository held within the vault and, more importantly, how it was protected. Leveraging the best and latest technology, he had studied their foolproof scheme to keep out hackers and those who would compromise their massive databases from outside the vault. While not privy to the contents of the information, what he had in his hand would be critical to his mission. He was told it contained an electronic list of the ELFs under control of the AI entity trying to crush The Good—they called her Aarden. Once it was loaded, every one of them could be deactivated or reprogrammed to obey orders from The Good.

Too important to trust to others, he personally took the device back to his private office. Using a retinal scan as well as a voice and handprint, the door opened. He entered and waited while the outer door closed and a guard in a remote location verified his identity.

"Go ahead, sir," a voice said, and the inner door latch clicked.

Homer crossed over to his workstation and pushed a button. A thin tray pushed out of the system, and he laid the pen inside. It fit perfectly, and the tray retracted. He selected an icon on the screen. "There you are, my darling," he said aloud. It didn't take long before a message appeared.

> *Application loaded.*

And then things changed. Homer knew his life and his world would never be the same. In the distance, he heard the klaxon, the alarm bells, and his screens went blank for a moment. A second later, a smiling face appeared. It looked remarkably like a beautiful woman he had met not long ago. She was smiling.

"Hi, Aarden," he said, as if greeting an old friend.

"Hello, Homer. Thanks for your help."

"Sir?" someone said over the intercom. "Something has defeated the security system. The firewall is down and the vault door is opening. The only thing we can access is some old TV show called *Hee Haw*."

Homer rocked back in his chair, put his feet up, and closed his eyes. *Mission accomplished.*

Forty-six—The Rescue Team

*J*ulijana didn't know Cynthia or the boy. From what Evard had told her, he had not known them very long, but they had grown very close. He had likened Cynthia to an innocent flower picked up by a storm, carried into their world of insurgents through no fault of her own. Was Evard in love with her? Quite possibly. If Cynthia didn't survive the day, it wouldn't make much difference—not that any of the time alterations they had made so far had made any significant difference. For once, Julijana thought what she was doing here inside this massive complex was more important than any of their fruitless expeditions that left her with nightmares and frustration. She and Vili had spent decades of their lives trying to alter time in vain attempts to undo what past generations had done, or not done—still leaving the planet on its knees, battered, bruised, and bleeding to death.

Julijana wondered if any of them would live out the day. Unlike the ELFs, she had no "restore" option. The humans were living their last lives, their only lives, and perhaps their last minutes. *But so was Felicity.*

"I think this is it," Ben said. He had been leading the way using a tracker Liam had given him. He had found a dark stairway leading down into the lower regions.

She looked over the railing, but could not see the bottom. "There must be twenty floors."

"More like fifty. I wonder what they're doing down there?"

They descended down one level. When they heard approaching footsteps, they tucked themselves into a convenient closet. In the tight space, her chest pressed up to his, she felt him breathing and recalled the night they spent sitting side by side on a buckboard. "I think they're gone," she said, but she didn't open the door. "Let's take this up a bit later."

He nodded and gave her a kiss before they stepped into the corridor.

"That way," he said. His face was blushing as he pushed down on a bulge in his pants.

In the distance behind them, a klaxon sounded again. "Is that the vault door alarm?" she asked.

"I expect so." Ben checked the device. "The boy is that way." He pointed off down the hall.

This is it. 102. "Go find the boy. I'll take care of Cynthia."

"You sure?"

"Go. I'll be fine."

* * *

Ben didn't want to leave Julijana behind, but there were so few people around and time was of the essence. She should be fine. Following the tracking device, he found it took him back to the stairway and down two levels. He opened a door that led to a catwalk. Below him, a vast room stretched out into the misty distance. *It must be fifty hectares.* The room was alive with an automated assembly line. At first, it was hard to tell what was being manufactured, but the acrid-sweet smell of gardenias burned his nose. He followed the line with his eyes, and at the other end of the room he watched the final product stand and step on a conveyer belt, which took the bot to a lower level. *Warrior bots! By the tens of thousands. Shit.*

When an alarm bell rang, everything stopped—the machines, the bots in mid-step, and the transport belt.

The boy. He checked the tracker. It led him to a door off the catwalk. Inside, he found a number of large body scanners. *The boy.* He spotted a boy lying on a table under one of the machines. Next to him lay another boy, which could have been his twin.

"What are you doing here?"

Ben turned to see a man in blue scrubs. "I might ask you the same question. What have you done to the boy?"

"We saved his life. He was injured, and we weren't sure he would recover, so we built a clone."

"Is he still alive?"

"The boy? Yes, he's just fallen asleep. His surgery went well. He'll be fine in a few days. His clone is also complete. I was just beginning to choose options for him. They're basically the same in most respects."

Ben read his name badge. "Doctor Ackers, you work for Verner?"

"I didn't have a choice. He's holding my family hostage."

"Perhaps that will change. Did you notice your little assembly line down there has stopped?"

"It has? Someone must have taken control of the—"

"Yeah. That's us. Get the boys dressed. We're going upstairs to meet their mom."

Forty-seven—The Reunion

*J*ulijana checked the knob. *Locked.* Using Vili's gadget, she unlocked it and slipped inside. Verner's quarters were lavishly furnished, with an artificial fire taking the chill off the room and providing a modicum of warm light. *Nobody here. Maybe in the bedroom?*

She crossed the room and put her ear against the door. *Nothing.* In the field, she and Vili rarely carried firearms. Killing or even wounding people in other eras caused countless issues for the future—but this *was* the future, at least what was left of it. She pulled out another device from Vili's pouch, flipped off the safety, and stepped inside.

A half-dressed middle-aged woman with bandaged arms lay spread-eagle on the bed, gagged, her ankles and hands tied to the bedposts.

"Cynthia?"

She nodded. Her eyes screamed fear and despair.

"We're here to get you out of here," Julijana said. She cut her feet free and began working on her hands, leaving her gag for last. Cynthia kept wagging her head, trying to speak.

"Turn around slowly," said someone behind her. "Mrs. Wellborn is staying right where she is. I'm not quite done with her."

Julijana turned to find a man holding a pulsar weapon. Her own lay on the bed, out of reach.

"You must be Verner," Julijana said calmly, untying Cynthia's hand. She got up and removed her gag.

"I don't think we've had the pleasure," Verner said.

"I'm your executioner," said a voice from behind him.

As Verner turned to look, Tanya neatly removed his head with a laser sword.

Cynthia screamed.

"It's over, it's all over." Julijana embraced her, shielding her face from the carnage.

"It is." Tanya pulled a sheet off the bed and covered his body. "Aarden already took over their system and her control is spreading worldwide. There's nothing they can do to stop her."

Felicity rushed into the room, stepping over the draped corpse. "Cynthia, are you all right?"

Cynthia nodded. "I will be once I find Dan. Verner's done something with him. I know it. He tried to convince me Dan never existed."

"Ben tracked him to a room down—" Julijana began.

"Mom!" Dan exclaimed as he appeared in the doorway. He broke away from Ben and ran into her arms.

Another Dan stepped into the room. "Mom?"

"What's this?" Cynthia asked.

"One of these boys is an ELF. Can you tell which one?" Ben asked.

"Two? I have twins?"

"Basically. One doesn't eat much, but is pretty good at math. I think they'll get along like brothers."

Cynthia embraced them both and cried. Felicity stood to one side with a broad smile. It was the smile of a new mother or big sister.

A moment later, a bruised and battered Evard walked into the room. He looked into Felicity's eyes, but before he could say a word, she embraced and kissed him. .

"Felicity! I thought you were—" Evard began.

"I was. Aarden said she would protect me. She did."

Felicity put a black ovoid in his hand. "Keep this safe this time. It might come in handy." She embraced him again, but then reached out her arm and Cynthia joined in.

"Aarden says she can put things back so the Earth will survive," Felicity said.

"I hope to God she can," Julijana said.

"Cynthia, can I come home with you? My place is a wreck," Evard asked.

"I…I would love it," she said, "but I would rather go back to the old lodge overlooking the Falls and take a try at a life there."

"That sounds wonderful," Evard said.

"So, what about Sam and Avey? What does Aarden have in store for them?" Julijana asked.

Felicity just smiled.

Forty-eight—The Final Breath

"*How* are you doing?" Avey asked. She lovingly pushed back Sam's hair and straightened his comforter, making sure not to disturb the telemetry attached to his chest or the tubes dripping clear fluid into his arm.

"As well as can be expected for someone over ninety." His voice was raspy and weak.

"Is there anything you want?" she asked.

He looked up at her with a crooked smile and raised an eyebrow.

"Besides that. You know what the doctor said."

"Yeah, but what a way to go." He took her hand and put it in his lap.

She didn't resist, but glanced up at the monitors. His heartrate was slow but steady, but his blood pressure and O2 levels were still low and declining. *It won't be long now.*

"Did you hear from the kids?" he asked.

"Of course. They're nearby." She was used to Sam asking the same questions over and over. He had lost most of his short-term memory and had to be reminded of nearly everything. Ironically, he was able to recall every detail of how they met, and still told tall tales of their many adventures over the years. But in the last year or so, the details seemed to be more imaginary than factual.

They both remembered Aarden sending them back to their own time, to the tree on the UW campus where they met in the evenings after class. From time to time, they had to rewind their time threads when someone inadvertently discovered Avey's secret, but since they were careful, those incidents were easy to repair. They both returned to their research with a renewed vigor to prevent what they had witnessed in the distant future. And now, they had arrived there together—in 2084.

"What about the kids?" Sam said, after a brief coughing spell.

She handed him a cup of water with a straw. "They're outside—at least most of them."

"Thanks. And Vili?"

"He and Julijana are there, too. Do you want to see them?"

"Not yet." He squeezed her hand. "I just want to be alone with you for a few more years."

She tried her best to daub back tears.

"I'm glad Aarden harvested your eggs."

"Me too."

"Did you know when she—"

"No, I told you, it could have been anytime. Does it matter?"

"Not really."

Avey just held his hand as they enjoyed the scenery. Seattle had been reborn—it was nothing like the ravaged hellhole they both had experienced first-hand. Once Aarden had taken control of time, the world had been reborn, and Seattle was transformed into a dazzling futuristic metropolis. Now, the sky was clear and dotted with white puffy clouds, the Sound a dazzling blue, the forests as lush as ever. In the distance, a squall moved in from the Olympics with the sun painting a brilliant orange and magenta sunset behind it. A wide V pattern of Canada geese and a long line of flying cars silently glided by. In the distance, a school of orcas seemed to jump for joy as sailboats jibed, heading for home ahead of the rain. And the reformation had spread to the entire planet. The rainforests and glaciers returned, the storms abated, and flooded cities reemerged as if they were never inundated—because they weren't.

"Seattle's putting on a show tonight," he said.

"It's…beautiful," Avey said, tears falling on her cheeks.

"You didn't have to do it," Sam said.

"What?"

"Make yourself look old." He looked down at her wrinkled hand.

"I know, but it was easier on both of us this way."

"Tell me, are you going be young again and hook up with a rich doctor? What about that cute grad student from the U who's been trying to hack into Aarden?"

"Sam, please don't."

"You know I'm kidding."

"Sam, it's not too late. We both can be young again—together."

"Get uploaded? We've talked about this. My memory…my—"

"Remember? Aarden protected you about three years ago—before you started showing symptoms."

"She did?"

"Yes, and you can be uploaded into—"

"Yeah. I still don't think it's a good idea. I'm just as claustrophobic as Evard—maybe more so. I couldn't stand it."

Avey knew he was just making excuses. They had talked, and argued, and even said bitter words before she gave up trying to convince him to join her in immortality.

"Sam, we can still have a wonderful life together."

"Haven't we already?" he asked, looking into her eyes.

Avey nodded. "We have."

"Then I'm content. I want to make room for others—

my kids and grandkids."

"And great-grandkids. Julijana's expecting again."

Sam just stared out at the sunset where the stars had all but won over the sky.

She noticed her charge indicator flashing two percent. Her charger lay on the bedside table along with a note explaining everything. The black ovoid, which had once contained her last and only backup, had been crushed. What she hadn't told him was that she was following him to the other side. Just then, she looked up to see herself standing in the doorway with a shocked look on her face. She remembered witnessing this scene so many years ago when Sam was still in his twenties.

"Sam, you know I love you."

"You know I've always loved you," he said, squeezing her hand.

She gave him a lingering kiss.

"I'm going to miss you," he said.

"I hope not," she said.

"I think it's time to let them in," he whispered. They were his last words.

The End

The Series

Watch the author's Facebook page, blog and websites for announcements regarding the next book in *The Timkers* series. In the meantime, consider that today's authors depend and thrive on reviews, whether the books are published by an enormous New York publisher house or self-published. Of course, all authors love flattering, five-star reviews, but we really appreciate honest feedback highlighting our talents as well as our shortcomings. Reviews also help other readers decide if the author's books are just what they're looking for, or not a good match for their interests. So, please, take the time to post a review of *The Timkers—Borrowed Time.* To do so, go to Amazon, Goodreads, or your favorite online book site, navigate to the title and enter your feedback.

Finding your favorite author in a local bookstore or in the library can also be a challenge—especially for independently published authors, as it's difficult to get accepted. If you can't find my books where you shop for books, I encourage you to ask for me by name.

WR Vaughn